D1041220

National Bestselling Author

LINDSAY CHASE

portrays the choices and challenges of women who dared to follow their dreams—in twc very special novels . . .

THE VOW

Hannah Shaw had a mind for business—and a heart that yearned for more than her loveless marriage could give her . . . A triumphant novel of the choices that can change a lifetime.

"A WONDERFUL STORYTELLER. I READ THIS IN A DAY. I COULDN'T PUT IT DOWN."

—FERN MICHAELS

"TUMULTUOUS . . ."

—bestselling author JULIE ELLIS

"A PAGE-TURNER OF A NOVEL . . . [A] FAST-MOVING STORY."

—*Rave Reviews*

"A NOVEL OF PASSION AND THOUGHTFULNESS THAT REVEALS AN AUTHOR OF GIGANTIC SKILL . . . AN ABSORBING STORY."

—*Rendezvous*

THE OATH

Catherine Stone vowed to become a doctor—at any price. But when her wealthy husband forces her to choose between medicine and his love, she must make the boldest sacrifice of all . . . A moving novel of one woman's unwavering commitment to her dreams.

"IN THE TRADITION OF *MIDWIFE* . . . A FASCINATING PORTRAIT OF THE LIFE, TRIUMPHS, AND TRAGEDIES OF A WOMAN DOCTOR."

—*Rave Reviews*

"EXCELLENT!" —*Heartland Critiques*

Diamond Books by Lindsay Chase

THE OATH
THE VOW
HONOR

HONOR

LINDSAY CHASE

DIAMOND BOOKS, NEW YORK

This book is a Diamond original edition,
and has never been previously published.

HONOR

A Diamond Book / published by arrangement with
the author

PRINTING HISTORY
Diamond edition / February 1994

For information address: The Berkley Publishing Group,
200 Madison Avenue, New York, NY 10016.

ISBN: 1-55773-977-3

Diamond Books are published by The Berkley Publishing Group,
200 Madison Avenue, New York, NY 10016.
DIAMOND and the "D" design
are trademarks belonging to Charter Communications, Inc.

PRINTED IN THE UNITED STATES OF AMERICA

10 9 8 7 6 5 4 3 2 1

In memory of John April
The world was his stage

Prologue

New York City, 1897

The Statue of Liberty no longer symbolized hope and refuge to Dr. Catherine Delancy; it signified only impending disaster.

She trembled in spite of the warm April day. "Afraid?" Damon stood beside her on the deck of the *Copper Queen* and leaned into the strong westerly breeze. "It's not too late to go back."

London . . . where their hopes and dreams lay shattered beyond imagining.

She gripped the brass rail so tightly that her knuckles threatened to pop through her worn kid gloves. "We never should have run away in the first place. We should have stayed in New York and fought that self-righteous hypocrite."

"For the hundred-thousandth time, Catherine," Damon said with the exaggerated forbearance of a man who had lost his patience long ago, "we had no choice."

Tears scalded her eyes. "If we had stayed, William would still be alive and you'd still be running your company."

"And you'd be in prison."

"I'm going there anyway. And you, too, for helping me." When she thought of Damon, her proud husband, being locked away like an animal, deprived of his freedom and degraded, she shed helpless tears. She wouldn't turn to him for comfort, for she had demanded far too much of him already.

Damon placed insistent hands on her shoulders and forced her to face him. "We can't lose hope."

She removed a handkerchief from her sleeve and dried her eyes. "You're right. Perhaps attitudes have changed. Perhaps a jury will be sympathetic." She wished she could convince herself.

He grinned with his old self-assuredness. "Courage, Catherine. We'll hire one hell of a lawyer, and we'll win."

When he drew her into his arms and kissed her, she clung to him as if to life itself, for she knew that once the *Copper Queen* docked, they would be arrested.

She wouldn't feel the warmth and strength of her husband's arms around her for a long, long time.

Chapter 1

Boston, 1894

"We find the defendant—not guilty."

Honor scanned the smug faces of the "jurors," fourteen young men in old "Bloomers" Bloomfield's criminal law class. She wasn't surprised that they hadn't found in her client's favor. They rarely did. They would rather put ink on her chair and call her Steel Stays Elliott behind her back than admit a woman into their august circle.

Honor glanced at her opponent, seated two desks away. "Congratulations, Mr. Davis." She masked her bitter disappointment behind a cool professional smile.

Robert Davis, who had played defense attorney to Honor's prosecutor, leaned back in his chair, hooked his thumbs in the pockets of his threadbare waistcoat, and grinned. "Your case had so many loopholes, a baby could have crawled through, but I trust you learned something from me today, Miss Elliott."

Had it not been considered unseemly for an aspiring lawyer to commit murder, Honor would have wrung the strutting cockerel's neck with her bare hands.

"Mr. Davis, I wouldn't gloat if I were you," old Bloomers said from his desk at the front of the room. He removed his pince-nez to display his disapproving scowl to the entire class. "In fact, you should all be ashamed of yourselves. Even though Miss Elliott is a woman, and the majority of you have made it clear that you disapprove of female lawyers, you should have found in her favor."

Honor tried not to betray her astonishment.

Davis's grin vanished, and a dull, angry flush appeared above his wing collar, then shot up his clean-shaven cheeks.

Bloomers' chastising gaze pinned every student to his chair. "If I've taught you gentlemen anything, it's that you must put aside your personal prejudices and view each case objectively. You haven't, and I'm deeply ashamed of all of you. You make me feel that I have been wasting my time."

Davis grinned insolently. "What difference would it have made if our jury had found in Miss Elliott's favor? She's a woman. She'll never argue a criminal case unless she goes out west."

Several mutterings of assent rippled through the class, and Honor glared at her adversary, unaware that her rarely displayed anger brought a becoming blush to her pale cheeks and fire to her obsidian eyes. Damn, how she disliked him!

Old Bloomers made a face. "My dear Mr. Davis," he said in his best aggrieved tone, "I'm surprised at you. Miss Elliott's prospects are irrelevant. I expect everyone in my class to judge these mock trials objectively based on the evidence presented, not on the personalities involved. Her argument for the prosecution was excellent."

Honor raised her hand. "Professor Bloomfield, may I say something in my own defense?"

He nodded.

She rose and faced the class, quickly reading their faces to determine where each man's sympathies lay, then addressed them in her most commanding voice.

"I'm not going to lecture you gentlemen about the suitability of a woman to become a lawyer," she began, especially conscious of Davis lounging in his seat and staring at the ceiling, the picture of consummate boredom. "Many of you have considered me an oddity ever since I enrolled here three years ago."

Davis yawned.

"Many of you—not all, to be fair—have gone out of your

way to discourage me. And I would just like to say"—she paused—"thank you."

Davis started. Professor Bloomfield's bushy brows rose. Every eye was riveted on Honor.

She smiled sweetly. "Because you have made my chosen course so difficult, you gentlemen will be responsible for my success. You see, your determination to see me fail has made me even more determined to succeed."

She sat down, not expecting applause and not getting any.

Bloomfield cleared his throat and suppressed a smile. "Gentlemen, you have been put in your places neatly and ever so skillfully." He bowed to Honor. "Nicely done, Miss Elliott."

"Nicely done indeed," Davis said.

A compliment from the insufferable Robert Davis? Honor decided she must be going deaf, so she said nothing and turned her attention back to old Bloomers, who was telling the class point by point why they should have found in Honor's favor.

She savored her brief victory, for she knew the next one would be just as hard won.

At three o'clock, when Honor's classes were finally over for the day, she walked across the Boston University campus, conscious of the chilly late October breeze swirling a funnel of brown fallen leaves high into the air as the golden autumn light poured like warm honey over the stately red brick buildings.

She attracted curious masculine stares as much for her sex's scarcity on a university campus as for her tall, slender figure and fine patrician features, rescued from perfection by a blunt, stubborn chin. Weary and eager to return to her Back Bay home, she ignored the men she hurried past, never seeing their curiosity change to blatant admiration. She did, however, notice Robert Davis.

He was huddled in a doorway, where a stone arch offered him some warmth and protection against the biting breeze, the collar of his ill-fitting tweed jacket pulled up below his ears, his hatless dark head bent over an open book. He shivered.

Honor was about to turn and walk the other way when he looked up and caught her staring. His feline green eyes boldly dared her not to acknowledge him. She contemplated walking by with only a curt nod, but stopped when he snapped his book shut and approached her.

"Miss Elliott," he said in his deep, compelling voice, his gaunt cheeks pale from the chilly bite in the air. "Do you mind if I walk with you?"

"Yes, but I doubt if my wishes would stop you."

He chuckled at that, his eyes dancing with amusement, and extended his hand. "If we're to walk together, at least let me carry your books."

"I can manage." She tightened her grip as if she feared he'd take the two heavy volumes by force.

"Suit yourself." Davis adjusted his long stride to Honor's shorter one, and they walked side by side in silence.

Honor wondered why her corset suddenly felt tighter. She moved her right arm a fraction so she wouldn't brush Davis's jacket, for even that slight contact disconcerted her.

"Are you walking to the corner where the streetcar stops?" he asked. He held his arms locked against his sides, apparently for warmth.

"No."

Davis waited. "Where do you live? Perhaps we're going in the same direction."

Damn the man's impertinence! "I doubt that."

A smile tugged at the corners of his mouth. "I can tell where you live just by looking at you." His bold inspection started at Honor's old Redfern chapeau with its once-elegant pheasant feather, took in the short black velvet cape that Aunt Theodate had brought from Paris two seasons ago, and ended with her impeccably tailored long blue serge skirt. "Beacon Hill."

"The sunny side of Commonwealth Avenue." She would make no apologies to this annoying man for living on one of Boston's most exclusive streets.

"Commonwealth Avenue . . . my, my." Davis shivered again. "It's a mystery to me why a rich woman would go through such hell to become a lawyer. You're—what? Twenty-six?"

She was twenty-five, but she didn't see the need to correct him.

He persisted. "Aren't rich women from the Back Bay married to rich men and having a brood of rich children by the time they're your age?"

Honor thought of her father and felt the pain of an old wound reopened. "I have my reasons, and they're no concern of yours, Mr. Davis. Neither is my age nor my marital status."

"That's no secret. Anyone can tell that you're a spinster." Then he laughed, a hearty rumble that caused passersby to stare. "Old Bloomers was right, you know," he said. "The class should have found in your favor."

His admission caught her off guard, but she recovered herself quickly. "How generous of you to admit it."

Davis studied her. "Do you know why you'll never become as successful a lawyer as any woman can hope to become, Miss Elliott?" Before Honor could answer, he added, "You take every defeat as a personal attack. You lack a man's ability to separate himself from his work, and you hold a grudge."

Honor snorted delicately. "A most interesting theory, but quite absurd."

"Is it?" Davis demanded. "Take us for example. I know you don't like me."

She stared straight ahead. "I don't know you well enough to dislike you."

"Yes, you do, and do you know why? Because I usually defeat you in class, and you don't like to lose. So you've formed a hearty dislike for me without really knowing me at all."

He was right. She didn't know where he came from or where he lived now, though she suspected it was one of the poorer sections of the city. She didn't know if his parents were alive, if he had brothers and sisters, or how he spent his Sunday afternoons. She found herself wondering.

"If your behavior in class is any indication," Honor said coolly, "I know that you are arrogant and opinionated."

He flinched, then recovered himself. "I believe I've made my point. You refuse to see me as anything but an adversary."

"Why would I wish to see you as anything else?"

He flashed a teasing smile. "Because if you were to put aside your prejudices, Miss Elliott, you might have to admit that you were wrong about me, and we both know you'd hate that. I am quite a likable fellow, you know. And handsome."

Honor looked him over with the same critical eye he had used on her. Except for large green eyes that sparkled with intelligence and humor, he wasn't conventionally handsome, yet he radiated an infectious energy and competitive spirit that animated his nondescript features and commanded attention. He didn't try to fill out his gaunt cheeks with a beard or balance his full, sensuous lower lip with a mustache. His face seemed to say, "This is who I am. Take it or leave it."

"I wouldn't go so far as to call you handsome," she said.

He just laughed. "Actually, neither would I."

They reached the end of the street, where a four-passenger brougham waited.

"Yours?" His eyes roved over the gleaming black-lacquered four-wheel carriage.

Honor raised one hand to her hat to keep a sudden gust of wind from catching it. "My aunt's."

Davis idly ran his hand down the glossy hindquarters of one of the two matching black horses standing there, its head held by a liveried coachman. "These beauties must have cost a pretty penny."

Honor ignored his crass comment and regarded him with customary coolness. "This has been a most interesting conversation, Mr. Davis, but I really don't have any interest in pursuing an . . . acquaintanceship."

His jaw tightened. "So Robert Davis isn't good enough for the likes of you, Miss Steel Stays Elliott!"

His use of the epithet angered her, but she didn't show it. "I'm sorry if I offended you, but—"

"You're all alike, aren't you? Spoiled little proper Bostonians who think they can do whatever they please because Papa has money and they live in a fancy house and buy their fancy clothes every spring in Paris." He shivered again, this time with passion rather than the cold. "And you, Miss Steel Stays, are the worst kind, a rich woman going to school to ease her boredom, taking the place of some decent, hard-working man who just wants to better himself."

Honor's eyes narrowed. She was too well bred to correct him. Proper Bostonian women preferred plain, unostentatious clothes that had aged a bit, none of which were ever purchased from Parisian couturiers such as Worth—except by Aunt Theo, of course, but then, she would shudder to be mistaken for a proper Bostonian. As for a rich papa, Honor no longer had one, nor did she have a mother, for that matter. "If you'll excuse me, Mr. Davis . . ."

Robert Davis flung his books down with a clatter, grasped Honor around the waist, and pulled her toward him. She dropped her own books in surprise. Before she could step back out of danger or shove him away, he crushed her against his hard chest and his mouth came down on hers in a punishing kiss.

For a heartbeat Honor felt cold, smooth lips pressed against her own with a demanding insistence, and then an unexpected answering warmth flaring deep within her own body.

"Hey, stop that!" she heard Simms, the coachman, shout from far away. "Unhand Miss Elliott!"

Before Simms could accost him, Davis released Honor, taking only a second to glare at her triumphantly before scooping up his books and striding off without a backward glance.

Rage swept through Honor like a forest fire, and this time she couldn't hide it. She cupped her trembling hand around her mouth and shouted, "Damn you! I'll have you arrested!"

He turned around but kept on walking. "There's no law against kissing a woman in public."

Simms reached Honor's side. "He didn't hurt you, did he, miss?" he said, stooping to retrieve her books.

Honor shook her head, her indignant gaze still on Davis's retreating form. "He only kissed me," she shouted so he would hear her, "and a disappointing experience it was, at that." She turned to Simms. "Take me home."

Simms handed her into the brougham and they departed. When Honor glanced out the rear window, she saw that Davis was waving a mocking good-bye.

"The effrontery of that man!" She slammed her books down on the seat and settled herself against the soft leather squabs. Her heart still raced, and her lips still felt bruised from his kiss.

She was used to his obnoxious behavior in class, constantly arguing and contradicting her at every opportunity, like a tenacious bull terrier worrying a trouser leg. Yet just a few moments ago he had acted like anything but an adversary.

Honor nervously tugged at the gold engraved locket she always wore on a black satin cord. Gradually the heat of her anger cooled, and rationality took over. She put herself in her antagonist's place, all the better to understand him.

Davis obviously resented those of wealth and privilege, and judging by his ill-fitting, threadbare clothes and belligerent attitude, he had known neither. If that was the case, what was his motive in seeking her out after class?

She put him out of her mind. She had more pressing concerns than Robert Davis.

Unlike nearby Beacon Hill, with its narrow cobblestone lanes and elegant brick row houses in earlier Federal and Georgian styles, Commonwealth Avenue resembled a wide, airy Parisian boulevard with a tree-filled park running down its center and houses with decidedly Gallic flair.

Arriving at number 165, Honor paused to study her aunt's

house. She had never thought it particularly fancy. Well, perhaps the tall arched windows on the first and second floor qualified as fancy. And it did boast two drawing rooms, a casual one for the family on the first floor and a more elaborate one for receiving guests on the second, but then, so did every other house on the avenue. She supposed hot-water heating might be considered a luxury in Robert Davis's estimation if he was used to coal fires. To Honor, the four-story structure was simply home.

The moment Honor stepped into the paneled foyer, the butler materialized out of nowhere to take her cape. "And how was school today, miss?"

"Stimulating as always, Jackson, but not for the usual reasons." Peeling off her gloves, she noticed a large wooden crate in the foyer. "What is this?"

"Another painting from Paris."

"Aunt Theo didn't tear it right out of its crate the moment it arrived?"

"She wasn't here when it arrived, miss. She's gone hunting."

"Gone hunting" meant that Theodate Putnam Tree was off seeking a new addition to her art collection or her wardrobe and wouldn't return until she had bagged her quarry.

"Alone?" Honor asked, removing her hat and smoothing her glossy black hair with a practiced hand.

"With Mr. Saltonsall."

Who else? Honor smiled to herself.

After having gone upstairs to her own room to change into a comfortable tea gown, Honor was passing through the foyer on her way to the library to study when the front door suddenly flew open and her aunt Theodate came sweeping in like a blast of autumn wind.

"But you must admit he was vastly entertaining," she was saying to the tall young man beside her laden with several hatboxes of various sizes.

At forty, the widow Tree was as tall and slender as her

niece, with premature white hair that was a family trait and eyes as black and mysterious as midnight.

The moment her gaze alighted on the crate, she clasped her hands together with glee. "Oh, Wes, it's finally arrived!" She fluttered one gloved hand in Jackson's direction when the butler appeared. "Jackson, take those boxes and bring us something to open the crate with before I expire of suspense!" Her long skirts had barely settled before she was in motion again, sweeping across the foyer to kiss Honor on the cheek. "How was school today, sweet Portia? Did you win any of those mock trials?"

Honor smiled, exchanged greetings with Wes, who was still struggling to transfer the hatboxes to Jackson, and said to her aunt, "My professor thought so, though my classmates disagreed."

"They're only men." Theo tugged off her blue kid gloves and flung them at the long hall table. She missed and turned to Wes, who finally had his hands free. "Will you bring the painting into the drawing room so that we can unpack it?"

Wesley Saltonsall, who was Honor's age, spent more time squiring Theo around Boston than working for his family's vast shipping business. Though he did not possess a formidable intellect, he was a perfect specimen of masculine beauty and charm, with a talent for making people comfortable in any social situation.

He was also Theodate's lover, a well-kept secret that even Honor would never have guessed if she hadn't discovered them dallying upstairs one quiet afternoon.

He grinned, displaying irresistible twin dimples. "Of course."

Wes pulled the crate into the downstairs drawing room and unpacked while Theo watched impatiently. As soon as Wes slid the painting out of its protective crate, Theo tore off its paper wrapping with the eagerness of the child on Christmas morning. Then she stood back to admire her latest purchase.

She clasped her hands to her bosom. "How magnificent!"

The still life depicted plump oranges arranged on a blue and white cloth, with a bowl of apples in the background.

"They look good enough to eat," Honor said. "Who painted it?"

"Paul Cézanne," Theo said, darting this way and that to examine it from all angles. "This is the first of his works that I've purchased, but it certainly won't be my last."

They were so engrossed in admiring the painting that they didn't pay attention when the doorbell rang. Jackson did. He went to the door and returned seconds later.

"Excuse me, Miss Honor, there is a gentleman here to see you. He says his name is Robert Davis."

Robert Davis had never before encountered a butler. He wondered if they all looked as though they wore starched drawers.

"If you'll wait one moment," this one said, "I'll see if Miss Elliott is at home." He closed the door, leaving Robert to wait outside in a late afternoon chill growing colder by the second.

He clasped his arms for warmth. She had to be here. She told him she was going home. He had seen her get into the carriage.

The door opened. The butler said, "Miss Elliott will see you," and stood aside for Robert to enter.

The foyer was the same size as the one at his boarding-house, but there was no lingering odor of last night's cooking, just a subtle, well-bred hint of beeswax polish. The fine parquet floor and dark wainscoting had a soft, lustrous patina that betrayed their costliness. He wondered if the inhabitants ever took such luxury for granted. He knew he never would.

He barely had time to glance at a gold-framed oval mirror hanging over a narrow table placed to receive gloves and canes before a woman emerged from a doorway. Immediately her dynamic presence dominated the foyer.

"How do you do, Mr. Davis?" she said in a warm, refined

voice, extending her hand. "I am Theodate Tree, Honor's aunt."

Not a common Alice or Mary but an exotic *Thee*-o-date.

He stared. Her youthful, unlined face and dark brows clashed with that cloud of white hair. Then he remembered his manners and took her delicate hand in his large one. Should he shake it? Kiss it? Finally he just bowed over it. "Pleased to meet you, Miss Tree."

The black eyes, so similar to her niece's, twinkled. "Mrs. Tree. I'm a widow." Before he could comment, she turned in a crisp rustle of taffeta and headed back to the doorway. "Do come and join us."

Inside the drawing room, Honor and a tall young man stood admiring and discussing a painting of fruit. He wondered why they thought it worthy of such expansive praise. It was just a picture.

"Mr. Davis," Honor said coolly. "This is a surprise."

He swallowed hard. Gone was the uniform of prim white shirtwaist and long skirt she usually wore to class. Now she was dressed in a shimmering, loose-fitting gown with no corset to restrain her subtle curves, but she still wore her ever-present locket. She had let down her hair and caught it back with a green ribbon so that it tumbled past her shoulders in a soft black cloud. He wanted to wrap it around his fist and bury his face in it.

". . . and this is Wesley Saltonsall," Mrs. Tree said, "an old family friend."

"Davis," he said, extending his hand and smiling a perfect dimpled smile.

Robert sized him up as they shook hands, then dismissed him as nothing more than a good-looking Brahmin who probably had never pulled on his own drawers in his life. "Saltonsall."

Honor said, "To what do we owe the pleasure of this call, Mr. Davis?"

"I needed to talk with you."

She regarded him with the same expression he had seen so often in class, a thoughtful, assessing look that told him she was examining the issue from both sides and carefully weighing all possible outcomes. "And it couldn't wait until class tomorrow?"

"No."

"Very well. Follow me." She glided toward a door at the end of the hall, and he caught the faint, sweet scent of roses. "Aunt Theo, we shall be in the library. Don't be alarmed if you hear glass breaking."

Mrs. Tree's tinkling laughter echoed through the foyer. Robert kept his gaze on Honor's proud back.

Once inside the library, Honor closed the door behind her and turned to face him. "What do you want, Mr. Davis? After the way you insulted me this afternoon, I—"

"I didn't insult you. I kissed you." And I'd do it again, right now, if I thought I could get away with it.

"To kiss me without my permission is to insult me." She walked toward him. "I don't appreciate men I barely know taking such liberties."

He bowed his head and tried to look contrite. "I don't know what the devil got into me. After you drove off, I realized that I had behaved badly. That's why I'm here, to apologize."

"I beg your pardon?"

"You heard me. I'm here to say I'm sorry."

"I see."

"And you'd better accept this apology, because I won't make it again."

Her obsidian eyes flashed in a rare display of anger. "Contrary to what you may think, I don't carry a grudge. I accept your apology." She paused. "One thing puzzles me. Why did you come here to deliver your apology in person? You could have waited until class tomorrow."

"Just like a lawyer, always suspicious of motives." He grinned and looked around the room. "I wanted to see your fancy house for myself. I'll bet it has another parlor upstairs and hot-water heating."

"I rather doubt you came here just to make that observation. Come, come, Mr. Davis. What is your real reason for coming here?"

He looked at her. "I'm a blunt man, Miss Elliott. I don't hide behind flowery words and fine manners like your rich friend Saltonsall out there. Plain and simple, I'm here because I want another chance."

"Another chance to do what?"

"To prove to you that you're wrong about me."

He expected her to whirl on her heel and head for the door, but she merely folded her arms and regarded him with that unnerving, assessing stare. "Why do you care what I think of you?"

"I just do."

She fell silent for a moment, still studying him. "Contrary to what you may think, I'm not wealthy." She waved her hand, encompassing the room. "This is all my aunt's. I live here on her charity."

"Why would I care about that?" Then he understood her implication all too well. His face grew hot, and he saw red. "You think I'm some—some damned fortune hunter?"

"You wouldn't be the first," she said with an infuriating smile.

He strode over to her and stood so close he could see the gold sunbursts surrounding the pupils of her exotic black eyes, like eclipsed suns. "I don't need any woman's money, damn you. I'll make a pile of my own someday."

She didn't step back, and her gaze didn't falter. "Then I'm sorry if I insulted you."

He stepped away. "You should be." He straightened the lapels of his coat. "We can help each other, you know."

"Help each other? How?"

"I noticed you aren't doing too well in constitutional law."

She made a face. "You needn't remind me."

"Well, I excel at it, so let's negotiate. I'll help you study, and you'll give me a second chance."

At first he thought she was going to burst out laughing,

but she didn't. "If I agree and declare a truce, will you agree to stop badgering me in our other classes?"

"That point is not open to negotiation. My badgering is going to make you a better lawyer."

She looked skeptical. "Is that why you persist?"

"Of course. Once you're in a courtroom, your opponents won't treat you like a lady. They'll tear you to pieces and laugh while they're doing it."

Her expression froze. "I never expect preferential treatment from anyone."

He smiled. "Then don't expect me to stop badgering you for your own good."

She studied him, then said, "All right. We have a deal."

He extended his hand. "Shake on it."

She did so reluctantly, as if she expected him to pull her into his arms and kiss her again. She must read minds, he thought. He restrained himself, shaking her hand and releasing it just as reluctantly.

There came a knock. When Honor bade the caller enter, her aunt swept through the doorway.

"When I didn't hear glass breaking, I began to worry," she said.

"As you can see," Honor said, "the windows are intact, and we've just concluded our discussion."

"Splendid. Then Mr. Davis will be staying for tea?"

Robert hadn't eaten since breakfast, and the thought of his pennypinching landlady's usual fare of tough, stringy mutton and overboiled cabbage made his stomach growl. He thanked Mrs. Tree and said he'd be delighted to stay for tea.

Honor watched Robert Davis eat as though this were his last meal.

Wes had gone to the Somerset Club, so only Honor, Aunt Theo, and Davis sat down in the upstairs parlor to a sumptuous tea. Honor noticed that her aunt had thoughtfully augmented their usual light fare of buttered toast and muffins with more substantial offerings of cold ham and roast beef.

"Do help yourself, Mr. Davis," Aunt Theo said, pouring her specially blended tea from a silver pot into two Spode cups. She herself had changed into a dramatic tea gown of magenta silk that made her look like a vibrant tropical flower, and she eschewed her usual glass of beer for tea.

"Don't mind if I do." He filled his plate with meat and bread, then balanced it on his knees.

When Honor finished nibbling on a muffin, she said, "Do you come from Boston, Mr. Davis?"

"Lowell," he replied.

"Lowell is noted for its many textile mills," Theo said.

"I used to work in one of them," Davis said.

That explains why he resents the wealthy so much, Honor thought, sipping her tea.

"What type of work did you do?" Theo said.

Robert finished his roast beef and reached for more. "I started out as a weaver and worked my way up to foreman."

Honor said, "Very ambitious and determined."

He glanced at her sharply. "It's the only way to be if you want to get somewhere in this world."

"And where is this 'somewhere' you'd like to go?" Theo said.

He dabbed at his mouth with his napkin, then set aside his empty plate, no doubt to avoid appearing greedy. "I want to go to New York City and practice law for men like J. Pierpont Morgan and William Rockefeller. They need lawyers to help them make more money and keep what they have. I intend to be one of them."

"I want to defend the helpless," Honor said.

His gaze held hers. "Is that why you want to become a lawyer?"

She didn't want to tell him about her father. "I come from a long line of bluestockings." That was explanation enough.

Davis looked across the tea table at Theo. "But you're not a lawyer, Mrs. Tree."

"No, I'm not. But I passionately believe in education for

women, and I have always encouraged Honor to follow her own road."

Davis turned to Honor. "Do your parents live here too?"

"My parents are dead," she replied in a flat tone that plainly warned him this subject was closed.

He made a sympathetic noise.

"And yours?" she said.

"Dead also."

Honor said, "I'm curious as to why you wanted to attend law school. You could just as easily have served an apprenticeship with another lawyer and saved the expense."

"I did for a short time," he replied, "but I didn't learn much. School will give me an advantage." Resentment flared briefly in his eyes, then died. "I scrimped and saved for years. I can afford to attend law school."

But just barely, Honor thought, glancing at the frayed coat cuffs covering bony wrists and several loose buttons hanging by a thread from his waistcoat. He did not look like a man who took care of himself.

"Where are you living in Boston?" Theo said.

"A boardinghouse in the South End," he replied. Davis looked from Honor to her aunt as if daring them to comment. "My room's not even half the size of your parlor here, but the rent's cheap and it's clean, and once I graduate from law school, I'll never have to live in a boardinghouse again."

"I'm sure you won't," Theo said. She poured him a second cup of tea. "Please help yourself, Mr. Davis. If any food is returned to the kitchen, my cook takes it as a personal insult and feeds us all bread and water until we're properly chastened."

He didn't need a second invitation.

Later, when nothing remained but crumbs, their guest drained his teacup, patted his lips with his napkin, and thanked Theo for her hospitality. When Davis rose, Theo bade Honor show him out.

In the downstairs foyer, Davis turned to her. "You won't regret giving me a second chance."

She recalled his offer to share his expertise in constitutional law. "I don't intend to."

He grasped her hand and drew it to his lips. "Good-bye. I'll see you in class tomorrow."

"Yes." She showed him to the door. When she opened it, a sharp gust of wind rushed in, tugging at her skirt hem and causing her to shiver. The sun had already set, turning the horizon the deep blue of twilight. "I'd offer you the carriage, but it's been put away for the evening."

He shivered. "No need. I'll get home the same way I came."

On foot no doubt, Honor thought, resisting the impulse to slip him money for the streetcar.

Trotting down the stairs, he turned once to look back at her with a penetrating stare. Then he flipped up his collar and was gone, striding down the sidewalk.

Honor closed the door and went back inside to warmth and light, all too conscious of Robert Davis tackling the cold autumn evening as if it were his mortal enemy.

CHAPTER 2

THE NEXT DAY, HONOR arrived at her constitutional law class fifteen minutes early.

Several men were already there, huddled together and talking among themselves. They exchanged warning looks and stopped speaking the moment she walked through the door.

She wished them good morning, sat down near the front of the classroom, and opened her notebook. As the minutes passed, several more students entered the classroom. Honor heard low voices punctuated by snickering, but she ignored them.

When one of the men sat on the desk top right next to her, she looked up to find Hubert Adcock smirking down at her, his round face aglow with all the anticipation of a nasty little boy preparing to pull the wings off a helpless fly.

She suppressed a shudder of revulsion. "Yes?"

He addressed the rest of the class. "Gentlemen, your attention please." The room fell silent. "I'll bet none of you know that you're going to school with the daughter of a convicted murderer."

The blood drained from Honor's cheeks. For one horrible moment black spots danced before her eyes and she couldn't breathe.

Adcock grinned as surprised muttering filled the room. "Yes, gentlemen, our own lady law student here is the daughter of one Jasper Elliott, a rich Chicago meat-packer who was convicted of murdering a business associate and hanged for his heinous crime."

White-hot rage welled up in Honor, and she suppressed the urge to wring Adcock's scrawny neck.

Still grinning, he said, "Does the dean know we've got a murderer's daughter going to our law school?"

"Let's tell 'im!" someone shouted.

Adcock stuck his turned-up nose inches away from Honor's face. "What person in his right mind would want to be represented by the daughter of—" His sentence ended in a strangled squawk as an arm appeared out of nowhere and a large hand grabbed him by the collar and dragged him off the desk.

Robert Davis, his face livid and his eyes dark with rage, propelled the choking, goggle-eyed Adcock across the aisle and slammed him against the nearest wall. "Why don't you pick on someone your own size?"

Two of Adcock's cohorts jumped out of their seats and started toward him, fists clenched and faces aflame with retribution. Honor watched, helpless, as they bore down on her rescuer.

Before they reached him, a furious voice bellowed, "What's going on here?" from the doorway.

Everyone stopped and watched as "Pudding" Weymouth, the constitutional law professor, came waddling into the classroom. Though as portly as the Christmas pudding that gave him his nickname, he was seldom jolly, and now his stout frame shook with anger.

"I warned them there would be fighting if we admitted women." He waddled toward his desk, his forehead shiny with sweat. "But did any of them listen to me? Of course not. 'You're behind the times,' they said. 'Women have just as much right to an education as men,' they said."

Davis flung Adcock away as if he were poison. "He insulted the lady."

"Take your seats," Weymouth said to Adcock's cronies. "I'll not have hooliganism in my classroom, no matter who is responsible." Then he turned to the brawlers. "Did you insult Miss Elliott, Mr. Adcock?"

Rubbing his reddened Adam's apple and glowering at Davis, Adcock croaked, "I just told the truth about her."

Honor rose, her insides shaking. "A half-truth, Mr. Adcock."

Weymouth flung his pudgy hands into the air. "I think we've wasted enough time discussing this."

Honor held her ground. "I would like your permission to address the class, Professor Weymouth."

He sighed and rolled his eyes. "From what I've heard, no one can stop you."

"Professor Weymouth—"

"Oh, all right, all right, all right!" Weymouth mopped his brow with a handkerchief. "Just say your piece as quickly as possible, Miss Elliott, and be done with it. I do have a class to teach."

Honor faced the class, her head held high. "As aspiring lawyers, we're taught to think objectively and to assemble all the facts. You, gentlemen, have done neither.

"It is true that my father, Jasper Elliott, was convicted of murder in the first degree and executed in Chicago ten years ago. What Mr. Adcock so conveniently neglected to mention is that my father was framed. A year later he was vindicated when another man confessed to the crime."

She let her contemptuous gaze slowly rove around the classroom. "My father was innocent, and even if he hadn't been, his crime would have no bearing on my ability to practice law." Then she turned to Adcock. "I would suggest you get your facts straight before you make false accusations, Mr. Adcock, or someday you'll find yourself sued for slander."

She would not give them the satisfaction of seeing her bolt from the room in tears. She kept her features composed and forced herself to sit down, conscious of hostile stares boring into her back like daggers.

Weymouth gave her a contemptuous look that plainly said "Uppity woman," then turned his attention to his notes.

Adcock glared at Davis in thin-lipped hostility, then slunk off to his seat like a whipped cur.

"As for you, Mr. Davis," Weymouth said, "I'll have no

more brawling in my classroom for any reason, is that clear?"

"Yes, sir." Robert took the seat next to Honor but didn't so much as glance at her.

Honor couldn't concentrate. She remembered all too vividly those horrible weeks after her father's arrest when people she thought were her family's friends acted as though the Elliotts had suddenly contracted the plague. Neighbors whispered behind their hands and cut Honor and her mother in the street. Children who had been lifelong playmates threw stones and called her "the Butcher's Daughter."

Honor feigned rapt attention during Weymouth's boring lecture, but his words were nothing more than the unintelligible buzz of so many industrious bees on a hot summer day.

Finally, after what seemed like an eternity, the portly professor glanced up at the clock on the wall, assembled his notes, and said, "Gentlemen—and our esteemed Miss Elliott—that will be all for today."

Honor closed her eyes and breathed a sigh of relief. When she opened them, she found Robert Davis staring at her.

"Do you have another class today?" he said.

The gentle concern in his voice caught her off guard. She shook her head.

"Neither do I. Why don't you let me escort you home?"

Honor looked at him askance. "The last time you escorted me anywhere, you kissed me against my will."

He rose. "I promise to be the perfect gentleman this time. Perhaps we could study together."

"Fair enough."

She let Davis collect her books, and they left the classroom without incident.

Once outside in the cool autumn air, Honor forced her father from her mind. "I appreciate your defending me, but I can defend myself."

Davis gave her an odd look. "Don't you get tired of it?"

"Of what?"

"Being so strong all the time."

"I have to be strong," she retorted, "or fools like Adcock and Weymouth will eat me alive." She looked at him. "I would have thought you, of all people, would understand that."

"I do, but I also know that sometimes you have to put aside your pride and let other people help you."

Honor lifted the collar of her velvet cape to keep him from seeing how much his words had affected her. "The carriage is over here. My aunt won't mind if we study in the library."

Once inside the carriage, Honor closed her eyes and leaned her head back against the soft leather squabs. Damn Adcock to hell for resurrecting the story about her father! Honor bit her lower lip to keep it from trembling and revealing to Robert Davis how close she was to losing her precious self-control.

Seated across from her, he said, "Is what Adcock said about your father true?"

"For the most part."

Davis sat silently for what seemed like an eternity. Finally he said, "That must have been a terrible time for you."

"It was."

"Tell me about it."

She stared down at her clenched hands. "You must think me an ungrateful wretch after you so kindly came to my rescue today." She looked over at him. "But I've always found it difficult to bare my soul to strangers."

"I consider myself your friend, not a stranger, and friends confide in each other."

Honor considered his offer. Perhaps it was time she trusted someone other than her aunt.

"I'll never forget the morning my father was arrested," she began. "It was two days after my fifteenth birthday. We were halfway through breakfast when Moira, our parlor-maid, came flying into the dining room as though she had just seen a banshee. Three policemen followed her."

In a halting voice she told Davis how the father she adored rose from his seat at the head of the table and bellowed, "What is the meaning of this?" in his majestic baritone voice.

Honor retrieved her handkerchief from her skirt pocket and dabbed at her eyes. "When they told him that an associate had been murdered the night before and that they were arresting him for the crime, he shrank in stature right before my very eyes."

Davis asked, "What grounds did they have?"

"This associate was a financier who advised my father about investments. It was common knowledge that my father had lost a great deal of money because of bad advice, and that he and this man had been having bitter disagreements. They had quarreled often and loudly. Witnesses came forward to say they had overheard my father threaten to kill him." She shook her head in disbelief. "So when the man was found shot to death in his library, the police blamed my father."

"What proof did they have?"

"My father had called on the financier the night he was killed. Unfortunately, Father never told my mother or any of our servants where he was going. He swore that the man was alive when he left, but since the financier had given his own servants the night off, he and my father were alone. No one saw what really happened. No one could corroborate Father's story."

"What about your father's driver? Surely he saw something."

"Father sent him away and told him to return half an hour later. He didn't hear or see anything."

"And the neighbors?"

"They claimed they didn't hear a thing."

"What about the murder weapon?"

"Since Father often worked late, he kept a loaded gun in his desk at the office. When the police searched for the gun, they found it missing, so they claimed my father used it to shoot his business associate, then got rid of it. Unfortunately, Father's gun was of the same type as the murder weapon."

"So they convicted your father of premeditated murder and executed him."

Fresh tears filled her eyes, and she looked out the carriage window again. "My mother was devastated. She cried all the time and walked around in a daze. I tried to help her as much as I could, but she was inconsolable. Later she went into a decline and died of a broken heart."

She felt her hand enfolded in a warm clasp and found Robert Davis seated next to her. She resisted the urge to withdraw her hand and let herself take comfort in his strength.

"Did you go to the trial?" he said softly.

"Every day. Father's lawyer wanted me there to evoke sympathy in the jurors. I sat there day after day, listening to people who didn't know my father say vile, untrue things about him."

A picture of her father flashed through her mind. She saw him, white-faced with resignation, as he stood in his jail cell and said good-bye to Honor and her mother the night before he was hanged.

Davis squeezed her hand. "You said in class that someone else later confessed to the crime."

"The financier's wife had been carrying on with another man," Honor said. "She plotted with her lover to kill her husband so she would inherit his fortune, and the two of them framed my father. Her lover broke into my father's office and stole his gun. When the wife's plan succeeded and she got the money, she foolishly discarded her accomplice and married someone else. She assumed her former lover would keep their secret, for if he didn't, he would implicate himself as well. She didn't count on his obsessive love for her." Honor took a deep shuddering breath. "He confessed and implicated the both of them."

"Were they convicted?"

Honor nodded. "And hanged. Together. Fitting, don't you think?"

Davis muttered, "Hell hath no fury like a lover scorned."

"Too late to do my father any good," Honor said bitterly. "People never remember that he was exonerated, but they never forget that he was convicted of murder."

She unbuttoned the top button of her cape, pulled out her locket and opened the gold engraved oval. "This is a picture of my parents in happier times. Minerva and Jasper Elliott."

"You obviously inherited your mother's beauty." Davis sat back in his seat. "So you want to become a lawyer because of what happened to your father."

She closed the locket and smiled dryly. "As foolish as it may seem, yes."

"You think it foolish?"

"Isn't it foolish of me to subject myself to the Weymouths and Adcocks of the world when I could be married and caring for a husband and children, oblivious of the many injustices in this society? After all, my becoming a lawyer won't bring my father back."

Davis looked at her and said nothing.

"It's difficult to explain." She groped for the right words. "What happened to my father had a profound effect on me. Like most people, I was raised to respect the law. I thought that the guilty were always punished and the innocent always set free." She laughed mirthlessly. "Oh, what a naive fool I was! I saw my own innocent father convicted and sentenced to death for a crime he didn't commit.

"It wasn't supposed to happen that way. I was appalled and furious at the injustice of it. I wanted to do something to help him, but I was helpless." She pursed her lips. "I hated it."

"Considering the overwhelming evidence against him, there was nothing you could have done," Davis said gently.

"True. But if I become a lawyer myself, perhaps I can spare someone else such an undeserved fate."

Davis raised his brows in astonishment. "You realize that no woman lawyer has ever argued a criminal case on the East Coast."

"Then I intend to be the first," she replied coldly.

"As much as I admire your determination and idealism, I think the odds are stacked against you."

"I'll just have to stack them in my favor by working twice as hard."

"Did you come to Boston after your mother died?"

"Yes. Her only sister offered me a home. My father had lost much of his wealth when he made those bad investments, and Aunt Theo's husband had just died after a long illness, so she insisted that I come to live with her."

"You're lucky she was here for you."

"Very lucky. Aunt Theo has been like a mother to me."

They arrived at Honor's house, spent the rest of the morning studying together, had luncheon, and continued studying all afternoon.

That night she dreamed of her father.

The dream never varied. Snow always fell from a low gray sky, filling the prison yard. The damned black chessmen marred its pristine surface. Her father, his hands bound behind his back, walked alone toward the scaffold, leaving deep footprints in the snow.

Honor screamed his name and tried to save him, but the snow held her feet fast. He never turned around. He climbed the scaffold steps. His hands were suddenly free, and Honor stood beside him. She placed the noose around her own father's neck.

Honor screamed as he dropped through the trapdoor and the rope went taut. The scaffold vanished. Nothing remained but footprints and chessmen in the snow.

She awoke panting and bathed in a cold, acrid sweat, her cramped fingers clutching the sheets, her heart pounding irrationally. She lit a lamp and sat up in bed.

It was only a dream, she told herself, hugging her knees. Only a dream.

She knew sleep would be a long time coming. It always was, after the dream.

Two weeks later Honor sat in constitutional law class awaiting the results of the most recent test. She stared out the window at the pewter-gray clouds hanging low in the November sky and prayed that her frequent study sessions with Robert Davis had done her some good.

She held her breath when Pudding Weymouth rolled into class, dabbing at his sweating forehead, his bulging stomach preceding him like the prow of a ship. When he reached his desk, he removed the test papers from his valise and waddled around the room to distribute them.

Honor risked a glance at Davis, seated to her right. He gave her an encouraging smile.

Weymouth's slow, deliberate footsteps approached. Honor took a deep breath and uttered one last prayer.

Weymouth stopped beside her desk.

Honor looked up.

His mouth pursed in a thin line of disapproval above his three chins, he said, "You've improved since the last test, Miss Elliott." He handed her the papers.

The butterflies fluttering in her stomach disappeared when she saw the *A* written near her name. Grinning with elation, she could have even hugged Pudding, but she caught Davis's eye instead. He grinned back and held up his own paper with its *A*.

"Congratulations," he said later, once class was over and they were walking together across campus.

Still smiling from ear to ear, her cheeks flushed with a combination of cold and exultation, Honor said, "I couldn't have done it without your help, Mr. Davis."

He studied her, his green eyes twinkling. "Since you're now in my debt, the least you could do is call me Robert."

Caught off guard, Honor felt a rare warmth flood her cheeks. "All right. Robert it is. And you may call me Honor."

"I like your name. It has a solid legal sound to it."

For the first time since Davis had known her, Honor really laughed, an earthy, unladylike rumble that came from deep inside her and filled the air with joy. "Ironic, isn't it?" She paused. "Would you care to return to the house with me? We can have a celebratory luncheon."

"You and your aunt are always feeding me." His green eyes twinkled. "Not that I'm complaining."

"Aunt Theo thinks you need fattening up."

Davis patted his flat midsection through his threadbare overcoat. "Then I shall turn into Pudding."

They laughed and bantered all the way to where Simms and the black brougham waited. Once inside, Davis surprised Honor by sitting beside her and saying, "Do you mind if I give you a congratulatory kiss?"

She thought of the last time he had forcibly kissed her, and a delicious shiver of expectation rippled along her arms. At least he had asked her permission this time.

His gaze roved over her face. "You're not afraid of me, are you?"

Today her triumph in constitutional law made her giddy and reckless. "Should I be?"

"Oh, yes."

Davis turned in his seat and crooked his index finger to lift her stubborn chin, then studied her face with a hunger that sent Honor's heart to slamming against her ribs. He closed his eyes and reached for her mouth with his own. The moment Honor's lips touched his, desire hot and deep claimed her.

When Davis pulled away, ending the kiss, Honor felt strangely bereft, as if the blazing parlor fire had gone out on a cold winter's day. She wanted to pull him into her arms and kiss him again, but her courage failed her.

"Congratulations," he said.

"I owe it all to you. If you hadn't helped me study, I—"

"It was my pleasure."

They rode the rest of the way in silence.

One night three weeks later a stranger came to the front door of the brownstone and asked to see Mrs. Sydney Tree on a matter of grave importance. When Jackson saw the man's card, he nodded and admitted him at once, for he knew his mistress had been anxiously awaiting this call. Theo received the caller in the library. They spoke for an hour; then the man left.

Theo reread the report the visitor had prepared for her, then locked it safely away in the bottom right-hand drawer of her late husband's desk. She prayed that no one else would ever see it.

Chapter 3

With Christmas just two weeks away, Honor sequestered herself in the library to wrap Robert's gift, a pair of butter-soft cordovan leather gloves to replace his old, moth-eaten knit ones.

Just as Honor finished tying the ribbon, Aunt Theo appeared in the doorway waving a cream-colored envelope. "This just arrived for you, sweet Portia. It's from Penelope Grant and it looks like an invitation."

Penelope Grant had been Honor's best friend when she first moved to Boston, but had drifted away once she made an excellent marriage to an up-and-coming young lawyer and started having babies.

Honor opened the heavy vellum envelope and read the message: "Penny has invited me and a guest to attend a dinner party this Saturday."

Theo looked at her. "Will you go?"

Honor made a face. "I really don't have much in common with her anymore."

"Why don't you go anyway? You haven't seen your old friends in years, and your studies certainly wouldn't suffer if you took one evening off to relax and socialize."

Honor glanced down at the wrapped gloves. "I could ask Robert to accompany me."

Theo's brows rose. "Really?"

"I sense you disapprove. May I ask why?"

"Do you think he'll fit in?"

"He's got nothing to be ashamed of. He's not a mill worker anymore; he's studying to be a lawyer." Honor frowned. "Why the reservations, Aunt? I thought you liked Robert. You certainly enjoyed his company when he came for Thanksgiving dinner."

"You know how closed and stuffy Boston society is. They tolerate my eccentric behavior only because the Putnam family has been here for the last two hundred years and because I was married to one of the Trees, who've been here even longer." She smoothed her skirt with a restless hand. "Proper Bostonians can be so closed-minded and snobbish. I wouldn't want Robert to feel uncomfortable, that's all."

Honor contemplated her point in silence.

"I doubt that Robert even owns evening clothes," Theo added. "You can't expect him to go in his usual attire when all the other men will be wearing white tie."

Honor's spirits sank. "I hadn't thought of that. He can't even afford to pay fifteen cents for a new collar let alone buy expensive evening clothes."

She suddenly brightened. "I have it! Aren't some of Uncle Oak's evening clothes packed away in the attic?" she said, referring to her late uncle Sydney by his nickname. When Theo nodded, Honor added, "Perhaps something could be altered to fit Robert—that is, if you don't mind seeing Uncle's clothes on another man."

"I'd rather someone use them than let them rot away." Theo glided over to the fireplace. "Come to think of it, Oak was the same height and had almost the same build as Robert. But aren't you putting the cart before the horse? You don't know if Robert will even want to go."

"I shall ask him on Monday."

"Don't be disappointed if he refuses."

The following Monday, when Honor invited Robert to accompany her to Penelope Grant's soiree, he accepted. If the prospect of rubbing elbows with Boston's elite daunted him, he never revealed his misgivings. When Theo offered him the use of her late husband's evening clothes, he appeared reluctant to accept, until Honor convinced him otherwise.

To Theo, this was not a good sign.

"How do I look?" Honor turned away from the cheval glass to nervously present herself to Aunt Theo for her inspection.

Since green was Honor's favorite color, she had dusted off an evening gown of forest green velvet and ivory moire that stood up to her dark, exotic coloring in a way that pale shades never could. Their maid, Fiona, had dressed Honor's black hair in an intricate upswept arrangement and crowned it with a white aigrette. For tonight Honor left off her locket.

"I have the perfect finishing touch," Theo announced, and left the room. She returned moments later to offer her niece a pair of earbobs set with a king's ransom in emeralds.

Honor gasped. "Oh, Aunt Theo . . . I couldn't possibly accept these." She knew the earbobs were the last gift Uncle Oak had given to Theo just before he died. Her aunt could never bear to wear them.

"Nonsense," Theo replied, her voice husky. "They were meant to be worn."

Once the jewels hung from Honor's earlobes, Theo stepped back. "Perfect. They're all the adornment you need."

Honor hugged Theo in silent thanks, for she knew the significance of the gesture.

Fiona appeared in the doorway. "Mr. Davis has arrived."

He was waiting for Honor in the downstairs foyer. She paused at the top of the stairs, and when he slowly turned around and looked up at her, she felt her heart give a queer little flutter.

He wore Uncle Oak's recently altered evening clothes with a careless elegance as if he had been born to them. The black jacket and snowy white shirtfront provided a perfect foil for Robert's dark hair and green eyes, making him look almost handsome.

Those green eyes filled with admiration as they followed Honor's graceful descent down the stairs. "You look beautiful," he said, taking her hand and bringing it to his lips.

He would never qualify as handsome, but Honor could honestly say, "And you look quite dashing."

A self-deprecating smile twisted his sensuous mouth. "I've been told that a good tailor can make a silk purse out of a sow's ear. Now I know it's true."

Close upon Honor's heels, Theo said, "Come, come, Mr. Davis, let's dispense with the false modesty, shall we? You know you're a damn fine figure of a man. Confident. Self-assured."

His clean-shaven cheeks colored slightly, and he bowed. "If you say so, Mrs. Tree."

"I do." Theo handed Honor her purse. "It's six-thirty. You'd better be off if you want to arrive there by seven."

Jackson presented Robert with Honor's heavy black satin evening cloak, and once she was ready to leave, he put on his overcoat and borrowed silk top hat, and they left.

Seated beside him inside the brougham, Honor said, "I'm glad you could accompany me tonight."

"I'm looking forward to meeting your friends," Robert replied. Wealthy, influential people who could open doors for him.

"You look very distinguished."

He straightened his white tie. "I've never had clothes tailored for me." He planned to have more of them in the future, these expensive coats that didn't pull through the shoulders and trousers that were not too loose in the waist. "I always wore whatever my mother sewed."

"Aunt Theo was afraid you wouldn't accept them."

"I wasn't going to. Borrowed clothes make me feel like a charity case and I have my pride, but I wanted to dress right. I didn't want to embarrass you."

By the light of the carriage lamps, Honor's expression clouded. "You wouldn't have embarrassed me. I don't judge people by what they wear."

"Most do."

"Then they're fools."

Davis said, "If Pudding could see you now, he'd—" He stopped. "Never mind."

"What were you about to say?"

"Nothing."

"Robert, don't tease. Tell me."

"I was going to say that if Pudding could see you now, he'd rest his case against beautiful women lawyers in the courtroom. But I knew you'd be insulted."

Her eyes darkened. "I'm not insulted."

Tonight she was ravishing, a breathtaking study in black and white, with the rich satin sheen of her evening cloak and her own night-black hair shrouding her pale face in mystery. Only the green earbobs and her own red lips provided any color. Robert longed to kiss her, to feel those lips soften and part under the domination of his mouth.

He took a deep breath, filling his nostrils with her sweet rose scent and settled back against the soft leather squabs. The kissing, and perhaps a little more this time if Honor was willing as he sensed her to be, would have to wait.

When Honor and Robert arrived at the Grants' brick house on Beacon Hill, a maid took their wraps and showed them to the parlor where all the guests were admiring the perfect Christmas tree, its thick evergreen branches filled to groaning with white tapers all ablaze, paper cones stuffed with sugarplums for the children, shiny tinsel garlands, and an angel that nearly scraped its outstretched wings against the high ceiling.

"We hauled it all the way from Lexington in a wagon," Amos Grant said to Wesley Saltonsall in his loud, pompous voice. "A devil of a time with it, but couldn't disappoint the boys."

Conversation ceased the moment Honor and Robert appeared in the doorway. Penelope, a diminutive blonde, rose from the velvet sofa where she had been talking to a woman Honor recognized as the wife of Aunt Theo's banker.

"Honor," Penelope said, extending her hands as she glided toward them, "how delighted we are that you could come. It's been such a long time." She touched cheeks and looked at Robert expectantly.

"Penelope Grant, this is Robert Davis, a fellow law student."

Penelope smiled archly. "And such a distinguished one."

Robert returned the smile and bowed over her hand. "It's a pleasure meeting you, Mrs. Grant."

"Do come over and meet everyone else." She ushered them into the warm, cozy room, where logs crackled and burned in the fireplace, scenting the air with appropriately festive woodsmoke.

Since Honor already knew the other guests and felt at home among them, she focused on observing how Robert reacted to being thrown to the lions, and their reactions to him. If his background made him nervous among the lawyers, bankers, and shipping scions present, he didn't show it as he bowed over the ladies' hands and shook their husbands' with a firm grip.

Honor held her breath when they came to Wesley. Unlike anyone else present, he alone knew how Theo had turned a sow's ear into a silk purse.

He extended his hand, too gracious to betray them. "Good to see you again, Davis." He turned to Amos Grant. "If Cutter, Bailey and Rye need another lawyer, Davis here is your man." He smiled his dimpled smile at Honor. "Or Honor is your woman."

Honor returned his smile. "How generous of you to say so, Wes." But then, he always strived to put outsiders at ease.

Amos Grant, a young man already stretching his waistcoat across an ample belly, cleared his throat with a pompous harrumph. "Cutter and Bailey has never hired a female and never will."

Honor felt her hackles rise and had opened her mouth to deliver a scathing retort when Penelope, with a nose for averting social disaster, swooped down on them with offers of sherry and drew Honor aside to converse with the other women.

Honor was beginning to regret having agreed to come tonight.

Robert took the port decanter that Freddie Horsley, banker and avid sportsman, slid across the table to him, and measured a cautious two fingers' worth, no more, into his glass.

The sumptuous dinner was over, and the ladies had retired to the parlor, leaving the gentlemen to their port and Amos Grant's excellent Cuban cigars.

Leaning back in his chair and unbuttoning the bottom two buttons of his waistcoat to let out his bloated belly, Amos Grant cleared his throat with a loud harrumph. "So, Davis, you from Boston?"

"Maine, originally."

Grant puffed on his cigar. "I have a place in Bar Harbor. Penny and the boys go up there every summer, and I join them on weekends."

Now we're getting down to business, Robert thought. This is where they see if I'm one of them.

He considered fabricating an acceptable background, but then he realized that anything he said would get back to Honor or her aunt through Saltonsall. No, best to tell the truth. At least for now.

He sipped his port and hoped for the best. "My family owned a farm near Portland."

"How many acres?" Grant demanded. "Five hundred? A thousand?"

"Only two hundred." He saw Grant analyze that information and conclude that Robert Davis was "not one of us."

Freddie Horsley said, "There's good shooting up in Maine." The banker believed that most animals were put on earth to be shot, hooked on a line, or chased by hounds. Of the men Robert had met tonight, he had found Horsley to be the most likable and congenial. "Do you do much hunting, Davis?"

"I go shooting occasionally." A lie, but he doubted that it would ever be tested.

Saltonsall smiled. "To Freddie, hunting means riding to hounds."

Cleavon Frame, another lawyer and older than the other men present by a good twenty years, said, "Damn fool sport, fox hunting. Who wants to get up at the crack of dawn on a cold winter's morning to bruise his balls bouncing around on the back of a horse!"

"I do!" Freddie exclaimed indignantly. "Besides, the saddle doesn't bruise the old balls; it toughens 'em up for the ladies."

Robert joined in the collective ribald laughter.

Frame said, "It takes more than tough balls to please the ladies, Freddie. You should know that at your age." When the laughter finally died along with Freddie's good-natured indignation, Frame took a deep drag on his cigar and said to Robert, "How long have you known Honor?"

"Several months. We're classmates at the university."

Frame nodded. "She's spent the last two summers clerking at Royce and Ellis."

Grant gave a disapproving harrumph. "I'm surprised you allowed her in the door."

Frame bristled at the younger man's tone. "The Trees have been valued clients ever since the firm was founded, so we had to take her on or risk losing Theodate as a client. We had to hide Honor in a back office so she wouldn't distract the men." He chuckled lasciviously. "Especially me. She is one damn fine looking woman. We won't hire her when she graduates, of course."

"Is she incompetent?" Robert asked.

Frame shrugged. "She could be another Oliver Wendell Holmes and we still wouldn't hire her. It's just not done."

Grant cleared his throat. "Can you imagine what kind of impression a beautiful woman would make on a jury? They'd find for her client whether he was guilty or innocent! There would be appeals right and left."

"Not to mention the absurdity of having a woman put 'Esquire' after her name," Frame said.

Robert said nothing. No use risking his future defending Honor when their minds were made up.

Saltonsall sipped his port, obviously uncomfortable with the controversial nature of the conversation. "You're a lucky man, Davis. Honor is a woman any man would be proud of."

Robert grinned in agreement. "I am lucky."

Freddie said, "If she were my daughter, I'd have married

her off years ago. Her aunt gives her too much freedom. It's not good for a woman to have too much freedom. Before you know it, she'll start telling her husband what to do. Then she'll want to vote. When will it stop?"

Frame shook his head. "It's her aunt's fault for encouraging her. Theodate's husband left her with too much money instead of putting it into a trust and letting me control it. She always was a wild one."

Saltonsall shifted in his chair and said nothing.

Grant took a deep drag on his cigar and blew out a cloud of smoke. He regarded Robert superciliously. "Too bad you didn't go to Harvard. Cutter and Bailey only invites Harvard men."

The right family, the right school. Robert's resentment boiled, but he held it in check. "Harvard is too rich for my blood."

Frame nodded in approval. "So you're a self-made man then, eh?"

Perceiving an advantage, Robert pressed it home. "Yes, sir. I left the family farm without a penny to my name sixteen years ago and worked my way up to foreman at a textile mill in Lowell. After my parents died, I sold the farm to a lumber company at a tidy profit and paid my way through college and law school."

Freddie said, "Ambitious." He stubbed out his cigar. "Honor Elliott would be the perfect wife for an ambitious man—if you could get her to give up her fool notion about becoming a lawyer."

"And if you could curb her sharp tongue," Grant added, blowing smoke into the air. "A woman shouldn't say what's on her mind."

Frame nodded. "The world judges a man by the woman he chooses to marry. A beautiful woman can do wonders for a man's career, especially if she's well connected, like Honor."

Robert sensed the deep, rapid undercurrents, but he couldn't read them successfully so he didn't risk responding. Finally he said, "Honor and I are just friends. There's been no talk of marriage." Yet.

"You could do worse," Saltonsall said, emptying the last of the port and staring moodily into space, his mind obviously elsewhere.

Conversation dwindled and died with the last of the cigars. Their host hoisted himself out of his chair, cleared his throat, and announced that it was time to rejoin the ladies.

Later, after coffee had been served and consumed, Honor and Robert were the first to leave.

As they put on their wraps in the foyer, Honor turned to Robert with an apologetic smile. "I seem to have left my purse in the parlor. Will you get it for me?"

He nodded and returned to the parlor. He was just about to walk in when he heard Freddie Horsley say quite distinctly and contemptuously, "That Davis fellow is obviously a climber."

Robert froze. He hadn't fooled anybody. Honor's wealthy, influential friends had recognized him for what he was, a social climber.

He said loudly over his shoulder, "I think it's in here," more to save himself embarrassment than to spare the men when he walked back into their midst unexpectedly. Only Saltonsall had the grace to look ashamed, but the rest hid their hypocrisy behind innocent looks and bland social smiles.

"Has anyone seen Honor's purse?" he asked.

Saltonsall held up what looked like the missing item. "Is this it?"

Robert nodded, took the purse, and bade them all a good night when he really wished them all in hell.

Something was definitely troubling Robert.

Seated across from him in the brougham, Honor observed the line of anger between his brows and the uncharacteristic tightness about his mouth. There was no hint of pleasure or satisfaction in the depths of his green eyes, none of the warm afterglow of conviviality one usually experienced after a successful social affair. And he hadn't said a word to her since handing her into the carriage. Not one word.

"Did you enjoy yourself?" she asked.

He nodded without looking at her. "Did you?"

She shifted in her seat, causing her satin cape to rustle softly. "Not really."

"Why not? These are your friends."

"They are not my friends; they are people I know. There is a difference." Honor looked out the carriage window at the deserted streets and dark, silent houses. "I know that most people in the world out there are narrow-minded and prejudiced against anyone who is different." She smiled wanly. "This evening just brought their pettiness home, that's all."

She turned to Robert. "Was Amos impressed enough to offer you a position with Cutter, Bailey and Rye by evening's end?"

Robert laughed. "Hardly. He informed me they only invite Harvard men to join the firm."

Honor noticed the bitterness in his voice. "They were all rather horrible to you, weren't they?" Her cheeks flamed with embarrassment. "I'm so, so sorry. Aunt Theo warned me this would happen."

"It wasn't your fault."

"What did they say?"

"Nothing worth repeating." Judging by the resentful set of his jaw, he was lying to spare his own considerable pride.

"Damn them! I feel like going back there and giving them all a piece of my mind."

Honor looked at Robert helplessly, overwhelmed with feelings of protectiveness. She wanted to make up to him for this disastrous evening. She needed his forgiveness.

Honor gathered her cape and maneuvered herself over onto the seat next to him. He turned toward her, surprise written on the planes of his face.

She placed her gloved fingertips against his hard cheek.

"I'm sorry." She brushed her lips tentatively against his own, then pulled away, suddenly uncertain.

It was all the invitation he needed. He reached for her, drawing her against him with a welcoming sigh. She could feel the heat of his body through their clothes, and even by the dim light of the carriage lamps, she saw desire turn his eyes into twin glittering emeralds.

He cupped her face in his hand and stroked her cheek with his thumb. "You don't have to be sorry for anything," he whispered hoarsely, just before his mouth came down on hers.

Honor closed her eyes and savored the smooth, warm pressure of his lips coaxing pleasure into full bloom. She reveled in the heady warmth singing through her blood, the way her sense of touch and taste blossomed like wild tropical flowers after an unexpected rain.

When she felt his lips part and his tongue press against her teeth, making his intention clear, she jerked away in confusion, her face flushed with betrayal.

Breathing hard, Robert held her fast and placed a gentling hand on her burning cheek. "Let me kiss you the way lovers kiss," he whispered. "Please."

Lovers.

The tantalizing unknown beckoned, and Honor followed. She placed her lips against his, and felt his fingers curl around the nape of her neck, holding her fast. Still tasting faintly of after-dinner coffee, his tongue possessed her mouth with shocking intimacy. Honor felt an answering jolt of heat rage deep in her belly, then spread throughout her body like wildfire until she couldn't breathe and her last coherent thought melted away. She craved . . . what? She was still too new at this to know.

Robert withdrew, panting, and Honor barely felt his fingers at the collar of her evening cloak, deftly undoing the topmost buttons, until the garment parted and she felt the sting of cold night air against her hot flesh. She knew what Robert was going to do next, and she felt powerless to stop him.

Chapter 4

So this is what it feels like, Honor thought, to be seduced.

Robert's soft, sensuous lips moved down the side of her neck in a slow, enthralling dance, trailing fire that warmed Honor's skin and sent shivers skittering down her arms. Her heartbeat quickened, and an involuntary gasp escaped her lips when she felt Robert's questing fingers slip between the fabric of her parted cloak.

He kissed her deeply, his hand closing over her breast.

No one had ever touched her so intimately, and she was unprepared for the erotic surge. Her nipple strained against the fabric of her bodice, craving Robert's touch. A white-hot lassitude crept through her limbs, leaving them as weightless as if they were made of paper rather than hard muscle and bone. Reason took flight, leaving only deep physical hunger in its wake.

Honor groaned against Robert's mouth and buried her fingers in the thick softness of his hair. When they parted, both breathless and gasping, he murmured ageless endearments to her.

"You are so beautiful," he whispered and kissed her again.

Honor shivered, closed her eyes, and sighed contentedly, savoring the warmth and hardness of his mouth against hers. Her eyes flew open in alarm when she felt his fingers slip beneath the neckline of her gown. Her cheeks burned with mortification as she felt his warm hand pass lightly over her bare breast.

She gasped. "Robert! No!" She pulled his hand out of her bodice and bolted to the far corner of the seat like a frightened rabbit. In seconds the overwhelming panic subsided. Her heartbeat slowed, her blood cooled, and her erratic breathing became less ragged. Only the appalling embarrassment lingered.

Honor couldn't look at him as she straightened her bodice, but she could feel the weight of his gaze on her. She searched for something to say, but her mind remained blank.

"I know I took liberties," he said softly, "but I'm not sorry." When Honor sat there in stiff, affronted silence, buttoning up her evening cloak, he added, "I don't think you are, either."

She thought of Theo and Wes, and she realized that Robert was right. She smiled slowly but still kept her eyes averted. "I suspect we both were swept away."

"Honor, look at me." She turned her head. "You're not angry at me for being so brazen, are you?"

"Of course not. I'm not a child, Robert. I know that there is more to lovemaking than mere kissing."

He smiled slowly and seductively. "You're a woman in every way, you know."

She grimaced. "Just because I know about such matters doesn't mean I'm experienced when it comes to men, so you must pardon me if I act a little skittish."

Her ingenuous confession caught him off guard. He reached for her hand and drew it to his lips. When he released it, his gaze still held hers. "I'm not a fine gentleman like your friends. I say what's on my mind, and I do what my heart tells me." Or his body. He took a deep, shuddering breath. "I just can't help myself. When I'm with you, I always want to find the nearest secluded spot and make love to you."

Her eyes widened in panic. "Dear Lord, Robert. What a shocking thing to say!"

"Now I've offended you," he said, retreating to his corner of the carriage. He bowed his head. "You're a respectable gentlewoman, and here I am trying to seduce you."

She regarded him warily. "I have no intention of letting anyone seduce me." Even though his kisses and caresses made her ache inside. Even though his skillful touch banished all reason. Even though some wild, wanton part of her secretly wanted him to.

He raised his hands as if in surrender. "Then I won't try."

"I'm relieved to hear you say that. As astounding as this may seem, I have come to enjoy your company a great deal."

He smiled. "Then we're friends again?"

She smiled back. "Friends again."

The carriage slowed and came to a stop. Honor looked out at the Tree residence, its windows dark and shuttered, its inhabitants mercifully asleep. "Gracious. We're here already."

After a yawning Simms opened the carriage door, Robert handed Honor down and they went inside, where a solitary lamp burned on the hall table to welcome them home.

The lamp's soft glow didn't reach down into the hallway by the study, where a worried Theo stood as still and patient as a stalking cat. Ever since the servants had retired for the night hours ago, Theo had been waiting and dozing fitfully in the cold, dark downstairs parlor. When she heard the faint clopping of hooves, she had jumped up and peered through the curtains to make sure her brougham had indeed returned; then she had withdrawn to wait. She watched Honor and Robert walk into the foyer, their footsteps tapping loudly in the hushed silence.

She watched Robert Davis take Honor in his arms and give her a long, lingering kiss that she wholeheartedly reciprocated. Then he wished her a good night and left.

Theo watched Honor return to the foyer, remove her evening cloak, and drape it through the crook of her arm. She stood there stroking the satin absently, her eyes glazed as if her thoughts dwelt among the stars.

Theo hoped Honor wasn't falling in love with Robert Davis, because if she was, Theo would be forced to stop her.

Honor paused before her aunt's bedchamber door, then decided it was too late to wake her. Once in her own room, tucked beneath a mountain of coverlets, she closed her eyes and tried to sleep.

Her eyes flew open. She had allowed a man to kiss her with his tongue and touch her bare breast. Shameful heat crawled up her cheeks. All the schoolgirl tales told in whispers about loose women and their terrible fate welled up like a Greek chorus of censorious ghosts.

She stifled a laugh. She had no intention of sharing their fate. Aunt Theo hadn't, and neither would she.

Honor sat up and hugged her knees. Robert filled her thoughts to overflowing. She pictured his green eyes darkening with desire and felt the softness of his hair sifting through her fingers. She shivered deliciously.

Robert, Robert, Robert.

She wouldn't be seeing him again until Monday. She wondered how she would survive.

Theo didn't like this latest development one bit.

That morning, having gone to her niece's room to ask about her evening, she had found Honor glowing. She was obviously growing closer to Robert Davis.

Theo sat at her late husband's desk and looked down at the locked bottom right-hand drawer where she had hidden the papers that had the power to break Honor's heart. Should she show them to her? No, it was too close to Christmas, and Theo couldn't be that heartless.

She sat back in her chair. She would just have to bide her time.

"This Christmas is going to be the best one I've had since Father died," Honor said to herself, breathing in the fresh scent of the evergreen boughs gracing the mantel. "Robert will be here any minute. What could possibly spoil this day?"

Here in the upstairs parlor, the Christmas tree dominated one corner of the room and was laden with tasteful decorations—gold and silver ribbon bows and slim white tapers that had not been lit since the year the tree caught fire. Beneath the wide branches stood box piled upon box of opened presents.

Robert's cordovan leather gloves were waiting beneath

the tree along with an ivory-handled boar-bristle shaving brush and mug of imported French shaving soap from Theo. Honor hoped their gifts would not embarrass him.

Aunt Theo, whose striking hunter green velvet gown matched Honor's, ladled milky syllabub from the silver punch bowl into cups and handed one to her niece. "Try this."

Honor walked over to the bay window and looked out over the deserted street and the park beyond as she sipped the frothy drink. "It's delicious." She looked at her aunt. "Is Wes coming today?"

Though she tried to hide her disappointment, Theo's strained smile betrayed her. "I don't expect so. He has family obligations."

Honor turned back to the window. She suspected her aunt was falling in love with Wes despite her protestations to the contrary.

The arrival of the brougham pulling up to the curb caught Honor's attention. "Robert's here. He's wearing Uncle Oak's overcoat and carrying packages."

Aunt Theo joined her and peered over her shoulder. "Oh, dear. I hope the poor man hasn't bankrupted himself buying us gifts."

Robert saw them standing in the window, smiled, and trotted up the steps. Honor and Theo waited for him upstairs.

His face was pale and pinched from the cold, but he radiated his customary infectious energy as he wished them a merry Christmas. He thrust one box wrapped in newspaper and tied with coarse brown butcher's twine into Honor's hands, and gave the other one to Theo with the explanation that it was only peppermints.

Theo, who professed that peppermints were her favorite, wished him a merry Christmas and kissed his cheek. "Would you like something to warm your bones before dinner?"

He rubbed his hands together and suppressed another shiver. "That would be appreciated."

Once they were seated in the parlor and Jackson had brought Robert a steaming cup of hot buttered rum, Honor retrieved his gifts from under the tree. "These are for you," she said almost shyly. "I hope you like them."

He looked uncomfortable, a man obviously unused to receiving gifts. "You've done too much for me as it is."

"On the contrary," Theo said, "this is our small way of thanking you for tutoring Honor. She received an *A* in constitutional law, you know."

His eyes shone with pride. "I know."

He set down his cup and unwrapped the largest box. When he took out the shaving brush and mug, his eyes widened in awe. He looked up at Theo. "Words fail me."

Theo smiled. "I thought you would like them."

"I do. Very much."

"Now mine," Honor said. She held her breath, desperate for him to like the gloves.

When Robert saw them, he looked overwhelmed by more emotions than Honor could have named. "Gloves." He stroked the rich cordovan leather as tenderly as if it were Honor's cheek. Then he tried them on, and to Honor's delight, they fit perfectly.

He rose, went to Honor's chair, and brought her hand to his lips, his green eyes holding hers. "I've never owned anything so magnificent. Now open your gift." While Honor undid the twine, he added, "It's not much."

"I'm sure I'll adore it."

She opened the box. Inside was something neatly wrapped in more newspaper. When she unwrapped it, her lips moved, but her voice caught in her throat. Robert's gift was a small barn owl carved out of wood, its talons wrapped around a branch that served as a base, its wings spread out majestically for a downward swoop on unseen prey.

Honor stared at him, just as speechless as he had been moments ago.

"I whittled it myself," he said. "Since owls are supposed to be wise, it seemed appropriate for you."

It was the highest compliment she could ever have received from a man, to be thought wise.

"Wherever did you find the time?" she asked, fighting back stinging tears.

"Here and there." Precious moments he could ill afford,

stolen between studying, tutoring her, and doing odd jobs for his landlady.

"It must have taken you weeks." She stared at the carving, admiring feathers so painstakingly rendered that the bird's wings seemed to flutter in her hand.

"No one has ever given me a lovelier present," Honor said. "I'll treasure it always." A warm glow of contentment and happiness enveloped her. This Christmas was as perfect as she had hoped.

They all settled down to drinking and talking. Later Robert told a hilarious story about Pudding Weymouth, complete with the professor's waddle and dabbing of his forehead, causing Honor and Theo to laugh so boisterously that none of them realized another visitor had arrived until a visibly shaken Jackson suddenly appeared in the doorway.

"Madam, Mr. Saltonsall has arrived, and I'm afraid he's quite—"

"Drunk, old boy?" Wes was swaying so badly he staggered and had to lean against the doorjamb to keep from falling. His brown hair flew every which way, and alcohol and misery dulled his humorous blue eyes.

While everyone sat there in stunned silence, not knowing where to look, Wes focused on Robert. His eyes narrowed into slits, and his nostrils flared as he took a few more hesitant steps into the parlor. "Might have known I'd find you here, Davis, turning up like a bad penny."

Honor rose. "I'll thank you not to insult my guest in my own home."

Wes's lip curled in a sneer as he stood swaying in the middle of the room. "Guest? The man's a filthy climber!"

"Wes . . ." Theo cautioned, rising.

Robert turned red and jumped to his feet, but before he could say one word, Theo intervened. "Wesley Saltonsall, I will not tolerate rudeness no matter how drunk you are."

"Filthy climber." Wes glared at Robert with such vehement hatred in his eyes that Honor took an involuntary step between the two men. "You should have seen him at the Grants', licking Cleavon Frame's boots. Did they taste good, Davis? Disgusting. But we can smell a climber a mile away." He swayed again. "They all had a good laugh about it afterward." His voice trailed off. "Good laugh."

Theo snapped, "That will be quite enough!"

"Don't you see?" His voice rose to a shout that shook the ornaments on the Christmas tree. "He's after Honor only because he wants to get his filthy hands on your money!"

Honor itched to slap his face. "Jackson, please show Mr. Saltonsall out."

Self-pitying tears filled Wes's eyes, and his face crumpled. "Can't believe he's got you two fooled. Can't believe it." He let out a loud, heartfelt sigh and leaned heavily against a nearby side table for support. Then he looked up at Theo. "Father wants me to marry Selena Cabot."

If Wes's declaration moved Theo, she didn't show it. "Why are you so surprised? You know it's high time you married."

Her words must have finally penetrated his drunken stupor, because he straightened up, looking as bewildered and betrayed as a boy whose father had just sold his beloved pony. "But I don't love her. Can't love her. You know why."

Theo's black eyes turned even darker in her white face. "I know, but we'll discuss it later in private, when you're sober."

His broad shoulders slumped, and his chin dropped to his chest. When he raised his head, tear tracks scored his cheeks. Not a dimple appeared. His trembling fingers caressed Theo's cheek. "Hair like snow, eyes like midnight. Coldhearted bitch. You don't love me. You just want to fuck me."

Honor's jaw dropped and she gasped in outrage, while Theo recoiled as if struck. Davis growled, "You bastard," and stepped forward, his intention clear, but Theo motioned him to stay back with an impatient wave of her hand.

"Sorry. Didn't mean it," Wes whimpered, his voice catching on a sob. He grabbed Theo and pulled her into his arms, crushing her to him as if he would never let her go.

"Don't hate me. Don't throw me out. It's the drink. I'm not myself."

Honor felt so embarrassed for him that she had to look away.

Theo gently detached herself and took his tearstained face in her hands. "My poor boy, you're overwrought and need to sleep. I'm going to put you in the guest room."

She signaled to Jackson, and they escorted Wes out of the parlor.

Honor stood rooted to the floor, listening to their heavy footsteps until the sound faded away into silence. The atmosphere still felt thick and charged with emotion, as if a residue of Wesley's bitter, spiteful words still lingered, tainting the air and shattering Honor's perfect Christmas.

His accusations about Robert couldn't possibly be true.

Gradually Honor came out of her daze and looked at Robert, standing there rigid, his face a mask of barely suppressed rage. "I don't know what got into him," she said. "This isn't like him at all."

"If he wasn't so drunk, I'd ask him to step outside. And then I'd knock his teeth out."

Shocked by the raw menace in Robert's voice, Honor said, "I don't think he meant what he said."

"Oh, he meant every word of it. What's that old saying? 'In wine there is truth.' The drink gave him enough courage to say what he really thinks of me." Robert paused. "I take it that he and your aunt . . ."

"Are lovers?" Honor's cheeks turned pink. "Yes. In spite of the difference in their ages." She paused. "Does that shock you?"

"No, but I'm sure it would shock his family."

"They'd have Aunt Theo run out of town on a rail. Even the Tree name could not protect her from such a scandal."

"Their loss. Your aunt's a fine woman."

"One of the best." Honor picked up Robert's cup of buttered rum, now cold, and took a swallow, letting the alcohol burn the shock right out of her. "I must apologize for Wes. He's wrong about you."

Robert went over to the tree and stared at the ornaments. "No, he's not. I *am* a climber."

Honor's insides turned to ice. She set down the cup before it fell from her shaking fingers and turned to face him. "Please explain yourself."

"What is there to explain? I'm a nobody who's greedy for money and power." He shrugged. "I guess that makes me a social climber in Saltonsall's book."

Honor clenched her fists so hard the nails bit into her palms. "You're a social climber only if you use people to get what you want." She swallowed hard. "Do you?"

He was at her side in two strides, his hands on her shoulders. He shook them. "No! I'm not using you to get your aunt's money. Oh, I'll be rich one day, but it will be through my own hard work."

"That's all I wanted to know," she said, relief making her feel weak and giddy.

"I need you to believe in me." He gazed at her hungrily. Then he drew her into his arms and kissed her.

When they parted, Honor said, "After the Grants' party, you were moody in the carriage. You overheard them saying something uncomplimentary, didn't you?"

He walked over to the fireplace and leaned against the mantel. "When I went back to the parlor to find your purse, I overheard Freddie Horsley telling everyone that I was nothing more than a social climber. I had thought he liked me. All night he'd acted like my best friend." Robert shook his head. "Then to hear what he really thought of me . . ."

"I imagine you felt as if he had stabbed you in the back."

"Aptly put."

"Damned hypocrites!" Honor went over to him and placed her hand on his arm. "Why didn't you tell me?"

He smiled. "Because I knew you'd go back there and give them hell."

"I would have, too."

His smile faded. "I was half afraid old Horsley was right."

Honor slid her arms around his waist and leaned against

his back. "I wish we had never gone to that idiotic party. They're all a bunch of shallow hypocrites, and I don't care what they think."

Robert disengaged her arms and turned to face her. "The loss of your friends is a high price to pay for defending me."

"No price is too high when you know you're right."

He touched her cheek. "Honor Elliott, champion of the downtrodden."

She placed her hand on his arm. "You mustn't let anyone make you feel small. You've much to be proud of, Robert Davis. Men like Wes have always had everything handed to them on a silver platter, but you've gotten where you are through hard work."

Before Robert could comment, Theo swept into the parlor and interrupted them. "I've given Wes a headache powder, for I'm certain he'll be needing it when the alcohol wears off. Jackson is putting him to bed, so why don't we sit down to Christmas dinner?"

Throughout the delicious meal, everyone tried to pretend nothing unpleasant had happened, but the holiday had been spoiled and nothing could be done to revive it.

The following morning a somber, contrite Wes apologized to Honor, who told him in no uncertain terms what she thought of his ridiculous accusations. Watching her niece defend Robert Davis so passionately, Theo suddenly experienced a vague sense of uneasiness.

As the weeks flew by and winter gradually relinquished its cold, cruel grip on Boston, Theo noticed with a sinking heart that Honor's relationship with Robert was blossoming with the crocuses.

Perhaps the time to unlock the desk drawer was close at hand.

CHAPTER 5

A SPRIGHTLY GUST OF late April wind tugged at Honor's long skirts as she and Robert strolled through the Public Garden. They found a bench beside a bed of red and yellow tulips and sat down to watch a little boy in knickers running heedlessly across the lawn, trying to get his kite airborne.

Honor sat close to Robert in quiet contentment, listening to the excited shouts of playing children. Despite the cool breeze, the sun was a warm benediction on her shoulders.

"I can't believe I'll be graduating in June," she said. "Perhaps Cleavon Frame will offer me a position at Royce and Ellis."

Robert stirred and draped his arm along the back of the bench. "Do you honestly think he will?"

Honor stared out across the pond at the swan boat filled with passengers gliding serenely across the water's glassy surface. "I'm not optimistic, but I'm stubborn enough to ask."

"What will you do if they don't accept you?"

"Apply to other firms, of course. There's got to be at least one that will hire me, if only as a favor to my aunt Theo."

"What if there isn't?"

"Then I'll borrow some money and establish a private practice."

"Here in Boston?"

"Where else?"

"With me in New York."

Around her, all noise faded away except for Robert's words ringing through her mind as loud as a bell. Honor grew very still and listened. "You want me to go to New York with you?"

He nodded, his gaze focused on the ground, his body tense and stiff beside her.

She tugged on her locket. "As your mistress?"

He looked over at her in irritation. "What do you take me for? I want you for my wife." When Honor did not respond, he said, "In case you hadn't noticed, I just asked you to marry me."

"I must confess that I'm quite at a loss for words."

He drummed his fingers nervously against his knees. "If I weren't so unsure of myself, I'd enjoy the novelty."

The world was spinning out of control, and Honor fought to steady it. "We haven't known each other for very long. I know so little about you."

"What do you want to know?"

Honor smoothed her blue serge skirt. "You're a man of the world, Robert. I doubt that I am the first woman in your life."

"Oh, that . . ."

She caught his heroic attempt to suppress a smile. "Don't dismiss my concern as mere feminine jealousy. I expect an answer."

He sobered instantly. "I'm thirty-two. Of course there have been other women." He looked at her. "But not as many as you seem to think, and none I wanted to marry."

"That's reassuring."

"I know that I want to spend the rest of my life with you." He leaned forward, rested his elbows on his knees, and stared at the grass. "I also know you deserve better. I'm not rich. I don't come from some fine old Boston family. But I know I'd be a good husband to you."

Honor folded her hands in her lap and felt her equilibrium returning. "I don't care about wealth or background. I know you'd be a good husband." Her gaze sought the swan boat again. "But to be honest, I have my life all planned, and my plan doesn't include marriage to anyone."

Especially to a man who had never once said he loved her.

He said, "Plans can be changed."

She thought of how all her plans had changed abruptly after her parents died. "How well I know that."

"If you're waiting for a blueblood like Saltonsall to come along, I have an advantage."

"And what would that be?"

"You and I will both be lawyers. We understand each other's work and could help each other."

Honor paused to consider it. "That would certainly provide a sound foundation for a marriage."

"And I don't think your ambition is unladylike."

"Decidedly a point in your favor."

He looked at her. "I also have another reason for wanting to marry you."

"What is that?"

He squirmed in his seat for a moment, then pulled out his handkerchief and dabbed his brow, unconsciously imitating Pudding Weymouth. "Oh, hell, I'd better just come out and say it before I lose my nerve." He took a deep breath. "I love you. I've loved you from the very first day I saw you."

Her heart began to flutter. "In old Bloomers' criminal law class?"

"No. Three years ago when we first started law school."

Honor's eyes widened in astonishment. "Oh, that's a colossal fib if ever I heard one! You always avoided me. You never spoke to me unless we were on opposite sides of an issue in class."

"I couldn't get up the nerve until this year."

"You?" she scoffed. "Robert Davis, my nemesis?"

"Every man is a coward about something." He sat back and rubbed his clean-shaven jaw. "I've made a muddle of this, haven't I?"

"In what way?"

"I should have gotten down on my knees and proposed to you. I should have given you flowers." He bolted to his feet, strode over to the flower bed and pulled up a bunch of tulips by their roots.

Passersby stopped to stare. The little boy, who had undoubtedly been warned many a time by his governess not to pick the tulips under pain of a spanking, gaped at Robert in envy as his kite plummeted to earth.

Honor's cheeks burned in mortification. "Robert! That's public property. You'll be arrested!"

He walked back, dropped down on one knee, and thrust the flowers, dirt-covered roots and all, at Honor. "Miss Elliott, will you marry me?"

Glancing around uneasily for any sign of a policeman, Honor hissed, "I refuse to be a party to such wanton vandalism!"

Grinning, he rose and flung away the flowers. "Dull, dull, dull! Where's your spirit of adventure, Miss Steel Stays Elliott? What about romance?"

She found herself laughing in spite of herself.

He kissed her for all the world to see, and even after they parted, he still held her arms. "What's your answer?"

"I'll need more time."

Robert flung back his head and laughed, a deep, rich rumble that welled up from his shoes. "Spoken like a true lawyer."

"Don't mock me. Marriage is a momentous occasion in a woman's life, not to be undertaken lightly."

He sobered instantly. "You're right. Take all the time you need. At least until we graduate. Then I'll be off to New York with or without you."

While writing a letter to her art dealer in Paris, Theo paused a moment to look out the window at the trees tight with buds. She felt wonderful. Life couldn't have been any better. She and Wes were still lovers. Honor and Robert Davis were still nothing more than good friends. She returned to her scribbling, content with the world.

Then her niece walked in. Without stopping or looking up, Theo said, "How were the gardens today?"

Honor poured herself a cup of black coffee from the pot Theo kept within arm's reach during the morning, then sat down on the leather chesterfield sofa and took several sips. "Robert asked me to marry him."

The pen halted. Theo looked up and blinked several times. "Did you just say what I think you said?"

"Your hearing is fine. He proposed in the Public Garden."

Theo sat back, trying to hide her rising panic. She moistened her dry lips. "What did you tell him?"

"I told him I'd have to think about it."

"Very sensible." Theo put her pen back into its inkwell, blotted the letter she had been writing, and folded it. "Do you think you will marry him?" She held her breath.

Honor rose and strolled over to the window to gaze into the street at a passing motorcar honking its obnoxious horn. "He's certainly turned my world upside down." She shook her head as if to clear it. "I hadn't thought of marrying anyone. Now a man has said he wants to spend the rest of his life with me."

Theo rose, glided across the room, and placed a concerned hand on her niece's arm. "Do you love him?"

"I rather think it's more a matter of my desiring him," Honor said dryly.

Ah. All was not lost. "If you don't want to marry him, become lovers. It's much simpler."

"Robert says he doesn't want me for his mistress. He wants me for his wife."

"When your uncle Oak asked me to marry him, I was the happiest woman on the face of the earth. But I knew I loved him, you see, and I didn't want more from life than to be his wife." Theo patted Honor's arm. "You, on the other hand, positively overflow with unladylike ambition. You want to be a lawyer."

Honor tugged at her locket. "Robert says we respect each other's work and could help each other."

"That's true. Another man would expect you to give up your dream so he could achieve his."

Looking pensive, Honor strolled back to the sofa and sat down. "There's so much to consider. I'd have to leave Boston. I'd be living with a man I know little about, sharing his life and his bed."

"My dear, one can know a man forever, and he'll still behave like a stranger. That's part of the adventure of marriage."

"Then there are practical considerations."

"Such as?"

Honor's expression of distaste was comical to behold. "I've always had servants, but at first we'd be struggling and couldn't afford them. Will he expect me to clean house and cook?"

Theo burst out laughing. "Good reasons to remain a spinster if ever I heard any."

When Theo sobered, she said, "Life is a series of choices, sweet Portia. All choices have their consequences, and every choice has a price." How well she knew that.

Honor rubbed her temples, then rose. "I'm so confused. I have a great deal of thinking to do, Aunt Theo, so if you'll excuse me—"

"Wait." The moment she had been dreading was at hand.

With a heavy heart, Theo walked over to the desk, took a small key from the top drawer, and unlocked the lower right-hand drawer. She removed the incriminating papers and handed them to Honor. "Before you decide, I want you to read these."

Honor took the papers. "What are they?"

"I hope they'll help you to make up your mind about Robert Davis."

With a puzzled frown, Honor settled back on the sofa and read the first page. Theo watched the frown deepen and Honor's eyes gradually widen in shock and disbelief. Then Honor leaned forward, both hands gripping the papers intently.

Minutes later she finished reading and flung the papers down. Like huge black pools, her eyes dominated her ashen face, and she looked as though she might faint. "I don't believe this."

Theo sat down beside her and clasped her cold, lifeless hands. "Everything you've read is true. I wish to heaven that it weren't."

"How . . ."

"I hired the best private investigator in Boston. That is his report."

Honor pulled her hands free and jumped to her feet. "Aunt Theo, what a despicable thing to do!"

"I know you're furious with me, but I make no apologies for going behind your back. We knew nothing about Robert. I wanted to make sure there were no skeletons rattling in his closet."

Honor paced around the library, her brow furrowed. "Why didn't you tell me about this sooner?"

"I never intended to show you the report unless you became serious about him. Now that you're considering marriage, I felt you should read it and make an informed decision."

"These allegations can't be true."

"I admire your loyalty, but the detective told me that all the information in his report can be verified by people who knew Robert when he worked in Lowell. The investigator listed everyone he spoke to. If you wish to go to Lowell and talk to these people yourself—"

"That won't be necessary." Honor rubbed her forehead. "Robert never said anything about this."

"He obviously wanted to keep his unsavory past hidden." Theo rose and put her arm around her niece's shoulders. "Perhaps I am condemning him unfairly. He may have a good explanation."

"In life as in the law, there are two sides to every story. I can't condemn Robert without hearing his side."

"I hope for your sake that he can explain himself satisfactorily." Theo's arm fell away. "I know I've caused you pain, but I had to, for your own good."

Honor's eyes shone with sadness. "If this report is true, then he has betrayed my trust and played me for a fool."

"You mustn't blame yourself." She thought of Wes. "Love can blind us all."

"If you'll excuse me, I have to be alone to think about this." She walked toward the door, her footsteps heavy.

"What do you intend to do?"

She paused and turned. "I've invited Robert to dinner tonight. We shall see what he has to say for himself."

Walking down Commonwealth Avenue toward Honor's house, Robert couldn't stop smiling. She was going to marry him. He could feel the certainty in his bones.

His proposal today had taken her aback. She hadn't been expecting it. She struggled to be rational and logical, weighing the pros and cons of accepting it like a lawyer deciding whether to take a case, but he could tell that deep down inside, she wanted him.

When he arrived, he found Honor sitting on the sofa in the library and poring over her notes. She hadn't dressed for dinner but was still wearing the same flattering pale blue shirtwaist and dark blue skirt that she had worn to the park today. She smiled when he walked in, rose, and kissed him on the cheek.

"Does this mean you'll marry me?"

"I haven't decided yet. I still have some questions to ask you."

He rolled his eyes. "Do you ever stop being a lawyer?"

"Never. Would you like some sherry before dinner?" She poured him a glass, brought it over, and sat across from him in the wing chair instead of beside him on the sofa. That should have warned him. "Now tell me about your life in Lowell."

He shrugged. "I've already told you."

"Overseeing the whole mill must have been a great deal of responsibility for so young a man."

"It was, but I was good at it. I liked being the boss."

Honor sipped her own sherry. "An ambitious young man with so much responsibility . . . the ladies must have flocked to you in droves."

He studied her for a moment, but she had put on her inscrutable lawyer's face. "No, not in droves."

"But there were women who sought you out."

An annoying suspicion niggled at the back of his mind. "Yes, but as I told you this morning, they meant nothing to me." He set down his glass, rose, and stuffed his hands in his pockets, where he balled them into fists. "Why do you keep harping on this?"

She smiled disarmingly. "Oh, all women like to know about the other women in a man's past."

"Do I want to know about the men in yours?"

"There were none."

Many a time he had seen her take this tack in a mock trial, her manner guileless, making casual comments that lulled a witness into a false sense of security. He knew full well that she was leading up to something. But what? And why?

He looked at her. "I'm told a gentleman never discusses his . . . amours with a lady."

Honor set down her sherry, rose, and walked over to the desk as if deliberately seeking to create a gulf between them. She toyed with her locket and asked conversationally, "Who was Priscilla Shanks?"

The way she said that name sounded like the jaws of a trap snapping shut. The blood drained from his face, and a thin film of sweat rose on his skin. He tried to speak, but the words caught in his dry throat.

Honor's eyes never left his face. "Would you care to tell me about her?" she asked gently.

He cleared his throat to give himself time to collect his stunned and scattered wits. "How'd you hear about her?"

Honor picked up some papers lying on the desk and held them out. "It's all in here. Aunt Theo hired a detective to investigate you."

Why, that scheming two-faced old bitch . . . White-hot rage seared away his initial shock. He stepped forward and snatched the papers out of Honor's hands. When he finished scanning the damning sheets, he crushed them in his fist. "What's there to say? You've already tried and convicted me."

She shook her head. "I believe a man is innocent until proven guilty. I'm giving you a chance to defend yourself."

"What a sneaky, dirty, low-down trick!" His voice rang with contempt. "I thought you trusted me. And you have me investigated like a common criminal." He strode over to the desk. "What's the matter, Honor? Is your aunt afraid I'll run off with her precious money?"

All concern vanished from her face. "You're a fine one to talk about trust. You assured me that the women in your life meant nothing to you." Her voice hardened. "If what these papers claim is true, I hardly think getting a sixteen-year-old girl with child is nothing!" She took a deep, shuddering breath. "And for her to drown herself because you spurned her? How can you stand there and not accept some responsibility?"

He smacked the crumpled papers against his open palm. "You know what hurts the most? You're so quick to believe some damned detective over me."

His accusation took her aback. "That's not true. I believe cold, hard evidence, and these facts are easily verifiable. I want to believe you, Robert, so why don't you convince me?"

He bowed his head in defeat. There was too much at stake to lie. He sighed in surrender. "Everything these papers say is true. I was the father of her child."

He looked up to find that Honor had let down her guard and was regarding him with a disappointment more painful than disgust. "I liked Priscilla, but not enough to marry her. I was the mill's head man. I lived in a fine house and had a bright future."

Honor smiled wryly. "She didn't conceive a child alone."

He spread his hands in a gesture of hopelessness. "We got carried away one night. But it was only one night, I swear. When she told me she was with child, I offered to do right and support her and the baby, but she wanted marriage, so she could live like a lady."

"Why didn't you marry her?"

"I know it sounds cold, but I didn't love her. And I was planning to quit the mill and go to school. I didn't want to be saddled with a wife and child. Can you blame me?"

"No, I know how ambitious you are. But to abandon them . . ."

"I offered to pay." As if that excused him. "She never told anyone she would kill herself if I didn't marry her. If I had known she was going to do that, I would've married her and made the best of it. But it's too late now, isn't it?"

"Yes," Honor said sadly, "for several reasons."

A cold foreboding seeped into his bones. "What do you mean?"

She gripped the edges of the desk for support. "I don't know if I can trust you."

"What are you talking about?"

"Don't you understand? You were dishonest with me. By not coming forward and telling me about the girl yourself, you lied by omission. Did you think such an incident would mean nothing to me? Did you intend to tell me about her after we were married?"

She was slipping through his fingers. His temper flared. "If you don't want to marry me, just say so. Don't use this as an excuse to turn me down."

Her cheeks turned pink, but she stood her ground. "It's not an excuse. It's a matter of trust."

"Trust?" he barked. "What about you trusting me?" When she made no comment, he added, "Finally at a loss of words?"

"Yes, because there's nothing left to say. You've hurt me deeply." She glanced at the door. "I think you had better leave."

He made one last attempt. "All right. I made a mistake. I should have told you about Priscilla. I'm sorry."

Her lower lip trembled. "So am I."

He took a step forward. "I promise I'll never keep anything from you again." He waited for her to waver and crumble, to throw herself into his arms and beg his forgiveness. When she didn't, he swallowed his pride and said, "If you want me to crawl on my belly, I will. Won't you forgive me so we can move on?"

"I can't. I feel betrayed."

"I thought our love could overcome anything."

"A marriage takes more than love to be strong and solid.

It needs to be built on a foundation of mutual trust and honesty."

Desperate, he held out a supplicating hand. "Honor, don't hold this one little mistake against me. We're good for each other. You know we are."

"Were," she said.

"Please. You've got to forgive me."

Her pitiless lawyer's face remained in place. "I'm sorry it has to end this way. Good-bye, Robert."

He started forward, fully intending to sweep her into his arms and kiss and caress the resistance right out of her, but she brought him up short with a curt, "Leave!"

He stopped in his tracks, then stormed out of the study without a backward glance, slamming the door behind him.

Honor stood behind the desk and winced as the door's loud slam reverberated through the study. Finally, she closed her eyes, grateful for silence after the angry clash of voices. She needed to be alone. She needed to forget him.

Moments later, upstairs in her bedchamber, she locked the door, undressed, and put on a comfortable tea gown. Just as she was about to recline on her fainting couch, she glanced at the mantel and spied the carved owl.

Suddenly, sweeter memories from a more innocent time assailed her: Robert patiently tutoring her in constitutional law, Robert championing her against Hubert Adcock, Robert carving the owl. . . .

Honor closed her eyes and let the hot tears fall. He had said all men were cowards about something. She wondered if women were as well.

When she couldn't cry any more, she pulled herself together and dried her eyes. Oddly enough, she could forgive him for abandoning the hapless Priscilla Shanks, because men had their weaknesses, but she could not forgive him for hiding the truth and thinking it wouldn't matter.

Exhaustion finally claimed her. She closed her eyes again and slept.

* * *

The following day, Honor dreaded facing Robert in class. She needn't have worried; he sat on the other side of the room, kept his eyes trained on the professor, and took notes. When class was over, he disappeared before Honor had time to collect her books.

His behavior never varied during the ensuing weeks, and Honor knew their relationship was truly over.

Then one Monday morning in mid-May, she noticed that Robert was absent from all his classes. His chair remained empty on Tuesday and Wednesday as well. When he was absent on Thursday, Honor reassured himself that he was sure to return the following day.

Friday morning, when Honor walked into her estate law class, she searched every face. Robert's was not among them.

Something's happened to him, she thought. He would never miss a week's worth of classes. Never. His career is at stake.

"Miss Elliott?" Pudding Weymouth said. "Please see me after class."

When class was over, Honor went up to his desk. "Yes, Professor Weymouth?"

"You and Mr. Davis are friends, are you not?"

"Acquaintances."

"Friends, acquaintances . . . mere semantics." His three chins shook as he shifted in his seat. "Do you know why he has been absent all week?"

"No, I don't."

He gave a patronizing groan as if he didn't believe her. "This institution doesn't pay me enough to chase after delinquent students, Miss Elliott, but because Mr. Davis has a brilliant future ahead of him, I will make an exception. Tell him that if he doesn't have a good excuse for missing my class, I will give him a failing grade. And he won't graduate with the rest of you next month."

Chapter 6

"I really should get a Duryea motorcar," Theo declared, looking out the carriage window as she and Honor raced to Robert's rescue. "The traffic is so slow, it's taking us forever."

Honor, seated beside her, fiddled with her locket, reassuring herself that she worried about Robert needlessly. They would arrive at his boardinghouse and find that he had some perfectly reasonable explanation for missing classes all week.

You're deluding yourself, she thought. There are no reasonable explanations for him to miss class.

Why was she so worried about a man who had concealed an unsavory part of his past, a man she claimed she never wanted to see again?

When they arrived in the city's poor South End, they had little trouble finding Robert's address—a rambling frame boardinghouse, sandwiched between row houses in the middle of the block on a narrow street.

After disembarking from the carriage, Honor paused at the gate of a defiant white picket fence, noticing the small but well-kept front lawn and the clapboard house's fresh coat of white paint—Robert's meticulous handiwork, no doubt. She opened the gate, which squeaked a warning to the house's inhabitants, and marched up to the front porch with her aunt following at her heels.

Honor rang the doorbell while Theo uneasily scanned the run-down neighborhood with more curiosity than disdain.

The door opened just a crack. "What do you want?"

"I'm a friend of Robert Davis's," Honor replied. "He hasn't been to school all week, and I'm worried about him."

The door swung open, revealing a woman of about sixty-two, with every graying brown hair in place and her appearance as well tended as her property. She regarded Honor and Theo out of narrowed, suspicious eyes, but once she discerned they were gentlewomen, she said, "Come in," and stepped back to allow them to enter.

Once inside, Honor introduced herself and Theo while she glanced around the surprisingly genteel carpeted foyer, with its dainty floral wallpaper and a tall rubber plant in one corner. Only the faint odor of yesterday's cooking clashed with the carefully cultivated air of gentility.

"I'm Mrs. Routledge," the woman said, her tone turning warm and familiar, "and you must be Mr. Davis's young lady. He's spoken of you so often I feel as if I know you. But one can never be too careful answering the door these days. So many foreigners about, you know."

Honor forced herself to smile. "If Mr. Davis is here, please tell him that we'd like to see him."

Mrs. Routledge gave an aggrieved sniff. "He's sick."

Honor flashed her aunt a look of alarm. "Has he seen a doctor?"

The woman shook her head.

"Where is he?" Theo said.

"In his room," Mrs. Routledge replied. "Follow me."

Once upstairs, she stopped before a closed door. "He's in here."

Heart hammering, Honor flung open the door. Immediately the sour odor of warm, stale air and sickness almost made her gag. The small room appeared large because it contained only an armoire, a table cluttered with notes that served as his desk near the window, and a narrow bed where Robert lay.

Honor took a deep breath. She was too late. He was already dead.

Her wail of anguish caused Mrs. Routledge to jump. Honor hurled herself across the room to Robert's bedside. She stared down at him, lying on his back, his gaunt white face turned toward the wall, a thin, moth-eaten blanket pulled up to his scruffy bearded chin. He shivered.

Dead men don't shiver, Honor thought, hope galvanizing her.

"Robert," she murmured, touching his cheek. His damp skin almost sizzled beneath her hand. He stirred. His eyes rolled beneath their lids, but didn't open. She felt his neck for a pulse and went weak with relief when she found the faint throb.

Honor looked at Mrs. Routledge. "How long has he been this way?"

"Since yesterday," the woman replied. "Before that, he was just feeling poorly."

Honor peered under the blanket and saw that he still wore his shirt and trousers, apparently not having had the strength to remove them before tumbling into bed. The wrinkled clothes reeked of acrid fever sweat.

Honor looked at her aunt. "Let's take him home."

"Honor?" She found Robert looking up at her, his green eyes glazed with sickness and confusion.

Honor smiled and placed a reassuring hand on his shoulder. "Everything is going to be all right. Theo is here with me, and we're going to take you home with us so you can get well."

Theo said to Robert, "Do you think you can walk downstairs if we help you?"

He nodded, and Honor pulled off the blanket. The abrupt loss of its meager warmth caused a shudder to rack his body so hard that his teeth chattered. Still, he managed to swing his legs over the side of the bed and, with Honor's help, sit up.

Minutes later Honor and their driver, Simms, each took

an arm and managed to assist the weakened, feverish Robert out of the house and into the carriage, where he gave a long, shuddering sigh and collapsed in a corner.

Honor sat down and covered him with the blanket that Theo had taken from his bed. She drew his head down against her shoulder and placed her cheek against his hair.

Honor dipped a cloth in a basin of cold water and wrung it out before placing the cool compress on Robert's burning forehead. He lay in the wide guest room bed beneath a mountain of coverlets that he was constantly trying to throw off and that Honor kept replacing. For the moment he was sleeping.

She sat down in the chair by his bedside and closed her eyes. As soon as they had arrived home, Theo had summoned the doctor. He had offered them a prognosis: if Robert's rising fever broke soon, he would survive.

What if he dies? Honor thought.

Her eyes flew open and filled with tears. She brushed them away angrily.

"What is wrong with me?" she said aloud. "He concealed a reprehensible part of his past, which is tantamount to lying. I told him I never wanted to see him again, and yet the minute I heard that he was ill, I went running to him without a second thought."

She knew why: she loved him. She would never condone his callous treatment of Priscilla Shanks, but she loved him in spite of it. Surely everyone was entitled to one mistake.

As Honor removed the compress, now dry from his fevered flesh, and stared down at him, her loving gaze traced the straight sweep of his brows, the not-quite-straight line of his nose, and the sunken hollows in his gaunt cheeks. Though she tried not to admit it, she had missed him, and if he still wanted her, she would marry him.

If he lived.

"Honor! Don't leave me!"

She awoke with an unsettling jolt to find that she had

dozed off in the chair by Robert's bedside. The clock on the mantel chimed two in the morning. He was sitting up, staring at her out of bright, glittering eyes.

She rose and smoothed the damp hair away from his brow. "I won't leave you ever again."

His eyes focused on something only he could see. "Can't lose her," he muttered, his breath coming in short, shallow gasps. "Won't live without her."

Then she realized why he couldn't see her. His high fever had made him delirious.

"Honor!" His tortured cry tore at her heart.

She tried to push him back against the pillows, but he flailed his arms about with surprising strength, whacking Honor's own arm so hard that excruciating pain shot all the way up to her shoulder and she staggered back, managing to break her fall by grabbing the chair. She stood there, still reeling from the shock of his unintentional assault.

His arms jabbed the air several more times as if he were fighting invisible demons; then he groaned and fell back against the pillows, where he thrashed about. Gradually the delirium demon released its grip and the fight went out of him. His body relaxed. His head lolled to the side. He sighed deeply, as if taking his last breath.

Her arm still aching like a sore tooth, Honor slowly approached him. She extended a cautious hand to his forehead. Where she expected heat, she found coolness against her fingers.

The fever had broken. Robert would live.

She let him sleep until almost five o'clock the following afternoon, and then she brought him a light supper.

Honor hesitated in the doorway, feeling suddenly awkward after the acrimonious way they had parted. She took a deep breath, squared her shoulders, and walked into the bedchamber, where she found him sitting up in bed, propped up against a bank of pillows, his eyes closed.

"How are you feeling?" she asked, setting the tray down on the bed.

He opened his eyes, and the reserve she saw there saddened her. "I feel better."

"Cook made you some beef tea to rebuild your strength." She sat down at his bedside and watched him drink it.

When Robert finished the beef tea, he said, "Why did you come for me?"

"I was worried about you."

"Did I ask you to interfere?"

"Interfere!" She fought to keep her temper in check. "If we hadn't interfered, you would have died alone in that horrid room."

He set down the empty cup. "I suppose you expect me to thank you."

Why was he being so mean to her after she had just saved his life? Honor rose and set the tray aside, her expression blank. "I thought I was performing a kindness for a friend. Obviously I was mistaken."

"Why the concern? The last time we talked, you treated me like a criminal. You didn't care if I lived or died. Then I got sick and you ran to my rescue." His voice softened unexpectedly. "Why?"

Her gaze slid away. "You had been absent from classes all week, and when Pudding Weymouth told me that he would fail you if you didn't come to class on Monday, I had to let you know your law career was in jeopardy."

"You could have sent me a note," he pointed out with maddening logic.

"What if you didn't receive it?"

That brought a wan smile to his lips. "You're trying to avoid my question, so I'll repeat it. Why did you come for me?"

She couldn't avoid the truth any longer. "I was afraid something had happened to you."

"But why would you even care? You told me that you never wanted to see me again."

"Oh, this discussion is pointless." She turned away, only to find that Robert had grasped her wrist to prevent her flight.

"Why, Honor?" he said softly.

Her eyes filled with helpless tears. "I realized that I love you."

"What did you say?"

"You heard me."

"Say it again."

She swallowed her considerable pride and sat on the edge of the bed. "Ever since we parted, I've been miserable. I've tried to forget you, but I can't."

He sighed wearily and sagged back against the pillows. "Are you saying you want to marry me after all?"

She stared down at the third finger of her left hand. "Yes. If your offer still holds."

"Honor, look at me." When she did so, he said, "If you want me, you're going to have to forgive me for not telling you about Priscilla. You're going to have to forget about her. Are you ready to do that?" His voice hardened with resolve. "I'm sorry for what happened to her and the child. I admit that I made a horrendous mistake. But I don't want it ever thrown up in my face. Do you understand?"

She nodded. "No one is perfect, me least of all. You have so many other fine qualities, I can't hold this against you."

"I'll never make another one like it." Suddenly his face grew rigid with embarrassment. "With all my money going for school, I'm as poor as a church mouse right now. I can't even afford a betrothal or wedding ring."

"Then I'll just have to buy my own, now, won't I?"

He turned crimson with mortification. "A man should at least be able to give his bride a ring on their wedding day. What will your aunt think of me?"

"She'll think you love me enough not to let anything stand in the way of our marriage."

"But she hired that detective."

"You mustn't hold that against her. She was making sure I didn't get hurt."

"Still, I don't think she feels too kindly toward me these days."

"She went with me to the boardinghouse to find you.

She'll accept you into the family because you're my husband."

He stroked her cheek. "You are one woman in a million, Honor Elliott."

She took his hand and laced her fingers through his. "When I saw you lying there in the boardinghouse, I thought you were dead. That's when I realized how much I really loved you and what a fool I'd been for sending you away."

"Then I'm glad I got sick. It was worth it to bring you to your senses."

When Honor saw blatant desire leap into his eyes, she pulled away. "Oh, no, you don't, Robert Davis. You're still too weak for that."

He grinned and pulled her back so that she fell against him. "I'm still strong enough to kiss you."

She wrinkled her nose. "I'll not be kissing you until you've had a hot bath."

He raised his brows in mock indignation. "Are you telling me that I smell, woman?"

"I've known horses that smelled better." Honor laughed and pushed herself away. When Robert made a grab for her, she rose and darted out of reach.

Laughing, he collapsed back against the pillows. "So much for romance."

"Plenty of time for that later," Honor said, "once you're well. Now, if you'll excuse me, I have to tell Aunt Theo my wonderful news."

Theo hid her dismay rather well when Honor told of her intentions at teatime. While Theo felt that Robert Davis was unsuitable for her niece, she realized he was Honor's choice, and she would respect that. She knew all too well that logic was no match for the blinding power of love.

Still, she couldn't forget the detective's report. Robert's cold, callous treatment of the Shanks girl indicated a serious character flaw. She feared that it would only be a matter of time before this man broke Honor's heart.

Theo forced herself to smile, then hugged her niece and offered her heartiest congratulations.

* * *

On Friday, June 21, Honor awoke thinking, Today is my wedding day.

Just a week ago she had graduated, becoming Honor Elliott, Esquire, and today she would become Mrs. Honor Davis.

She rose, went to the window, flung open the curtains, and was delighted to discover a bright, clear summer day outside. "Happy is the bride the sun shines on," she recited to herself with a wide smile of anticipation. Then she took a small jeweler's box from her bureau, opened it, and stared at the plain gold wedding band she had bought for herself. At least no one else would know that the groom hadn't given it to his bride.

She put the ring away just as there came a knock on her door and Aunt Theo breezed in carrying a breakfast tray. "Good morning, sweet bride," she trilled, setting down the tray and hugging Honor. "And never has there been a more beautiful one, I declare."

Sudden tears sprang to Honor's eyes. After today she wouldn't be living in the house that had been her home for the last ten years. She wouldn't see her aunt every day.

Theo patted her cheek. "Why the tears? This is your wedding day."

"I'm just feeling a little melancholy, that's all." She hugged her aunt again. "I'm going to miss you so much."

"There, there. You may come back to visit whenever you wish. And who knows? I may have white hair, but I'm not so old that I can't make a trip to New York now and then."

Honor laughed through her tears. "I'll hold you to your promise." She dried her eyes. "I wish Father were here to give me away and Mother to share in my happiness. I know they'd like Robert."

"They'd both be so happy for you." Theo fished through her pockets. "Well, enough tears. I have to give you something."

Honor's eyes widened. Theo had already given Honor and Robert their law books when they graduated, along with a wedding gift of two thousand dollars. She was also paying for the wedding itself and letting them spend their honeymoon at High Water, the Tree summer house in the town of Manchester by the sea.

Theo drew Honor over to a chair and made her sit down while she rummaged through her pockets again and removed a small box. "These are for you, to make sure you don't have a child until you want one."

Honor opened the box to find dozens of strange rubber cups no bigger than her thumb. "What are these?"

"They are anti-conception devices," Theo said. "Pessaries."

Honor's eyes widened. "Where in God's name did you get these? They're illegal. If you got them by mail, you could be arrested and sent to jail."

Theo raised her brows. "Are you going to turn your own aunt in to the police for having them?"

"Of course not."

"As you begin your married life, sweet Portia, you'll discover that no issue is ever black and white. There are shades of gray. This is one of them. Such devices may be illegal, but they shouldn't be. They give a woman control over her own body and ultimately over her destiny."

If Priscilla Shanks had had one of these devices, perhaps she would have been alive today.

Theo said, "Since I've never been able to have a child, I don't need them, but I know you will. Would you like me to explain how to use them?"

Honor stared doubtfully at the rubber devices. "Perhaps I should discuss this matter with Robert."

"Robert is not the one who could conceive a child on your wedding night," Theo said dryly. "Robert is not the one who will have to give up practicing law to care for a child. I think that gives you more of a say in the matter, don't you?"

Honor sighed. "I have grave reservations, Aunt Theo. I hate keeping secrets from my husband."

Theo arched one brow. "All wives keep secrets from their

husbands. Has Robert demanded that you have a child right away?"

"We haven't discussed children at all."

Theo rolled her eyes in supreme exasperation. "I would suggest that you do, and soon." She added, "This is a serious matter, sweet Portia. If you should conceive a child, your future will be decided for you. You will become a mother, not a lawyer. Is that what you want?"

"Of course not. At least not yet." She did want children someday, when she and Robert were settled. "I've worked too hard to become a lawyer." Honor looked up. "Tell me how to use these."

And Theo did.

"I feel right at home here," Robert said, staring out over the green Atlantic Ocean sweeping away from the beach to a distant horizon. The sea air smelled fresh today, without the usual salty tang of brine.

Impatience had characterized Honor during their beautiful wedding ceremony in Trinity Church, and later at the sumptuous wedding breakfast held at the Parker House. She couldn't wait to begin her wedding trip, when she and Robert would be blissfully alone.

Now Honor smiled possessively at her new husband and squeezed his hand. "I've always loved this beach at sunset, when the day slows down. The ocean is so quiet, even the waves just whisper."

"Perfect for me and my bride." Robert started walking, the dry sand shortening his long stride. He stopped to look at the house nestled in a grove of pine trees beyond the dunes. "How long has your family owned this place?"

"Theo's husband gave her High Water as a wedding present," Honor replied, staring down at her wedding ring for the thousandth time and thinking how bare her hand had looked before.

"Generous man."

"We used to come here every summer for weeks at a time, and in the fall, too, when I wasn't going to law school." She looked up at the darkening sky streaked with wide bands of sunset purple and pink. "Now I'll spend my summers working in a law office."

Robert smiled. "It won't be long before we're spending our summer weekends in Newport with the likes of the Vanderbilts and the Astors." His eyes glimmered with grandiose dreams. "Perhaps we'll even own a Newport mansion ourselves."

She leaned over and brushed his lips with her own. "That's not important. Being together is what matters."

"You're right." He stopped, took her face in his hands, and kissed her, his soft, sensual lips insistent and arousing.

She pulled away. "Let's go back to the house."

The bedroom on the second floor faced the ocean, with two windows wide open to draw the cool summer sea breeze inside, the muffled sound of waves slapping against wet sand, and the occasional mournful cry of a sea gull wheeling overhead.

Honor stood by the windows, waiting for her husband in the fading rose light. Even though she and Robert hadn't discussed children, she had taken her precautions with one of the anti-conception devices, then unpinned her hair and dressed in a white silk peignoir that felt cool against her warm, expectant skin. She shivered as a sudden gust of wind blew in, billowing both the curtains and her nightgown out like sails.

Robert emerged from his dressing room and stood entranced in the doorway. Honor, usually concealed by high collars, leg-o'-mutton sleeves, and skirts hanging past her ankles, a corset protecting her from questing fingers like armor, now looked enticingly unfettered, so light she could float away. Still unaware of his presence, she stood in profile, her hair as glossy as glass tumbling down over her shoulders in a soft black cloud. The breeze fluttered the frivolous blue satin ribbons on her lace-trimmed nightdress and pressed the light material against her naked body.

Robert felt the familiar stirring and tightening at the

silhouette of full, upturned breasts, flat belly, and long thighs. He imagined himself imprisoned and squeezed breathless between those strong legs. He had so much to teach her.

"You're all mine now."

Honor started at the sound of Robert's deep, resonant voice, and turned to find her husband standing in the doorway, watching her out of glittering eyes. He wore nothing underneath his hunter-green silk dressing gown.

"Don't be afraid," he said softly, as if he could read her mind. He walked over to the maple bed and extended his hand.

"I'm not." The physical act of crossing the room bolstered her courage, and she placed her trusting hand in his. She lowered her gaze and blushed. "Well, perhaps just a little. I've never—"

"You know I would never hurt you," he whispered, lifting her chin and looking into the bottomless depths of her eyes.

"I know."

He tangled his fingers in her hair and rained soft kisses on her forehead, her eyebrows, her closed eyelids, the tip of her nose, and finally settled on her mouth, where he tormented her parted lips with tender nibbles that left Honor's head spinning.

"You are so beautiful," he said in a hushed, almost reverent tones, "and I can't believe you're mine." He drew her down to sit on the edge of the bed and undid the tiny white pearl buttons running down the front of her nightgown.

He looked down at her bare breasts, his eyes darkening at the splendid sight. Priscilla had been as big as a cow, always trying to smother him. "You are perfect."

To Honor's surprise, he knelt at her feet while she still sat on the edge of the bed. He reached up to fill his hands with her breasts, his touch both hot silk and fire. Honor closed her eyes, her head fell back, and a groan inadvertently escaped her.

The welcome tense knot of pleasure slowly started to

unravel deep within her belly, enslaving her senses. When Robert's mouth closed over a straining nipple, Honor cried out, unprepared for the intensity of her response, and buried her fingers deep in his hair.

Abruptly he rose, untied his dressing gown, and let it fall open. He was a slender, broad-shouldered man, but his illness had left him too thin. Except in one respect. Honor stared out of astonished eyes.

She extended her hand to touch him, but he stayed her curious fingers. "I wish only to please you," he said. "Undress. Now."

Honor rose, removed her peignoir, and pushed the nightgown off her shoulders. She had thought she would be embarrassed, standing naked before a man for the first time in her life, but she loved him so much that all she felt was pride that she could cause such hunger in his eyes.

She slipped into bed, savoring the contrast of cool sheets against hot skin. Robert let his robe drop and slid in beside her.

He explored every plane and hollow of her body with deliberate, maddening slowness. When she tried to reciprocate, he always stayed her hand. "You must let me worship you."

"But I want to give you pleasure, too."

"You do, just by being my wife."

Honor was so ready for him that she barely felt any pain as she welcomed him into her body. When he began to move within her, he murmured, "Mine," with every thrust, until the word became a drumbeat keeping time with Honor's rising passion.

When her climax sent her exploding into thousands of shards of light, she screamed Robert's name, and he threw back his head and crowed in triumph. She was his, forever and ever.

Later, after he made love to her again and still refused to let her make love to him in return, Honor lay there in the growing darkness and wondered why she felt both possessed and a possession.

CHAPTER 7

New York City

HONOR STOOD BEFORE THE closed door, stared at the name Jedediah Crawley, Esq., painted in bold black letters on frosted glass, and tugged at her locket nervously. He had to hire her.

In the three months that she and Robert had been living in New York City, Honor had lost count of the number of law firms she had gone to seeking a position. Armed with ample self-confidence and letters of reference from Cleavon Frame and several other prominent Boston attorneys and judges, who had written them as a favor to Theo, Honor stormed the legal bastions of the city. She soon discovered that all of them, from the largest firms with dozens of attorneys to the smallest one-man firm, had raised the drawbridge against her.

She took a deep breath, opened the door, and went inside.

Honor liked Jedediah Crawley the moment his receptionist showed her into his small, cluttered office. A barrel-chested man with a booming voice as wide as his smile and a bone-crushing handshake, he reminded her of her father. "Sit down, Mrs. Davis, sit down," he said. "I always have time for a fellow Bostonian."

When they were both seated, he said, "So you're Sydney Tree's niece. I left Sid's company shortly after you came to live with Theodate, but I remember you." He shook his head. "The company was never the same once Sid died, never the same. Just as profitable, but never the same. How is Theodate?"

"She still misses Uncle Oak, but otherwise she's fine." Wes saw to that.

He nodded. "She's quite a woman, your aunt, quite a woman. If Sid hadn't gotten her first, I would have asked her to marry me."

Honor smiled. "All men want to marry Theo."

"Indeed. She's that kind of woman." The niceties dispensed with, Crawley said, "Now, I'm assuming you're here for some legal advice, Mrs. Davis, so how may I help you?"

Honor leaned forward in her chair. "Actually, I'm here seeking employment, Mr. Crawley."

"Employment?" His smile widened. "Anything for Sid's niece, anything. Are you a typewriter? A stenographer?"

"Neither. Like you, I'm a lawyer."

The shock pushed him back in his chair, his bulk causing it to groan and squeak. "A lawyer?"

Honor nodded, and before he could say another word, she recited her qualifications as she had a hundred times before since coming to New York City, and spread out her credentials and letters of reference on his desk.

Unlike most of the attorneys she had approached, Jedediah Crawley at least gave her the courtesy of reading her credentials. "This recommendation from Cleavon Frame is most impressive, Mrs. Davis, most impressive. He was just a young pup starting out when I left Boston."

Honor sat there stiffly, not daring to move a muscle for fear of betraying her expectations.

Crawley heaved his bulk out of his chair and walked over to a window overlooking Wall Street, where he stared out into space for what seemed like an eternity.

Finally he turned. "Didn't anyone ever warn you?"

"Many tried," she said, knowing exactly what he was talking about, "but I'm a thickheaded Putnam. I refused to believe no law firm would hire me."

Crawley's face registered such sadness that Honor felt tears sting her eyes. "I'm afraid they were right."

She sat there, watching her dream go up in smoke.

"Do you know that there are no women practicing law in

all of New York City?" he said. "No women at all. The city bar association won't even admit them."

"So I discovered when I applied," Honor said. "I was hoping to be the first."

She knew that without admission to the city bar association and to the gentlemen's clubs that catered to the legal establishment, she would be deprived of vital contacts needed to succeed.

"I'm told you'd have better luck if you went out west, to Wyoming or Idaho," Crawley said helpfully. "They need lawyers so badly, they don't care if you are a woman."

She thought of Robert and his dreams of working for a wealthy financier. "I'm afraid that's impossible right now."

Crawley lowered his bulk back into his chair. "I wish I could help you, Mrs. Davis, but I can't."

Honor rose, trying to keep the desperation out of her voice. "Could you at least hire me as a clerk, to do research for you? Take depositions? Write briefs? Anything?"

Regret filled his eyes. "I'm sorry, but I've already got one clerk." He cast an embarrassed glance around his own small office. "There's only me, you see, only me." He paused, then named several other firms.

"I've tried all of them," Honor replied, collecting her credentials and slipping the worthless pieces of paper back into her valise. "And the answer was always the same."

Crawley nodded sympathetically. "I'm sorry, Mrs. Davis. I truly am."

Honor wished him a good day and left with her tattered self-confidence and dashed hopes.

She was too despondent to go home to an empty apartment right away, so she took a streetcar to the red brick Criminal Courts Building on the corner of White and Centre streets to observe a trial.

Hurrying down Centre Street, she looked up to see a convicted prisoner being escorted across the Bridge of Sighs, which spanned Franklin Street and connected the court building to the adjacent Tombs jail, and she shuddered, not envying the man his destination—a narrow windowless cell. She knew just how hopeless he must have felt.

The moment Honor stepped inside the building's huge central rotunda, she remembered the first time Robert had come here. He had wrinkled his nose in distaste and questioned her sanity in wanting to work here. Tier upon tier of dim mezzanines and corridors rose from the rotunda all the way up to a great soot-encrusted glass roof that let in watery, soiled light. The thick air was rancid with garlic, cigar smoke, sweat, and the odor of the prisoners' lunch. Perhaps her husband was right.

She stepped over to the side to avoid being trampled by a policeman hustling his prisoner past, and observed the ebb and flow of humanity. She watched mustachioed Italians, men with their eyes and jaws bandaged, Chinese in their long pigtails and blue smocks, black-bearded rabbis, grim-faced policemen, and lawyers chomping on thick, odiferous cigars. She listened to lawyers' runners extolling the virtues and successes of their masters, and she wished she could afford one to drum up business for her. She overheard a judge and an attorney agreeing to meet at "Pont's"—Pontin's Restaurant on Franklin Street, and she knew that she would never be welcome there.

She was just about to leave the building when she noticed a family standing out of the way on the other side of the rotunda. A neatly dressed young man in his early twenties knelt talking to a little blond girl while a pretty young woman kept dabbing at her eyes with a handkerchief, her face the picture of fear and resignation that Honor recognized so well. She wished she could offer them her services, but she knew that at this stage of the legal process, they already had counsel. She hoped their lawyer was a damn sight better than her father's had been. Finally the man stood up and hugged the woman fiercely. Then a policeman led him away.

Honor stood frozen to the spot, her thoughts suddenly flying back to her own father's trial. He had knelt before her just as this man did, while his despondent wife cried silently. Then a policeman had led him away.

When her thoughts returned to the present, determination

added spring to her step, and she strode through the rotunda and out the door.

To hell with them all. Somehow, some way, she would practice law.

When Honor arrived at her third-floor apartment at the Osborne, she found Robert seated in the parlor, reading the *World*. The moment he saw her, he set the newspaper aside. "Any luck today?"

Honor pulled out the hatpin, took off her hat, and threw it in disgust down on the nearest chair. "No luck."

Robert went to her and put his hands on her shoulders, his eyes soft with sympathy. "Don't give up hope."

She rested her head against his shoulder. "No matter how cruel and thoughtless the world is, I know I can always count on you to comfort me and give me strength."

He had been her anchor ever since they arrived in New York City in early July, right after their blissful honeymoon at High Water. He found this spacious, comfortable seven-room apartment on the West Side, and when Honor expressed reservations about its expense, he insisted it would repay them tenfold by becoming their oasis in an often unfeeling city. The ensuing weeks of rejection and bitter disappointment had proven him right. Shutting the door on the outside world and entering these welcoming, familiar rooms, Honor knew her spirit would replenish itself.

Robert smiled with suppressed excitement. "Well, I have some news that will make you happy." He paused for effect. "I've got a job."

Honor gave a shriek of elation, flung herself into his arms again, and kissed him. "Oh, Robert, that's wonderful! Who hired you? What will you be doing? When—"

He stopped her stream of questions by lifting her off her feet and spinning her around until they were both laughing and breathless with dizziness. When they stopped, he said, "A law firm called Fitch, Martin and Fogg on Wall Street hired me this morning."

Honor brushed his mouth lightly with her own. "Oh,

Robert, I am so happy for you! You've worked so hard for this. You deserve it." She took his hand and led him over to the sofa. "Come sit down and tell me all about it."

Robert sat down and turned his body toward her, his face glowing with excitement. "Fogg himself interviewed me, and at first I thought he was going to tell me he only hired Harvard or Yale men. But once he read those letters from your aunt's lawyer friends, I could tell he wanted me."

So if Fogg was one of the firm's founders, it was a new firm. Founders of old established firms like Boston's Cutter, Bailey and Rye were long dead, though their names would remain firmly affixed forever.

"Fogg specializes in corporate law, so as his clerk, I'll learn a lot from him." He rose and paced back and forth, his restless energy filling the room. "This is only the beginning for me, Honor."

She tugged at her locket and looked away. "At least someone was willing to hire you. I'm usually laughed out the door because I'm a woman."

He stopped his pacing. "You knew you'd face incredible obstacles when you decided to become a lawyer."

She smiled dryly. "That I did." She rose. "And I've decided that since no law firm will hire me, I'll just have to establish my own practice."

Robert rubbed his jaw. "Have you thought this through?"

The doubt in his voice took her aback. "I once told you that if I couldn't find a position with a law firm, I would go into private practice."

He went to her and took her hands. "Don't be angry with me. I wasn't doubting you. It's just that there are so many law firms in this city, you'll be a little fish in a big pond filled with sharks. I wonder if you won't be swallowed up."

Honor pulled away. "You've always been so encouraging. Why the sudden change?"

"I'm merely being realistic. I don't want to see you hurt." He sighed. "Plus there's the expense of renting an office and hiring someone to help you. We can't afford that just now."

"I'm sure we can. There's the money Aunt Theo gave us

for a wedding gift." An account that Honor had opened in both their names. "Even after we pay our rent and expenses, there's still a goodly amount left over."

"That has to last us until I become established and we can replenish it. No lawyer ever got rich writing wills."

Honor tried to hide her anger and failed. "Are you saying that you don't have faith in my abilities, Robert?"

"I have every faith in you, my darling, but I am also more realistic than you are." He smiled indulgently. "You're a dreamer, Honor, not a realist like me. I just don't want to see you hurt."

She tugged on her locket. "This revelation quite stuns me. I never knew you considered me an unrealistic dreamer."

"You are level-headed about the law. But I think you won't face the realities of being able to practice it. You've been so sheltered you think you can do anything."

"That's not true!"

He came over to her and put a placating hand on her shoulder. "If you want something to do, you can do legal research for me."

"I don't want 'something to do.' I want to practice law."

His hand fell away. "I was only trying to help." He returned to the sofa and his newspaper. "I'm sorry if I hurt you, but I'm giving you my honest opinion. Husbands and wives should be honest with each other."

She thought of Priscilla Shanks, but held her tongue. "Are you forbidding me to open my own practice?"

Robert looked up at her over his newspaper. "Of course not. I'm merely asking you to be prudent."

Honor turned and walked away, feeling for the first time in her marriage that she was truly alone.

We've had our first marital spat, Honor thought.

She took her cup of tea that Tilly, their live-in maid-cook, had made for her and sought refuge in the apartment's library, a small room about half the size of the one in Aunt Theo's house, with a wall of empty shelves waiting to be filled with books when they could afford them. She closed the door behind her with a dismal sigh and sat down in the room's most comfortable chair, but her anger followed her like a dark, malevolent specter.

Robert's betrayal gnawed at her. She especially resented his depiction of her as a spoiled, sheltered little rich girl.

But aren't you? a little voice whispered.

Her aunt had sheltered her with love, money, and influence. No matter who put ink on her chair, no matter how many men closed ranks and doors against her, she knew she could always return to the loving, sheltering embrace of her aunt.

Yet Robert's assumption that her private practice would fail still rankled. She knew she could be just as good a lawyer as any man in this city. All she needed was a chance to prove herself.

"Are you still angry with me?" Robert asked softly from the doorway of their bedroom.

Honor, seated at her dressing table and searching for premature white hairs, didn't know the answer. She had avoided him for the rest of the afternoon, until he finally went out somewhere and left her and Tilly alone. When he returned for supper, they had sat at opposite ends of the long oak table and eaten in an icy silence that settled between them like a thick, impenetrable fog. Neither of them had spoken for the duration of the meal. Honor had returned to the library to read, then decided to retire early.

She turned and faced him. "I don't want to be angry, but you said some very hurtful things to me this afternoon."

"I was only being honest." He looked at her. "All husbands and wives get angry with each other now and then. But it passes. If you're going to hold this against me forever, I'll sleep in the library."

Suddenly the coldness, the silence, the awkwardness between them seemed so pointless. "No, I'm not angry with you anymore."

"I knew you couldn't be." He crossed the room to her dressing table, drew her to her feet, and took her in his arms.

The touch of his lips against hers melted away the last vestiges of anger and hurt, and she slid her arms around his waist to draw him into her forgiving embrace.

When they parted, he murmured, "I want to make love to you." That was as close to an apology as such a proud man would ever come.

Honor kissed him again. "Then why don't you undress while I get ready?" She went to the bathroom to take her usual precautions, and when she returned, she turned off the gaslight and slipped into bed beside her waiting husband. When she tried to touch him, he stayed her hand, as always.

Why should she complain that he never allowed her to love him in return? He always satisfied her, and he derived great pleasure from her ecstasy. So she let him burn away her anger in the fires of passion.

Late that night the dream came to her.

As always she stood in the prison yard with the scaffold in the center and black chessmen scattered in the snow. Again she watched her father walk inexorably to his doom. Again she placed the noose around his neck. Again she awoke gasping and bathed in cold sweat.

Sitting up in the darkness with her knees drawn up to her chest while her husband slept on, blissfully unaware, Honor knew what she had to do. Hadn't Aunt Theo said all wives kept secrets from their husbands?

The next day Honor told Robert that she was going to down to the Criminal Courts Building to observe. In reality she went in search of an office.

Robert was unimpressed with the office Honor rented three weeks later, two small rooms above a photography studio on bustling Broadway, but when she stood in the outer office where her stenographer would one day work and looked into her own larger room with its desk, and with her diploma hanging on the wall, she swelled with satisfaction and pride.

Now all she needed was a client.

She was still waiting for them a month later.

Standing at her office window and watching scurrying pedestrians bob and weave in the cold, steady October rain, she heard a familiar British-accented voice say, "Are you in your lair, you lovely creature?"

"Waiting to lure unsuspecting photographers to their doom, John," she replied, turning around to find her downstairs neighbor standing in the doorway of her office. "What can I do for you on this dreary day?"

He grinned. "I think I've found you your first client."

Honor's eyes widened. "You have? Who?"

John Townsend's august clientele consisted of society women and theater people, and he had promised Honor that he would recommend her legal services.

"Come downstairs to my studio with me."

All Honor saw in John's studio was a tall, swarthy man with a muscular barrel chest, and arms and thighs as thick as tree trunks, clad only in a leopard-skin tunic that barely covered his privates. Honor turned red with embarrassment.

"Honor Davis," John said with a flourish, "may I present Man Mountain Mountford, the Strongest Man in the World, the current attraction at the Hippodrome."

Honor extended her hand. "How do you do, Mr., er, Mountford. I've seen your playbills. They don't do you justice."

He beamed and held her hand with surprising gentleness for so large and muscular a man. "How do you do, Mrs. Davis? Call me Fred." His voice was soft, and his speech was polished. "Townsend here tells me that you're a lawyer."

"Yes."

"Well, I'm due to sign a new contract, but there are some things management wants me to do that I don't. I need a lawyer to read it for me and make sure I'm not cheated." He looked at her out of shrewd eyes. "Townsend says you're good."

"One of the best," Honor replied. In law school, she amended silently and crossed her fingers.

His eyes narrowed. "You're too damn pretty to be a lawyer."

"That gives me an advantage, Fred. My opponents tend to

underestimate me. By the time they discover how tough I really am, it's too late."

Fred grinned. "We circus folks don't care what you are as long as you can do the job. Townsend here says you don't charge much."

Honor sensed that the price of her services was a prime consideration. "No, I don't."

He grinned. "Good. I'll bring my contract over tomorrow morning."

Honor shook his hand again and left him flexing his muscles for Townsend's camera.

When she went back upstairs and entered her outer office, she was startled to see a woman standing at the window, her back to the door. "May I help you?"

The woman turned around. "I hope so, sweet Portia."

"Aunt Theo!" Honor shrieked, flinging herself into her smiling aunt's outstretched arms and hugging her. "It's so good to see you!" She stepped back. "Whatever are you doing here in New York? How did you find my office?"

Theo paced around the room, as restless as ever. "I stopped at your apartment, and your maid gave me the address."

"How long have you been here?"

"I just arrived yesterday, and I'm staying at the Waldorf."

"Why didn't you tell me you were coming?"

"I wanted to surprise you." She stopped her energetic pacing. "My main reasons for coming are to go shopping and to tell you that I am going to Italy for the winter."

Honor rocked back on her heels. "Italy? Why for the entire winter?"

Her aunt's black eyes became unnaturally bright. "I can't bear Boston and have to get away for a while." She looked away. "You see, I've ended my affair with Wes."

Honor grew very still, and she moistened her dry lips. "Oh, Aunt Theo . . . I—I don't know what to say."

Theo managed a brave smile and began pacing the office again like a caged lioness. "It's for the best. Marriage between us would have been a disaster. He's so young and has his whole life ahead of him. If he stayed with me, he'd be living my life instead of his own. It just wouldn't be fair."

"He's never cared about that. He loves you. He must be devastated."

Unwitting tears sprang to Theo's eyes. "We had such a frightful argument." She sighed. "In any case, he's going to marry Selena Cabot in the spring, and you and I have happier things to talk about." She dried her eyes. "How is married life?"

"Just wonderful," Honor replied. As badly as she wanted to discuss Robert's sudden lack of faith in her professional abilities, Honor couldn't send her aunt off to Italy with another burden on her shoulders. Though Theo tried to pretend that she didn't care about breaking off with her young lover, Honor could almost see the gash in her aunt's heart.

Theo smiled wanly. "I'm delighted to hear it."

"You'll have to come to dinner every night while you're here. I'm sure Robert will want to see you, though he often works late."

"I'd like that."

Honor said, "If you don't mind braving the rain, there's a delightful little shop called Maillard's where we can have tea and ice cream."

"I do adore ice cream." Her strained voice belied her enthusiasm, and her eyes had lost their sparkle.

Honor decided she would put it back. Drawing her aunt's arm through her own and leading her out of the office, she said, "Let me tell you all about my first client, Aunt Theo. His name is Man Mountain Mountford, the Strongest Man in the World. . . ."

Robert laughed when Honor told him about Man Mountain Mountford, but not in Theo's presence, so she enjoyed her stay in New York City and left for Italy under the illusion that her niece's marriage was perfect.

Laugh as Robert might at the circus strong man, Mountford became a satisfied client who paid his bills on time and recommended Honor to his fellow performers, and throughout the winter her reputation as a tough contract negotiator grew throughout the Broadway theater district.

Then, in April of 1896, Honor met a woman who was to change her life.

CHAPTER 8

"HE BROKE MY HEART."

Honor looked up at the dejected, weeping young woman seated across from her desk. With her golden hair, desolate green eyes, and a lovely, malleable face quick to reveal soulful despair, Lillie Troy would have a judge and jury eating out of her hand when she told them her heart-wrenching tale of true love betrayed. After all, she was an actress destined for greatness if only some enterprising theater manager could see beyond her series of minor roles on the Broadway stage and give her a break.

Honor said, "Mr. LaRouche also violated an unwritten contract, Miss Troy. He once promised to marry you, and now he has reneged on that promise. He's broken the law and caused you much mental anguish. You are entitled to receive monetary compensation for alienation of affection."

Lillie dabbed at the corner of her right eye with her monogrammed handkerchief. "No amount of money can repay me for the loss of my Nevada."

"Nevada . . . what an unusual name."

"He was born there. He used to be a cowboy."

Honor raised a skeptical brow at this bit of information.

"He seldom spoke to me of his youth out west, but that was before he came to New York with his friend and business partner, Damon Delancy. Have you heard what happened to the Delancys?" When Honor shook her head,

Lillie leaned forward and lowered her voice as if she feared being overheard. "It was quite a scandal. Damon Delancy was married to this lady doctor who was arrested. Rather than risk having her go to prison, he spirited her and their baby boy away to England." Lillie sighed. "Isn't that romantic?"

"Breaking the law is not romantic, Miss Troy," Honor said, for she had no patience with lawbreakers. "It catches up with you sooner or later."

The actress colored at Honor's rebuke. "Well, you would feel that way, being a lawyer and all. I was just leading up to the fact that with Mr. Delancy out of the country, Nevada has been running their company."

Honor scribbled a few notes on her tablet. "So Mr. LaRouche is obviously wealthy."

"I daresay Nevada's one of the wealthiest men in New York. You should see the Fifth Avenue mansion he lives in. It's—"

"I'm sure it's most impressive," Honor said, continuing to write. She looked up. "Here we have a wealthy man taking advantage of a hapless, trusting young woman. He woos her with promises of marriage, and when he tires of her, he coldly casts her aside."

Lillie's eyes grew luminous with tears. "That's exactly how it happened, Mrs. Davis."

"Now tell me about Mr. LaRouche."

Lillie's expressive face reflected puzzlement and a trace of suspicion. "He's in his late twenties or early thirties. I never did get around to asking, but—"

"I meant, what kind of man is he? I need to know as much as possible about him so I'll know what I'm up against." Honor also wanted to see just how well the actress really knew LaRouche, or if she was playing Honor for a fool.

She patiently sat through Lillie's rapturous description of her former lover as "tall and ever so handsome, with hair the color of summer wheat and eyes as blue as a prairie sky."

Lillie added, "He's a gentle man, for having lived out on the wild frontier. And he's real quiet, even when he loses his temper." She shivered. "He becomes so still, like the air just before a thunderstorm, until you wish he'd just yell and get it over with."

"Did he lose his temper often?" Honor asked.

Lillie smiled a self-satisfied, blatantly sexual smile. "I never gave him any cause." Her expression changed to one of bewilderment. "He's a secretive man, hard to know. When I asked him how he got those scars on his body, he just smiled and told me not to worry my pretty little head about them." Lillie's eyes widened in awe. "I've always suspected he got shot in several gunfights."

At least Honor now knew that Lillie had known the man well enough to see him unclothed, giving credence to her claim that she had been his devoted mistress.

Lillie smiled another dreamy smile. "He has a beautiful voice, low, quiet, with a musical drawl. When he talks, he speaks prairie poetry. He once said my hair was the color of desert sand and that I was as pretty as a Colorado sunrise."

Honor suppressed a smile and made a few more notes. "How do you think Mr. LaRouche will react to the possibility of a lawsuit? Will he settle out of court, or will he fight your claim?"

Lillie's lovely face went blank. "He was always very considerate of me up until he decided to give me my walking papers. And he never struck me as nasty or vengeful, the way a lot of men are when they don't get their way." She wrinkled her brow in concentration. "He's a decent, honorable man. I think he will settle."

Honor rose and walked around her desk. "You've given me all the information I need, Miss Troy. I'll make an appointment with Mr. LaRouche before I file a writ summons and complaint, and then I'll let you know if he wants to settle or if we're going to have a fight on our hands."

Privately, Honor hoped he chose to fight, for if he did, this would be her first court case. She hadn't become a lawyer just to write wills and negotiate contracts.

Honor leaned back in her chair. "Would five thousand dollars be adequate compensation for you?"

The prospect of so much money made Lillie Troy's lovely face brighten. "That would certainly help mend my broken heart."

"It's a fair settlement."

The actress rose and dabbed at her eyes one last time. "I am so grateful to you, Mrs. Davis. Now I don't feel so helpless and alone."

"There are laws to protect the helpless, Miss Troy." Even if they had failed to protect Honor's own father. Then she wished her client a good day and showed her out.

When Lillie Troy's footsteps died away, Honor turned to Elroy Crisp, the stenographer and assistant she had hired a month ago. "What were you able to find out about our Miss Troy?"

"Not much, boss," the freckle-faced young man replied. "She's not one of those women who make a habit of suing former suitors. The people I've talked to all said she is a sweet young girl who honestly thought LaRouche was going to marry her."

"That's gratifying. She's my client and I'll protect her best interests, but I will not tolerate a client who lies to me."

After telling Elroy to make an appointment with Nevada LaRouche, Honor returned to her office to plan for their confrontation.

Three days later, immediately upon Honor's arrival at the Wall Street offices of Delancy and LaRouche, a woman ushered her into the inner office and announced, "Mrs. Honor Davis to see you, Mr. LaRouche."

He stood before a tall arched window bathed in spring sunlight, with his back to Honor. "Thank you, Miss Fields. If I need anything, I'll call."

Lillie Troy's description of his voice as low and musical didn't do it justice. Seductive, Honor thought, a drawling velvet voice that could soothe a high-strung horse and then, in the same breath, charm the pantalets off a duchess. She raised her guard.

He turned, and Honor's first thought was that he looked out of place amid the uncluttered pedimented desk and cabinets, the banal accoutrements of commerce. His tall, lanky frame, which topped Robert's six feet by a good two inches, didn't account for it, and neither did the fact that he wore his sun-streaked blond hair and mustache longer than current male fashion decreed. The hand-tooled black leather cowboy boots he wore certainly set him apart from the average New Yorker, but the reason for that other indefinable quality kept eluding her.

When he nodded curtly and said, "Mrs. Davis," she realized that while his eyes were as blue as Lillie Troy's fanciful prairie sky, they had wild, untamed depths that conjured up in Honor's own mind equally fanciful images of wide open spaces inhabited by rough, lawless men.

Be careful, Honor. This man will be a formidable opponent. She returned his nod. "Mr. LaRouche."

He walked toward her, his step light and soundless on a plush Turkish carpet. He smiled, a disarming white grin even more charming than his voice. "I know lady doctors, but I've never met a lady lawyer before."

She braced herself for lavish references to her beauty and was relieved when he made none. Then she surprised him by extending her hand.

When he placed his hand in hers, she shook it firmly. "I'm something of a rarity, but I can assure you that I am indeed a fully qualified lawyer, and I represent Miss Lillie Troy." Honor watched him carefully for any sign of recognition, and when his eyes turned wary and he quickly released her hand, she said, "I see you know Miss Troy."

He indicated a comfortable leather chair, then rounded his enormous desk, where he remained standing, his thumbs hooked in his belt, his weight resting easily on one leg. "Ma'am, I don't deny knowing Lillie. I'm just puzzled as to why she needs a lawyer and why that lawyer has come calling on me."

Honor opened her valise and removed her notes. "She claims you knew each other so well that you promised to marry her." She looked up at him. "Is this true?"

He reached up to stroke his drooping mustache. "Mrs. Davis," he said softly, "what in damnation is this all about?"

"I'd advise you to have your own attorney present while you hear what I have to say."

"No need, ma'am. I fight my own battles."

"Suit yourself." She leaned back in her chair. "Miss Troy intends to sue you for breach of promise."

"Come again?"

Honor scanned her notes as a delaying tactic, hoping to rattle him into saying something imprudent that she could use against him to her client's benefit. "Miss Troy claims you led her to believe that you wanted to marry her, then reneged on your offer. Is that true?"

He sat down, stretched out his lanky frame as if even this large room were too small to contain him, and studied Honor with the maddening deliberation of a cat stalking a mouse. "I'm not one to use coarse language in front of a lady, and I don't mean to offend you, ma'am, but—"

"Candor does not offend me, Mr. LaRouche," she said. "In fact, I would find it most refreshing."

"Lillie was my—my *petite amie*." He stumbled over the French phrase, giving it an odd, flat pronunciation.

"Your mistress."

He inclined his head slightly at her blunt use of the word. "I set her up in her own apartment, and for the last six months I paid all her bills, which were considerable, without complaint. A man keeps a woman, he pays her bills. Fair exchange for services rendered." He leaned forward. "But I was always honest with her. I never led her to believe that I would marry her, especially when I found out that I couldn't trust her."

"She claims you did deceive her."

"Then one of us is lying." He rose, came around his desk, and leaned against its edge so he was only a few feet away from her. "Did I give her a betrothal ring?"

She refused to let his disconcerting nearness intimidate her, for he was one of those men whose quiet demeanor was more intimidating than raving and hollering would have been. "No, you did not."

"Did I tell my friends that I intended to marry her?"

"I don't know. Did you?"

"No! You can ask every last one of them."

"Why should I believe your friends? Of course they would take your side."

When he looked chagrined, Honor softened her voice regretfully. "Mr. LaRouche, you don't have to convince me of anything. It's obvious that it's your word against Miss Troy's, but the courts will decide who's telling the truth." Honor paused. "Unless, of course, you choose to settle this dispute out of court."

Comprehension dawned immediately. The cold disdain in his eyes would have made lesser opponents rise and leave the room while they still had their skin intact, but Honor thought once again of all the men who had put ink on her chair, and then she steeled herself for battle like a war-horse smelling cannon fire.

He gave a knowing nod. "So that's what this is all about. Blackmail."

"Justice for a defenseless woman, Mr. LaRouche," Honor retorted just as coldly.

"How much?"

"Five thousand dollars, which I think is only fair."

He grew very still, though the very air around him thrummed with suppressed rage like the calm before a thunderstorm. "So you think that's only fair."

"I do, and Miss Troy agrees."

The disdain in LaRouche's eyes turned to pure contempt. "You seem like a decent woman, ma'am. How can someone who claims to uphold the law be a party to out-and-out blackmail?"

Honor raised her chin and looked him in the eye. "As a lawyer, I am bound to represent my client to the best of my ability."

"But she's lying to you."

"So you say, but I choose to believe she's telling me the truth."

"Did she tell you why I broke off with her?"

"She wanted marriage, and you didn't."

He gave her an exasperated look. "I went to the apartment

intending to surprise her, but I was the one who got a surprise. I found her entertaining another man, and they weren't playing cards, if you get my drift."

She suppressed a smile at his choice of words. If Nevada LaRouche had found his paramour in bed with another man, then Lillie hadn't been totally honest with her lawyer after all.

"Miss Troy's fidelity or lack of it has nothing to do with the fact that you promised to marry her and broke that promise."

LaRouche shook his head in palpable disgust. "Damnation! You mean to tell me that you could defend a woman who would cheat on her man and still expect him to marry her?"

"That's your version of what happened. Why should I take your word over Miss Troy's?"

"Because I'm telling the truth."

"I would consult with your lawyer, if I were you," Honor said, "though if you want my advice, I would pay up the five thousand and select my mistresses more carefully in the future." She returned her notes to her valise and rose. "Be warned that if you choose to go to court, we will ask for an even larger settlement, and we will insist that you pay Miss Troy's court costs and my legal fees."

He crossed his arms and raked Honor from bonnet to hem with an insolent gaze that made her itch to slap him. "You have the face of an angel and the heart of a sidewinder, ma'am."

If that's his idea of poetry, Honor thought, then I've read better written on the side of a barn.

She smiled coldly. "I'll give you seven days to come to a decision, Mr. LaRouche. If I don't receive a settlement check by then, my client and I will start proceedings against you and we'll next meet in court. Good day."

She didn't bother to extend her hand, for she had the uneasy feeling it would be akin to sticking it into the jaws of a lion.

As she turned to go, LaRouche said, "Mrs. Davis," and extended his hand.

Honor had no choice but to shake it or risk appearing afraid of him. "Mr. LaRouche." When she tried to withdraw her hand, he held it fast without hurting. Honor remained still and returned his cool, challenging stare.

"I don't take kindly to people who try to cheat me," he drawled in a calm, quiet voice that sent chills down Honor's spine. "I tend to want to get even."

"And I don't take kindly to rich, powerful men who think they can take advantage of helpless women and threaten their lawyers."

"You don't strike me as helpless."

"I'm not. I was referring to Miss Troy."

He smiled and released her hand.

Honor turned and showed herself out. She forced herself to remain calm and didn't start shaking until she was out on the street.

Once the lady lawyer shut the door behind her, Nevada seated himself behind his desk, took a photograph out of the top drawer, and studied the bespectacled young woman seated next to a silly grinning skeleton, its bony hand resting on her shoulder as though they were boon companions, which they had been through medical school and her later practice. Though she had posed that way to make him laugh, the picture had turned into an ironic premonition of her own mortality. The photograph was all he had left of her, except memories both sweet and sad, so he kept it.

"Damnation, Sybilla," he muttered. "Why'd you have to go and die on me?"

He leaned back in his swivel chair and put his feet up on his desk. Sadness and longing sure could make a man stupid. He had taken up with that scheming Lillie Troy only because she bore a remarkable physical resemblance to his Dr. Sybilla, with the same golden hair and green eyes. He soon discovered any resemblance ended right there. After six months of Lillie's endless spending and cheating, he couldn't wait to be rid of her, like a tick on a hound's ear.

Now the venal little bitch was trying to extort money out of him with the aid of that she-devil in a shirtwaist.

Nevada stroked his mustache and smiled in spite of

himself when he thought of Honor Davis. She had stood up to him when most men would have had the good sense to back down. He admired strength and courage in a woman, and this one had a backbone made of steel.

Perhaps that was what made her appear cold in spite of her dark, warm beauty. Or perhaps she only seemed that way because she had kept her features composed and neutral, never revealing her emotions even when baited.

He wondered what kind of man had dared to marry her.

Nevada put Sybilla's photograph back in the drawer. As much as he would relish watching the formidable Honor Davis in a courtroom, he decided that paying Lillie off would be preferable to holding himself up for public ridicule. He was a private man who shunned the limelight, and he knew he had been foolish and indiscreet. He didn't need to see his shortcomings written in headlines screaming across every newspaper in New York City.

Despite her strength and courage, Honor Davis should count herself lucky that their paths wouldn't cross again.

Honor sat before her dressing table mirror, inserting the emerald earbobs into her earlobes. Tonight she and Robert were sure to impress Hartford Fogg, his boss, who had invited them to dinner at his Madison Avenue home. Honor smiled at her reflection and turned to look at her husband struggling with his pearl shirt studs.

"We're sure to cause a sensation," she said, turning back to her mirror, "as the only married couple in New York City who are both lawyers."

Robert made no comment. When he succeeded in conquering his shirt studs, he came over to Honor's dressing table and placed his hands lightly on her bare shoulders. "Honor, do you love me?"

She looked up at his tight, solemn face reflected in the mirror. "What a silly question. You know I do."

"You'd do anything for me?"

She hesitated, trying to ignore the little alarm bell going off in the recesses of her mind. Because she always strove to be a good wife, she replied, "Anything—within the limits of the law, of course."

His grip tightened a fraction. "When we're at the Foggs', promise me you won't tell anyone you're a lawyer."

All she could do was stare at him as though he had spoken in a foreign language. "You want me to do what?"

His jaw clenched. "You heard me."

First came pain scraping every nerve ending raw, followed by anger so virulent that it grabbed Honor by the throat and shook her until she couldn't breathe.

She shrugged out from beneath his hands and rose to face him. "I can't believe you could ask me to do such a thing. You, of all people, who know how hard I struggled against the Hubert Adcocks and Amos Grants of the world to become a lawyer!" Her voice grew louder and more incredulous. "And now you want me to deny it?"

"You don't understand," he said, raising his voice to match hers. "All of the men at the firm are just like Amos Grant and Cleavon Frame. They're married to women who are just like Penelope Grant. They don't understand women like you."

Then Honor understood all too clearly. "You haven't told them, have you?" His gaze slid away, and a guilty flush stained his lean cheeks.

"Damn you, Robert Davis! You've been working there for over six months, and you still haven't told them that your wife is a lawyer." He said nothing. "You're ashamed of me."

"That's not true. I'm proud of you."

"As long as your cronies don't know about me, is that it?" A bubble of hysterical laughter escaped her lips. "I feel like a kept woman hidden away in a back street flat. I'm fine under the covers, but never good enough to be seen in public."

Robert turned livid, his anger gathering around him like a whirlwind. "That's not true, and you know it. For heaven's sake, Honor, I'm asking you to do this one little favor to help advance my career."

"You're asking me to lie by omission. Do you think Fitch, Martin and Fogg won't find out about me eventually? They must have noticed that a woman applied for admission to the city bar. Perhaps one of them even wrote that curt letter informing me that women are not admitted to the Association of the Bar of the City of New York."

"Of course they all noticed. It was the talk of the office for weeks. Luckily, no one made the connection."

"One day they will, and everyone will know that you lied."

Robert just glared at her.

Honor said, "I may not have the august clientele that they do, but I'm slowly building a solid reputation among theater people."

Robert gave a derisive snort. "Circus strongmen and second-rate actors."

Stung, Honor retorted, "They're still paying clients." She reached up and pulled out one earbob, unmindful of the pain. "Since you're obviously ashamed of me"—the other earbob came next—"you can go to your precious dinner party alone."

Robert looked panic-stricken. "You've got to come. I told Fogg you were coming. Everyone wants to meet you."

Honor glared at him, her fingers defiantly pulling hairpins from her hair, ruining the elaborate coiffure that Tilly had spent an hour devising.

Robert moistened his dry lips. "Honor, be reasonable."

She tossed her head defiantly, letting her hair tumble free.

Anger hardened Robert's eyes to shards of green bottle glass. "Steel Stays was just the right name for you. You cold, selfish little—" He caught himself. "Always thinking of yourself, never of me."

"That's not fair."

"Fair! You're a fine one to talk about fairness. You don't give a damn about me and what I want. How many other men would allow their wives to practice law once they were married? Wesley Saltonsall? Sydney Tree? Even your own precious father? Never."

He pointed a proud finger at himself. "But I did. I've never forbidden you to do anything, which is my right as your husband. I've been lenient and indulgent with you, Honor, and now you won't even do this to help me get ahead."

"Lenient? Indulgent? Is that how you see yourself?" She shook her head. "I can see I've been laboring under the delusion that our marriage was a rare one among equals, not parent and child."

Robert muttered, "I don't know why I even bother trying to explain anything to you. You're going to do as you damn well please, as you always do, without any consideration for anyone else."

Guilt tugged at Honor's resistance. "Wouldn't it be better to tell the truth right away? They will find out about me eventually, and when they do, they'll know you lied."

"I'll tell them about you once I become a partner."

"The way you were going to tell me about Priscilla Shanks once we were married?" She knew she had made a mistake the moment the hurtful, heedless words flew out of her mouth.

Robert said coldly, "I was wondering how long it would take you to throw that up in my face."

"I'm sorry. I didn't mean—"

"But you did mean it. And you claim you love me."

"I do." In spite of her momentary anger, she realized that she did love him.

"Then you'll do this for me."

"What about my feelings? You know how much I hate dishonesty and lies."

He glared at her. "I seem to remember that when we were in law school, you wanted to keep our relationship secret from the other students. I wanted to tell the world, but you were afraid that people would think you went to law school just to catch a husband. And didn't I agree to go along with your deception?"

"That was different. We were just students. Now I'm a

practicing lawyer, and the sooner your bosses know it, the better."

"If you won't do this, Honor, then our marriage is a sham. You may as well go back to Boston."

She grew so still that she fancied she could hear her blood pumping furiously through her veins. "Are you saying you'll leave me?"

He grasped her arms before she could evade him, his face a mask of torment. "Of course not. I love you too much to ever leave you. But I will be very disappointed."

She knew that if she didn't comply, he would make her regret her decision in a thousand little ways. They would engage in the most civilized of wars—a cold silence here, a cutting word there—until they chipped away at each other's self-respect and their love turned to dust.

"All right," she said with a bitter, resigned sigh. "If it will please you, I'll go and pretend I'm Penelope Grant. But don't ask me to like it."

A triumphant smile lit Robert's face, and he kissed her cheek before Honor could step away.

"Only this once, Robert," she warned him, lest he think his victory was absolute. "You had better think of some way to tell your bosses about me, because I will not lie for you again."

He took a step back, his features unreadable. "Get ready. We have to leave in a few minutes so we won't be late. I want to make a good impression." He turned and left the room.

Honor returned to her dressing table and brushed out her hair in long, painful strokes that scraped her scalp. After twisting her hair into a simple, elegant chignon that displayed her long, slender neck to best advantage, she replaced her earbobs, then tugged at her bodice to lower the neckline and expose more of the snowy swell of her breasts.

She took one satisfied look at her reflection and rose with a smile. If he wanted to treat his beautiful wife like a showpiece to decorate his arm, she would give him exactly what he wanted and more than he bargained for.

* * *

If you want to scintillate at a party, Aunt Theo had once advised her with a mischievous twinkle in her eye, look at every man in the room and speculate about how he makes love.

Well, I'm going to seduce every man here tonight, Honor thought the moment she and Robert stood in the doorway of the Foggs' crowded parlor and felt all eyes upon her.

She had never deliberately used her beauty to draw people to her, seeing it as a liability in her attempt to be taken seriously. Tonight her reckless mood, fueled by her lingering anger at her husband's betrayal, made her want to test her powers. She wanted to dazzle. She wanted to conquer. She wanted to leave hearts broken and bleeding at her feet.

A short, gray-haired couple who could have been twins approached them.

"Davis," the man greeted them, displaying small yellow teeth as he shook Robert's hand. "Mrs. Fogg and I are delighted that you and Mrs. Davis could come tonight."

Mr. Fogg, Honor decided, made love in the dark and quickly. She suppressed a giggle.

When Robert introduced Honor to his boss, she dazzled him with her smile, then complimented his wife on her lovely gown and her beautiful home.

Mrs. Fogg flashed yellow teeth, thanked her, and said, "Why don't you come and let me introduce you to our other guests?"

Most of the twenty or so guests seated or standing were lawyers and their wives, though several were clients whom Fogg was trying to woo. Honor burned to discuss cases with them, but restrained herself for Robert's sake. To keep away from temptation, she sat with his bosses' wives, earning a pleased, encouraging smile from her husband, which she did not return.

After making sure Honor had a glass of champagne, Mrs. Fogg introduced her to the other women present, and they chatted pleasantly about the differences between Boston and New York.

Activity by the parlor doorway caused Mrs. Fogg to say, "Ah, I see our last guest has finally arrived."

There stood none other than Nevada LaRouche.

Honor froze, her champagne glass halfway to her lips, a sense of doom clenching the pit of her stomach and making her dizzy with apprehension. Her charade was over. Soon everyone in this room would know that her husband was a liar.

She cast a look of mute appeal at Robert, but he remained deep in conversation with Clarence Martin and didn't notice her distress.

She watched helplessly as her host and hostess went to welcome the man who could ruin everything.

LaRouche looked as handsome as the devil tonight, his somber black evening attire providing a striking foil for his fair coloring. Yet for all his surface polish, he still looked out of place.

Suddenly he looked straight at Honor, those remote blue eyes pinning her to the sofa. He started, obviously surprised to find her here. Then his eyes narrowed, sending a chill down Honor's spine. She didn't dare allow herself to speculate about how this quiet, purposeful man made love.

Honor had only one small hope of salvaging the evening. She rose.

Nevada watched her approach, thinking to himself, What in damnation is she doing here?

A low-cut evening gown in a flattering shade of forest green had replaced her prim shirtwaist, revealing creamy shoulders and a stunning figure worthy of a long, lingering look. In fact, even men engaged in conversation followed her out of the corner of their eye as she moved across the room with a floating, seductive grace, but she appeared oblivious to the attention her cream and jet beauty attracted.

As she drew closer, he could sense panic and desperation about her like that of a horse trapped in a burning barn.

"Why, Mr. LaRouche," she said with a too-bright smile, "what a pleasure to see you again."

Pleasure? He would hardly call their meeting in his office a pleasure. More like having a tooth pulled. He smiled mirthlessly. "I suppose you could call it that, ma'am."

Mrs. Davis said to the Foggs, "Mr. LaRouche recently made a very generous donation to the Florence Night Mission for Fallen Women."

He rocked back on his heels and opened his mouth, ready to refute her absurd assertion, when he caught the silent plea in her eyes.

What kind of game is she playing? he wondered.

Intrigued in spite of himself, he smiled and decided to play along. "Mrs. Davis here will do anything to rescue fallen women."

Only he noticed her little sigh of relief at disaster averted.

Mrs. Fogg beamed. "A truly worthy cause, my dear."

His hostess then took him around the room to introduce him to everyone, including the lady lawyer's husband, Robert Davis.

Davis said, "Nevada LaRouche of Delancy and LaRouche?" When Nevada responded in the affirmative, Davis said, "One of the few companies that didn't lose their shirt in '93," referring to the devastating depression that had gripped the country. "A real feat."

"My partner had more to do with that than I did," he said. "He's the brains of the outfit."

"Nonsense. I'm sure you're too modest."

Now, there's a man who wants something real bad, Nevada thought after he excused himself and continued on his rounds. Once he had spoken his quota of social inanities, he cornered Mrs. Davis and maneuvered her into a quiet corner of the parlor where they wouldn't be overheard.

"What in damnation was that all about?" He smiled and looked out over the room so no one would think he and this duplicitous woman were having anything but an innocent conversation.

"Thank you for not giving me away." She fanned herself

nervously. "Mr. LaRouche, I must ask a great favor of you."

"A favor? I—"

"Please. No one here must know that I'm a lawyer."

"Why? Are you trying to find someone else to blackmail?"

She looked out over the assembled guests. "For the thousandth time, Lillie Troy isn't blackmailing you. I am keeping my profession a secret for personal reasons."

"You have some gall, asking me to help you after the way you cheated me." He stroked his mustache. "If I agree to help you, you have to tell me what's going on."

The look in her eyes told him she'd rather trust a rabid wildcat. "I can't."

He shrugged. "Suit yourself, but I can't guarantee I'll keep my mouth shut."

"Oh, all right!" She stepped closer to him and whispered behind her silk fan, her sweet rose perfume and midnight eyes distracting him momentarily. "Please don't tell anyone here that I'm a lawyer."

"Why not? Aren't you proud of being one?"

She bristled. "Of course I am."

"Then why keep it a secret from all these other lawyers?"

Her direct gaze fell away, and she looked troubled. "My husband just started working at Fitch, Martin and Fogg a little while ago. Unfortunately, most lawyers are downright hostile to women in the legal profession. They regard us as oddities."

The bitterness in her voice spoke volumes, and he felt an unexpected twinge of sympathy. He knew all about women who were considered oddities. His Sybilla. Damon's wife, Catherine. Both dedicated doctors.

"So you're doing this for your husband?"

"To advance his career."

"Hasn't he told the people he works with that you're a lawyer?"

"I begged him not to, and he reluctantly agreed to go along with my request until he becomes more established."

"That could take a while."

"I know. But if they find out that his wife is a lawyer, they might dismiss him. He's worked so hard for this position, Mr. LaRouche. I'd hate to see him lose it because of me."

Her explanation was so full of holes that he doubted it would hold up under closer scrutiny, but she was riled enough without him pressing her further. "I can understand a man needing to work."

She swallowed hard. "Then you won't tell? I can count on your discretion?"

He stroked his mustache. "If I keep your secret, what will you do for me?"

She fanned herself, and her shoulders drooped slightly in resignation. "What's your price? As if I don't know."

"Talk Lillie into dropping her suit." Even as he made his request, something told him that she would refuse.

"And you accuse me of blackmailing you." She raised her stubborn chin. "I will not, so do your worst, Mr. LaRouche. Tell my secret to the world. See if I care."

"You wouldn't turn your back on Lillie to save your own skin?"

Without hesitation, she replied, "No, Mr. LaRouche, I could not. It's a matter of ethics."

His eyes narrowed. "Why would you be so loyal to Lillie? What's she to you?"

"She's a client. She trusts me to represent her to the best of my ability, and I owe her my loyalty." She looked around the room with an air of fatalism. "Well, I got myself into this and will have to suffer the consequences. If you'll excuse me . . ."

She moved away, but LaRouche stayed her with the brief touch of his hand on her arm. "I'll keep your secret, Mrs. Davis. For now." He grinned, for he couldn't resist turning the tables on her. "But now you're in my debt, and I intend to collect."

She swallowed hard. "I've already told you that I won't urge Lillie to drop her suit."

"That's not the price I had in mind."

"Oh? What do you want from me?"

His grin widened. "I haven't figured that out yet, but when I do, you'll be the first to know."

He was going to enjoy thinking of a suitable punishment for Honor Davis.

With a brief nod, he turned and walked away.

Later, when Honor and Robert were back in their apartment and he was unhooking her gown, he said, "You were wonderful tonight, Honor. Everyone there adored you, and I know Fogg was most impressed by my beautiful wife."

His beautiful wife, not his accomplished wife.

All I had to do was be party to a lie, she thought, stepping out of the dress and laying it across a chair for Tilly to clean and iron in the morning.

"I'm happy you're pleased," she said, unhooking her corset and letting her compressed insides return to their natural, comfortable state so she could breathe deeply again. Now there would be no arguments. As much as she loved arguing cases, she hated arguing with her husband. She reached for her nightgown.

Robert undid his shirt studs. "You and Nevada LaRouche seemed to hit it off. I saw you in a corner talking like old friends." He removed his shirt. "If I were a jealous husband, I'd have a few words with him for monopolizing my wife."

"That's because I had met him once before," she replied, slipping her nightgown over her head and seating herself at her dressing table. "There is no cause for you to be jealous. We're hardly old friends."

Robert looked at her. "Oh? You never told me. When did you meet him?"

Honor creamed her face and told him as much as she could about Lillie Troy's breach-of-promise suit.

Robert's hands stilled, and he stared at her out of displeased eyes. "You let some second-rate actress sue a prominent man like LaRouche?"

She turned slowly in her seat, expecting the worst. "Why shouldn't I? She had a good case, and she's my client."

Robert shook his head. "Didn't you stop to think that you've made us a very powerful enemy?"

"Us?" Honor wiped the cream from her face with hard strokes. "No, Robert, I'm afraid I didn't think of that at all. The woman needed a lawyer, and I agreed to represent her, which I did to the best of my ability."

Chagrin twisted his features. "Well, there go my chances of ever working for him, thanks to my idealistic wife."

Honor yanked out her hairpins and brushed her hair so vigorously it crackled. "I'm sorry if I've spoiled your opportunities yet again, but I didn't know the man's good opinion meant so much to you." And even if she had, she still would have taken Lillie on as a client.

He came up behind her and stroked her hair. "Idealism has its place, but you have to be prudent. There are people in this world who can hurt you, and there are those who can help. I know you've been sheltered, but you have to learn the difference if you're to survive in the legal profession."

She tied her hair back with a ribbon and then rose. "I shall remember that in the future." Not that she would ever allow personal convenience to override her principles. "Now, if you'll excuse me, it really is late, and I'm exhausted."

She slipped into bed, closed her eyes, and prayed he wouldn't touch her tonight, when there was still the residue of anger as solid as a wall between them. He didn't.

Exhausted as she was, she lay awake in the darkness, wondering why she had taken the blame for Robert's lie tonight. Wifely loyalty, she supposed, and pride. Like most women, she didn't want anyone to think ill of her husband.

Nevada LaRouche remained an enigma. He could have exposed her, but he hadn't, and not for any altruistic reasons. He wanted her in his debt, to pay her back for helping his former mistress. Quid pro quo. Something exchanged for something wanted. The thought of owing such a man a favor caused a shudder to ripple across her skin.

Three days later she learned exactly how he intended to be repaid.

CHAPTER 9

NEARLY BURIED AMONG THE opened and unopened law tomes scattered around her desk, Honor barely looked up when she heard the knock on her door. "Come in," she said as she kept on writing.

"Can you put down that pen long enough to hear my good news?"

She looked up and smiled. "Robert." Then she glanced at her clock in puzzlement. "It's not even noon. Why aren't you at work?"

His green eyes shone with triumph as he swaggered over to the chair. "I don't work for Fitch, Martin and Fogg anymore."

Honor sat back in shock. "You don't? What happened?" She prayed they hadn't discovered that his wife was a lawyer and fired him.

"Starting tomorrow, I'll be working for Delancy and LaRouche."

Her mouth went dry. "Delancy and LaRouche?" She tugged at her locket. "Nevada LaRouche offered you a position?"

"Just over an hour ago."

"Why?"

Robert's smile froze. "Why do you think?" he snapped. "I'm a damn fine lawyer, and he's impressed with me."

Honor rose and placed a placating hand on his arm. "I didn't mean to imply that you aren't. I'm just surprised he would offer you a position after I represented a woman who was suing him. That could be construed as a conflict of interest."

Robert dismissed her point with a wave of his hand. "Men don't hold grudges the way women do. His company needed another lawyer, and he knew I was looking for a new position." He shrugged. "He said he'd even consider you."

Help Nevada LaRouche twist and circumvent the law to increase his vast wealth? Never.

"That's most generous of him," Honor replied, "but you know I've never been interested in working for a financier. Besides, it would be much too distracting to work with my own husband."

Robert's eyes tasted her, and he smiled slowly. "You're right. I'd be kissing you in the coatroom every chance I got."

The sparkle of desire in his eyes made Honor's blood race. "When did you tell him you were interested in another position?"

"Saturday night at the dinner party. I told him I had been with the firm for eight months, and at this rate I'd be an old man before I became successful. He said he admired a man who wanted to get ahead, and to come and talk to him. I did, and he hired me."

Oh, Robert, she thought, your ambition has blinded you. You've taken the bait. He's got us where he wants us. "What did Hartford Fogg say when you told him you were leaving?"

Robert's cocksure laughter filled the small office. "He was so furious I thought he was going to have an apoplectic fit. He said that I was too young and didn't have enough experience under my belt for such a position, that I was too ambitious for my own good." He sobered. "I am ambitious, Honor, but I know I can handle whatever LaRouche throws at me."

Honor smiled and rose. "I know you can, too." If Nevada LaRouche doesn't destroy you first.

Robert stood and rounded her desk, taking her into his arms. He kissed her long and hard, like a victorious warrior claiming his prize after battle. He released her. "There's no limit to what I can do. This is just the beginning."

Or the end, she thought.

After her husband left, Honor sat at her desk and stared at the bare opposite wall. Despite what Robert had said about men not holding grudges, she was willing to bet her law degree that Nevada LaRouche had an ulterior motive for hiring him. After all, he blamed Honor for costing him five thousand dollars. She wished that she had never asked him not to tell anyone she was a lawyer, but at the time, she couldn't risk exposing her husband as a liar.

"Now you're in my debt," LaRouche had said to her at the Foggs' party, "and I intend to collect."

Did he plan to hurt her through her husband? Perhaps in several months he'd tell Robert that his work wasn't satisfactory and dismiss him without a reference, making it harder, if not impossible, for him to find another position in the city.

"I wouldn't trust that man as far as I could throw him," she muttered. "I've got to stay one step ahead of him." She rose and went to the door. "Elroy?"

Her assistant stopped typing and looked up. "Yes, boss?"

"I want you to investigate someone for me. He's a powerful, wealthy man, so you must be very discreet."

Elroy's freckled face brightened, for he secretly yearned to be a detective like his idol, Sherlock Holmes. "Discretion is my middle name, boss. When do you need my report?"

"As soon as possible. I want you to investigate a man by the name of Nevada LaRouche."

By the end of the week, Elroy had finished his investigation.

He sat in the chair across from Honor's desk, a sheaf of papers in his hand, and began his report while Honor listened with rapt attention. For the first twenty minutes he reiterated what Lillie Troy had already told Honor about LaRouche's early days out west.

Elroy stuck his pencil behind his ear. "He really struck pay dirt when he teamed up with Damon Delancy, the so-called Wolf of Wall Street. Delancy made his fortune in Arizona copper and has been making more money ever since."

Honor said, "I understand Delancy has been living in

England. Something about his wife being arrested. Did you unearth anything about that?"

"Quite a bit, boss. His wife, Dr. Catherine Delancy, was arrested for violating the Comstock Act. She gave her patients anti-conception information, which she received through the mails."

During her weekly visits to the Criminal Courts Building, Honor had often seen Anthony Comstock, president of the New York Society for the Suppression of Vice, gleefully hauling into Special Sessions some violator of the federal anti-obscenity law that bore his name. As a special agent of the post office, he was empowered to search the mails for what he considered obscene literature or items. Anti-conception literature and rubber goods, like the pessaries that Aunt Theo had given Honor, were fair game for seizure and prosecution.

Honor personally thought Comstock a zealot and his law outdated, but receiving such items through the mail was a misdemeanor punishable by a fine and up to five years in prison.

"According to all reports," Elroy continued, "the woman is a saint."

"A saint? Surely you jest."

"I'm serious, boss. No one in this city has a bad word to say about her except Anthony Comstock, and we all know he's a crazy old coot. Dr. Delancy was so dedicated to her patients that she often risked her life for them. Most were poor immigrants who lived in the East Side tenements. She treated them without ever charging them a dime."

"Commendable."

"Comstock didn't think so. When he couldn't trick her into giving one of his flunkies anti-conception devices, he got a warrant, searched her office, and found so-called obscene literature that had been sent to her through the mail. Before the doctor could go to trial, she, her husband and their son, flew the coop to England."

"I wonder just how much Mr. LaRouche did to aid and abet them?"

"He claims he didn't know what they were planning."

Honor gave a snort of derision. "And I'm from Texas."

Nevada LaRouche obviously thought he could flout the law and get away with it.

She said, "What about the other women in LaRouche's life?" One could tell a great deal about a man from what he thought about women.

Elroy sifted through his papers until he located the one he wanted. "He used to frequent a high-class brothel called Ivory's north of Gramercy Park."

That didn't surprise her, for both bachelors and married men patronized the city's brothels. She did wonder why LaRouche chose to patronize ladies of the evening instead of maintaining a mistress. Did he prefer a variety of women? Did he want immediate physical gratification rather than long-term intimacy?

Elroy said, "Then he courted Catherine Delancy's friend, another lady doctor named Sybilla Wolcott."

So he had committed himself to one woman after all. "Where is she now?"

Elroy's features turned somber. "Dead. She was murdered."

Honor felt the breath knocked out of her. "Murdered!"

"That's what it said in the *World*. She was strangled in an alley while going to treat a patient."

"Did the police ever catch her murderer?"

"It was a banker named August Talmadge. He blamed Damon Delancy for the failure of his bank in the depression of '93 and had intended to kill Delancy's wife that night. He sent a little girl with a note for Dr. Delancy, saying that the child's mother was gravely ill and to come at once. But Dr. Delancy wasn't there, so Dr. Wolcott went in her place. The alley was dark. Talmadge killed her by mistake."

"How horrible." Honor shook her head. "The poor woman."

"Later the banker tried again to kill Dr. Delancy in her office, but her husband and LaRouche got there just in time to save her." Elroy looked up. "LaRouche killed the banker."

Honor grew very still. "Was he arrested?"

"No, boss, he was never charged. According to the police report, he acted in self-defense. While fighting with LaRouche, the banker accidentally fell, hit his head, and broke his neck. The Delancys swore to it."

"How convenient. Have there been any other women in LaRouche's life?"

Elroy shook his head. "Nothing serious. He stopped patronizing Ivory's a while back, and then he met Miss Troy." He sat back. "I learned that she looks like the lady doctor who was murdered. That might explain why he took up with her."

"Trying to recapture his lost love?" Honor smiled. "You are such a romantic, Elroy."

He blushed beneath his freckles. "Nevada LaRouche leads a dull life, boss. Before Delancy left, LaRouche mostly stayed in his shadow. Now he keeps the company on an even keel in Delancy's absence. He's not the Wall Street wizard Delancy was, though. Delancy sends him daily cablegrams from London, and LaRouche just follows orders."

"Most illuminating. Is that all?" When Elroy nodded, Honor extended her hand for his notes. "You've done a splendid job. Sherlock Holmes would be proud."

Elroy grinned. "We aim to please." He rose and returned to his own desk.

Alone, Honor rose and went to the window to look down on the teeming street that was now as familiar to her as sedate Commonwealth Avenue. A shiver slithered down her arms, a cold seeping into her bones, though the April sunlight warmed the room.

Murdered . . .

She ran her hands up and down her arms. It always amazed her how one new bit of evidence, hidden or unknown, could suddenly alter one's perception of a person or incident when it finally came to light. She had thought she knew Robert as well as anyone until she learned of Priscilla Shanks. Now the knowledge that the woman Nevada LaRouche once loved had been brutally murdered touched the most vulnerable corner of her woman's heart.

Murdered . . .

Losing her father to the hangman was the same as his being murdered, a life suddenly wrenched from the world of the living, whether by an individual or by the government. For years afterward, the knowledge that he had died so horribly would suddenly overwhelm Honor, leaving her with a sadness so profound she wondered if it would drive her mad. She suspected all loved ones left behind experienced the same lingering, aching sense of loss.

She turned away from the window. "Don't!" she chided herself. "Don't let sentiment cloud your judgment."

While she sympathized with the man's loss, she couldn't afford to let down her guard, because he had the power to destroy all she held dear. She prayed that Nevada LaRouche would just leave her and Robert alone.

Her prayers went unanswered.

When she returned home early that evening, an excited Robert told her that LaRouche had invited them to spend the following weekend with him and several other guests at Damon Delancy's Hudson River estate.

Honor knew better than to argue, so she feigned suitable wifely enthusiasm. Deep inside, she dreaded going.

"It's not exactly Newport," Robert said when he first saw Coppermine, the country estate named after the source of Delancy's vast wealth.

From her seat in the open victoria that had been sent to the train station to collect them late that Friday afternoon, Honor decided she vastly preferred this small Georgian-style house built of white granite to Newport's opulent French châteaux, staid English manor houses, and Italian villas so sprawling that one could spend days wandering the hallways. This house had been designed for comfort and intimacy rather than to flaunt its owner's wealth. That a powerful man like Damon Delancy preferred graciousness to ostentation both surprised and impressed her.

As the carriage rattled over an arched stone bridge that spanned a racing, gurgling stream, Coppermine seduced Honor with its bucolic serenity. Taking in the acres of well-kept green lawn stretching out on either side and the stately elm and oak trees rising up to the spring sky, the thick knot of apprehension in the middle of her chest began to unravel.

Beyond the bridge, the victoria swept down the long circular drive. Robert said, "This is the back entrance. The front overlooks the Hudson River, and I'm told the view is quite magnificent." He grasped her hand. "Someday we're going to have a summer home even grander than this."

Though a summer home really didn't matter to Honor, she respected Robert's right to cherish his own dreams. "Someday we shall."

The moment the victoria came to a stop at the door, Nevada LaRouche himself came out and sauntered down the porch steps with his usual predatory grace. Attired for the country in a white shirt with no cravat, unbuttoned waistcoat, and brown twill trousers, he nevertheless still wore his cowboy boots.

He smiled, and Honor felt the serenity vanish.

"Davis, Mrs. Davis . . ." He walked over to the carriage and extended his hand to help Honor disembark. "Welcome to Coppermine."

"Thank you for inviting us," Honor said, avoiding his cool, amused gaze by focusing all her attention on the complex task of gathering her skirt in one hand. She was thankful that her gloves shielded her fingers from the warmth of his clasp as he helped her down. Again Honor avoided looking at him by studying her surroundings. "This is a beautiful estate, very serene and restful after the bustle of New York City."

"That's what my partner had in mind when he built it," LaRouche replied. "Maybe tomorrow you'd like to see the dairy farm and orchards, or go riding."

Honor managed a small polite smile. "I'm sure Robert and I would enjoy that."

"Do you come up here every weekend?" Robert asked after he stepped down.

"As often as I can get away, especially in the summer." As the footmen began unloading his guests' bags from the carriage, LaRouche drifted toward the house. "Why don't you come in and meet the others?"

Robert drew Honor's arm through his, and they followed their host into the house, passing first through a small foyer, then into a spacious central atrium that soared past the second floor.

Honor tilted her head back to stare at the stained-glass skylight made up of squares of translucent white glass in the center and bordered with vivid green grape leaves and twisting brown vines.

She smiled, thinking how much Aunt Theo would adore the artistry and craftsmanship of the stained glass. "That's lovely."

"I've always thought it right pretty myself," LaRouche said in his soft drawl. "The rest of the guests are in the drawing room."

Three men rose the moment they entered the room, and their wives turned interested faces on the newcomers.

LaRouche said, "I'd like you all to meet Robert Davis, the company's newest lawyer, and his wife, Honor, who is the only lady lawyer in New York City."

Her secret was out. Amid the murmurs of polite surprise and admiration rippling among the guests, Honor caught a sniff or two of disapproval. She was not surprised.

She kept her face blank but shot Robert an apologetic look. His expression remained impassive. Honor concentrated on the introductions.

A short, swarthy man with a clipped English accent and his shy, forgettable wife were the Herrons, visiting from London. The large woman with the haughty air turned out to be Maria Morelli, the temperamental opera singer, and her companion, a florid middle-aged man who couldn't take his adoring eyes off her, was named Jeffrey Something-or-other. But the guests who most intrigued Honor were the tallest man in the room and his diminutive redheaded wife.

With wild dark brown hair down to his broad shoulders and a full beard down to his chest, Gordon Graham reminded Honor of a fierce lion. Though he bared his teeth in a smile when introduced, his dark eyes glittered with disapproval. One huge paw rested on his wife Genevra's shoulder as if to restrain her should she try to flee. The woman looked as terrified and resigned as Honor's father the day before he was to go to the gallows.

Introductions made, their host said, "Maybe you'd care to see your rooms and rest up before dinner?"

Robert thanked him, and he and Honor followed a servant upstairs to a large, spacious room decorated in warm tones of pale yellow.

When Honor was alone with her husband, she said, "I'm quite relieved that Mr. LaRouche told everyone that I am a lawyer. I know you didn't want anyone to know just yet, but I was tired of pretending."

"I only didn't want Fogg and the others to know," Robert said with an offhand shrug. "LaRouche's not like them. He doesn't care that you're a lawyer."

That surprised her. "I'm relieved to hear it."

Robert went to one of the windows and drew open the curtains. "Sweet Jesus, will you look at this view? You can see the river and the land on the opposite side." He turned. "Did you notice that I'm the only employee he invited up here?"

"Mr. Herron and that Graham man don't work for him?"

Robert shook his head and smiled. "Just me. That's got to mean he has big plans for me."

Honor felt sick to her stomach as she wondered what those "big plans" could be.

At dinner, when Honor saw LaRouche had seated Robert in a place of honor at his left, she decided to use this social occasion to glean more information about their host and turned her attention to her own dinner partners, the Englishman Mr. Herron on her left and Gordon Graham on her right.

As the soup course was being served, Honor said to Herron, "How do you happen to know Mr. LaRouche?"

"We have mutual friends in London," he replied, "Damon Delancy and his wife, Dr. Catherine."

She sipped a spoonful of the delicious beef consommé. "I had heard they were living in London." Evading the law. "Does Dr. Delancy still practice medicine?"

Herron dabbed at his lips with his napkin. "She works for a dispensary in the city's East End. Are you familiar with London, Mrs. Davis?" When Honor replied that she wasn't, he continued, "The East End is a very poor section, and medical care is a luxury its inhabitants can ill afford. Catherine and the other dispensary doctors go out into the slums and care for those who need it without cost."

Elroy had said she was a saint.

"How . . . selfless of her," Honor said.

To her right, Graham muttered, "Foodhardy, if you ask me."

Honor turned toward him. "Why would you think that, Mr. Graham?"

He looked at her, his dark eyes glittering with that disapproval Honor had sensed earlier. "Slums are dangerous places for women alone." He looked meaningfully at his wife seated between Robert and the opera singer's companion. "I know I wouldn't want my wife going into dangerous places at all hours of the night. A woman could get beaten . . . or worse."

She could be murdered, like Dr. Sybilla Wolcott.

Honor darted a glance at Nevada LaRouche, but he was deep in conversation with Maria Morelli and hadn't heard Graham's remark.

Genevra Graham looked at her husband with a sparkle of defiance in her hazel eyes. "That may be true, but you know as well as I do, Gordon, that if it hadn't been for Dr. Delancy and Dr. Wolcott, our son wouldn't be alive today." Her defiant gaze faltered and slid away, and she muttered, "Nor would I, for that matter," almost as an afterthought.

Intrigued, Honor leaned forward. "May I ask how Dr. Delancy saved your lives?"

"I was having a particularly difficult delivery," Genevra Graham explained, her cheeks coloring at mentioning such a delicate subject at the dinner table. "Catherine's friend Sybilla performed a rare, dangerous operation that saved us both." She resumed eating her soup, effectively closing the conversation. Honor noticed that her fingers trembled.

Mr. Herron said, "Dr. Catherine tried to open a private practice in London, but very few would go to a woman doctor, so she went to work for the dispensary." He turned to Honor. "You must have faced similar prejudice, Mrs. Davis, being the only woman lawyer in New York City."

Honor thought of the men in law school who had put ink on her chair and all the lawyers who had refused to hire her, and she suddenly felt a kinship with a woman she had never met.

She sat back so the footman could remove her soup bowl. "I think that for all their difficulties, women doctors are accepted more readily than female lawyers."

Conversation around her suddenly ceased. Honor became aware that eight pairs of eyes were riveted on her.

Nevada LaRouche said, "Why would you say that, Mrs. Davis?"

Honor met his clear blue gaze with a challenging one of her own. "People believe that caring for the sick, whether as a nurse or doctor, is a basic part of a woman's gentle, nurturing nature, so they are willing to accept it more readily. But if women are allowed in the courtroom, they threaten the legal power men have held for themselves for centuries."

Gordon Graham looked at Honor, the disapproval in his eyes turning to frank dislike. "Women don't need power. They've got their fathers and husbands to protect them and give them everything they need."

His wife made no comment, but her lips tightened.

"I quite agree," Maria Morelli said in her rich, melodic voice. "A woman, she loses her womanliness when she tries to be like a man, no?"

Honor looked past Mr. Herron at the opera singer. "But you yourself are an independent woman, Miss Morelli. You earn a living by performing on the stage. You travel around the country."

"That is true, but I am always a woman before I am a singer. The man, he always comes first with Maria Morelli." She placed a dramatic hand on her ample, quivering bosom. "I would give up singing tomorrow to please the man I love." She beamed at her companion. "That's so, eh?"

Jeffrey Something-or-other beamed back. "Very true, *ma bella*. But I would never be so selfish as to deprive the world of your beautiful voice."

Honor looked at Robert, hoping he would support her, but he merely continued eating without saying a word. Too proud to prompt him, Honor hid her disappointment by sipping her wine, all too aware of Nevada LaRouche's eyes on her.

Their host looked around the table. "Well, having known some remarkable women in my life, I say that if a woman wants to be a doctor or a lawyer, no one should stop her."

Honor gave him a look of surprise tempered with suspicion and skepticism. No matter how enlightened Nevada LaRouche professed to be about women, Honor still didn't trust him.

She raised her wineglass. "You are a prince among men, Mr. LaRouche."

He caught the edge of sarcasm in her voice, for he frowned, his blue eyes turning to ice and promising retribution.

Honor turned her attention back to her plate and spent the rest of the evening engaging in bland, uncontroversial conversation with the other guests and deliberately avoiding Nevada LaRouche.

Chapter 10

The following morning Honor rose quietly at first light, dressed quickly in her blue striped shirtwaist and a plain skirt, brushed out her hair so that it flowed down over her shoulders, and left the bedroom to the melodic accompaniment of Robert's snores.

After walking through the hushed house without meeting so much as a servant, she let herself out through the front door and found herself in an eerie, fog-enshrouded world that smelled wonderfully of damp grass and bark, where even a sigh reverberated loudly, and she could barely see six feet in front of her. Honor shivered, pulling her cashmere shawl closer about her to ward off the predawn chill, and strode away from the house. The wet grass seeped through her thin kid slippers and dampened her skirt's hem, but she didn't turn back, finding the silence and solitude and unremitting grayness comforting after her foolish behavior at dinner last night.

What had possessed her to insult Nevada LaRouche? He was their host and her husband's employer. He held Robert's future in the palm of his hand.

Even if you don't trust him, she told herself, you've got to swallow your animosity and be polite. For Robert's sake.

Luckily for her, Robert hadn't overheard her sarcastic toast to LaRouche. When they retired for the evening, he had praised her for being a credit to him. Sitting at the dressing table and creaming her face, she had told him that she was disappointed in him for not defending her at dinner.

He had kissed the nape of her neck until she went all soft and shivery, then said, "You defend yourself better than I or anyone else ever could," and later redeemed himself by making wild, passionate love to her.

She found a narrow, well-worn dirt path leading across the lawn and into a lightly wooded area beyond, so she took it. As she walked farther and farther away from the main house, more trees materialized out of the mist and were swiftly swallowed up behind her as she hurried past them.

Honor hadn't been walking more than ten minutes when she heard the unmistakable sound of footsteps behind her. Heart pounding wildly, she whirled around and came face to face with Nevada LaRouche.

He stood in the middle of the path, a tall, forbidding figure silhouetted against a solid wall of gray mist.

"Mrs. Davis." Even his soft drawl sounded loud and forceful when trapped by the surrounding fog.

"Mr. LaRouche." Honor attempted a smile and failed. "What are you doing out so early in the morning?"

Noticing the man's tousled hair and the light golden stubble on his lean jaw, Honor assumed that he, too, had dressed hastily.

The grayness of the predawn fog turned his blue eyes to ice. "I wanted a chance to talk to you. In private."

"So when you saw me leave the house, you decided to follow me."

"Something like that."

"You must be an early riser."

"When I have a lot on my mind."

Though she already knew the answer, Honor said, "What do you wish to speak to me about?"

The surrounding fog and trees enclosed them like the four walls of a small room. He took a step forward and hooked his thumbs in his belt. "When you're around me, you act as ornery as a cow pony with a burr under its saddle. I'd like to know why."

Honor pulled her shawl closer about her and decided to

lie yet again for Robert's sake. She forced her expression to remain impassive. "I don't know what you're talking about. I have been politeness itself to you."

"Politeness?" He smiled, a wolfish baring of too many white teeth. "Ma'am, if that's what you call polite, I'd hate to see you when you're ornery." He studied her with a disconcerting frankness. "You don't like me very much, do you?"

Honor raised her brows. "You are certainly direct, sir."

"I believe in laying all my cards on the table."

"How do you expect me to answer such a question? I would hardly be stupid enough to admit a dislike for my husband's employer, now, would I?"

"So you do dislike me."

"Don't be exasperating. I don't know you well enough to form an opinion."

He raised one brow. "You strike me as a woman of strong opinions, one who doesn't sashay around."

"You're right. I don't. I, too, like to lay all my cards on the table." Honor took a deep breath. "It's not that I dislike you. I simply don't trust men like you."

He didn't take offense. "Is that because of what happened to your father?"

The blood rushed to Honor's cheeks so fast that she felt momentarily dizzy. She tugged at her locket so hard that the cord finally snapped. "Damn!" she swore softly as her treasured memento fell to the ground.

Before Honor could take another breath, LaRouche swooped down and picked up the locket in his long fingers. "It's wet," he said, taking a handkerchief from the breast pocket of his coat and gently wiping the gold engraved face before handing it back to Honor. "You should put that on a chain."

"I did," she replied, slipping the locket and broken cord into her skirt pocket, "but they all broke eventually."

She tried to gather her scattered wits and failed. She turned and blindly started down the path, only to be stopped in her tracks by a gentle restraining hand on her arm. She stared straight ahead at distant sunlight slanting through the trees like a direct road to heaven, burning off the fog. "Did my husband tell you everything?"

"Yes," LaRouche said softly at her elbow.

Was nothing sacred to Robert in his attempt to ingratiate himself with this man? "I see."

He released her. "I know it must have been terrible for you to lose your father that way, and I'm sorry. But I'm not like the man who swindled him."

Honor composed herself and turned around. The sympathy in his eyes almost undid her, but she refused to let it touch her heart. "Aren't you?" she blurted heedlessly. "You're a wealthy, powerful man—"

"I may be wealthy, thanks to Delancy, but powerful?" He shook his head. "You flatter me, ma'am."

Honor plunged on. "Don't deny that you harbor a grudge against me for helping Lillie Troy. And don't deny that you said I owed you a debt of gratitude for helping me the night of Hartford Fogg's dinner party. How do you expect me to repay that debt, Mr. LaRouche? Unless, of course, you're planning to ruin my unsuspecting husband."

He rocked back on the heels of his cowboy boots. "Is that why you think I hired him, to get back at you for helping Lillie?"

"Didn't you?"

He looked genuinely shocked. "No, ma'am, I did not." He stroked his long mustache and studied her with that unsettling intensity. "I hired him because I heard he's a damn fine lawyer."

That unexpected admission stunned her into silence.

"Don't you think your husband is good enough to be hired for his abilities?"

She bristled. "Of course I do. I'm relieved to hear you appreciate his talent."

"I'll admit that I was annoyed with you for helping Lillie." He shook his head. "That woman has given me more headaches—"

"Annoyed? That day in your office you said that you didn't take kindly to people who tried to cheat you." Honor swallowed hard. "You threatened to get even."

Shock and surprise mingled on his features. "I only said that to scare you a little, ma'am. I didn't think you'd take it to heart. I've got more important things to worry about then petty vengeance against Lillie and her lawyer." His gaze locked with hers. "If I really wanted to get even, you'd know it."

Honor shivered at his implied threat.

"Cold?"

She suspected he knew damn well that she wasn't, but he took off his tweed jacket anyway and slipped it around her shoulders. The garment, still warm from the heat of LaRouche's body and smelling pleasantly of damp wool, hugged her like a strong embrace. She fought the seductive comfort of it.

He suddenly loomed too close, and she stepped away. "I also know that you've broken the law."

His long mustache twitched with the effort of suppressing a smile. "I reckon I've broken all sorts of laws in my lifetime, ma'am, some more serious than others. Which specific one did you have in mind?"

She clenched her teeth at the teasing mockery in his voice. "I heard that you helped Damon Delancy and his wife flee the country when she was about to stand trial for violating the Comstock Act."

The amusement in his eyes died. "Hold on, there. As I told the police, Delancy never told me what he was planning until it was too late for me to stop him."

"Oh, come, come, Mr. LaRouche. Do you really expect me to believe that? You were his partner and his closest friend. I'm sure he told you everything."

"Not in this case, ma'am. Whether you believe it or not, it's the truth."

"They did break the law. It was only a misdemeanor, but—"

"Misdemeanor?"

"A crime less serious than a felony."

He shook his head, frankly puzzled. "I'm not a lawyer, ma'am, and I don't know what those words mean. You'll have to explain them to me."

So while LaRouche listened, Honor explained that misdemeanors were crimes such as unlawful entry and adultery, while felonies included more serious crimes such as murder.

"I guess they did commit a crime," he said, "but I don't blame them for running. I've never known a man to love a woman more than Delancy loves the doc." His lip curled in contempt. "He couldn't risk having her go to prison for breaking some stupid law."

"As stupid as it may be, it's still the law, and the three of you conspired to break it."

His eyes narrowed. "Does it matter that the doc saved lives and didn't deserve to go to prison? Does it matter that her little boy would have lost his mama for Lord knows how long?"

"Five years. That would have been her prison sentence if convicted."

LaRouche looked appalled. "You call that justice?"

Honor sighed. "I'm not saying that all laws are good or just. But your friends should have stayed and fought."

"They did what they thought was best."

Arguing with him was pointless. Honor looked around. "The sun's coming up. As much as I enjoy arguing with you, Mr. LaRouche, I have to get back. My husband will wonder where I am."

Honor turned and walked down the path. LaRouche shortened his long stride to fall into step beside her.

She broke the tense silence with "I'm sorry about Dr. Wolcott."

He stopped. "What do you know about Sybilla?"

Honor faced him. She felt a small jolt of triumph that she had finally succeeded in throwing the remote Nevada LaRouche off-balance, quickly followed by shame when she saw the pain she had raised in his eyes. "I know she was murdered."

"How'd you find that out?"

Honor looked away, debating whether to tell him. "I had my clerk investigate you."

He grew as still as a stag sensing danger. Not a muscle quivered. Only his eyes narrowed.

Honor regarded him defiantly. "I'm not ashamed of what I

did. You threatened me with retribution, Mr. LaRouche, and I needed information that I could use against you if I ever had to protect myself or my husband. Surely you can understand that."

"You would use a man's misery against him?" he said, his voice ragged and dangerous.

"I would never do that," she quickly replied. "Personal tragedy was not the kind of information I sought." She shrugged. "It was in all the newspapers, and my zealous clerk found it." Her gaze faltered. "I wish he hadn't."

"Why?"

She looked up at him. "It's a very sad story."

A bit of color returned to his face. "It was, but it's in the past. As much as it hurts, there's nothing I can do to change it." He started walking slowly down the path. "I'll always miss her, but she wasn't the kind of woman who'd want me to pine away."

Honor thought of her father and her vivid recurring dream of the gallows and the chessmen in the snow, and felt an unwanted bond with the enigmatic man walking beside her. "When you lose someone you love so tragically, it haunts you for a long, long time."

"The pain goes away. Eventually."

"Oh, no, it never goes away. It lessens, but it's always there."

"You miss your father, don't you?"

"Every day of my life." She couldn't tell him that her pain went beyond a simple loss.

Suddenly the house loomed before them out of the fog. Honor handed him back his coat and thanked him coolly. "Well, now that we've laid all our cards on the table, Mr. LaRouche, does my husband still have a position, or has his outspoken wife ruined his career?"

He gave her a slow, wolfish smile. "If having your husband work for an outlaw doesn't compromise your high principles, Mrs. Davis, he's got a job for as long as he's able to do it to my satisfaction."

Honor felt rare heat burn her cheeks. "I may not approve

of some of your actions, but as long as you don't expect Robert to do anything illegal, I'm sure we'll get along."

He grinned and inclined his head in a courtly nod. "Yes, ma'am, whatever you say."

Then he put on his coat and strode off toward the stables.

Still trembling with relief from her confrontation with Nevada LaRouche, Honor quietly returned to her room.

Just as she reached for the doorknob, a voice whispered, "Mrs. Davis?" and Honor turned to see Genevra Graham hurrying down the hall toward her. Before Honor could say another word, the other woman slipped a piece of paper into her hand, held a warning finger to her lips for silence, and disappeared back down the hall as quietly as a wraith.

Once inside her own room, Honor unfolded the note: "Mrs. Davis, please meet me in the guesthouse at six o'clock tomorrow morning. *Tell no one.* It is a matter of life and death. Genevra Graham."

An image of the frightened woman and her vigilant, disapproving husband flashed through Honor's mind, followed by the desperate underlined words *"Tell no one."*

Honor put the note in her pocket and went to wake her sleeping husband.

Nevada LaRouche stood at the tall study windows and watched his guests play a spirited Saturday afternoon game of croquet on the front lawn.

Honor Davis claimed most of his attention.

The woman played to win. She wasn't hapless, like Herron's shy wife, or a halfhearted player like Genevra Graham. Honor studied her opponents' moves as well as her own and whacked that poor wooden ball with competence and determination. When she scored, she grinned and clasped her hands in childlike glee, much to the chagrin of her husband, who was losing.

Watching the dappled sunlight rain down on her, LaRouche was glad he had followed her outside this morning. With tiny beads of dew caught in her wild black hair and her black eyes filled with ageless mysteries, she had reminded him of an Indian medicine woman who had once saved his life.

He had been a fool to threaten Honor Davis. He should have known such a strong-willed woman would fight back with all of the weapons she could find. Except the tragic loss of the woman he loved.

He smiled to himself. So the tough lady lawyer had a weakness after all.

Her admission that she had investigated him knocked the starch right out of him. He hadn't been expecting it. He was learning that Honor Davis was a woman of many surprises.

Watching her lift one hand to absently brush a stray tendril of witch-black hair away from her alabaster cheek, he wondered if a man could ever share a simple, uncomplicated friendship with a woman of such strength and passion. He'd have to get her to accept him first, and considering the lady's contempt for lawbreakers, he had about as much of a chance of accomplishing that as a prairie dog had of surviving in a nest of rattlers.

He had to admit that he enjoyed Honor Davis's company. He liked talking to her. Hell, he especially liked teasing her and watching her get all fired up. She belonged to another man, so they would never become lovers. But then, he wasn't looking for a dalliance, and he could tell she wasn't the dallying kind. She would want a man free and clear.

Suddenly he caught her staring at him. She hurriedly looked away and turned her attention back to the wooden ball at her feet.

He smiled slowly to himself and decided it was time he showed Honor Davis how an outlaw played croquet.

At six o'clock the following morning, while everyone else was still sleeping, Honor went to the guesthouse, a small stone lodge not far from the main house, where extra guests stayed when they outnumbered the bedrooms.

Inside, she went directly from the small foyer to a receiving room furnished with several sofas and chairs. Even in the dim early morning light seeping through the windows, she could see the room was empty.

"Hello?" she called. "Is anyone here?"

There came a rustling of silk and a light tapping of footsteps, and Genevra Graham emerged from an adjacent room. Her frightened eyes darted anxiously to the doorway beyond Honor's shoulder. "Did anyone see you?"

"No," Honor replied. "Everyone sleeps late on a Sunday, and I was very careful." She paused. "A note slipped into my hand, a clandestine meeting . . . Why all the mystery, Mrs. Graham?"

The poor woman was trembling uncontrollably. "I—I want to divorce my husband."

Honor knew that even though society leader Alva Vanderbilt had legitimized divorce among her set when she divorced William K. Vanderbilt just the previous year, women like Genevra Graham still thought twice about undertaking the dissolution of their marriages.

She must be desperate, Honor thought.

She went to her and grasped her cold, stiff hands. "Come sit down and tell me why."

Once they were seated, Genevra Graham cast a nervous glance toward the door before proceeding. "Gordon and I used to be very much in love, even though he is so much older. When he found out that I once had a"—she took a deep breath—"an abortion and never told him, that love quickly turned to hatred."

Honor could understand why. To not tell a man you were carrying his child and then to secretly abort it . . .

A shudder rippled through Genevra's narrow shoulders. "He's been a monster to me, Mrs. Davis. I live in a constant state of terror."

"Has he beat you?"

She shook her head. "No. But he refuses to speak to me or let the servants speak to me for days on end. Sometimes he tells my friends that I'm not at home when they call and makes me watch while they leave. Sometimes he locks me in the attic. He won't give me any money for new clothes, and worst of all, he threatens to take my son away from me."

Genevra Graham burst into tears. "If I don't get away from him, I'll go mad!"

Honor patted the distraught woman's shoulder. "Mrs. Graham, has your husband ever committed adultery?"

She dabbed at her eyes with her handkerchief. "How would I know that?"

"Pray that he has, because in New York State, you can obtain a divorce only on those grounds."

Genevra's hazel eyes widened. "But—but he's so cruel to me! And any love I had for him is dead and gone. Can't I divorce him for that?"

Honor shook her head. "I'm afraid not. While some states accept cruelty as grounds for a divorce, New York does not." She paused. "Perhaps your abortion is just an excuse for his cruelty. Perhaps his real reason is that he has a mistress."

Genevra frowned. "If he wanted another woman, I would gladly give him a divorce, but he hasn't asked me." Her gaze hardened. "He would rather keep me his prisoner out of spite."

A sudden sound caused the woman to leap to her feet and stare at the door in terror. When her husband didn't come barging in, she sighed heavily, then began pacing the room. "What am I going to do? What am I going to do?"

Honor rose. "Your situation isn't hopeless, Mrs. Graham. If you wish me to take your case, I'll start investigating your husband. If we can prove he has committed adultery, we may have a case."

"And if you can't?"

"Then I'd advise you to take up residency in another state such as Connecticut, where the divorce laws are more lenient."

"I can't. I don't have the money. Gordon even took away all my good jewelry, so I can't even pawn my diamonds."

"Don't you have any friends who will lend you the money?"

"All of their husbands are Gordon's friends. And they wouldn't dream of defying their husbands."

Honor said, "Then how do you expect to pay the court costs and my fee?"

Genevra Graham gave her a sheepish look. "I thought you might be persuaded to waive your fee."

Honor experienced a flash of resentment. Didn't the woman realize that Honor had rent and Elroy's wages to pay as well as other expenses? Then she calmed down. "I can't do that, but if I win your case, I'll ask the judge to have your husband pay your legal costs as part of your settlement. If I lose, you'll owe me nothing. Fair enough?"

"Fair enough." Genevra looked relieved. "I was afraid that I'd be doomed to spend the rest of my life in a living hell with that monster."

"I'll do the best I can, but no promises." Honor paused. "Are you sure you don't want someone more experienced to represent you?"

"You're the only lawyer I know," Genevra said, "and since you're a woman, it will be easier for me to meet with you. I can always pretend I'm making a social call. If Gordon even suspects that I'm planning to divorce him . . ." She shuddered.

Honor patted her hand. "I'll do my best to keep it a secret until it's too late."

Genevra began trembling again. "We'll have to be very, very careful. Gordon is a powerful man. He's also got a wicked temper, and he might try to harm you if he knows you're helping me."

Honor raised her stubborn chin. "No man is above the law. Now, assuming that it's too dangerous for us to meet in my office, is there somewhere else in the city where we can meet without being seen?"

A frown marred her brow. "I think Gordon has been having me watched, but perhaps we can meet at the home of a mutual friend. Provided, of course, that he is in one of his generous moods and lets me out of the house."

Honor gave Genevra her card. "Just tell me where and when."

She left the guesthouse first and returned to the main house, unaware that she was being observed from an upstairs window.

CHAPTER 11

TWO MONTHS LATER, ON a balmy June evening at eight o'clock, Honor sat in the library writing to Aunt Theo while waiting for Robert to come home from work.

Since Theo's return from Italy in the spring, her letters had been light and humorous, with amusing anecdotes about the many paintings she had bought as well as her adventures terrorizing the horses and dogs of Boston in the new Duryea motorcar, but Honor sensed a false brightness to their tone. She could tell that her aunt missed Wes.

She looked up to find Robert standing in the doorway, one hand on the knob, and she smiled warmly in welcome. "Long, hard day? You look tired. Tilly's been keeping supper warm."

Robert didn't return her smile. "Is it true that you're representing Genevra Graham in a divorce case?"

Honor set down her pen and rose. "Yes. She approached me while we were at Coppermine in April, and I agreed to take her case."

"Why didn't you tell me?"

"There was no need for you to know."

Honor hadn't even been sure that Genevra had grounds for divorce until last week, when her clever, persistent sleuth, Elroy, had discovered that Gordon Graham was keeping a mistress named Araminta deGrey in high style at the posh Spanish Flats across from Central Park.

Her husband's green eyes hardened to glass, and his hand tightened with white-knuckled intensity on the doorknob. "Whatever possessed you to take the case?"

Honor stiffened and mentally girded herself for the argument she could see looming between them. "The woman wants to divorce her husband and asked me if I would represent her. I jumped at the chance. It will be my first court case, and I'm heartily looking forward to it."

"Honor, Gordon Graham is a wealthy, powerful man."

"Why should that make any difference to me?"

"It should make a great deal of difference to you! Not only does he have the money and influence to hire the best lawyers in New York City, but he also has the power to ruin us."

Honor tugged at her locket on its new cord. "What about his wife?" Her voice rose. "Am I supposed to leave her twisting in the wind because I'm afraid of offending her almighty husband?" She paced around the small room to dissipate some of her anger. "Everyone is entitled to legal representation, Robert. Or have you so quickly forgotten that?"

His cheeks turned crimson."I'm only concerned for you. You don't have the experience. His lawyers will tear you to pieces in the courtroom."

"You didn't let your lack of experience keep you from taking a position with Delancy and LaRouche."

"That was different. I never go into court."

"Thank you for your concern, but I've got to undergo my baptism of fire sooner or later. Mrs. Graham has faith in me in spite of my inexperience, and all I can do is my best."

Robert crossed the room and grasped her hands. "I'm asking you to drop the case."

Honor pulled away. "Why? Because you're concerned about me or because Gordon Graham is Nevada LaRouche's friend?" When Robert turned a guilty shade of red and said nothing, she added, "Did LaRouche pressure you to ask me to drop this case?"

"He hasn't said a word about it."

Somehow she doubted that. "Good. Because I refuse."

Robert whirled away and stood by the bookshelves, anger

emanating from him in palpable waves. "Don't you ever think before you act? Don't you ever consider the possible consequences of your actions?"

Honor crossed her arms, seeking to put a physical barrier between them. "Of course I do. But I don't accept or reject cases just so someone who is wealthy and powerful will think kindly of me."

"Well, you should—if not for your sake, then for mine."

"For your sake? What does this case have to do with you?"

He shrugged. "You never know. I may want to go to work for Graham some day."

Honor flung up her hands in exasperation. "You, you, *you*! You're the only one who matters in this marriage." She fought to control her rising temper. "I have to move to New York City because you want to work for a man like J. Pierpont Morgan. I have to keep my profession a secret from your bosses because they are prejudiced against women lawyers. Now I'm supposed to give up my first important case because you may want to work for Graham someday."

He glared at her. "I've never heard you complain before."

Honor shook with anger. "Well, you're hearing it now."

"Honor—"

"There's nothing I wouldn't do for you, Robert, but don't ask me to give up this case, because I can't, and I won't."

"Fine," he snapped. "Tell Tilly not to hold supper. I'm going out, and I don't know when I'll be back."

Honor took a hesitant step forward. "Don't leave with these bad feelings between us."

"I need some time alone." He turned on his heel and stormed out of the library. A minute later Honor winced when she heard the apartment door slam. Then silence.

She stood in the center of the library, breathing deeply until her anger vanished. Then she sat at her desk to finish her letter. She found she couldn't concentrate, so she put her pen down, leaned back in her chair, and rubbed her neck.

"How dare he!" she muttered, her annoyance returning.

The preparations for Genevra Graham's divorce case were proceeding better than Honor hoped. Once Elroy discovered Graham's adulterous liaison, Honor and Genevra had begun meeting secretly. The moment Honor had enough information to file for the divorce, Genevra took their son and left her husband. Only Honor knew that her terrified client had fled to the house of friends in Rhinebeck, New York, just three days ago to await the trial's August court date.

Matters had progressed too far for Honor to let Genevra down, no matter how badly her own husband or Nevada LaRouche wanted her to step aside.

Two days later Honor was sitting in her office surrounded by a fortress of law books piled on her desk when there came a knock at her door.

"Door's open, Elroy," she said without looking up.

The door swung open, but no Elroy came rushing in like a whirlwind. Even as Honor continued writing, she became aware of the hand-tooled black cowboy boots.

She looked up, tried to hide her surprise, and failed. "Mr. LaRouche."

"Morning." He was dressed for Wall Street today in a black frock coat, waistcoat, and black striped cravat. He held a silk top hat. Honor thought a black Stetson would have been more appropriate with his longish fair hair curling around the back of his collar. He glanced toward the outer office, where Elroy should have been. "No one was out there so I took the liberty of letting myself in. Hope you don't mind."

She pushed a stray lock of hair away from her cheek and rose, resenting the way this out-of-place man became right at home in her office the moment he stepped through the door. "Of course not." She indicated one of the chairs across from her desk. "Do sit down."

"Don't mind if I do." LaRouche waited politely until she sat back down, then eased his tall, lanky frame into one chair and set his hat on the other.

Honor leaned back in her chair so she wouldn't feel overpowered by LaRouche's quiet, unnerving presence. She looked him right in the eye. "I know you've come to discuss the Graham divorce."

He gave a low appreciative whistle. "You don't beat around the bush."

"If you're here to try to persuade me to drop the case, you may as well turn around and walk right out that door."

LaRouche shook his head, his eyes bright with an amusement at odds with his serious demeanor. "You sure do jump to conclusions, ma'am. Might be a serious failing for a lawyer."

Honor kept her features composed. "If you're not here to discuss the Graham divorce, then why are you here?"

"To invite you and your husband to the opera."

Her jaw dropped. "The opera?"

"You heard me. Maria Morelli is singing at the Metropolitan tonight, and since Delancy still keeps his box, I thought you and Davis would like to come along. After dinner at Delmonico's, as my guests."

Honor felt as disoriented as Lewis Carroll's hapless Alice when she tumbled down the rabbit hole. What other surprises did Nevada LaRouche have up his sleeve?

He smiled slowly. "Judging by the look on your face, I'd say you're wondering how a simple fellow like me could enjoy opera."

Despite the fact that her corset suddenly felt too tight, Honor said, "I would never make the mistake of thinking that you're a simple fellow, Mr. LaRouche. On the contrary, I think you're quite complex."

Heat flickered in the depths of his eyes for just a second, then disappeared. "Actually, I don't understand a word of it, but the music is right pretty." He studied her for a moment with that disquieting gaze. "Would you and your husband like to go?"

"Of course. I'm sure Robert would enjoy it as well." Any opportunity to impress his employer.

"Good." He rose. "My carriage will call for you at six."

When he reached for his hat and looked ready to leave, Honor rose and said, "About the Graham divorce case . . ."

He paused expectantly.

"I realize that Gordon Graham is your friend, and I hope you won't hold it against me or my husband that I'm representing his wife."

LaRouche rested his head against the back of his chair. "Your husband came to me today and said the same thing."

If Robert had been standing there, Honor would have strangled him. "He shouldn't have done that. For him to discuss my case with you could be construed as a conflict of interest."

LaRouche shrugged. "Who you represent is your own business, ma'am. It's not my place to interfere unless you attack me or mine personally, and I told your husband as much."

So that was why he had come here, to reassure her. He must have known she would worry about jeopardizing Robert's position if she took this case. Honor let out the breath she had been holding. "I'm relieved to hear that."

A troubled frown marred his brow, and he shook his head sadly. "I had heard that the Grahams were having difficulties, but when they came to Coppermine for the weekend, I could see it for myself." He fell into a reflective silence for a moment. Then he said, "That Genevra used to be a little ball of fire, always laughing, full of life. Damn shame she's changed. Now she just shakes like a calf being stalked by a cougar."

Honor made no comment.

He stroked his mustache. "I never thought of Gordon as particularly terrifying."

An image of Gordon Graham's towering, powerful frame, his leonine presence, and his dark eyes glittering with disapproval flashed through Honor's mind. She could well understand his wife's terror.

LaRouche shook his head. "A wife shouldn't have to fear her husband."

"I quite agree."

He picked up his hat, nodded, and smiled. "Six o'clock, then?"

Honor smiled back. "Six o'clock."

"I'll be looking forward to it." Then he bade her good day and left.

Attending an occasional concert with Aunt Theo in Boston hadn't prepared Honor for an evening at the Metropolitan Opera. Bostonians attended concerts to listen to the music; New Yorkers attended the opera to see and be seen.

Seated between Nevada LaRouche—who had stunned Honor by not bringing a guest to make their little party a foursome—and her husband in Damon Delancy's box, located in the exclusive Diamond Horseshoe, Honor had a front row seat for both performances—the one on stage and the one in the audience.

The female members of society's elite Four Hundred, seated in nearby boxes, all wore lavish thousand-dollar Worth gowns that most Bostonian women would have eschewed as too vulgar and ostentatious. The moment they sat down, they whipped out their opera glasses and swept the audience like searchlights seeking social transgressions. More than once Honor saw lips tighten in envy or widen into smiles of malicious satisfaction. More than once Honor felt herself the subject of their intense scrutiny.

She placed her hand on Robert's and leaned closer so he could hear her above the din. "I feel like a sparrow among peacocks."

She wore her favorite four-year-old summer gown of Nile green silk, which had not been made by Worth, and the emerald earbobs. No king's ransom of diamonds or even pearls graced her neck, just her locket.

Robert brought her fingers to his sensuous lips. "You're still the most beautiful woman here tonight," he whispered, "and someday you will wear diamonds."

To Honor's left, Nevada LaRouche shifted in his seat.

Honor smiled at her husband. Now that the Graham divorce case didn't threaten Robert's standing with his new employer, harmony had returned to their marriage.

Just as the curtain rose on the stage set of Lucia di Lammermoor's Ravenswood Castle, a park of rocky woods with a lake painted on the backdrop, Honor glanced over several boxes to her left and froze.

Gordon Graham sat glaring at her, the malevolence in his eyes reaching across the space that separated them to send an icy chill running down Honor's spine.

"What's wrong?" Nevada LaRouche whispered.

How does he always know? she wondered in astonishment. Did he feel the air stir when she shivered or stiffened? Did he hear the subtle change when her breathing quickened?

On the stage below, a group of guards searched the castle grounds, but the operagoers' conversations didn't cease and the opera glasses continued their blatant spying. Even the opera itself could not deter the noisy upper crust from visiting each others' boxes, much to the chagrin of the true music lovers in the audience, who would often look up and glare.

Honor leaned over and placed her lips close to his ear. "Gordon Graham is here."

"Where? He doesn't go to the opera as a rule."

"Well, he's here now, in the third box to our left."

"Must be somebody's guest." LaRouche turned his head. When he found Graham, he nodded slightly in acknowledgment and turned back to Honor. "He won't bother you."

Honor wished she could share his confidence as she gave her full attention to the opera.

All through La Morelli's first-act performance, Honor felt Graham's cold, hateful gaze crawling like a slug down her hair, her cheek, her shoulders, her breasts. Her fingers itched to brush it away, but she kept her eyes focused on the stage and didn't give him the satisfaction. Finally Graham looked away.

Five minutes later the rear door to the box opened, and Nevada LaRouche rose to face their visitor. "Evening, Gordon. I didn't expect to see you here. Something I can do for you?"

Honor turned in her seat, and Robert also rose.

Graham entered the box, his glittering, baleful stare

focused on Honor. "What have you done with my wife and son?" he said in a voice just loud and furious enough to cause the heads in neighboring boxes to turn in blatant curiosity.

"If you have anything to say to me, Mr. Graham," she said coolly, "you can speak through your attorney."

Graham's face turned purple with rage, and his hands balled into fists at his sides. The moment he took a threatening step toward Honor, Robert stepped in front of his wife, and Nevada LaRouche neatly blocked Graham.

"I don't recall inviting you to join us, Gordon," he said.

"Do you know what she's trying to do?" Graham roared. "She's trying to take my wife and son away from me."

"This isn't the place to discuss it," LaRouche replied.

Graham looked from Honor and Robert back to LaRouche. "So that's it. You're on her side. And you call yourself my friend. You two-faced son of a bitch! Delancy never would've sold me down the river."

"Delancy isn't here, and I don't take kindly to anyone threatening my guests."

Graham pointed a warning finger at Honor. "You're going to regret this." Then he turned on his heel and stormed out of the box, slamming the door behind him so loud that even some of the singers on stage heard the noise and looked up in irritation, their concentration broken.

LaRouche turned, noticed that people in the adjacent boxes were staring, and said, "Show's over, folks," before resuming his seat next to Honor, who spent the remainder of the evening counting the seconds until the interminable opera ended.

Later, seated across from Nevada LaRouche in his carriage, Honor said, "I'm afraid I've cost you a friendship."

Robert cast an accusatory glance at her, followed by an apologetic one to his employer. "I warned my wife something like this might happen if she took the case."

LaRouche stroked his mustache. "I've got to hand it to Gordon, though."

Honor understood at once. "You think that little confrontation was a show of his own, don't you?"

LaRouche nodded. "He made damn sure a lot of people heard him tonight."

Robert said, "He's gathering support."

"Looks like it to me."

Honor asked, "What do you think he'll do next?"

"Tell some overeager newspaper reporter his side of the story."

Honor swore softly under her breath. "Just what we need, a society divorce scandal."

Robert looked at her. "This is going to get dirty, and I don't think you're up to it."

"I've never been one to run away from a fight. You know that."

"In case you didn't notice, Graham threatened you tonight."

Honor gave him an annoyed look. "I think his bark is worse than his bite."

The remote look returned to LaRouche's eyes. "Don't underestimate Gordon. Any man is capable of violence if pushed hard enough."

Honor said nothing, wondering if he was talking about Gordon Graham or himself.

Several days later Honor arrived at her office building to find John Townsend lying in wait for her in the lobby.

When she wished the photographer a good morning, he replied, "You've got a surprise waiting for you upstairs, my beauty."

Honor paused, her foot on the barrier step. "Oh, dear. What kind of surprise?"

The man practically licked his chops. "Several surprises actually. From the *World*, the *Sun*, the *Herald*, and probably the *Sleepy Hollow Snorer*."

Honor groaned and rolled her eyes. "Newspaper reporters."

"The same, your loveliness."

She took a deep breath to steel herself and started up the stairs. "I may as well get this over with."

Upstairs, she found the faithful Elroy braced against the office's outer door while a pack of newspaper reporters held up the corridor's walls. The moment Elroy saw her, he said, "Here's Mrs. Davis now."

Before Honor had a chance to take another step, the reporters swarmed around her, pencils poised over their notepads.

She kept on walking. "Good morning, gentlemen," she said with her brightest smile. "Dare I hope that you're here to write about women lawyers?"

"Never knew there were any," one muttered.

"There most certainly are," Honor replied. "I have a law degree from Boston University and passed the New York State bar examination, so I'm just as qualified to practice as my male colleagues." She didn't add that she had fewer opportunities.

Another added, "I'll write about lady lawyers if they're all as pretty as you!"

One young man at Honor's left elbow didn't crack a smile at his colleagues' sallies. "Liam Flynn of the *Sun*. We're here about the Graham divorce case."

Honor stopped and faced them. "As I'm sure you know from the court calendar, Genevra Graham has filed for a divorce from her husband, Gordon, and I am representing her."

"On what grounds?" Flynn asked.

"You know very well there is only one ground for divorce in this state."

"Adultery," someone said.

Flynn said, "Who's the adulterer, Graham or his wife?"

"I'm sure you gentlemen are bright enough to figure that out for yourselves."

Another reporter said, "Jensen from the *World*. Graham claims he's innocent, that he dearly loves his wife and wants her and his son back."

Flynn added, "He claims you're hiding them somewhere."

Honor held her tongue. "Mr. Graham may say whatever he likes. The truth will come out in court. That's all I'm going to say on the matter, gentlemen, so if you'll excuse me, I have to go to work."

Mutterings of protest rose around her, but Elroy managed to usher her through the office door. "You heard the lady," he told the reporters. "She has nothing more to say."

When the footsteps died away, Elroy stepped into the outer office and closed the door behind him. "Damned pack of jackals."

Honor couldn't stop shaking. She suddenly knew what a fish must feel like when surrounded by hungry sharks. She breathed a sigh of relief. "They're a sly bunch, aren't they?"

And so was Gordon Graham. LaRouche had been right when he warned her not to underestimate him.

"I wonder what they'll say about you?" Elroy said.

She smiled dryly. "We'll soon find out."

Honor found out when she went home at the end of the day.

Robert greeted her at the door with a kiss on the cheek and the afternoon edition of the *Sun*. "There's an article about you on the front page."

Honor didn't even bother taking off her hat. She read "First Woman Lawyer in City" as she walked into the parlor. "How droll," she said to Robert. "They've put an article about me right next to one about a sea serpent sighted in Long Island Sound. I suppose a female lawyer is considered as odd as a sea serpent."

"You know people are fools," Robert muttered.

"Quite." Honor sat down on the sofa and continued reading, though soon her cheeks were flaming and she threw down the paper in disgust. "This whole article is about my looks, not my qualifications to practice law! Listen to this: 'Mrs. Honor Davis, a tall beauty with raven black hair and captivating black eyes—' "

"He's right about that," Robert said with a teasing grin.

"Your eyes captivated me from the moment I first saw you."

She glared at him and continued, "'is sure to spellbind any judge and jury.' Damn that Liam Flynn! He implies that I'll win cases because of my looks, not my legal skills."

Robert placed a comforting arm around her shoulders. "You knew this would happen, so get used to it."

She sighed. "You're right."

He kissed her on the cheek. "I have some good news for you."

"I'm delighted one of us does. What is it?"

"LaRouche is sending me and another lawyer to Philadelphia next week to conduct some very important business for him."

Honor kissed him back. "That's wonderful. He obviously thinks highly of your work. How long will you be gone?"

"Next Tuesday through Thursday. So, as much as I hate to leave you, you'll be on your own."

"Don't worry about me. I'll manage just fine."

The following Tuesday, Honor decided to work late on a contract she was revising for another temperamental actor. Robert had left for Philadelphia just that morning, and Tilly was in New Jersey nursing her sick mother, so the prospect of going home to an empty apartment held no appeal. Since it was July and the balmy summer days were longer, she didn't have to worry about going home in the dark.

At six o'clock she sent Elroy on his way and returned to her contract.

Fifteen minutes later she heard the door to the outer office open, followed by hesitant footsteps. Honor rose. "Elroy?"

No response.

She walked out of her office to find two men standing by Elroy's desk. The burly one, who wore a loud yellow and black checked suit with a red tie and a horseshoe pin, reminded her of Man Mountain Mountford. His smaller companion looked like a ferret. Both reeked of fried onions, stale hair oil, and unwashed skin.

"May I help you?"

"You the lady lawyer?" the smaller man asked.

"Yes."

"That's all we need to know."

They rushed at her.

Before Honor had time to think another coherent thought, the burly one stood behind her, pinioning her arms, leaving her helpless and defenseless against the smaller man. Honor didn't need to ask what they wanted. She knew the instant she saw the smaller man raise his hand.

The first backhanded blow hit her jaw just hard enough for her teeth to cut the inside of her cheek and let her taste her own blood. The pain was beyond imagining. Honor cried out, but was still too shocked to struggle.

The second blow hit her other cheekbone, snapping her head back and causing her to see dancing stars. Her assailant hit her again. And again.

Her existence became defined by a red haze of pain. From far away she heard a frantic, tearful voice begging them to stop, please stop. Finally she could endure no more. She crawled away into a quiet, dark place deep in her mind and wove the blackness tight around her. The frantic pleas for mercy stopped.

After what seemed like an eternity but was in fact two minutes, they released her. Without support, her knees buckled and she collapsed to the floor. Just when she thought her torment had ended, something slammed into her side and the world exploded before she slid into blissful unconsciousness.

Nevada LaRouche alighted from his carriage in front of Honor's office building. With her husband away, he had decided to take a chance that she might be working late and would be amenable to joining him for dinner at Delmonico's. He suspected that she might refuse, for she was still standoffish, but it was worth asking.

Just as he reached the entrance to the building, two men came hurrying out, brushed past him without so much as a by-your-leave, and headed down Broadway. Just the sight of them made the hair rise on the back of LaRouche's neck.

Upstairs, he tried the outer door to Honor's office, and when it opened readily, he smiled. So she was working late after all.

He stepped inside. Then he looked down and saw her.

A hunter's instinct finely honed in a savage time and place overroad shock and rage. He froze and listened, sharp eyes darting into corners where an assailant could hide. His nostrils flared to catch the commingled odors of terror and excitement.

The two men. They were long gone by now, so it would be useless to give chase.

He looked at the woman lying face down on the floor, and the hunter in him died.

"Damnation!" His rage almost choked him. He dropped down onto one knee and felt for a pulse in her neck. She was alive.

LaRouche eased her onto her back. He had seen unspeakable violence in his life, but when he saw what those two men had done to her . . .

As bad as Honor's injuries looked, LaRouche knew that if the bastard had used brass knuckles or even a closed fist, he would have ensured that no one would ever again look at Honor Davis without cringing.

They hadn't taken her locket or rifled through desk drawers, so robbery wasn't their motive. No, she had been beaten with exquisite care by someone skilled enough to know how to warn without maiming.

LaRouche brushed a stray lock of disheveled black hair away from her bruised cheek, then carefully lifted her in his arms and took her home.

The first sound Honor heard as she cautiously emerged from the dark, safe place in her mind was the low, anguished groan of an animal crazed with pain. With the return of her senses came the realization that the pitiful sound emanated from her.

She felt as if a horse had kicked her in the face. Or as if a man had struck her with the back of his hand.

Not a man, two men. She whimpered in terror and struggled to open her eyes. Only one obliged.

"Easy," said a familiar drawl that sounded more ragged than soft. "You're safe now. No one can hurt you any more."

She turned her head slowly toward the voice, felt a lightning bolt stab her ribs, and cried out. She found her own hand clasped firmly by warm fingers offering silent strength and courage. When the pain subsided, she opened her good eye again and saw Nevada LaRouche.

The soft glow from a lamp she couldn't see cast the planes of his face in sharp relief. Concern warred with rage in his eyes.

"Sorry," she whispered, forcing the word through sore, stiff lips puffed to twice their size. "Hurts."

"Yell all you want if it makes you feel better."

Where was Robert? Why was Nevada LaRouche being so solicitous when he knew she didn't trust him? "Where am I?"

"My house—actually it's Delancy's—on Fifth Avenue. I brought you here because it was closer than your place, and I don't trust hospitals."

He didn't need to tell her she was lying in a strange bed, wearing a stranger's soft, comfortable nightgown that smelled faintly of lemon verbena. Catherine Delancy's, perhaps, left behind when she fled to England? Honor was in too much pain to wonder who had undressed her or to consider the propriety of being in a bachelor gentleman's house no matter what the circumstances.

He said, "It's nearly midnight, so why don't you try to sleep? We'll talk in the morning."

"Can't sleep."

He guessed why, for his features smoldered with anger for a moment before he brought it under relentless control. "The doctor left laudanum."

"Later." Suddenly a horrifying thought almost sent her sitting upright. "My face!"

"Hush," he murmured again, his hands moving up and down her arms lightly as if he were gentling a restive horse. "I know your face hurts like hell and it looks even worse, but the doctor said it's just bruised. Your jaw and your nose aren't broken, and none of your teeth were knocked out or loosened. You have a couple of broken ribs where the bastard must have kicked you, but the doc said you're not bleeding inside and he taped them up. You'll be fine before you know it."

She heard his unspoken words: You're damned lucky.

The shocking realization that someone had deliberately hurt her washed over Honor in waves, making her shiver uncontrollably. Though she hated to display weakness to this man, helpless tears ran down her cheeks.

Still gripping her hand, LaRouche reached over to a night table to retrieve a handkerchief. He dabbed her tears away with surprising gentleness.

"Did two men do this to you? A big fellow in a checked coat and a little one who looked like a weasel?" he said, his voice strangely gruff.

She shuddered violently, as if her assailants had suddenly materialized at the foot of her bed. "How did you know?"

"They were coming out of your building just as I was going in."

"Why were you there?"

A ghost of a smile played about his mouth, though it never reached his cold, remote eyes. "I thought you'd be working late, so I stopped by to invite you to supper at Delmonico's."

She tried to shift to a more comfortable position, and another spasm of pain hit her ribs. Later she would wonder about this dinner invitation, but right now all she felt was gratitude that he had happened by when he did. Otherwise no one would have found her until morning.

"Thank you." When the spasm passed, she said, "Those men . . . hired?"

"I'd stake my life on it," he replied. He scowled. "I think we both know who hired them."

Honor shuddered. "No witnesses. Can't prove it."

"No, I don't reckon we can." He straightened and looked down at her. "I'll send a telegram to your husband tomorrow morning and get him back here on the next train. Right now you need to sleep and let your body heal."

Honor watched him pour some laudanum from a brown stoppered bottle into a glass. He gently slid his left hand beneath her head to lift and support it, and held the rim of the glass carefully to her lips so she could swallow. The liquid opiate stung the cuts in her mouth, but she grimaced and drank it all down like an obedient child, seeking blissful oblivion.

Then she closed her eyes. Sensing a benevolent, protective presence watching over her like a guardian angel, she allowed herself to drift off into a safe, dreamless sleep.

Once Honor was asleep, LaRouche stalked out of the room. He closed the door and leaned heavily against it, breathing deeply until he could control his murderous rage.

He went out to the stable, with its dark, comforting smell of hay and horses, and began brushing Comanche, his chestnut gelding, who regarded his master out of reproachful, sleepy eyes, but snuffled softly through his nose in welcome and submitted to the grooming.

LaRouche brushed the horse's neck with long, firm strokes until his anger subsided. Damon Delancy had always kidded him about wearing out a horse's hide, but LaRouche figured that grooming his horse was a productive outlet for whatever ate at his insides. His horse got a glossy coat, and someone stayed alive.

He thought of the woman in the guest room and rested his forehead against Comanche's neck for a moment.

"Why in God's name did they have to do that to her?" At least he had been able to help her. Sybilla had died alone, knowing that the man she loved would never come.

He brushed and brushed and brushed, then returned to the

house to doze in a chair by Honor's bedside while she slept soundly, one hand curled between her breasts where her locket usually hung. Whenever some noise disturbed him and he jerked awake, he would look at her poor battered face and his heart would ache for her. Brave woman.

At daybreak he saddled Comanche and headed for Central Park, where he knew he would find Gordon Graham taking his usual morning ride.

The treed area of the park was deserted at this ungodly hour, save for a few hardy souls pretending they were riding through the wilderness. LaRouche found a secluded spot near a big oak tree where there would be no witnesses and waited. Five minutes later Graham came riding down the path right on time.

He stopped his horse when he saw LaRouche, but said nothing, obviously remembering their confrontation at the opera.

LaRouche stared at the other man, searching for any sign of guilt or remorse, but all he saw was a face as guileless as a choirboy's.

You heartless bastard, he thought.

"'Morning, Gordon," he said amiably, deciding that the element of surprise would give him a distinct advantage over the bigger, heavier man. "Fine morning for a ride, isn't it? Not a soul around."

"Just one two-faced son of a bitch," Graham replied.

LaRouche wanted to inflict on Graham every punishment his boys had inflicted on Honor Davis. Pay him back blow for blow.

He touched his heel to Comanche's side and rode forward as if to move past him. When he was within reach, he pulled up his horse and his fist shot out, hitting a startled Graham hard in the mouth, unbalancing him so that he tumbled out of the saddle.

LaRouche dismounted, rubbed his skinned knuckles, and waited for the other man to haul himself to his feet. Then he hit him again, harder. First a split lip, now a black eye. This time Graham was ready for him. He recoiled from the blow with a grunt, but came back swinging. LaRouche didn't move fast enough, and pain exploded in one side of his face. He ruthlessly pushed the discomfort aside with practiced ease and drove his fist as hard as he could into Garham's stomach.

With a "woof" of surprise, the bigger man went crashing to earth like a felled redwood, clutching his middle and trying desperately to suck air into his lungs.

Savoring the sweet taste of victory, LaRouche hunkered down beside him. "I don't hold with beating women." He rose, his lip curled in a contemptuous sneer. "I would break a few of your ribs, but unlike your boys, I don't kick a man when he's down."

He mounted his horse and rode away without looking back.

Honor didn't awake until afternoon.

She opened her one good eye to find her host dressed and standing patiently at the foot of her bed. She wondered how long he had been watching with the quiet intensity that so unnerved her.

"How are you feeling?" he asked.

It still hurt to talk, so she spoke slowly, enunciating each word. "A little better."

"I'm right glad to hear that."

"Where's . . . Robert?"

"I sent him a telegram. He should be here in another hour." LaRouche rounded the bed. "Since you can't be moved, he can stay here until you get better. There's plenty of room in this pile of stone, and it's real quiet with the Delancys gone."

The unguarded wistfulness in his voice made Honor blurt out, "You miss them?"

She caught him unawares, for his lean cheeks colored slightly. "'Course I do. They're my friends." Then he retreated into polite silence.

Honor took a deep breath. "Can't impose."

He gave her a superior masculine look. "You're not going

anywhere until you're better, ma'am, so don't even waste your breath arguing. I stopped by your office and told that clerk of yours what happened. He's feeling right guilty that he left you alone, but he said he'll hold the fort down until you get back."

"Not his fault." For the first time, Honor noticed the bruise on LaRouche's left cheekbone. "What happened to you?"

"This?" He touched his cheek and winced. "Ran into a door." His unwavering gaze defied her to contradict him.

"A door named Gordon?"

His mustache twitched as he suppressed a triumphant smile. "If you think I look bad, you should see the door."

Heat infused Honor's cheeks, for she didn't want to be beholden to this man for anything. She certainly didn't want him thrashing people on her behalf, no matter how richly they deserved it.

She looked at him. "Shouldn't have."

The laughter in his eyes faded. "I do regret not giving your husband first crack at him, and I hope he won't hold it against me."

Honor remembered Hubert Adcock in Pudding Weymouth's class and wondered what Robert would do.

"Graham will press charges against you," she said.

LaRouche widened his eyes innocently. "Poor Graham. I hear he was attacked by thieves while taking his morning ride in Central Park. Shame there were no witnesses."

Frustrated and angry even as she was grateful to him, Honor shook her head. "Why did you do it?"

"Sometimes you don't find justice in a courtroom, ma'am."

Robert turned ashen when he first saw her.

"Sweet Jesus," he muttered. He sat by Honor's bedside, grasped her hand, and pressed it to his cheek. He clenched his teeth to keep from breaking down. "LaRouche told me what happened. Thank God you're alive."

"LaRouche thinks Gordon Graham hired the thugs who did this."

Robert released her hand and rose. "Damn it, Honor, if you hadn't taken Mrs. Graham's case, you never would have angered her husband and this never would have happened to you. A powerful man like Graham doesn't like being crossed. What were you thinking of?"

His words hurt more than her bruises. Honor stared at him, aghast. "Are you saying that this is my fault? That I brought this on myself?" She took a deep breath. "Robert, how could you? My own husband!"

He took her hand, and she didn't have the strength to pull away. "Don't excite yourself, my dear. Of course it's not your fault. I didn't mean to imply that it was. You're my wife. I don't want anything to happen to you."

Somehow his declarations rang hollow, and she knew he was just mouthing what she wanted to hear. She averted her head and closed her good eye. "Please leave. I'm tired." She wanted him out of sight.

Robert kissed her on the cheek and left.

Lying there alone with her thoughts, Honor wondered why Nevada LaRouche had felt compelled to thrash his friend. Honor meant nothing to him. She was the outspoken, unconventional wife of one of his employees, nothing more. He could have looked the other way and denied Graham's responsibility, thus keeping his friendship. But he had chosen to end it by siding with Honor.

The man frankly puzzled her. He had admitted to breaking the law on several occasions and had helped the Delancys escape to England. Yet Honor's beating had outraged him and he had avenged her.

No man had defended her since Robert took on Hubert Adcock, but that seemed a lifetime ago.

Still, LaRouche was wrong about one point: justice could be found in a courtroom, as Gordon Graham would soon discover.

CHAPTER 12

"I'D LIKE TO SEE a mirror, please," Honor said to her host.

Five days had passed since the brutal attack. Honor could now breathe deeply and smile without excruciating pain. Though she had risen to use the bathroom where, oddly enough, there wasn't a mirror to be seen, she hadn't the courage to face her reflection in the shiny faucets. Now she was ready.

Standing at the foot of the bed with his thumbs hooked in his belt and his weight resting on his right hip, Nevada LaRouche regarded her solemnly. "Not just yet."

Honor managed a small smile to hide her self-consciousness at being alone in a bedchamber with a strange man. "Do I look that bad?"

He returned her smile. "Better, but I'd give it a few more days."

She toyed with the lace running down the front of Catherine Delancy's bed jacket. "I promise I won't scream or swoon."

"I don't expect you would, ma'am, but you'd feel bad, and that might keep you from healing."

To hide how much his gentle concern disconcerted her, Honor said lightly, "I'm sure I'll be fine in no time, Mr. LaRouche, and out of your house once and for all."

He removed his thumbs from his belt and straightened,

looking oddly crestfallen. "You're no burden, Mrs. Davis. I'm right sorry if I've made you feel that way."

"You haven't," she said hurriedly. "You and your staff have been kindness itself to me. But it's time my husband and I stopped imposing on your generous hospitality." Robert especially, who spoke of nothing but the marble floors, the mahogany furniture, and the army of servants at his beck and call.

"You're not imposing," LaRouche said. "You're staying until you heal, and I won't take no for an answer."

Honor's gaze slid over to a carved rose on the bedpost. "I don't know what to say."

He flashed her a wide white smile. "Lawyers aren't often at a loss for words, are they?" He consulted his pocket watch. "Time for me to go to the office."

LaRouche wished her a good day and left.

Alone, Honor lay back against the pillows and stared at the ceiling. Since the assault, she had seen another side to Nevada LaRouche, an unexpected sensitivity so at odds with his untamed personality. He had taken her to his home and cared for her. He had avenged her by fighting Gordon Graham. Several nights ago, when he thought she was sleeping, he had quietly removed both the mirror over the dressing table and the one near the bathroom sink just so she wouldn't glimpse her battered face.

"You're a man of many surprises," she said to no one in particular as she rose carefully and took a few tentative steps across the room.

She wondered if Nevada LaRouche would ever demand that his wife lie for him or violate her principles so as not to offend someone powerful.

Such heretical thoughts made her feel disloyal to her own husband, but they refused to remain submerged and floated to the top of her consciousness. Robert had asked her to keep her profession a secret from his employers. Robert had discouraged her from handling Lillie Troy's suit and Genevra Graham's divorce because he was afraid of offending someone and hurting his own career. What had stripped the veil of illusion from her eyes once and for all was his thoughtless and unforgivable intimation that if she hadn't angered Gordon Graham, she wouldn't have been beaten.

Honor stopped before a window overlooking Fifth Avenue and caught her reflection in the glass. "Not bad, Honor old girl," she mused when she saw the pattern of fading purple and yellow bruises. "He needn't have removed the mirrors."

Still, she appreciated the gesture.

Nevada LaRouche tried to concentrate on the cablegrams from London spread across his desk, but Honor Davis continued to haunt him.

He put up his feet on the desk, leaned back in the swivel chair, laced his hands behind his head, and stared into space. That exasperating woman had insinuated herself into his thoughts from the moment she had boldly strode into his office with the news that Lillie Troy intended to sue him. He had a weakness for strong, courageous women with high principles, and he hadn't met one like Honor Davis since Sybilla.

LaRouche sighed. Damn shame she was another man's wife. He had never poached on another man's preserve, and he wasn't about to start now. It wasn't right.

No sooner did he take his feet off the desk than a knock sounded on the door. When he bade the caller enter and his worried-looking assistant appeared, LaRouche sensed trouble brewing. "Something wrong, Goddard?"

"Yes, sir," Goddard replied. "We lost the refinery. Cavanaugh outbid us."

LaRouche sat back in his chair. "That's impossible. Our bid was more than generous. No one could have possibly topped us."

"Well, Cavanaugh did, but not by much."

"Damn!" LaRouche rose and paced around the room. "He couldn't have."

"I'm afraid he did, sir."

LaRouche stopped. "He's always so cautious."

"Not this time." Goddard opened his mouth as if to say something, then closed it.

LaRouche looked at him. "If you have something to say, spit it out before you choke on it."

Goddard said, "It's almost as if he knew what our bid would be."

LaRouche went still. "Are you saying that you think Cavanaugh had inside information?"

"I can't prove it yet, but yes, I do."

"Do you have any suspects?"

"Not yet."

"When you do, let me know."

Goddard gave a worried bob of his head and left.

LaRouche swore under his breath. So someone in his own company, a trusted employee, had been supplying information to competitors. Delancy had been counting on this refinery deal going through, and he wasn't going to be pleased to hear that it hadn't.

LaRouche smiled grimly to himself. At least such a crisis would keep his mind off the intriguing Honor Davis.

As the days passed and July slid effortlessly into August, Honor's fading bruises finally disappeared and she was able to get back to work on *Graham v. Graham.*

Since Gordon Graham had already forcefully demonstrated to Honor what his wealth and power could do, she remained nervous and on edge, wondering just what he would do next to thwart his wife's plan to divorce him. Pay his mistress to disappear? No, Elroy reported that the lovely Araminta deGrey remained a defiant resident of the Spanish Flats, though she surely knew by now that she would be named corespondent in court. Would Graham bribe the night attendant and the tenants who were willing to swear that they had seen him entering and leaving Miss deGrey's apartment in the evening? Elroy said they all claimed no one had approached them about changing their stories, and they were still willing to testify.

He obviously thought Honor could not prove that his wife

had grounds to divorce him. When she met his lawyer, she knew why.

Honor felt the eyes of a dozen clerks following her as she walked to Salem Frick's office.

"So that's the lady lawyer everyone's talking about," one of them said, making no attempt to keep from being overheard.

"She is a stunner," another said.

"Looks won't save her," a third added. "When the boss gets through with her, she'll know why they call him Frick the Prick."

The clerks snickered openly, and Honor felt her cheeks grow hot, but she kept her head held high and her back ramrod straight as she ran their gauntlet of stares.

Her burning face cooled by the time she was shown into Frick's private office, a cavernous, lavishly appointed room at least ten times the size of Honor's.

The very best money can buy, she thought.

"Mrs. Davis to see you, Mr. Frick," the male secretary announced.

"Send her in."

When the secretary nodded and left, Honor saw one man seated behind a mahogany desk wider than Nevada LaRouche's and another seated in a leather club chair. When he turned, Honor saw that it was none other than Gordon Graham.

Neither of the men rose as she entered, a bit of rudeness no doubt calculated to intimidate her. She ignored it and strode across the plush Turkish carpet to stand before the desk.

After nodding to Graham who sat there glaring at her in blatant hostility, Honor turned her attention to the renowned Salem Frick, whom she had heard of but never observed in a courtroom. Now she wished she had.

In his early forties, Frick was not physically imposing, a fact that might lead his adversaries to underestimate him. Though he remained seated, Honor guessed he was of average height and build, his looks just as average. His eyes, however, were like a snake's, a pale, unblinking blue that mesmerized his victims before he struck.

"Mr. Frick," she said in a clear, professional voice, extending her hand, "I am Honor Davis, Genevra Graham's counsel."

Instead of shaking her hand, Frick deliberately ignored it and proceeded to take a cigar from a humidor on his desk and light it with exaggerated care.

So that's your game, is it? she thought, withdrawing her hand. She resisted the urge to tug on her locket.

He did not offer her a seat in another club chair, and she did not give him the satisfaction of glancing at it as though she expected to be seated. Instead, she consulted her lapel watch and said, "I am very busy, Mr. Frick. You may waste exactly one more minute of my time before I walk out that door."

Anger flared in the depths of his unblinking stare. "My client wishes you to inform his wife that she may as well withdraw her petition for a divorce and return to him."

"I'll convey your message to Mrs. Graham, but I know for a fact that she will not withdraw her petition and has no intention of returning to her husband."

Frick blinked. "I would strongly urge you to do so, my dear girl. You haven't a hope or a prayer of proving that my client committed adultery with Miss deGrey, and you know it." He smiled, a patronizing baring of teeth. "But then, considering your lack of experience, my dear girl, perhaps you don't know that you're doomed to lose this case."

"I know nothing of the kind."

Graham gave a soft snort, and his lip curled in disdain.

Frick moistened his lower lip with a flick of his tongue, and his unblinking stare roved insolently over Honor. "You're a beautiful woman, Mrs. Davis, but like the rest of your sex, you simply don't belong in a courtroom. An adversary of my experience and stature will cut you up into little pieces and feed you to the fishes."

Honor delicately smothered a yawn with her fingertips.

"Your aimless chatter is quite boring, Mr. Frick, and I can see that my coming here has been a waste of time. If you have nothing of importance to discuss, I'll be on my way."

Something akin to pity softened those strange unblinking eyes, and he shook his head regretfully as one would when arguing with a recalcitrant child. "Mrs. Davis, my dear girl—"

"I am not your dear girl," Honor said coldly, and turned to leave. "Good day to you, Mr. Frick. I shall see you in court the Monday after next."

Without warning, Gordon Graham bounded out of his chair and blocked her path with his tall, leonine presence. "I heard you were assaulted in your office, Mrs. Davis. I'm glad to see that you've recovered. A woman alone in such a big city can never be too careful."

Honor's heart raced as she remembered that evening when she thought she was going to die, but she kept her features composed so they wouldn't reveal her rising panic.

She took a deep breath and stared right into Graham's dark eyes. "I'm quite recovered, thanks to Nevada LaRouche. I understand that you were also attacked while riding in Central Park."

Something flickered in the depths of Graham's eyes. "I was, but as you can see, I am also fully recovered."

She gave him her coldest smile. "Perhaps the two men who assaulted me attacked you as well."

His face turned crimson, and he stepped aside without a word.

Her point made, Honor wished both men a good day and left.

If Honor thought that Salem Frick was a formidable opponent, she revised her opinion when she went to court to present her credentials to the judge who would be hearing Genevra's case, Justice X. Thornton West.

At first he refused to see Honor because he didn't believe a woman could be a lawyer, and when he finally relented after she threatened to take root outside his office, he lectured her for a full half hour about the unsuitability of women lawyers in his courtroom. Honor listened courteously and tried not to yawn.

When she calmly pointed out that women had been allowed to practice law in New York State since 1886 and that her client had a right to select whomever she pleased to represent her, or even to represent herself if she so desired, he resentfully agreed to let her appear before him.

Leaving the courthouse, Honor was relieved that the case would be heard in camera, with no spectators allowed and the records sealed, so Genevra's reputation wouldn't be tarnished further by scandal.

Justice X. Thornton West sat high on his dais and scowled down at the jurors, twelve men whom Honor and Frick had finally agreed upon after two days of voir dire.

"Gentlemen of the jury," he said, while the court stenographer recorded every word, "before these proceedings begin, I must warn you that just because Mrs. Davis is a gentlewoman, you must not let her beauty influence you. In other words, just because she's pretty doesn't mean she's right. You must reach a verdict based on the evidence presented and on that evidence alone."

Seated at her table with a skittish Genevra, Honor wore her expressionless lawyer's face, even though she was seething inside that Justice West would issue such a warning. Out of the corner of her eye, she watched the unblinking Frick suppress a smile while Gordon glowered at his wife.

Though this was Honor's first trial, her clerkship with Cleavon Frame at Royce and Ellis and the many hours she had spent observing trials had prepared her well for what was to follow. Her main concern was four men unknown to Genevra whom Frick intended to call as witnesses.

Finally the trial got under way and Honor was told to make her opening statement.

Rising, she approached the jurors. She did not smile, lest she appear coquettish. She scanned their faces and made note of the wariness and flagrant hostility written on every one.

"Gentlemen of the jury," she began, "like any other contract, the marriage contract can be broken, and like any other contract, it can be dissolved. The dissolution of the marriage contract is known as divorce.

"When the Grahams married, they promised to be faithful to each other. That was part of their contract. If one spouse is unfaithful to the other, the contract is broken."

Honor strolled before the jury box. "Gentlemen, I shall prove that Gordon Graham was unfaithful to his wife and that, under the laws of the state, has given Genevra Graham grounds for dissolving their marriage."

She made eye contact with each of the jurors. "I would ask you to keep in mind that Mrs. Graham is not yet thirty years old, still a young woman with a long and fulfilling life ahead of her. Why should she remain shackled to a man who broke their solemn marriage vows? Whatever love Mrs. Graham felt for her husband has been destroyed. Whatever respect she once had for him has turned to contempt. Whatever happiness she experienced has now soured."

Honor spread her hands in supplication. "Pretend for a moment that Genevra Graham is your own daughter. Would you condemn your own child to such a sterile existence? Of course not. Then I ask—no, I beg you to grant Genevra Graham a divorce."

When she sat down, Salem Frick rose to make his opening statement.

"Gentlemen of the jury," he began, resting his hands on the box's partition and leaning forward as if having a conversation with old friends, "I am sure you were all moved by Mrs. Davis's depiction of Genevra Graham as a wronged wife seeking her freedom from a callous husband. But nothing could be further from the truth."

Honor leaned forward in her chair, eager to hear just what her opponent planned.

Frick stepped back, his unblinking stare still scanning the jury as if gathering them to his side by the sheer force of his will. "Contrary to what Mrs. Davis would have you believe, Gordon Graham has always taken his marriage vows quite seriously. I will prove to you that this most devoted of husbands and fathers—this pillar of the community—would no more commit adultery than willingly give up his beloved little boy."

Honor watched doubt suddenly creep into the expressions of the men her opening statement had swayed to her side, but she didn't panic. She had seen jurors pulled first one way and then the other by opposing testimony, but it was early yet. What mattered was their verdict.

Frick strolled away from the jury. "I will also prove to you that the plaintiff is not the innocent Mrs. Davis would have you believe." He shook his head. "Like your own daughters, indeed," he scoffed, his snake's eyes suddenly bright with withering contempt. "Mrs. Graham is as unlike your own virtuous daughters as night is to day. You will see that she"—he whirled around and pointed an accusing finger at Genevra—"is the guilty party in this divorce action, not her husband."

Genevra started like a frightened rabbit, but calmed down the moment Honor placed a reassuring hand on her arm. Honor had warned her not to lose her temper or her composure no matter how hard Frick rode her.

As Frick wound up his opening statement, Honor thought carefully about what he had said. If he intended to prove that Genevra was the guilty party, no doubt the four mystery men on his witness list would play a pivotal role.

Honor called Genevra to the stand.

Dressed demurely in a summer gown of rust-colored linen that accented her auburn hair and matching straw bonnet, Genevra looked the very picture of a wronged wife with her sad hazel eyes and lower lip that wouldn't stop quivering. She kept darting fearful glances at her husband while she placed her hand on the Bible and swore to tell "the whole truth and nothing but the truth" in a quavering voice, something Honor hoped the jury noticed.

"Mrs. Graham," Honor began, "how long have you been married?"

"Eight years."

"Do you have any children?"

"A six-year-old son," she replied, her eyes brightening for the first time. "Stone Wolcott Graham."

"Would you say that your marriage has been happy?"

"Yes, until about a year ago."

"Will you tell the court what happened at that time?"

Genevra glanced nervously at her husband, seated with Frick. "My husband changed. He used to treat me with love and respect. Now all I feel is coldness and contempt."

"Would you elaborate?"

Genevra repeated exactly what she had told Honor at Coppermine—that her husband locked her in the attic, refused to let the servants speak to her for days on end, and lied to her callers, saying that she was not at home when, in truth, she was.

In the middle of Genevra's recitation, Salem Frick objected. "This is irrelevant, Your Honor. Even if Mrs. Graham's account of her husband's behavior is true, cruelty is not grounds for divorce in this state."

Honor said, "I will show the relevancy of this testimony shortly, Your Honor."

Justice West wrote something down. "I will allow it. Continue."

After Genevra finished, Honor said, "Do you have any idea why your husband changed?"

Genevra glanced at Gordon and swallowed hard, her eyes filling with tears. Even though Honor had coached her about what to say, it was apparent to everyone present that the woman was in great distress. Finally she blurted out, "I think it's because he learned that I had an—an abortion several years ago and never told him."

One of the jurors gasped. Justice West stared at Genevra in blatant disapproval. Gordon Graham closed his eyes, bowed his head, and buried his face in his hands.

Whether the men were upset because Genevra had an

abortion or because she kept it a secret from her husband, Honor couldn't tell, but she cynically suspected it was the latter.

"Was he upset when he found out?" she said.

"Yes." Genevra dabbed at her eyes with a handkerchief. "He flew into a towering rage. He called me a—a slut and a—a damned whore, and then he stormed out of the house. He returned a stranger. I threw myself at his feet and begged him to forgive me, but he refused." She sniffed. "That's when my life became a nightmare."

Honor gave her an encouraging smile. "Mrs. Graham, please pardon the indelicacy of my next question, but after your estrangement, did you and your husband engage in marital relations?"

Several gentlemen of the jury coughed, and others shifted in their seats.

Genevra's pale cheeks turned a dull, embarrassed red. "No, we did not. Gordon couldn't bear to touch me."

"At any time did you suspect that your husband might be seeing another woman?"

"Not at first. On the nights when he didn't come home, I thought he was staying at his club. But as the months passed and he never claimed his—his husbandly rights, I did become suspicious." She colored again. "He used to be quite . . . insistent in that respect, so the change in him was noticeable."

Honor said, "Have you ever been unfaithful to your husband, Mrs. Graham?"

"Never," she snapped indignantly.

"And you have never given him cause to think you unfaithful?"

"Never."

Honor smiled and thanked Genevra for her testimony, then told the justice she had no further questions and returned to her seat.

Frick rose and turned his unblinking stare on Genevra. "Mrs. Graham, you are considerably younger than your husband, are you not?"

"Yes."

"Did you marry him for his money?"

Genevra glanced at her husband. "No. At the time, I loved him."

Frick raised his brows in surprise. "If you loved him, why did you abort his child without telling him?"

Stay calm, Genevra, Honor silently pleaded. Don't let him rattle you into making an outburst.

"I was fearful of bearing another child," she replied, her voice steady. "I almost died giving birth to our son, and I was afraid that if I did have another child, I would surely die."

"Did you ever stop to consider your husband's wishes?"

Genevra's hazel eyes hardened. "No. He had no consideration for my fears. He just wanted me to give him one child after another, so why—"

"Just answer the question, Mrs. Graham."

"No, I never stopped to consider my husband's wishes."

Frick paused and stared at her. "You have testified under oath that you believe your abortion caused your husband to turn away from you. Is that true?"

"Yes."

He leaned forward. "But isn't there another reason, Mrs. Graham?"

Genevra looked confused. "I can think of no other."

"Oh, I can." Frick took another quiet stroll around the courtroom, letting his cryptic words sink in. When Justice West looked impatient, Frick stopped in front of the witness box, his unblinking stare pinning Genevra to her seat. His voice rang out: "Isn't it true that your husband suspected you of having illicit affairs with other men?"

Honor sat up straighter.

Genevra turned as white as plaster. "That's not true!"

Frick walked back to his table, picked up his notes, and made a great production out of studying them. "I have statements here from several of your servants swearing that they overheard your husband accusing you of seeing other men."

So that's Frick's sordid little game, Honor thought. "Objection, Your Honor. This is hearsay. Just because Mr. Graham was overheard accusing his wife of adultery doesn't mean she committed it." Still, Frick had just planted a seed of doubt in the jurors' minds. That had obviously been his intention all along.

"Sustained."

Frick's snake eyes narrowed. "What is your relationship to Nevada LaRouche, Mrs. Graham?"

Genevra turned a guilty shade of red. "What do you mean?"

Genevra and LaRouche lovers? Honor hadn't even considered that possibility. She shook off her doubts at once. That weekend at Coppermine, they had been nothing more to each other than host and guest. Besides, they would have told her.

Frick said, "Is he an acquaintance, a business associate of your husband's, a friend . . ."

"He is—was—a good friend of my husband's," she replied cautiously.

"Do you consider him your friend as well?"

"Yes, I do."

"You have spent several weekends at Mr. LaRouche's Hudson Valley estate as his guest, have you not?"

"Yes." Lest the jurors get the wrong impression, she quickly added, "Along with my husband and several other couples."

Honor objected at once. "I don't see how Mrs. Graham's friendship with Mr. LaRouche has any bearing on this case." Other than to discredit Genevra by insinuating that she had an affair with him.

"I quite agree," Justice West said and sustained her objection.

Frick all but winked lasciviously at the jury. "I have no further questions of this witness."

Determined not to let Frick get away with his character assassination of her client, Honor rose and asked for permission to approach the bench. Standing before Justice

West, she said, "Your Honor, I would like to request a short recess to summon another witness who isn't present at the moment."

"And who would that be?" the justice demanded.

Honor glanced at her opponent. "Nevada LaRouche."

A half hour later, Nevada LaRouche strode into the courthouse, his impatient gaze cutting through the crowd to find Honor pacing around the edge of the rotunda. When he reached her side, he said, "I got here as fast as I could. What's this about you wanting me to testify?"

"Gordon's lawyer has intimated that you and Genevra were lovers," Honor said, steeling herself for the explosion that was sure to follow.

A rare red flush flooded LaRouche's cheeks, his usual composure deserting him. "Why that low-down good-for-nothing . . . He's lying." He stared hard at Honor. "You don't think—"

"Of course not." She didn't tell him about her momentary doubts in the courtroom.

Honor was surprised to see relief flare briefly in the depths of his eyes. "His lawyer is too wily to actually accuse you," she said, to mollify him, "but even though he can't prove anything, he's planted a seed of doubt in the jurors' minds. If they think Genevra is as guilty of committing adultery as her husband, they won't grant her a divorce."

LaRouche rubbed his jaw. "You think my testifying will help?"

Honor nodded. "All you have to do is tell the truth. I doubt if Gordon's attorney will want to cross-examine you, but if he does, please don't lose your temper."

LaRouche's jaw clenched. "Afterward, Gordon and I are going to have a few words."

"Don't waste your breath. He's not worth it."

"I don't take kindly to someone telling lies about me."

"I realize that, but please restrain yourself."

"I'll do my best."

In the courtroom, Honor watched Frick when LaRouche

took the stand and was sworn in, and was delighted to see that her opponent did not look too pleased.

"Mr. LaRouche," Honor began, "how did you come to know Genevra Graham?"

"Mr. and Mrs. Graham were friends of my business partner, Damon Delancy."

"And you socialized often?"

"Yes. Mr. and Mrs. Graham were often Delancy's guests at his home here in New York and for weekends at his country estate."

"And during these weekends were you ever alone with Mrs. Graham?"

LaRouche bristled with barely restrained annoyance. "No, ma'am. There were always other people present."

"Pardon my frankness, Mr. LaRouche, but were you and Mrs. Graham ever lovers?"

"Absolutely not!" he growled, glaring at Gordon. "I don't make a habit of sleeping with other men's wives, and any man who says I do is a bald-faced liar."

Justice West admonished LaRouche to refrain from making personal comments, but Honor had made her point to the jury and turned the witness over to Frick, who prudently declined to cross-examine.

Honor's next witness was Gordon Graham's mistress.

CHAPTER 13

A BREATHLESS HUSH FELL across the courtroom when the alleged "other woman" was called to the stand.

Honor couldn't resist looking over her shoulder as Araminta deGrey entered the courtroom and glided up to the witness stand as regally and contemptuously as a queen, leaving just a sigh of Parma violet perfume in her wake.

Even Elroy's awestruck description of Graham's *petite amie* as "the most beautiful woman I've ever seen" didn't do her justice. First of all, there was nothing petite about her. Nearly six feet tall, Araminta deGrey displayed a lush hourglass figure that was already impressing the gentlemen of the jury.

Dressed in a modish ensemble of cornflower-blue faille that matched her spectacular eyes, she possessed a slender, patrician nose and a Cupid's bow mouth that begged to be kissed. A flawless ivory complexion and hair the color of sun-ripened wheat gilded an already impressive lily.

But underneath all that golden glitter is pure brass, Honor thought.

There was nothing remotely wifely or domestic about the woman. Her lush hothouse beauty evoked secret trysts in a house of assignation and tributes of priceless jewels from a grateful, satisfied lover, one Gordon Graham. At least Honor could see it. Now all she had to do was convince the jury.

Once Araminta deGrey took the stand and was sworn in, Honor approached her with a conciliatory smile.

"Miss deGrey, what a lovely ensemble you're wearing. Was it designed by Redfern?"

"No. Worth," the woman replied in a low, soft voice more suitable to the boudoir than to the courtroom.

A juror snickered. Justice West rolled his eyes and said, "Mrs. Davis, this is a courtroom, not a dressmaker's salon."

"Sorry, Your Honor." Although men would fail to see the significance of this seemingly frivolous line of questioning, Honor had her reasons for pursuing it. She strolled over to the jurors' box. "Miss deGrey, I understand that you are an actress."

"I used to be. I haven't appeared on the stage for several years."

"Are you employed now?"

The cornflower-blue eyes sparkled at some secret joke. "No."

"I understand you own an apartment at the Central Park Apartments, also known as the Spanish Flats. Is this true?"

"Yes."

"How long have you lived there?"

"A year and a half."

"You're not married?" When the woman answered in the negative, Honor smiled and added, "And you're not an heiress."

Araminta deGray smiled back. "No, I'm not an heiress, Mrs. Davis."

Honor made sure all the jurors could clearly see her puzzled frown. "Quite frankly, Miss deGrey, I'm confused. How can a woman who is not married, not employed, and not an heiress afford a thousand-dollar Worth ensemble like the one you're wearing, and a four-thousand-dollar cooperative apartment?"

An expectant hush fell over the courtroom. Twelve jurors leaned forward in their seats. Even Justice West looked eager to hear the answer.

Araminta deGrey batted her long eyelashes, smiled, and

said, "I have an . . . admirer, Mrs. Davis. He bought me this Worth ensemble, the apartment, and many other things."

Her brazen admission that she was a kept woman caught Honor unawares. She had never expected her to admit it. Never. Honor prayed her face didn't reveal her shock at this unexpected turn of events.

She thought fast. "And is Gordon Graham, the man seated over there, your admirer, Miss deGrey?"

"No."

"If he isn't, who is?"

Frick rose. "Objection, Your Honor. Since the witness has denied that Gordon Graham is her admirer, the man's identity has no relevancy to this case."

When the judge sustained the objection, Honor said, "Miss deGrey, I have witnesses who will testify that Gordon Graham has been seen visiting your apartment quite frequently, often late at night. Do you still deny that he is your . . . admirer?"

The witness tried to suppress an unladylike smirk and failed. "I deny that Mr. Graham is my admirer, but I've never denied knowing him. As a matter of fact, we are good friends." She gave Graham a bold glance that was anything but platonic, then said to Honor, "There's no law against a simple friendship between a man and a woman, is there? I may break the laws of propriety by allowing Mr. Graham to visit me late into the night, but that doesn't mean he is my lover, Mrs. Davis."

Honor nodded graciously when she really wanted to wring the woman's perfect swanlike neck. "Thank you for clarifying your relationship, Miss deGrey." She paused. "What do you do when Mr. Graham visits?"

"We dine, we talk, we play poker," she replied smoothly. "And nothing else."

"What does your admirer think of your friendship with Mr. Graham?"

"Oh, he understands perfectly."

"How fortunate for you. No further questions, though I

would like to reserve the right to recall this witness, Your Honor."

As Honor returned to her seat, she saw that both Frick and Graham were trying hard to keep from laughing. They were deliberately taunting her with Araminta deGrey. Honor wasn't surprised when Frick declined to cross-examine this witness. He didn't need to prove anything.

Honor's next witnesses were the doorman at the Spanish Flats and two neighbors of Miss deGrey's. They all swore to having seen Gordon Graham coming and going at all hours. When Frick cross-examined them, he forcefully brought home the fact that none had actually witnessed Graham fornicating with the beauteous Araminta. So how could Honor prove him guilty of adultery?

Her only hope was to force one of them to confess.

But how?

At home late that night, as she lay in bed beside her snoring husband and tried to sleep, something Araminta had said kept going around and around in her mind like a dog chasing its tail: "We dine, we talk, we play poker."

"Poker . . ." Honor muttered. "I'll bet my law degree that woman has never played a game of cards in her life." Unlike Honor, who had been taught by her cardsharp of an aunt.

Honor sat bolt upright. Cards! She hugged her knees and planned just how she was going to trap the smug Araminta deGrey.

The following day it was Frick's turn to call his witnesses. Several of the Graham servants testified that their mistress was a nervous and high-strung woman who had imagined her husband's cruelties. Several character witnesses then swore that Gordon Graham was a pillar of the community. They were followed by a man named Hamilton Adair who swore that Genevra Graham had slept with him several times while summering in Newport.

Hamilton Adair was one of the four mystery names that

Genevra hadn't recognized on Frick's witness list. Now Honor knew why.

"He's lying," Genevra whispered desperately to Honor. "I don't remember ever meeting him, never mind sleeping with him."

"That's obvious," Honor whispered back, "but no matter what happens, don't panic. It isn't over until the jury reaches a verdict."

With her client calmed down, Honor studied Frick and wondered what he was going to do next. First he had intimated that Nevada LaRouche had been Genevra's lover, and now this man was testifying in another attempt to discredit her. Honor wondered if the other three unknown witnesses would also conveniently turn out to have been Genevra's alleged lovers.

When Frick was through with Adair, Honor declined to cross-examine because she didn't know how the witness would answer her questions. Frick then called the other three men to the stand, and just as Honor had suspected, all of them claimed that Genevra Graham had been their lover. Again, Honor thought it best not to cross-examine.

After a short recess for luncheon, when Honor tried to cheer up a despondent Genevra, they returned to the courtroom, and Graham himself took the stand.

Gordon impressed the jury of his peers with his commanding, leonine presence, which exuded wealth, success, and respectability. He painted a picture of himself as a devoted, concerned husband and father who loved his wife and child more than life itself. No, he couldn't understand why his wife wanted to divorce him. Even though her secret abortion and her many infidelities had devastated him, he was still willing to forgive her.

When it was Honor's turn to cross-examine, all she said was, "Mr. Graham, according to Miss deGrey's testimony under oath, when you visited her you dined, you talked, and you played poker. Is this true?"

While he looked the very picture of innocence, his hostile, disapproving eyes mocked her. "Yes."

"How would you describe her poker-playing skills?"

He looked surprised for a second, then recovered himself. "I would describe her skills as excellent. When we play for small stakes, she often beats me."

Frick rose. "Your Honor," he moaned, "what bearing does Miss deGrey's skill at cards have on this case?"

"Everything," Honor retorted, "as I will soon prove to the court. Your Honor, I'd like to recall Araminta deGrey."

Today she wore a more subdued but equally expensive ensemble of dove gray mousseline de soie, making no attempt to disguise her status as a well-kept woman. Again she regarded Honor with thinly veiled disdain.

Honor said, "Miss deGrey, we've just heard from your . . . friend Mr. Graham that you are an excellent poker player and often beat him. Is this true?"

"Yes."

Honor walked over to her table, removed five playing cards from her purse, and fanned them out in her hand before walking back to the witness stand. "Since you are such an expert poker player, Miss deGrey, you won't mind identifying the hand I'm holding."

The witness's cornflower-blue eyes widened in alarm. "Of—of course not." She studied the cards, her delicate brow furrowed in concentration. "You're holding a full house."

Honor showed the hand to the jury. "As you see, gentlemen, I hold an ace, king, queen, jack, and ten of hearts. Is that a full house?"

"It's a royal flush," one of the jurors replied.

Honor looked at Araminta deGrey, who was no longer smiling. "Let's give the . . . lady another chance." Honor returned to her purse and selected another hand.

"Your Honor," Frick wailed, "I fail to see—"

"Well, I do. Overruled."

Honor showed the cards to the witness, who moistened her lips and threw Gordon Graham a panic-stricken look before saying, "That's a flush."

Honor turned to the jury. "Gentlemen, would you call a deuce, three, four, five, and six of clubs a flush?"

"No," her card expert responded, thoroughly enjoying himself. "It's a straight flush."

"Sir, would you enlighten the court as to the difference between a flush and a straight flush?"

"A flush is a deuce, five, six, jack, and king of clubs."

Honor pocketed her cards and faced the witness with the cold, deadly calculation of a cobra about to strike. "Miss deGrey, both you and Mr. Graham have testified under oath that you are an expert poker player. Yet when I asked you to identify two hands that any card player—myself included—would know, you could not accurately identify them. Can you explain this discrepancy to the court?"

The witness's gloved hand fluttered and she batted her lashes helplessly at Judge West. "I—I'm so nervous about testifying that I made a mistake."

"Twice? Oh, come now, Miss deGrey!" Honor said, her voice edged with steel. "Not once during your entire testimony have you appeared the least bit nervous. If anything, you've been extremely confident of yourself—confident to the point of arrogance. No, I think you're not an expert poker player at all. I'd bet my law degree that you have never played a game of cards in your life." She approached the stand and glared at the witness. "In fact, I think that you've been lying. You and Gordon Graham don't play cards when he comes calling. You go to the bedroom and—"

"Your Honor!" Frick cried, jumping to his feet.

Looking like a fox finally cornered by the hounds, Araminta deGrey sputtered, "Even if we didn't tell the truth about playing cards, we are not lovers!"

"Then why did you lie under oath, Miss deGrey? That's perjury, punishable by a fine, a prison term, or both. Have you ever been in prison, Miss deGrey? I can assure you that it's most unpleasant." Honor let her contemptuous gaze rove over the woman's flaunted finery. "There are no Worth gowns in prison, Miss deGrey, and you'll face imprisonment if you don't tell the truth."

Araminta deGrey flashed another silent desperate plea for deliverance in Graham's direction, but all he could do was glower helplessly.

"I am telling the truth," she insisted. "We are not lovers."

"Prison cells are very small, Miss deGrey. Those in the Tombs are seven feet long and three and a half feet wide. There's barely enough room to stand up between your cot and the wall." Honor smiled. "Not exactly the Spanish Flats, is it?"

The woman swallowed hard, but remained tight-lipped and silent.

"No running water and only a bucket for sanitation."

"Your Honor," Frick said, "Mrs. Davis is trying to terrify this witness into making a false confession."

"On the contrary. I am doing her a service by describing what she will face if she's guilty of perjury." When the justice overruled Frick, Honor added, "It's such a shame that there are no fine face creams or perfumes in prison."

Doubt slowly shadowed those cornflower-blue eyes. Araminta deGrey nervously bit her lower lip.

"Once again, Miss deGrey," Honor said coldly, "are you and Gordon Graham lovers?"

Her iron resolve finally failed her. The lovely face crumpled. "Yes! Yes!" She burst into tears. "Don't send me to jail. Please."

Honor, whose nerves were strung as tight as a wire, almost collapsed with relief. "Thank you, Miss deGrey. That will be all."

She had proved Gordon Graham guilty of adultery by his mistress's own admission.

Honor took a deep breath and faced the jury to deliver her summary, her final chance to sway them to her side.

"Gentlemen of the jury," she began, "during the past two days you've heard a great deal of conflicting testimony.

Your responsibility will be to sort through that testimony and arrive at the truth. But what is the truth?"

She looked at each man. "Although Mrs. Graham is not on trial here today, my esteemed opponent, in an attempt to discredit her in your eyes, has insinuated that she, not her husband, is the guilty party in this marriage.

"He has called four witnesses to the stand—not counting Mr. Nevada LaRouche—who have all testified that they were Genevra Graham's lovers. Mr. LaRouche supposedly carried on with her at his Hudson Valley country estate, another man chose Newport for their alleged trysts, a third claimed he slept with her in the Berkshires, a fourth at a New York hotel, and a fifth traveled all the way to Connecticut."

Honor took a moment to glare contemptuously at the defense table before turning back to the jury. "It would seem that the lady has a lover stashed away in every country house." Honor fanned her face with her hand. "An exhausting prospect, is it not?"

Several jurors snickered, as Honor had hoped they would.

She rested her hands on the bar. "While these four men claim Mrs. Graham committed adultery with them, the defense has failed to prove it in every instance. No witnesses have come forth to corroborate their testimony, so it all boils down to their word against my client's. In fact, Mr. LaRouche, one of the men my esteemed opponent implied was Mrs. Graham's lover has emphatically denied the charge."

Honor stepped back. "Gentlemen, does the defense counsel really believe that you are so gullible as to be easily duped into believing that this sweet, innocent gentlewoman, a mother who loves her little boy and only wants what's best for him, has taken *four* lovers?"

The members of the jury shifted in their seats and looked downright uncomfortable.

"Four!" Honor said, holding up that many fingers for emphasis. "A veritable male harem, gentlemen. Only courtesans and streetwalkers heedless of their tender, feminine nature collect so many men. Yet Mr. Graham would have you believe that his gentle wife has the morals of a courtesan." She shook her head. "It's absurd. First of all, it goes against a well-bred lady's nature to be promiscuous. All you have to do is look at Genevra Graham seated over there to see that she is certainly a lady. Second, how could any lady possibly love four men at once?

"On the other hand, gentlemen, you have heard Miss Araminta deGrey, who is obviously not a lady, confess under oath that she is Gordon Graham's mistress."

Honor turned and pointed an accusing finger at a glowering Gordon Graham. "It's plain to see that he is the one who is guilty of adultery."

She turned back to the jury. "At the beginning of this trial, Justice West warned you not to be unduly influenced by the fact that I am a woman. I believe his exact words were 'Just because she's pretty doesn't mean she's right.'" She ignored West's scowl. "But just because I'm pretty doesn't mean I'm wrong, either. By extracting a confession from his mistress, I've proven that Gordon Graham is guilty of adultery, and I'm asking you to grant his wife a divorce on those grounds."

She thanked them and sat down.

Frick's closing remarks were all bluster as he tried to punch holes in Honor's arguments, but she couldn't tell if he was swaying the jury to his side.

When Frick finished, the jury went out to begin their deliberations. One hour later they returned.

"How do you find?" Judge West asked the foreman.

Honor held her breath and prayed.

"We find for the plaintiff, and grant Genevra Graham a divorce on the grounds of adultery."

Nevada LaRouche raised his champagne glass and grinned. "To the best lawyer in New York City."

Honor and Genevra were celebrating their victory with Robert and LaRouche in the parlor of the Fifth Avenue mansion.

Genevra's hazel eyes shone with grateful tears. "I never expected to win custody of my son, let alone the house and ten thousand dollars a year in alimony."

"You should have gotten more," Honor declared. "Gordon can afford it." She smiled wickedly. "Of course the smug Araminta may have to do without her Worth gowns for a while."

LaRouche's remote gaze hardened. "Considering what he paid those two thugs to beat you, I'd say Gordon got off real easy."

"I quite agree," Honor said, suppressing a shiver. "I just wish I could have proven that he hired them."

Genevra said, "One thing puzzles me, Honor. Why didn't you cross-examine Hamilton Adair and those other three men and expose their lies for what they were?"

"It could have harmed our case," she replied. "Cleavon Frame, the Boston lawyer I clerked for, drilled it into me that a lawyer is not obligated to cross-examine every witness who takes the stand. Frick thought that because I wasn't as experienced as he, I would fall into the trap of trying to prove you innocent of adultery. Instead, I didn't waste time cross-examining his mystery witnesses, and I let Frick hang himself."

Nevada frowned. "But what if the jury had believed those low-down liars?"

"By not cross-examining them," Honor replied, "I let their testimony pile up to the point of nausea. Frick's attempts at character assassination finally disgusted the jury, and when I pointed out the absurdity of his assertion that a well-bred lady had taken four lovers, they saw Frick's ploy for what it was."

LaRouche raised his glass to her again. "Very clever."

Robert frowned. "So Frick hired those men to lie."

"To give the devil his due, it wasn't his idea," Honor said. "Out in the corridor after the trial, I overheard Frick calling Gordon a damn fool for insisting that they hire those men."

Genevra's eyes widened. "Gordon was responsible?"

Honor nodded. "He not only wanted you to lose, he

wanted to exact revenge by depicting you as a loose woman. And he wanted it badly enough to disregard the advice of his expensive counsel."

LaRouche shook his head in disgust.

Robert raised his glass to his wife, his green eyes shining with some emotion Honor couldn't name. "That was also a clever strategy with the cards."

His compliment amazed Honor; he gave her so few these days.

"I know I tried to discourage you from taking the case," he went on, "but I can see now that I was wrong." He toasted her again. "My apologies for doubting you."

Honor didn't know what to say. His apology in front of Nevada LaRouche and Genevra touched her deeply, for Robert was not a man to admit his mistakes easily. Perhaps he realized how much he had hurt her in the past and this was his way of making amends.

Perhaps there was hope for their marriage after all.

Chapter 14

One warm mid-September evening, Honor was about to sit down to dinner when Robert pulled a piece of paper out of his breast pocket and handed it to her. "Oh, I almost forgot. This telegram came for you this morning. It's from some doctor."

The blood drained from Honor's face when she read the cryptic message. She grasped the locket with shaking fingers. "Aunt Theo is ill. Her doctor wants me to come immediately." She rose from the table, her thoughts scattered, her knees shaking, her soup untouched. "There has to be a night train leaving Grand Central for Boston."

Robert looked peeved. "Do you have to leave this minute? You haven't touched your supper."

Her nerves stretched to the limit by shock and thoughts of impending disaster, Honor glared at him. "For all I know, my aunt may be dying. Of course I'm leaving tonight!" She headed for the dining room door, stopped and turned. "Will you come with me?"

"I can't possibly get away," he replied. "LaRouche wants me to go over some important contracts with him tomorrow morning."

Honor tugged at her locket. "He's a very understanding man. I'm sure he wouldn't object to your taking several days off under the circumstances."

Robert dabbed at his lips with his napkin. "I wouldn't presume by asking for preferential treatment."

"Robert, please come with me," she said, hating the desperation in her voice. "I need you."

He rose, crossed the room and grasped her hands so tightly Honor winced. "Haven't you been listening to a word I've said? I've told you that I can't possibly get away."

"Perhaps if I asked Mr. LaRouche—"

"No!" He dropped her hands and stepped away, his sensuous mouth tightening into an obstinate line. "I can't go with you, and that's final."

"Robert—"

"Damn it!" he roared. "Don't argue with me!" He returned to his seat at the head of the table and resumed eating his soup. "Tell your aunt that I send my warmest regards and wish her a speedy recovery."

Eyes blazing, Honor whirled on her heels and stormed out of the dining room. What a fool she had been to think he had changed. Men like Robert never changed, they merely altered course.

Passing the kitchen, she said, "Tilly, come to the bedroom at once. I'm leaving for Boston tonight and need you to help me pack."

The maid looked up from carving the roast. "But madam, what about the master's dinner?"

"It can get cold for all I care."

"But it will only take me a minute to—"

"Didn't you hear what I said? The master's dinner can wait."

A subdued Tilly set down the carving knife and followed.

Once in the bedchamber, Honor sat at her desk and dashed off an explanatory note to Elroy, telling him that she had been called away to Boston on a family matter. He should cancel her appointments and manage the office for a week or two. After she finished writing, a disturbing thought occurred to her. "Tilly, what time did the telegram arrive?"

Carefully folding a shirtwaist so its leg-o'-mutton sleeves

wouldn't be crushed in the suitcase, the maid replied, "Around ten o'clock this morning, madam."

Honor slammed down her pen. "Dear God, Tilly! Why in heaven's name didn't you bring the telegram to my office immediately? Didn't it ever occur to you that it might be important?"

The maid recoiled as if struck, and tears filled her eyes. "I brought it to Mr. Davis's office the minute it arrived, madam. I thought if it contained bad news, your husband should tell you."

Robert had known about her aunt's illness all day. All day. And he hadn't thought to inform Honor until tonight.

I will never forgive him for this, she thought. Never.

"I'm sorry for being such a shrew, Tilly," she said after her anger died. "I didn't mean to snap at you. My aunt has been like a mother to me, and I'm just worried about her."

"That's understandable, madam."

Ten minutes later, after giving Tilly the letter to deliver to Elroy first thing tomorrow morning, Honor emerged from the bedchamber, her suitcase in hand. If she wasn't so desperate to leave, she would have given her husband a tongue lashing he would never forget.

The moment Honor entered the dining room, Robert said, "Where is Tilly with the rest of my supper?"

"She had to pack for me," Honor replied. "She'll have the rest of your supper in a moment." And I hope it's ice-cold.

Robert glanced at her suitcase. "All ready, are we?" He rose from the table and reached for her bag. "Let me take that downstairs for you."

"You needn't trouble yourself," Honor said coldly, grasping the handle as if preparing for a tug-of-war. "I can manage." She headed for the door, adding over her shoulder, "I don't know how long I shall stay in Boston."

"Stay until your aunt recovers," Robert said. Now that he had gotten his own way, he was all smiles and generosity. "Honor, wait."

She turned, plainly irritated with the interruption.

Robert came over to her, grasped her arms above the

elbow, and leaned forward to kiss her. Honor averted her face at the last moment and received a peck on the cheek.

"I have to be on my way," she said, pulling away, delighted to see her husband's startled look at her rebuff. "I shall miss my train."

Without a good-bye or a smile, Honor left for Boston.

Not a carriage could be seen up or down Commonwealth Avenue, which was bathed in silvery moonlight, for it was past midnight by the time an exhausted, worried Honor arrived at her aunt's brownstone. While the cab driver fetched her suitcase, she paused at the foot of the steps and felt a lump form in her throat as she stared up at dark windows.

Home.

She paid the driver, who lugged her suitcase up the steps and departed. Honor opened the front door with the key Aunt Theo had insisted she keep "just in case." Once inside the foyer, Honor turned on the gaslight. To her relief, nothing had changed. The wainscoted walls still boasted the same mellow beeswax sheen. The silver salver on the hall table waited to receive calling cards. A welcoming warmth so lacking in her life enveloped her, and tears stung her eyes.

She lit a lamp, went up to the third floor, and knocked softly on her aunt's door before calling, "Aunt Theo?" and opening it.

"Honor, is that you?" Light flooded the bedchamber as Theo lit a lamp, got out of bed, and hurried across the room.

"Yes," Honor replied.

The two women quickly embraced, for they hadn't seen each other for almost a year. When they parted, Theo held Honor at arm's length. "Let me look at you." Her dark, penetrating gaze assessed and stripped away Honor's carefully cultivated defenses. "You don't look happy."

Theo didn't look so well herself. Aside from an inordinately pale complexion, new lines of sadness deeply scored the corners of her eyes while their depths held an emptiness that Honor knew only Wesley Saltonsall could fill. But Wes was gone, lost forever.

Honor ignored her aunt's observation. "Never mind about me. What's wrong with you? Are you going to be all right?"

Theo closed her eyes and nodded. "I'm in no danger. The doctor said I had a minor inflammation of the bowels. I was in such agony last night that the poor man panicked and sent you the telegram." She smiled sheepishly. "I feel just like the boy who cried wolf. I've summoned you all the way to Boston when there was no need."

"Nonsense. A visit to Boston is never wasted. I should have come back months ago, but I've been so busy."

"Yes, I read about your successful divorce case, and I make a point of throwing it in Amos Grant's pompous face at every opportunity."

Honor smiled. "Well, now that I am here, I plan to stay until you've fully recovered."

Theo looked over Honor's shoulder. "It's obvious that Robert didn't come with you."

"He couldn't get away."

"I see."

Honor suspected that her aunt saw all too well.

Theo said, "You look exhausted. Why don't you get some sleep and we can talk in the morning?"

Honor kissed her on the cheek and tiptoed out, going back to her old room, where she undressed quickly and tumbled into bed, putting all thoughts out of her exhausted mind.

Theo set down her coffee and said, "I have had quite enough. Sweet Portia, what's wrong?"

Honor turned away from the fireplace. "Why, nothing."

"Don't 'why, nothing' me. You haven't mentioned Robert once today. You're a million miles away, and if you tug on that damn locket one more time, you'll not only break the cord, I swear you'll drive me clear out of my mind!" Theo rose in an agitated rustle of violet silk. "It's not like you to keep secrets from me."

Honor's eyes filled with tears, but before they could fall,

she brushed them away angrily with the back of her hand. “I’ve discovered that I take second place to my husband’s ambition.”

“That should not come as a shock to you. Most women do.”

Honor managed a bitter smile. “That may be true, but it’s still quite a humiliating experience, one I prefer to keep to myself. That’s why I haven’t told you.”

Theo made a soft sound of sympathy, led Honor to the sofa, and sat her down. “Talk. Perhaps I can offer my usual sage advice.”

Honor laced her fingers together to keep from tugging on her locket. “Robert says he loves me, but he always puts his concerns ahead of mine.”

Theo sipped her coffee and listened intently while Honor told her about the time Robert wanted her to keep her profession secret from his bosses, and then about how he had urged her to drop several cases so as not to incur the wrath of someone rich and powerful.

Honor stared down at her wedding ring when she related the next incident. “After I was beaten, Robert told me that if I hadn’t taken the divorce case, I wouldn’t have angered someone as powerful as Gordon Graham and I wouldn’t have been beaten.”

“Oh, my sweet Portia . . .”

Honor looked at her, tears stinging her eyes. “My own husband implied that I had brought such punishment on myself. My own husband!” Honor leaned back against the sofa. “When I so desperately needed him to comfort and defend me, all he could do was imply that I got exactly what I deserved.”

“My dear, I don’t know what to say.”

Honor smiled. “Did I ever tell you that the man who found me—Robert’s boss, Nevada LaRouche—later fought with the man he suspected of hiring those thugs?” When Theo shook her head, Honor said, “A stranger defended me. Not my own husband but a man I barely knew and didn’t even fully trust.”

Theo placed a hand on Honor's shoulder. "You've learned a hard, cruel lesson."

Honor raised her head. "Robert never fails to disappoint me. When I most need him, he's never there."

Theo set down her coffee cup. "Have you told him how you feel?"

"Once, when we were arguing about my dropping the divorce case, but it was like talking to a brick wall."

"Do you still love him?"

Honor sighed. "Part of me still loves the man I married, but another part of me does not love the man he has become." She shook her head. "Sometimes it's like living with a stranger, a cold, selfish stranger."

Theo smoothed her skirt with a restless hand. "What do you intend to do now?"

"I can either accept the fact that Robert will never give me what I need, or"—she uttered the unthinkable—"I can leave him."

"You know that you're always welcome here with your old aunt." Theo gave her an arch look. "But you're hardly an old crone, my dear. You would marry again, perhaps to that Nevada person who championed you?"

Honor stared at her out of wide, shocked eyes. "What an absurd thought! He's just like the man who destroyed my family."

"You know him better than I."

"I do. Charming as he is on the surface, he's unprincipled and has led quite a lawless life."

"He sounds more intriguing by the minute." Theo shook her head. "Life is too short to settle for crumbs." She rose and paced the parlor. "You know what will happen if you do settle, don't you? Robert will disappoint you again and again. You'll make excuses for him and tell yourself that you love him in spite of his faults, but each time he fails you, you'll die a little inside. And make no mistake, sweet Portia, he will fail you. Such men always do." Theo stopped. "Soon you will feel nothing inside except bitterness and resentment. I'd hate to see that happen to you."

Honor closed her eyes and rubbed her forehead where a headache was forming. "I'm so torn."

"You're home now," Theo said. "Take all the time you need to make a decision. You know I will support you, whatever you decide."

Honor rose and kissed her aunt on the cheek. "That means a great deal to me." When she returned to the sofa, she said, "What about you, Aunt Theo?"

Theo frowned. "What about me?"

"Is there a new man in your life?"

Theo's dark eyes suddenly filled with sadness. She smiled with forced brightness. "No, there is no one. Did I tell you that Wes has a son, a little heir to the Saltonsall shipping dynasty? Wes's father couldn't be prouder. He tells everyone who'll listen that he couldn't ask for a better daughter-in-law than Selena. Rumor has it that she's expecting another child."

But was Wes happy? Honor doubted it.

"You know you should have married him," she said softly.

Her aunt stiffened. "Don't reproach me," she snapped with uncharacteristic ire. "I did what was best for him. Someday he will realize that, when he's old with his grandchildren gathered around him. Now, if you'll excuse me, it's time for my afternoon drive. Will you come?"

"As tempting as your offer is, the thought of terrorizing Boston in your motorcar holds little appeal. Besides, I have a great deal of thinking to do."

"I understand," Theo said.

Half an hour later, Honor watched in some trepidation from the doorway as her aunt, covered from head to toe in duster, hat, and goggles, went rattling off in a puff of exhaust down Commonwealth Avenue. When the car disappeared from view, Honor went back into the house to decide what to do about her marriage.

Honor returned to New York five days later to tell Robert that their marriage was over and that she had decided to leave him.

Unlocking her apartment door and stepping inside, she called out, "Robert? I'm home."

Silence.

Where was he on a Saturday at four o'clock in the afternoon? Even if he had decided to go to his office, surely he wouldn't be working this late.

"Tilly?" Honor called, carrying her suitcase into the parlor and setting it down.

No answer.

She paused and listened for a footstep, a door closing, a voice. Nothing. Absolute silence filled the apartment.

Frowning, Honor went into the kitchen, for that was where she usually found Tilly, preparing the evening meal. She scowled when she found nothing but unwashed dishes in the sink, for Tilly was too conscientious to neglect her duties. The maid had obviously left quickly.

"Where have they gone?" Honor muttered to herself, heading for her bedchamber.

She stepped through the open door and stopped cold. Every drawer of Robert's bureau had been pulled open and emptied, the top stripped bare of the brushes and combs he kept there. Honor's heart raced. She walked slowly into the room, fighting to make sense of this. She stopped when she noticed the open armoire door.

His half of the armoire was empty.

Knees shaking, Honor walked around the room one more time, searching for any sign that Robert had ever been here at all, but she found not a shoe, not a shirt, not a note of explanation.

A note. Surely he had left her a note.

Honor frantically searched the bedchamber. When she found nothing, she systematically combed every other room in the apartment.

Nothing.

Returning to the parlor out of breath and in a daze, she sat down on the sofa to think.

"There has got to be a reasonable explanation."

Perhaps he had gone on another business trip for Nevada

LaRouche. If so, why had he taken all of his clothes? Why was Tilly missing?

Honor trembled as a thought too horrible to contemplate assailed her. What if Robert and Tilly had met with foul play? What if Gordon Graham had hired some thugs to kidnap and murder them in retaliation for Genevra's divorce? As much as she wanted to be rid of Robert, she didn't wish him to come to harm.

"There would be signs of a struggle," she reminded herself. "Furniture would be overturned. Clothes would not be missing."

Honor spent the next several hours talking to her neighbors. They stood in their doorways and listened out of curious or suspicious eyes. No, they hadn't heard anything out of the ordinary. No, they hadn't seen anything out of the ordinary. No, they didn't know where her husband and their maid could have gone.

The doorman, however, reported that he hadn't seen Robert in several days.

Dusk had fallen while Honor knocked on doors and asked the same desperate questions over and over, and now, as she stood in her parlor, staring out into the gathering darkness, she decided she needed some help.

Honor's heart sank when she saw that every downstairs window in the Delancy mansion blazed with light. A line of carriages waited ahead of her cab to let their passengers disembark beneath the porte cochere. Whenever the front door opened, faint strains of music poured out along with more golden light, illuminating smiling ladies in Worth gowns and dazzling jewels, and dashing men in white tie.

Growing impatient, Honor stepped down from her cab, asked the driver to wait, and walked to the front door. Party or no party, she would see Nevada LaRouche.

Ignoring the embarrassed, curious glances cast at the wrinkled, dusty traveling attire she had worn since this morning, she eased past a young woman dithering with her skirts and entered the expansive foyer that had so impressed Robert.

LaRouche, handsome in his severe black evening clothes, stood near the ballroom door conversing with several of the newest arrivals. He looked up, those remote blue eyes boring right through Honor as if she were a stranger. He did not smile. He excused himself and strode toward her.

Honor stepped back a pace, suddenly overwhelmed by the uncharacteristic coldness emanating from him.

"Good evening, Mrs. Davis," he said, a noticeable hard edge to his soft drawl. Before Honor could reply, he slipped an insistent hand beneath her elbow. "I need to talk to you. My study is this way."

Honor let him guide her down a long corridor. When they stopped at a closed door, she pulled away. "Where is Robert?"

A puzzled frown appeared between his brows. He opened the door and indicated that Honor should precede him. "I don't know. Isn't he at home, with you?"

"When I returned from Boston this afternoon," she began, entering the room where a light had been left burning, "he wasn't at the apartment." She shivered. "All of his clothes are missing, and the doorman hasn't seen him for several days."

"I think I know why." LaRouche closed the door. "Please sit down."

Honor's frayed nerves finally snapped. She balled her hands into fists and took a menacing step toward Nevada LaRouche. "I don't want to sit down! I want to know what in God's name has happened to Robert!"

His hands shot out, grasping Honor's arms with a touch that was both firm and gentle. "Easy, ma'am. I know you're worn out with worry, but if you'll just sit down, I'll try to ease your mind."

"Then you do know what's happened to him." Honor's knees buckled, and she sagged against him, feeling suddenly drained. Before she could fall, LaRouche eased her down into a corner of the leather sofa. "I just want to know what has happened to him."

She had to find Robert to tell him their marriage was over.

LaRouche sat down beside her, angling his lanky body sideways so that he faced her. "Something happened while you were away."

She looked at him. "Something to do with Robert?"

LaRouche nodded. "I had to fire him."

Honor ignored the sinking feeling in her stomach. "Why? I thought you were pleased with Robert's work."

"I was, until I caught him selling confidential information to our competitors."

"Dear God!" Honor stared at him in disbelief. "Robert? Doing something dishonest?" She laughed—a high, shaky sound, so unlike her. "That's absurd. You must be mistaken."

"I wish I was."

She shook her head. "I can't believe it. That position meant everything to him. He wouldn't risk losing it by doing something so—so underhanded."

"I couldn't believe it either when my people told me. I liked Davis and thought he was a loyal employee. We took our time investigating so as to give him the benefit of the doubt, but the evidence against him was overwhelming."

While Honor listened, LaRouche related what Robert had done. "I had no choice but to give him his walking papers."

"When?"

"Three days ago."

While Honor was in Boston.

"What did he say?"

"He denied everything at first, but we had him dead to rights. He asked for another chance." LaRouche looked away. "You understand that I can't work with a man I don't trust."

"Of course."

"He asked for a reference, but I told him I couldn't give him one. I did agree not to blackball him."

Honor knew that a man as powerful as LaRouche could

have seen to it that Robert never worked again. Filled with bitterness and shame at what her husband had done, she said, "Why didn't you?"

His blue eyes warmed with unexpected heat. "I didn't want to see you tarred with the same brush."

Honor struggled to keep her features composed and not to betray her inner turmoil. "If you didn't drive him away, why did he leave?"

"He's a proud man. Perhaps he was too ashamed to face you, or maybe he thought I'd change my mind and have him arrested." A knock on the door caused LaRouche to snap, "What is it?"

The door opened to reveal his butler. "Begging your pardon, sir, but your guests are asking for you."

"Hold the fort a little while longer." When the butler left, LaRouche said, "Will you stay? We can talk some more after my guests leave."

Honor moistened her dry lips with the tip of her tongue. "Why would you want to have anything more to do with me? After the unspeakable way my husband repaid your generosity, I'm surprised you let me through the door tonight."

LaRouche leaned back. "Now, hold on one minute, there, ma'am, I knew you couldn't have been a party to his betrayal."

His vehement assertion brought a faint blush to Honor's cheeks. "When you saw me walk in just a few minutes ago, you looked as though you wanted to escort me right out the door."

"That was because I thought you had come to plead for him, and it made me angry."

Honor didn't dare ask him why. "If I had known what my husband was doing, I would have reported him to you myself." She paused. "Wifely loyalty has its limits, Mr. LaRouche, especially when it's undeserved."

Tension danced between them. "I figured you'd feel that way."

Honor looked down at her clasped hands. "I appreciate your confidence."

"You'll stay then?"

A self-conscious hand went to her hair to find that it was beginning to come down. No wonder all the ladies had given her strange looks. "I'm not dressed for the occasion." It was as good an excuse as any.

"You look fine to me."

She ignored the warmth in his voice and rose. "I—I can't stay." She couldn't possibly accept his hospitality after what Robert had done. "I'm exhausted after my trip, and I have to be alone to sort all this out."

He had risen with her and regarded her with concern in his eyes. "You sure you'll be all right?" When Honor nodded, he said, "I can't leave my guests, but I will have my driver take you home."

"There's no need. I have a cab waiting."

Once they were back out in the foyer, now quiet and devoid of guests, LaRouche said something to his butler, who then stepped outside the front door.

Honor said, "A mere apology can't compensate for my husband's betrayal, Mr. LaRouche, but I am sorry. If he's caused any financial loss to your company, I shall do my best to repay it, though it will take a while."

"Don't talk nonsense." LaRouche startled her by taking her hand and bringing it to his lips. "It wasn't your fault."

"No, but he is my husband, and I feel his shame as acutely as if it were my own." Before LaRouche could comment, Honor bade him good-bye and left.

When she arrived at the Osborne, she discovered that Nevada LaRouche had ordered his butler to pay her cab fare.

Sitting alone in her quiet parlor in the middle of the night, Honor studied the owl Robert had carved, a symbol of happier times. She set it down. Those times were gone.

For the first time in months, she thought of Priscilla Shanks, the young Lowell woman Robert had seduced and abandoned. She wondered why she hadn't seen this major flaw in his character, his predilection to escape unpleasant situations by running away instead of facing them. She supposed she had been blinded by love.

The coward hadn't even had the decency to leave her a note. He had just bolted. Disappeared. She wasn't going to waste her time wondering where.

He had left without knowing that she was going to leave him. He had robbed her of even that pleasure.

She returned to the sofa and picked up the owl again. "Oh, yes, you loved me, all right, you craven bastard. The only person you've ever loved is yourself, and I was too blind to see it." She chucked the owl into a nearby wastebasket. Her wedding ring followed. "My eyes are wide open now."

Creaming her face before retiring and finding two white hairs among the black, Honor thought of Nevada LaRouche. She had sensed the tension in him tonight, so at odds with his usual easygoing manner. All during their conversation in his study, she'd had the impression he was keeping some strong emotion in check.

She wiped off the cream, noticing the dark circles beneath her eyes. Now that her husband no longer worked for Delancy and LaRouche, Honor wouldn't be seeing Nevada LaRouche again.

The startling thought that she would miss him sprang unbidden into her mind. He had tended her after her beating and had removed the mirrors from her room. He had celebrated her victory in the Graham divorce trial. He could have had Robert arrested for his crime, but he hadn't. Each time Honor tried to dismiss him as an unscrupulous financier, like the man who had caused her father's downfall, he redeemed himself with a selfless act of kindness. She was beginning to suspect his motives.

"What does he want from you?" she asked her reflection in the dresser mirror.

Not finding the answer, she rose and went to bed.

Honor didn't realize how much she missed Tilly until the following morning when she awoke and her daily cup of coffee wasn't forthcoming. She padded on bare feet into the kitchen, stared at the black cast-iron monster known as a stove, and decided that its mysteries were far beyond her.

After bathing and dressing, she went out to eat, since the alternative was starvation. When she returned to the Osborne, the doorman informed her that a Nevada LaRouche had called and left his card. On the back he had written, "Sorry to have missed you. Please call on me this afternoon and stay for dinner."

Still feeling ashamed of what her husband had done, she ignored LaRouche's invitation.

On Monday Honor learned the true extent of Robert's treachery when she stopped at the First Manhattan Bank before going to her office.

A clerk regretfully informed her that her husband had withdrawn all their funds and closed the account several days ago.

For the first time in Honor's life, she fainted.

Chapter 15

"You avoiding me?" The deceptively quiet drawl filled Honor's office.

She glanced up from her pile of paperwork to find Nevada LaRouche filling her office doorway. Frustration simmered just beneath his calm, steady surface like a kettle ready to boil. She nonchalantly turned her attention back to her work. "I've been very busy, and I am still very busy, so if you'll excuse me . . ."

He closed the door on Elroy's curious gaze and crossed the room to her desk. He leaned over, forcing her to look up at him. "In the last two weeks I've called at your apartment four times. Each time the doorman said you weren't home. I've invited you to dinner six times. You've declined. I've stopped by your office every morning. This is the first time you've been in." He paused. "Why are you avoiding me?"

His face was so close to hers that if Honor had leaned forward just a little, she could have kissed him. That realization made her sit back in her chair. "I haven't been avoiding you. I've been looking for a new place to live."

He gave her a curious look. "You don't like living at the Osborne?"

Honor rose and decided that lies would only lead to more questions from this maddeningly persistent man, so she swallowed her Putnam pride and said, "The Osborne is fine, but I can no longer afford it. You see, when Robert left, he took all our money with him."

The remaining one thousand dollars of Aunt Theo's wedding gift, another five hundred in legal fees that both he and Honor had earned—Robert had taken every red cent and left her with nothing.

The anger in LaRouche's eyes dimmed in sympathy for her, then flared fierce and bright. "The bastard!"

A bastard she had once loved.

"So with both the home rent and the office rent due and with Elroy's wages to be paid, I'm afraid I haven't had the time for social niceties, Mr. LaRouche."

"I can understand that." He stroked his long mustache and cleared his throat. "I know you're a proud woman, ma'am, but I'd be more than happy to stake you until you get on your feet. Just a loan, you understand."

An embarrassed warmth flooded Honor's cheeks. "I appreciate the offer, but my aunt in Boston has sent me enough to tide me over, and as soon as several clients pay their bills, I'll be solvent again."

"Then will you have dinner with me?"

Honor's gaze slid back to her desk. "I don't think that would be wise."

"Why not?" He frowned thoughtfully. "If I have done something to offend you, tell me right now and let's clear the air."

Her head came up and she stared at him. "You've done nothing to offend me. If anything, you've always been too generous." She rose, walked over to the window, and stared down at the pedestrians hanging on to their hats and leaning into the brisk October wind as it heedlessly whistled down Broadway. Now was as good a time as any to tell him.

"There's something you should know," she said. "When I was in Boston, I decided to leave my husband."

He said nothing for what seemed like an eternity. Finally he cleared his throat. "I'm sorry to hear that." But he didn't sound sorry or even surprised.

Honor turned and smiled wanly. "Unfortunately he beat

me to it. However, in the eyes of the law, I am still a married woman. Even though I feel less and less married with each passing day, I don't think it would be . . . seemly for me to be seen in the company of a bachelor gentleman like you. I have to guard my reputation. People would talk, and I might lose clients."

"I hadn't thought of that. Well, I wouldn't want to be the cause of your losing clients, but there's no harm in two friends sharing a meal, is there?"

So he considered her a friend. "No, but—"

"Mrs. Davis, please don't turn me down again." He crossed the room to stand before her. "I haven't enjoyed an intelligent woman's company as much as yours since my Sybilla died and the doc left for England." He bowed his head and added softly, "I find that I sorely miss it."

The pain and loneliness in his bald admission caught her by surprise. She wasn't prepared for the warm rush of sympathy. She forgot that he had helped the Delancys to break the law and had no doubt broken countless laws himself. She ignored the fact that he had patronized a brothel called Ivory's and kept a mistress named Lillie Troy. She overlooked her own wariness of him. All she saw standing before her was a proud, lonely man begging for her company.

What could be the harm? With Robert gone, she filled every second of her evenings with work to stave off her own loneliness. Yet there always came that time between activity and sleep when it stood before her, demanding to be acknowledged.

"Very well," she said, wondering why the room suddenly felt too warm. "I will accept a friend's dinner invitation."

He raised his head and stared at her as if he couldn't believe she had finally agreed. "Delmonico's?"

She shook her head. "Too many lawyers dine there."

"Sherry's?" he said, mentioning another popular restaurant.

She wrinkled her nose in distaste.

"The Waldorf?" The hotel renowned for its Peacock

Alley, where New York's Four Hundred strutted on public display.

"Much too public."

LaRouche grew very still. "If you want someplace private, that leaves Delancy's."

Nevada's home. Dining alone with him in his home. By eliminating the other possibilities, she had all but suggested it herself and he knew it.

Honor Elliott Davis, you must be out of your mind. "Delancy's it is. For dinner and conversation." Nothing else. He would surely understand that.

"Dinner and conversation." He bowed his head slightly with a certain courtly grace. "I'll have my carriage call for you at half past six." The remoteness in his eyes failed to hide the glimmer of anticipation.

"I'll be ready."

Her contract with the devil signed and sealed, Honor wished him a good day and watched him stride out of her office, pausing to smile at her before he left.

Honor, resplendent in a new dinner gown of emerald velvet that provided a dramatic and stunning foil for her earbobs, found Nevada LaRouche waiting beneath the mansion's porte cochere to hand her down from the carriage. The moment his strong, lean fingers closed over her gloved hand, Honor realized that she should not have come tonight.

"Quickly!" LaRouche said, suppressing a shiver as a gust of chilly autumn air elbowed its way between the carriage and the front door. He ushered Honor into the warm foyer, where he removed her black velvet cape as impersonally as a butler. She made some banal comment about the coolness of the evening to hide her growing unease.

He, however, remained as polished as silver. He bowed, flicked an appreciative glance at her dress and said, "Pretty," without heat or innuendo. Before she had a chance to thank him, he slipped his hand beneath her elbow. "We'll have supper in the library."

Honor's heart sank. The thought of a mile-long mahogany dining room table and elaborate centerpieces separating them held a certain appeal.

The small table set for two stood before the library fireplace where logs crackled and burned, more to create a reassuring coziness than to ward off the chill. Amid the precise arrangement of china, silver, and crystal stood not an elaborate pyramid of pears for Honor to hide behind but a simple vase artlessly stuffed with bright golden marigolds. The flowers reminded her of that spring day in the Public Garden when Robert had picked tulips for her and won her heart.

Overcome with emotion, she fought back tears as LaRouche held her chair for her. "The flowers are lovely."

"They're from the little garden out back," he replied, tugging on the bellpull. He didn't need to say that he had picked them himself, yanking them out of the ground with a man's impatience and lack of finesse. "I've never been one for hothouse flowers. Seems unnatural seeing roses in the fall and winter."

He took his seat and ran one finger up and down the stem of his crystal wineglass as if searching for something to say. "Your practice seems to be doing real well."

"I've gotten half a dozen new clients since the Grahams' divorce," she replied. "Success does breed success."

There came a discreet knock, followed by the butler and a footman bearing a soup tureen. While the footman ladled fragrant, steaming soup and the butler poured white wine for the master's approval, Honor sat quietly and wondered why LaRouche suddenly made her feel like a doe being stalked by a wolf.

She scoffed at her own analogy. She was not a frightened, quivering deer but a strong-willed woman rarely intimidated by men. Then why did she suddenly perceive this man as threatening? He certainly gave her no cause to feel that way. Tonight he embodied politeness.

Her host pronounced the wine perfect and indicated to the butler that he should pour Honor a glass. Their duties completed, the servants discreetly disappeared, and LaRouche said, "I don't know why he does that. The wine always tastes fine to me."

Most of the men Honor knew would have died before appearing unsophisticated, but not Nevada LaRouche. She said, "It's customary."

He raised his glass in a toast. "To strange customs and your success."

She clinked her glass against his. "To yours as well." She sipped the wine, savoring the fruity bouquet and crisp, light taste.

He picked up his soup spoon. "The chef makes a real good oxtail soup."

Honor tasted the rich beef broth. "Delicious."

They ate in silence. As Honor sipped her soup and wine, a pleasant, contented warmth enveloped her. Surrounded by hundreds of books that smelled richly of paper and morocco leather bindings, listening to the logs snap and hiss as a shower of sparks flew up the chimney, tasting such delicious food and drink, she felt cosseted. Pampered. Soothed. She suppressed a smile.

His sharp eyes missed nothing. "What is it?"

"I'm afraid I'm not the stimulating company you expected tonight."

"It's early yet. We haven't even finished the soup." He grinned disarmingly and leaned toward her. "By the time we reach the roast beef, I expect we'll be talking each other's ears off."

Honor laughed, the wine emboldening her to say, "You've always struck me as a man of few words, Mr. LaRouche."

He put one elbow on the table and leaned closer. "I've never seen much point to talking when you have nothing to say."

Oh, you are very eloquent, Honor thought, but you speak with your body rather than words. "In that case, you'd make a terrible lawyer."

"I suspect so, ma'am." He wiped his lips with his napkin and said out of the blue, "The name's Nevada, by the way."

Whether the fire or the wine caused her cheeks to grow warm, Honor couldn't tell. "I'll call you Nevada if you'll stop calling me ma'am. It makes me sound like a—a schoolmarm."

His eyes danced with mirth. "You're not like any schoolmarm I've ever known . . . Honor."

The sound of her name on his lips brought another flush of warmth to her face, and she turned her attention back to finishing her soup. Her lawyerly composure was fast deserting her tonight.

When the butler and footman answered their master's next summons, they bore large ramekins filled with sherried lobster. When they left, LaRouche said, "I've never been to Boston. What's it like?"

Honor spent the next fifteen minutes drawing comparisons between the Hub of New England and New York City. LaRouche listened intently, interrupting her to ask intelligent questions about the city long after they finished their fish course. Finally the butler interrupted them with dishes of lemon ice to clear their palates.

"You lived there with your aunt?" LaRouche said.

"Yes. Theodate Putnam Tree," Honor replied, giving her aunt's name a certain proper Bostonian imperiousness. Then she smiled. "Despite her name, Aunt Theo is quite unconventional. She collects French paintings of the Impressionist school, terrorizes Boston in her motorcar, and once took a young lover."

The minute she realized what she had said, her hand flew to her mouth in horror and she turned crimson. "I'm so sorry," she muttered, looking over at the fire, down at her lemon ice, anywhere but at the man seated across from her. "I didn't mean to say that. Do forgive me. It's the wine."

He didn't embarrass her further by catching her eye or smirking. "I'd like to meet your aunt Theodate one day. She sounds like a most unusual lady." Then he went over to the bellpull to give Honor time to compose herself.

When the main course was served and the butler was

about to pour the burgundy, LaRouche said, "No wine for Mrs. Davis, Winston."

Honor stared at him, surprised by his uncharacteristic display of masculine presumption.

The moment the servants left, LaRouche said, "You can cuss at me all you want, but it won't do any good. I never serve spirits to women who can't hold their liquor."

Her annoyance dissipated like smoke. Mollified, she regarded him with a grudging respect. "I know far too many men who would have let me drink myself senseless." And taken advantage of her afterward.

"I don't know why. Can't converse with a senseless woman."

After taking a bite of the delicious rare roast beef, Honor said, "I've committed the cardinal sin of monopolizing the conversation. Now it's your turn to tell me about yourself."

Wariness flickered in the depths of his eyes. "Not much to tell."

Honor grinned. "You don't like talking about yourself, do you? Well, that's too bad. You'll just have to humor me."

His mustache twitched, and he smiled almost shyly. "As I said, there's not much to tell."

"You're too modest. Were you born in Nevada?"

He nodded.

Honor leaned forward, bursting with curiosity. "Where? In a mining town? On a ranch?"

"I was born in a Virginia City whorehouse."

Her fork stopped halfway to her mouth. Surely she had misunderstood. "I beg your pardon?"

He repeated himself, never taking his eyes off her, daring her to look away.

She set down her fork and stared at him for what seemed like an eternity. "I—I don't know what to say."

Again that diffident shrug. "My mother was a dance hall girl who sold herself to whoever was willing to pay." His gaze didn't flinch. "She was a whore. Life dealt her a bad hand, and that's how she survived. I never held it against her, but that's what she was. I didn't know my father."

"I can imagine you had an . . . unusual upbringing."

A faint smile touched his mouth. "You could say that. I learned a whole lot about women and even more about the mindless cruelty of men." His smile died, and a faraway look glazed his eyes as if he were looking back into a turbulent, troubled past.

Sitting there quietly, Honor envisioned him as a little boy always seeing too much, hearing too much, and learning things that only a grown man should know, and her heart went out to him.

"Honor?"

The sound of her name brought her back to the present. She found Nevada LaRouche regarding her with a frown of concern.

"I didn't mean to make you feel bad," he said. "I should have spared your feelings."

She reached across the table and placed her hand on his. "I asked you to tell me about yourself, and you did. I much prefer the truth to a falsehood, however well intentioned." She took her hand away. "Where is your mother now?"

"Dead."

"I'm sorry."

"No need. It happened a long time ago."

She didn't dare ask how his mother had died. "How old were you?"

He sipped his wine. "Twelve. After the funeral, one of my mother's best customers, a local rancher, took me in and taught me everything he knew about ranching because I was Chantal's son and I reckon he had loved her in his fashion. When I turned sixteen, I took off on my own."

"Sixteen." Still more boy than man. "How did you survive?"

"By using my wits and my hands." He stroked the stem of his wineglass. "Sometimes my gun."

What had he said to her that foggy morning at Coppermine, that he had broken more than one law in his lifetime?

She took a deep, shuddering breath, for the four walls

suddenly closed in on her. She had to know. "Did you ever kill anyone?"

He placed both hands palms down on the table as if daring her to find blood on them. "Only when I had to." His shoulders tensed. Did he expect her to recoil in disgust or slap his face or denounce him as a murderer?

She envisioned the little boy he had once been, raised among loose women and rough men. "You'd better eat," she said softly. "Your food will get cold."

The clock on the mantel chimed midnight. In the fireplace only glowing embers remained. The servants had cleared the table long ago, then discreetly retired for the night.

Honor sat too close to Nevada on the sofa as he sipped his brandy, her velvet skirt covering part of his leg. The lateness of the hour and the hushed, shadowed library lulled her into soft conversation and shared confidences.

Nevada had just finished telling her how he first met Damon Delancy, who had saved him from three men intent on shooting him and stealing his horse.

"So he saved your life, and you became friends," she said.

"More like brothers." He stared into the depths of his brandy glass. "He took me under his wing and made me his partner. Taught me everything he knew."

She brushed an errant lock of hair away from her cheek. "You know so much about commerce now. Have you ever thought of starting your own company?"

"Can't say that I have. I make all the money I could need or want working with Delancy." He gave her a quick self-deprecating smile. "I reckon one of my biggest faults is that I lack ambition."

"Don't!" Her vehemence made the word ricochet through the hushed room like a shot. She placed a hand on his arm. "Don't you dare think of it as a fault! You're a strong, steadfast man whom people can depend on. If you hadn't been there after I was beaten, I—" She stopped. Her hand fell away, and she sat back.

"What about your husband?" he said softly, his eyes shadowed.

Honor rose and turned her back so he wouldn't see her tears. "He had enough ambition for ten men, but I could never depend on him." Rows of book spines swam and danced before her eyes. "Robert and I may have been married, but we were not . . . not . . ." She groped helplessly for the right word.

"Mated?"

The animalistic word evoked an image of two loping wolves silhouetted against the vast, endless night sky. "Yes," she said, "we never . . . mated. Our spirits never connected. Whenever I really needed him, I always found myself alone." She shivered. "And it made me angry."

She didn't hear Nevada rise. She felt a warning rush of air against her back just a second before his warm hands rested lightly on her bare shoulders. He said nothing, demanded nothing.

Not this, she thought. Not with this unlikely man.

Honor turned, her heart thudding so loud she feared he could hear it in the surrounding stillness. His hands resettled on her shoulders with a gentle persistence. Suddenly unsure, she raised her gaze no higher than his white tie, still loosened. When he whispered her name, she looked up into the eyes of a stranger.

The remoteness had vanished, unmistakable desire now smoldering in its place. Honor had never seen cool blue eyes turn so hot, and she felt the heat both weaken and strengthen her. She wanted to run. She wanted to stay and burn.

His hands slid down her arm in a light, questioning caress. She could feel him holding back, sense the tension stretching taut within his lanky frame. He watched and waited.

With a soft sigh of surrender, Honor went to him and felt herself tenderly enfolded in his embrace. He fit her to his lean, hard body, holding her close in the circle of his arm while he tucked her head against his shoulder.

Steadfast, she thought, inhaling the faint spruce scent of

his shaving soap mingled with freshly starched linen and clean male skin. She slid one arm around his waist while he took her other hand and held it against his heart.

She closed her eyes. Her pain eased. Her loneliness vanished.

Nevada stirred. He placed his fingers beneath her chin so he could tilt her face upward. Honor opened her eyes, then let her gaze drift down to his mouth, half hidden by his mustache. She stood on tiptoe and parted her lips in blatant invitation.

Nevada accepted with alacrity. The moment he covered her mouth deftly with his own, his warm, hard lips tasting sweetly of brandy and desire, Honor's blood ignited. Her hand slid up to cradle his hard, warm cheek. He moaned deep in his throat at her touch, and kissed her harder.

Suddenly he stiffened and broke the kiss, but still held Honor in his arms. "Shouldn't do this," he whispered raggedly, his cheek pressed to hers.

She moved back to look at him. "Because I'm married?"

"I'm not in the habit of taking another man's woman. It's not right."

Honor stepped away and crossed her arms, daring him to trespass. "I'll have you know that I am not for anyone's taking, Mr. LaRouche."

He stared at her in keen silent appraisal. "I can see that. Either you give yourself to a man or he doesn't get you at all."

"Exactly. In the eyes of the law, Robert and I are still married and will remain so until I can divorce him, but I no longer regard myself as married." A bittersweet smile touched her mouth. "I know I should feel some regret that my marriage has failed, but I'm too angry with myself for having used such poor judgment in marrying him in the first place."

"We all do things we later regret." LaRouche stirred. "What if he comes back?"

"I don't think he will. For all his bravado, he's a coward. He couldn't face me after what he had done. When my maid

Tilly came to collect her back pay, she said that Robert just left and told her to find a new position because he was leaving me and I wouldn't be able to afford to pay her wages. Can you blame me for never wanting to see him again?"

"Can't say that I can."

"He even wanted me to lie for him." She told LaRouche about the night of the Foggs' dinner party and how Robert had wanted her to keep her profession a secret.

"You took the blame yourself so your husband wouldn't look bad?" When Honor nodded, he muttered, "I thought your story was full of holes. You're not the kind of woman who hides her accomplishments."

"Not when I've worked so hard for them."

Honor shivered, and not from the room's sudden chill. Discussing Robert had conjured him up like an unwelcome guest sitting in the corner, spoiling the rest of the evening for her. "It's late, and I have to be at the office early tomorrow. Perhaps you'd better take me home."

"Only if you agree to have dinner with me again," he said, catching her hand.

If I accept, there will be no turning back, she thought. She smiled. "I'd like that."

Honor missed him the moment she locked her apartment door and the emptiness closed in on her once again.

She undressed, creamed her face, and slipped into bed, but found that sleep eluded her. She rose and returned to the parlor, where she sat in a corner of the sofa, hugging her knees and thinking of Nevada LaRouche.

Her growing attraction to the man astonished her, especially since every instinct warned her to put a thick, high wall between them. He wasn't her kind. He broke the very laws she had sworn to uphold. He probably engaged in questionable business practices, like the man who had destroyed her father.

He also disdained hothouse flowers and guilelessly confessed he lacked ambition, not realizing that his contentment with himself was even more attractive. He refused to let her drink too much and made her heart ache for the child raised in a brothel.

Steadfast, she had called him. Strong. Dependable.

He was the kind of man who could capture her heart if she wasn't careful.

She saw him every day after that. He called at her office, took her riding in Central Park on Sunday afternoons, and even arranged to have her move to smaller quarters in an apartment hotel that provided meals in a dining hall and maid service, so she didn't miss Tilly. If Honor didn't have paperwork to do at home in the evenings, she joined him for dinner several times a week. They talked for hours as if they had known each other all their lives. Afterward they shared sweet kisses. That was all.

She found herself looking forward to their times together.

Then came the raw, rainy fourth of November that Honor would never forget.

That afternoon she stood at her office window staring glumly at the flat gray sky and the driving sheets of slanting water. Below her a sea of black umbrellas bobbed and wove as pedestrians scrambled for shelter in the nearest doorway.

Behind her she heard her office door open. "Don't you believe in knock—" The remonstrance died when she turned and saw Nevada standing there.

Water plastered his fair hair to his skull and dripped off the ends of his mustache. Just one look at his ashen face and dazed expression, and Honor knew his world had come to an end.

"What's happened?" She went to him and grasped his hands, wet and ice cold. "Tell me."

He said nothing, just looked at her helplessly and shuddered. She wrapped her arms around him and drew him close. He clung to her so tightly she feared he'd crack her ribs.

"Tell me," she murmured, rubbing his back with sure,

steady strokes, suddenly afraid for him. He was soaked to the skin. What news could be so terrible that it had sent him rushing headlong into the cold and rain without an overcoat or hat?

"Let's get this off before you catch your death," she said, stepping back and removing his frock coat while he stood there, silent and shivering. Honor took her warm woolen cape from the rack and flung it around his shoulders, then made him sit down. She stroked his wet hair and saw the devastation in his bright, red-rimmed eyes. "Say something, please. You're frightening me."

He took a deep breath and forced out the words between his chattering teeth. "The Delancys' son is dead."

"Oh, dear God." Honor pulled him against her and held him, returning the strength he had so often offered her. She knew that the Delancys' son, William, had been a baby when they fled to England, so how old was he now? Three? Four? Poor Catherine. Poor Damon. Honor's eyes filled with tears. "My poor Nevada."

She held him until his shudders subsided. Then she released him and knelt beside his chair. "I'm so, so sorry," she said, grasping his hands. "How . . ."

"Cholera. I just got the cable. Sorry to barge in on you, but I didn't know where else to go."

She touched his cheek, still wet with either rain or tears. "I'm glad you came to me."

He sighed deeply and cradled his head in his hands. "I only remember little Wild Bill as a baby, so I suppose I'm grieving for Delancy and the doc all alone in a strange country, with no kin to share their grief."

Honor placed one reassuring hand on his shoulder. "They have each other, and they know your prayers are with them."

Nevada said nothing, just stared into space, his thoughts in a place that Honor couldn't reach. She knelt beside him quietly, comforting him with her silent presence. Finally he gave one deep, heartfelt sigh, flung off the cape, and helped Honor to her feet.

"I need to go to Coppermine for a few days," he said, retrieving his wet frock coat and preparing to leave.

"You shouldn't be alone at a time like this." She took a deep breath. "May I come with you?"

He raised his brows, his surprised gaze boring into hers. "Much as I would appreciate the company, what about your reputation? There won't be any other guests there this time, just old Mr. and Mrs. May, the winter caretakers."

Honor knew that to spend a weekend in the country with a bachelor gentleman and a houseful of other guests was perfectly acceptable, but to go off alone with a man amounted to an illicit tryst. "I understand that, and I would still like to come."

He grew very still and eyed her as warily as a hawk. "You're sure?"

Unspoken between them glimmered the tacit understanding that if she went with him, they would become lovers. "I'm sure."

Nevada kissed her swiftly, his lips cold. "I would welcome your company."

That was all he said. He wouldn't ask her to go.

Honor went over to the window and tugged at her locket as she looked out at the pouring rain. She turned to face him. "Can we leave this afternoon?"

"What about your clients?"

"I have no appointments for several days. If there are any emergencies, Elroy can refer my clients to another lawyer."

His cool eyes burned. "Just let me send a telegram to the Mays to let them know when to expect us, and we'll be off."

CHAPTER 16

THEY ARRIVED AT COPPERMINE after dark, in the pouring rain.

Once inside the atrium, Nevada removed Honor's damp cape and handed it to Mrs. May while her husband shuffled off with their bags.

Nevada took off his own coat and gloves, rubbing his hands together to warm them. "It's cool in here," he said to Honor. "Shall we have a sherry in the library?"

"My shoes are soaked through, and my skirt is wet," she replied, shaking it out to avoid catching his eye. "I'd like to go to my room and change."

"Of course." He turned to Mrs. May. "I know I don't need to ask if our rooms are ready."

"They were readied the minute we learned you were coming, sir."

"I can always count on you, Mrs. May." He placed his hand beneath Honor's elbow and guided her upstairs, stopping in front of a closed door. Honor noticed that this was not the same room that she and Robert had occupied.

Nevada opened the door and stepped back. "My room is right next door."

Honor didn't comment or even look at him. She entered the room and closed the door. A freshly trimmed lamp burning dimly on the nightstand revealed what she hoped to find, a connecting door.

She closed her eyes and took several deep, calming

breaths. Oh, Honor, she thought, I hope he wants you as much as you want him.

She searched her heart and realized that this was more than a case of mere wanting. She loved him. She hadn't expected to fall in love with him, but she had, and now that love justified her presence here.

On the bed her suitcase waited like Pandora's box.

He knew she would come to him tonight.

He had known ever since that brief electrifying moment in her office when she asked if she could join him, ostensibly to share his grief. Behind that most innocent of motives, he had recognized the decisive air of a woman finally embracing the inevitable.

He knelt on one knee before the fire to put on another log. He listened to the rain beating against the roof and the November wind moaning through the trees. He shivered, but not from the cold, for his room was warm and cozy. For her comfort.

The women he'd known had taught him that lovemaking was more than knowing when and where and how to touch a woman. Gentleness and caring were as important as filling the hollows in a woman's heart, even if just for the night.

He jabbed at the logs with the poker. Grief had left a few hollows in his own heart that needed filling.

Nevada stared at the connecting door. What was taking her so long? What if he had misread her and she was down in the library waiting for him and that sherry?

Above the roaring rain, he heard the unmistakable sound of a doorknob turning. The connecting door opened. His heart gave a queer little lurch at the sight of her.

Honor's thick, lustrous hair, usually pinned up so demurely, cascaded wild and free down over her shoulders to her breasts. Spellbinding black eyes held a potent mixture of defiance, anticipation, and a nervous fear of the unknown.

Nevada rose, stepped forward, then extended a hand in wordless invitation.

Honor closed the connecting door and crossed the room

in a soft rustle of blue silk. She solemnly placed her hand in his, her long delicate fingers ice cold.

He rubbed warmth into them as he stared into the dark depths of her eyes. "You don't have to do this."

"But I want to." Her gaze shifted to the bed. "Unless you don't."

"I wouldn't have agreed to let you come here if I didn't." He cleared his throat. "If you're worried about conceiving a child—"

"I—I've already taken care of that possibility," she said, blushing to the roots of her hair.

"Good." He knew unresolved issues hung between them, but desire overrode caution. He simply couldn't resist. He drew her into his arms, reveling in the uncorseted, yielding softness of her through the smooth, cool silk of the tea gown she wore. He sought her mouth with his own.

She entwined her arms around his neck and pulled him even closer, parting her lips in sweet surrender. He teased her tongue with his own, tasting her, and felt her tremble with delight, while her soft rose scent evoked images of spring and renewal.

His head spinning, his body aching and taut with desire, Nevada broke their kiss just long enough to push the hair away from her face, where several wild strands had gotten caught against her lips.

"Black-eyed witch." He kissed her again, feeling her smile against his mouth, and strained the bonds of his self-control almost to the breaking point. He tested her resolve by stroking her breast, raising the nipple through the silk with an erotic flick of his thumb. Her smile died and she moaned deep in her throat, but did not pull away, giving him her tacit permission to continue.

Though the bed beckoned from the far side of the room, Nevada ignored it, tossed some pillows from a nearby chair onto the floor, and pulled Honor down beside him in front of the fireplace. Tucking the pillows beneath her head and fanning her glorious hair about her, he propped himself up on one elbow and stared down at her, feeling himself go gloriously hard. He wanted to give her pleasure such as she had never known. He wanted her to will him her soul.

He kissed her forehead, her eyelids, then her mouth again, while undoing the tiny pearl buttons running down the front of her tea gown.

To his surprise and delight, she opened the gown herself, offering him a gift of her bare breasts. No corset or chemise impeded his ardor. Honor's eyes closed, her lips parted, and she arched her back in invitation.

He caressed her breasts tenderly, watching her expressive face. She struggled and cried out, a gratifying sound of feminine torment and mounting excitement.

When he moved away, her eyes flew open and he saw both need and desire. It was time. He rose, unbuttoning his shirt with trembling fingers. He looked down at her lying among the scattered pillows like a tantalizing newly opened gift on Christmas morning, in a tangle of pale blue silk, with her dainty bare feet and slender ankles exposed.

He grinned. "If the gentlemen of the jury could see you now . . ."

Honor grabbed a pillow and flung it at him. "I would win every case."

"You surely would." He removed his shirt and watched her carefully as he unfastened his trousers.

Honor could not tear her eyes away. His shirt came off to reveal a hard, lean torso, lighter than Robert's physique, but roped with muscle. And scarred. She counted five scars—two round, puckered bullet holes and three knife slashes. Instead of fascinating Honor, as they had Lillie Troy, the scars angered her.

She rose and stared at the long, raised white slash just beneath his rib cage, her eyes dampening. "That someone would dare to hurt you . . . I'm appalled."

He caught her hands and held them tightly. "They don't hurt anymore. They belong to my past. Different time, different place, different man. So don't cry over them."

She smiled and nodded. When Nevada released her hands to remove his trousers, she shrugged out of her tea gown. It slid down her naked body to the floor in a beguiling whisper of silk.

His sharp gasp of surprise pleased and excited her, as did his lean, powerful body and proud, insistent arousal. He drew her into his arms, hot skin touching hot skin, hardness against softness. Honor tucked her head against his neck, holding him. He smelled deliciously of woodsmoke and male arousal.

I'm going to make love to a man who is not my husband, she thought. I am committing adultery, so why don't I feel ashamed?

Because I do love him. I don't know how or why it happened. I don't even know if he loves me in return or just desires me. For tonight I don't care.

Nevada swung her into his arms and carried her to the bed, where the light from the fireplace barely reached the dark corners. He set her down gently on the cool, smooth sheets and slid in beside her.

He kissed her, then trailed his lips down her throat and breasts, all the while stroking her rounded hip and long thigh with light teasing fingers. Her breathing grew more ragged, and she moaned at his touch, but made no effort to return his caresses.

How odd, he thought, that a married woman . . .

He paused, suddenly afraid. What if her husband had mistreated her in their marriage bed, turning her cold and unresponsive?

He propped himself up on one elbow and stared down at her. "Does my body repulse you?"

"Repulse me? Of course not. I—I think it's beautiful."

He guided her hand to his chest. "Then touch it."

"You like being touched?"

"You seem surprised. I like it just fine."

She turned her head away. "Robert never wanted me to touch him . . . that way."

Nevada grew very still. "Never?"

"Never. I—I thought all men disliked being touched intimately."

Few things penetrated his calm and drove him to rage. He

fought against it to no avail. He couldn't speak. He released her hand and sat up, jabbing his fingers through his hair. "God damn him! If I had his good-for-nothing neck between my hands right now, I'd—" He calmed down and placed his hand on Honor's shoulder. "I don't know what kind of twisted game he was playing with you, but most men like to be touched that way."

"Oh." Honor stared down at the sheets for a moment, then looked up at him. "In that case, you're really the first man I will love."

Her touch was shy and tentative, and she watched him warily for the slightest sign of displeasure. His eyes darkened and glazed with passion when she touched him here. He bit his lip when she touched him there. The moment she felt his body tense helplessly beneath her hand, Honor's reserve fell away and she finally relished the feminine power she had never known as Robert's wife.

Time stood still as they pleasured each other relentlessly. They never noticed the rain drumming harder against the roof, the fire dying, and the room growing cool.

Almost delirious with wanting and need, Nevada possessed her, fitting her as perfectly as if he had always been her lover. He moved slowly at first, holding himself back, bringing her just to the brink of ecstasy time after time.

"Please!" she finally begged, on the verge of madness, her nails raking his shoulders in painful supplication.

Her need made him lose control, and he rocked faster and deeper against her. Finally he felt her whole body shudder as she cried out his name. Then his own climax hit him like a tornado, swirling him upward, and then letting him float back to earth.

He sighed in satisfaction and drew her against him, still intimately joined, then pulled the covers over them to ward off the night, and slept.

During the night they awoke and made love again.

The rain had finally stopped, and now the thin gray light of dawn flooded the room through the curtains they had forgotten to draw last night. The fire had died long ago, but Honor felt snug and warm in his wide bed, the musky scent of their lovemaking still clinging to their bodies.

Now she knew what she had been missing as Robert's wife. By never allowing her to physically love him in return, he had kept her at arm's length. Oh, he'd made it appear that her pleasure alone was his sole unselfish concern, but now she understood that he derived a twisted satisfaction from thwarting her attempts at intimacy.

She had known only half a marriage.

Honor rolled onto her side and studied Nevada. He lay on his back, still asleep, one arm flung across his forehead. The arm was lean but strong, the wristbones prominent and finely sculpted. She thought of how tightly and securely that arm had held her last night, and smiled.

My lover, she thought.

She lifted the covers to take a naughty peek at the rest of him. He lay sprawled across the sheets in rangy masculine display, as sleek as a racehorse. Honor's gaze traveled down his flat belly and narrow hips, and back up his body.

She nuzzled Nevada's cheek until he opened his eyes and smiled the sensual, lazy smile that made her feel all warm and fluttery inside. "Did I please you?" she whispered, already knowing the answer, but needing to hear this laconic man say it.

He pushed the hair away from her face. "You pleased me so much," he said, "I'm never letting you out of my bed."

She giggled. "Never?"

"Never, so get used to it."

Never had a man wanted her so badly. Bursting to know more about him, Honor stroked his shoulder and said, "How old were you when you first slept with a woman?"

"You think of the damnedest questions to ask a man at the damnedest times." He kissed the tip of her nose. "Not until I was fifteen. Surprised? Just because I lived in a whore-house doesn't mean I spent every waking hour rutting like a stallion. My mother's friends all knew enough to keep their hands off me. When she died and I later became a paying customer, that was different."

"My, oh, my, they did teach you well, Mr. LaRouche."

He grinned. "Not meaning to brag, but they used to say I was their best student."

"I can't argue with that." Eyes shining with mischief, Honor said, in her best imitation of Nevada's soft drawl, "Why'd your mother name you Nevada? Why not New Mexico or Colorado?"

He gave her an exasperated look. "She didn't. Nevada isn't my real name."

"What is it? You can trust me. I won't tell a soul."

He raised one brow. "Trust a lawyer?"

Honor lightly punched his shoulder. "I resent that slur upon my profession. I'll have you know I'm extremely trustworthy, so tell me your real name." When he hesitated, she said, "I'll tell you my nickname in law school if you tell me your real name."

He grinned. "You first."

"The men used to call me Steel Stays Elliott behind my back."

His smile died. "Not a very flattering nickname."

"I took it as a compliment."

He stared at her as if he didn't believe her. Finally he said, "I know I'm going to regret this, but it's Clovis."

"Clovis? That's your real name? Clovis?"

"A moniker to be proud of, isn't it?"

Honor tried to control herself. The corners of her mouth twitched with the superhuman effort. Her shoulders started shaking, and without warning, she burst into whoops of laughter. "N-no wonder you changed it!"

He narrowed his eyes in mock affront. "A man's name is no laughing matter, woman."

Honor roared helplessly, clutching her aching sides. "It is when it's so funny. Cl-clovis . . . I've never heard such a ridiculous name in all my life."

He gave a long-suffering sigh. "I guess I'll just have to teach you some respect."

He reached for her, kissing her laughing mouth and fondling her sweet body until her laughter dwindled into an appropriately respectful silence.

Later, nestled against his shoulder, Honor said, "What was Dr. Wolcott like?"

Nevada wondered why women always waited until they got a man into bed and turned his brains to mash with their loving before asking such questions. Perhaps because a man was more apt to let down his guard and tell them the truth.

"She was a lot like you."

"Really? In what respect?"

"She was intelligent and strong-willed, unlike many other women. Very feminine. Liked to wear pretty clothes. Passionate about helping people. She didn't suffer fools gladly, either." He grinned. "And, like you, she realized what a splendid fellow I am."

Honor yanked on his chest hair. "Conceited oaf." She paused. "How are we different?"

"Well, she was fair, with pretty blond hair and green eyes. You're more serious. Sybilla used to make up her own swearwords. You had to be a doctor to know what they meant, but they sounded funny when she said them just the same. And she had this skeleton from medical school that she named Bonette. Hung it in her office and treated it like a pet cat or dog."

Honor smiled. "A skeleton named Bonette . . . that is funny." Her smile died. "I wish I had known her."

"You would have liked each other."

"If she's anything like me, we would have fought over you."

Nevada rolled over on his side so he could face her. "Sybilla's gone. A part of me will always love her, but you've gone a long way toward filling the hole in my heart. I'm not with you because you remind me of her."

"I wouldn't be here with you if I thought I was a replacement for another woman," she said softly. "I also want you to know that I'm not here with you just because my husband left me and I'm lonely."

He ran his fingers down her arm in a gentle caress. "What will you do now? Divorce him?"

She smiled ruefully. "I'd have to find him first."

"You don't know where he's gone?"

She shrugged helplessly. "I haven't a clue."

"Maybe he went home to be with his kin. Where's he from?"

"Maine, but I doubt if he'd return there. His parents are both dead, and he sold their family farm a while back. He lived in Lowell, Massachusetts, for a time, but I doubt if he'd go back there, either, because of the scandal." While Nevada listened, she told him the tragic story of Priscilla Shanks.

He just shook his head. "No offense, but he's not an honorable man, your husband."

"No," she agreed softly, "not an honorable man at all."

Nevada pulled the covers closer about them. "So you won't be free of him until you find out where he is and serve him with legal papers stating your intention to divorce him."

"That's how the law works, but I won't be able to do that until my financial situation improves. I also have no grounds."

"Grounds?"

"Legal reasons for divorcing." Honor told him why she had no grounds for divorce. She smiled ruefully. "After tonight he has grounds to divorce me, but he'd never want the world to know his wife slept with another man. So I guess I'll remain married whether I want to or not."

"That's a kind of slavery."

She shrugged. "It's the law."

He slipped his hand behind her neck and pulled her toward him for a kiss, a plan to free her beginning to form in his mind.

After a late breakfast, Honor and Nevada strolled arm in arm through the grounds, following a path high on the cliff overlooking the Hudson River.

Honor looked over at Nevada's sharp profile and touched his arm. "Feel better today?"

He placed his hand on hers, resting in the crook of his arm. "I do, thanks to you."

Honor ignored the wet leaves clinging to her skirt hem. "It's terrible for a parent to lose a child, but for its mother to be a doctor and not be able to save him . . ."

"The doc always was the philosophical sort. She said that death is a part of life, but a child's death always hit her doubly hard because the child's promise would never be fulfilled." His eyes grew hard and bright. "Now death has claimed her own little boy."

Honor sought to distract him. "Why did she become a doctor, then?"

"Sybilla once told me that when Catherine's ma gave birth, the doctor in charge left her too soon because he was in a hurry to get to a social engagement. Catherine's ma started bleeding, and they couldn't stop it. She bled to death. As she grew up, all Catherine could think about was becoming a doctor so other women wouldn't die so senselessly."

Honor thought of her father. "I can understand that."

Nevada glanced at her. "You became a lawyer because of what happened to your father."

She took a deep breath, her eyes brimming with tears. She couldn't keep her terrible secret locked inside any longer. "I'm to blame for his death."

Nevada stopped in the middle of the path and turned to her. "What did you say?"

"I—it was my fault." The words tumbled out, faster and faster. "He wanted to play chess with me on the night of the murder, but I was furious with him about some inconsequential childhood slight, and I refused. So he went to that man's house instead, and you know the rest." She stared at Nevada. "Don't you see? If I had only played chess with him that night, he'd still be alive."

Nevada grabbed her shoulders. "You don't know that."

She bobbed her head. "But I do. The murderers were counting on him being there."

Nevada wrapped her in his arms and held her close, his cheek pressed against hers. "Maybe he would have gone there anyway after your chess game, or maybe he would have stopped playing to keep his appointment. Did you ever think of that?"

Honor pulled away. "When I grew older, I realized that what you say is true. My father would have stopped playing chess to keep his appointment. It was his destiny. But somehow the child inside me still blames herself."

Nevada grasped her shoulders again, giving them a little shake. "It's easy to look back and see what you should have done. If I had thrown out the drunken cowboy who was my mother's last customer, he wouldn't have cut her throat."

So that was how his mother had died. Honor shivered. "Did you blame yourself?"

His expression grew bleak. "'Course I did. Even after the law caught the sidewinder who killed her."

"What happened to him?"

"They tried him, found him guilty, and hanged him. Actually, they let me slap his horse's rump, so you could say that I hanged him. Then I put the incident behind me and moved on." He stroked her cheeks with his thumbs. "Did you ever tell anybody—your mother, your aunt—you felt this way?"

Honor shook her head. "My mother was so devastated by what had happened that I couldn't bring myself to tell her I thought I could have prevented it. I feared she wouldn't love me anymore."

"Honor, that's a terrible burden for anyone to bear alone. It must have torn you up inside."

She told him about her recurring dream. Trying to describe her father going to the gallows made her stumble over the words. They came faster and faster, tumbling out of her as she described her own helpless terror and impotence, and the black chessmen scattered in the snow, mute reminders of her own culpability.

When she finished, uncontrollable sobs of acceptance and release shook her shoulders, and tears streamed down her face. The harder she cried, the lighter her omnipresent burden became.

"Let it go," Nevada murmured, taking her in his arms and holding her until she had no more tears to shed. "Just let it go."

She envisioned the prison yard. The gallows was gone. Her father smiled at her before his image faded, then vanished.

It's not my fault, she thought. I'm really not to blame for my father's death.

Dream snow melted in a blaze of warm, healing sunlight. The chess pieces disappeared. The walls of the prison crumbled, and when Honor opened her eyes, she was standing on the riverbank, held safe in Nevada's arms.

They separated. She gave him a shaky, wondrous smile. "I feel as though the weight of the world has been lifted from my shoulders. Strange. I hadn't felt like telling anyone—until now."

His brows rose in surprise. "Not even your husband?"

"Especially Robert." Honor stared out across the river to the steeply sloping opposite bank. "I think I feared he would dismiss it as trivial."

Nevada gave her a curious look. "Then why tell me?"

Her gaze fell to his cravat. "I don't really know. I must trust you."

His lips brushed her forehead in silent thanks.

A wry smile touched her mouth. "It's ironic. I remember facing you in these very woods the first time I came to Coppermine and brazenly insisting that I didn't trust you."

"You had your reasons."

"Foolish ones. All of them."

His expression turned serious. He took her face in his hands, holding her fast so she couldn't evade him. "That day in the woods I told you that I'd broken laws, done things I'm not proud of. Are you telling me that you don't hold that part of my past against me?"

"I can't," she replied. "You're not the same man you were then."

He looked skeptical, but released her and searched through his pockets. "I've got something for you."

"For me?"

He took her hand, turned it palm up, and placed a small envelope there.

When Honor opened the packet and saw what was inside, she smiled. "Nevada LaRouche . . . a chain for my locket." Her first gift from her lover, a gift from the heart. She dangled it from her fingers so the thick, sturdy gold links gleamed in the sun. "It's beautiful."

He smiled. "This chain won't break like the others."

Honor kissed him too quickly to be aroused. "Strong and solid. Just like you." She opened her cape, removed the locket, and replaced its cord with the chain.

"Allow me," he said. He took the locket and slipped it over her head.

She gave it an experimental tug. "It should withstand any abuse."

He slid his arms around her waist and pulled her against him so he could kiss her.

Honor wrapped her arms around his neck and molded her body against his, trying to feel him through her thick woolen cape, her shirtwaist, her damned confining corset. In the cold morning air his mouth burned hers. Desire shrieked through her blood.

Honor pulled away, breathless. "Shall we go back to the house?"

A teasing smile warmed his eyes. "I thought you wanted to go for a walk."

"It's too cold."

"Then let's go inside where it's warmer."

A week after returning from Coppermine, Honor stopped at Nevada's office on her way to court. She had something important to ask him, and she didn't know how he would react to her request.

Kept waiting by Miss Fields, who said that Mr. LaRouche was in a meeting, Honor tried to remain nonchalant, but her thoughts kept turning to Nevada behind that thick oak door. What would he say when she asked him?

She stirred. What was taking him so long?

Fifteen minutes later his office door finally opened and several men filed out, each glancing at her. When the last man closed the door behind him, Miss Fields rose from behind her typewriter and went into Nevada's office to announce Honor.

"Send Mrs. Davis in," Honor heard him say through the open door, "and don't disturb me for any reason."

"Mr. LaRouche will see you now," Miss Fields said.

Honor rose and went inside. She barely had time to close the door before Nevada grabbed her, bent her head back, and plundered her mouth with ruthless abandon.

Laughing, she pushed him away. "Please. I'm due in court. What will the judge and jury think if I arrive looking as though I've just come from your bed?"

He glanced at his desk, his eyes gleaming wickedly, his intention plain.

Honor recoiled in panic. "You wouldn't!"

"Don't tempt me." He kissed her again. "Will you come to the house tonight? Or shall I come to your apartment?"

She sighed regretfully. "I have too much work to do tonight. And you're so distracting."

He stroked his mustache and sighed. "How about tomorrow night?"

"I'll make sure I'm free." She tugged on her locket with its sturdy new chain. "I'll be going to Boston to spend Thanksgiving with my aunt. She has invited you also."

He looked at her, plainly surprised. "You want me to meet your aunt?"

She nodded and held her breath.

"Why would she want to meet me?"

"She's dying of curiosity about the man who has been so kind to me," she replied. The man who saved her life after the beating. The man who offered a strong shoulder after Robert deserted her.

"It's an important occasion when a woman takes a man to meet her family," he said softly. "Means she has strong feelings for him."

Honor's heart raced at the look in his eyes. Suddenly overcome with doubt, she stepped back and turned away so she would have time to compose herself if he refused. "If you don't want to go, I'll understand."

Nevada placed his hands on her shoulders and whispered in her ear, "That would depend on exactly how strong your feelings are."

Honor smiled. "Very, very strong." Regaining her confidence, she turned to face him with a defiant toss of her head. "I wouldn't be sharing your bed if they weren't, now, would I?"

"No, ma'am." A devilish twinkle danced in his eyes. "Will your aunt put us in separate bedrooms?"

"Of course. She may be unconventional, but she wouldn't want to shock the servants. Once everyone is asleep, you could"—she ran one fingertip across his lower lip—"visit me."

He grasped her hands and brought them to his lips. "How can I resist such an invitation?" When he released her, he said, "Did you think I'd refuse?"

"For a minute or two," she admitted. "I can see it was foolish of me to doubt you. You've never disappointed me."

"And I never will."

She kissed him on the cheek and stepped back. "I really have to get to the courthouse before the judge finds me in contempt."

She bade him good-bye and left.

Once alone in his office, Nevada sat at his desk and stared at the closed door. He could still smell the faintest trace of her rose scent clinging to his collar. Still feel her, soft and warm in his arms.

He realized the significance of her invitation only too well, and it pleased him mightily. But why had she thought he would refuse to accompany her? Was she still so uncertain of him?

He was determined to find out.

CHAPTER 17

THE TALL, NARROW HOUSE in Boston reminded Nevada of New York's brownstones. Like the rest of this cradle of American civilization, it radiated an air of unostentatious dignity and gentility.

Old money, he thought. Money so old it's grown whiskers.

A light, leisurely snow had been falling since they arrived at the train station in Delancy's private railway car, and now it dusted the steep steps. Standing there with Honor on his arm, Nevada shivered, but not from the cold. He rarely cared what other people thought of him, but he desperately wanted the approval of Honor's aunt.

"Nervous?" Honor whispered, squeezing his arm. Snowflakes clung to her black fur collar, and several melted on her lower lip.

He cleared his throat. "Why should I be nervous? I'm only going into your home to meet the woman who took you in." Suddenly he felt like a Clovis, gauche and bumbling, with hay sticking to his shoes.

Honor's eyes gleamed with amusement. "Are you telling me that the brave Nevada LaRouche, who has stared death in the face more times than he can count, is afraid to meet a harmless woman?"

"If she's anything like you, she's not harmless."

She kissed his cheek. "Oh, stop fretting, Clovis. She's not

an ogre. She'll love you." Honor pulled at his arm, guiding him inexorably to his doom.

He assisted her up the steps, steadying her so she wouldn't slip on the slick snow. When they reached the top, before he had a chance to ring the bell, the front door swung open to reveal not the butler but a regal, beautiful woman who looked too young to sport that upswept coif of shocking white hair.

"Sweet Portia!" the woman shrieked with delight, opening her arms wide, unmindful that the November air swirling about them was too cold for her light silk tea gown.

"Aunt Theo!" Honor flung herself into her aunt's arms for a lingering hug while Nevada stood watching them in silence and wondering why Honor's aunt called her Portia.

When they parted, Theodate Tree regarded him with a mixture of curiosity and interest. "And you must be Nevada."

At least she hadn't called him Mr. LaRouche, surely a good sign. He tipped his tall silk hat. "Yes, ma'am."

She smiled warmly. "I'm Honor's aunt Theo." She took his hand in both of hers and pulled him through the doorway. "Come inside before you catch your death."

The foyer was perhaps one-quarter the size of the one in Delancy's mansion and lacked a marble floor, but its elegant simplicity made Nevada feel welcome. He especially admired the bowl filled with branches heavy with small bright orange berries.

"Did you have a good trip?" Theo asked as Honor unbuttoned her coat.

Honor gave Nevada a mischievous look. "We came by train in Nevada's private railway car."

"Delancy's private railway car," he corrected her.

Now the butler made his appearance to exchange warm greetings with Honor and take their coats.

Theo said, "Let's go into the parlor, shall we?"

Once upstairs, Honor looked around the parlor at all the new paintings Theo had acquired and said, "You certainly have been busy in my absence, Aunt Theo. You have so many paintings one can hardly see the wallpaper."

"My friends tell me that if I keep on going the way I am, I'll have enough paintings to open my own museum."

Honor gave all the paintings a cursory glance, but stopped at the one hanging over the fireplace. "What a lovely painting!"

Theo's eyes sparkled with pleasure. "I just received it two weeks ago."

Nevada stepped forward to admire the portrait of Theodate Tree. "It's by John Singer Sargent, isn't it?"

Two pair of eyes regarded him with unabashed astonishment.

Theo recovered first. "Honor didn't tell me you were knowledgeable about art."

"I don't know a thing about art," he replied with a self-deprecating smile. "I've seen other portraits by Sargent, and I've always liked the way he captures a woman's spirit as well as her likeness, that's all."

Theo beamed. "That is exactly why I adore him myself."

"As you can see," Honor said, "art is Aunt Theo's passion. Don't encourage her, or she'll go on for hours and show you every painting she's ever collected."

Theo gave an indignant sniff. "I resent your implication that I bore my guests with my passion." She paused, studied Nevada for another agonizing second, then nodded. "Nevada, would you like a beer?"

She caught him by surprise, but he recovered quickly. "Bourbon, if you have any."

"Indeed I do," Theo said, going over to the bell pull to summon the butler. "My late husband was a bourbon man. Honor, I suppose you want tea?"

"Of course."

Though Nevada shared Theodate Tree's appreciation of Sargent's work, he still sensed that the woman disapproved of him.

He had an uneasy feeling that before this holiday was

over, he and Honor's beloved aunt were headed for a showdown.

It came sooner than he expected.

That evening the three of them were sitting in the upstairs parlor after dinner when Theo rose. "Honor, would you mind taking Mrs. Jameson one of the pumpkin pies that Cook baked for Thanksgiving? She always asks for you, and I think she'd enjoy the company." Theo smiled at Nevada. "Mrs. Jameson is an elderly woman who lives next door and doesn't have many callers. Surely you wouldn't mind keeping me company while Honor dashes off for a few minutes, would you?"

"Of course not." Out of the corner of his eye, he saw Honor roll her eyes at the obviousness of her aunt's ploy.

Theo beamed. "I knew you were an understanding man the moment I met you. Off with you, sweet Portia, on your errand of mercy."

"Anything to brighten someone's holiday," Honor muttered, casting an apologetic glance at Nevada before rising and leaving for her call.

When Nevada and Theo were alone, he said, "That's right neighborly of you, to cheer an old lady."

She smiled coolly. "The pumpkin pie was merely an excuse to leave us alone, as I'm sure you're well aware."

"The thought had occurred to me." He rose and went to stand by the fireplace. "I think you wanted to get me alone so you could talk to me about my intentions toward your niece."

"First I'd like you to tell me about yourself." Before Nevada could reply, Theo added, "Honor told me about your background when she was last here. I want to know what kind of man you are."

Now he knew how Honor's father must have felt facing the gallows. He took a deep breath. "I like to think of myself as a decent man, Mrs. Tree, trustworthy and loyal to my friends. I'm more successful than some, less successful than others. I would never hurt your niece or ask her to lie for me."

Theodate Tree drummed her restless fingers against the arm of her chair and sat in silence as if collecting her thoughts. "Honor is a bright, strong-willed young woman who has chosen an unconventional path in life. Are you able to handle the challenge of such a woman?"

He thought of Sybilla. "Yes."

"I've been told Honor is a good lawyer."

"She's still green, but I've heard she shows promise."

"Even as a child she was always very level-headed and clear-thinking." Theo rose to stand behind her chair. "Unfortunately, she's as emotional and soft-hearted as any other woman when it comes to love and men."

Nevada grew still. "I'm not Robert Davis, Mrs. Tree."

"That is very reassuring. She is as dear to me as the daughter I never had, and I would hate to see her make another mistake in judgment." She took a deep breath. "Honor's told you what happened to her father and to the man who brought about his downfall?"

"She has. And I can understand your mistrust of wealthy men involved in commerce."

She looked around the room. "I have nothing against wealth or commerce. I wouldn't be living a life of privilege and ease in such elegant surroundings if it hadn't been for my husband's vast wealth. It's dishonesty that I abhor. Many financiers are ruthless and don't care who gets trodden beneath their heels as long as they profit."

Nevada stirred uneasily. Damon Delancy wasn't called the Wolf of Wall Street for nothing. He could be ruthless when the occasion demanded. Would Theodate Tree consider Nevada guilty by association?

Honor's aunt said, "If you are not an honest man, Nevada, you and Honor will never suit. Her husband expected her to lie and compromise her values so that he could profit. He fooled us with his false sincerity and underdog charm, but I will not be fooled again."

"It's not my intention to fool anybody." Wasn't it? He had

never dared tell a soul the truth about August Talmadge, the banker who had murdered Sybilla.

Theo walked over to him. "Honor told me how you cared for her after she was beaten and what you did to the man responsible. For that alone I'll be forever in your debt."

"I just did what needed doing, ma'am."

"No, you did more than that." She moved about the room in a feminine rustle of silk. "Tell me, has Honor received any word from her no-account husband?"

"Not a word. He just vanished without a trace."

"So she can't divorce him?"

"Not until he's found."

Her black eyes flashed. "He is beneath contempt for such cowardice. Honor will never be free of that—that albatross around her neck."

"Maybe not"—he looked at her—"but I've hired a Pinkerton detective to search for Davis. I haven't told Honor because I don't want to get her hopes up."

Theodate Tree's brows rose. "A Pinkerton detective . . . You must be very fond of my niece to incur such an expense."

"I am right fond of her."

She smiled with genuine warmth for the first time since they had begun their discussion. "I can see that you are." She extended her hand. "I must admit that I had reservations about you, but you've laid my misgivings to rest."

He took her hand and bowed over it. "I'm relieved to hear you say that, Mrs. Tree."

"Theo, please."

He smiled. "As I was saying, Theo, I couldn't live with myself if I caused a rift between Honor and her kin."

"You needn't worry about that. I can see that you're an honest, decent upstanding young man."

Nevada shifted uneasily. Would she still think so if she knew the truth about the night August Talmadge died?

By the soft light of the lamp on the nightstand, Honor waited impatiently in her bedroom, her gaze trained on the door. The clock on the mantel chimed midnight, reminding her that they had all retired an hour ago and Nevada still hadn't come to her.

What was keeping him?

She sat up in bed, hugged her knees, and wiggled her toes. Perhaps his personal code of honor restrained him from making love to her beneath her aunt's roof. She smiled and flung back the covers. In that case, she would have to go to him.

No sooner did her bare feet touch the floor than the doorknob slowly turned. She rose, one hand held against her racing heart. The door opened just wide enough for her lover to slide through, then he shut it quietly behind him.

Honor stood there poised at her bedside, studying him. His blue wool robe was loosely belted at the waist, revealing a tantalizing expanse of chest, and he was barefoot, all the better to move with silence and stealth down the hall. In the dim lamplight, Nevada's blue eyes blazed with a desire matched by Honor's own.

They moved together with the impatience of lovers too long denied, meeting in the center of the room in a tangle of limbs.

Honor entwined her arms around Nevada's neck and pressed her body tightly against his, resenting even the barriers of silk and wool. "I thought you weren't coming," she murmured between kisses.

He sifted his fingers through her hair, his gaze roving over her face. "I wanted to make sure everyone was asleep."

She slid her hand beneath his robe, caressing his chest until he shuddered. "I feared you were having second thoughts about making love to me in my aunt's house."

He grinned. "Some men would, but I want you too badly."

Honor ignited at his arousing touch. She pulled back, but only long enough to strip off her peignoir, then allowed Nevada a few seconds to stare his fill before she grasped both his hands and drew them to her breasts.

He caressed her until she groaned. "Not so loud," he whispered, "or you'll wake someone."

Honor stifled a shuddering gasp as his fingers tormented her with consummate skill. She wanted to scream in glorious abandon, but the prospect of discovery paradoxically deterred and aroused her even more. When Honor's knees finally buckled under the strain of restraint, Nevada lifted her effortlessly into his arms and strode over to the bed. He set her down gently, shrugged off his robe, and slid in beside her.

She kissed him hungrily, her hands stroking and tickling, reveling in the masculine textures of rough hair and hard muscle covered by smooth skin. Except for deep, ragged breathing, Nevada manfully made not a sound until Honor's hand closed over his aroused flesh.

"Hush," she said with a mischievous smile, "or you'll wake someone."

"You do try a man's patience, woman," he muttered between clenched teeth before his mouth closed over hers, and he covered her body with his own.

Honor's last coherent thought before she succumbed to her rising passion was that she had slept in this bed as a child, and now she was making love in it as a woman.

Later, when they both lay sated and spent, Honor whispered, "What did my aunt have to say to you when I went to Mrs. Jameson's?"

Nevada rolled over and propped his head on his hand. "She wanted to make sure I wasn't a no-good varmint like your husband."

Honor suppressed a smile. "You evidently succeeded in convincing her. I noticed the way she kept beaming at you for the rest of the evening."

"That's because we reached an understanding."

Honor stroked his smooth cheek. "I'm delighted to hear it. I wanted her to approve of you."

"And if she didn't?"

Her fingers sought her missing locket. "She would force me to choose between you, and she would lose."

He brushed her cheek with his fingertips. "You were skittish about asking me here. Why? Were you afraid she wouldn't accept me?"

Honor's mouth went dry, and she suddenly felt chilled. "No. I was afraid you'd think me too forward and refuse my invitation."

A puzzled frown appeared between his brows. "Too forward? Why would I think that?"

Honor turned her head away, focusing on the fireplace concealed deep in shadow on the other side of the room. Why could she be so eloquent on behalf of a client, yet have so much difficulty expressing herself in matters of the heart? Finally, she said, "I'm afraid I'm hopelessly in love with you, Nevada LaRouche."

His mustache twitched with his smile. "Took you long enough to admit it, but I've always known."

"You have?"

"I grew up with women who could make love to a man without loving him, but you're not that kind. You wouldn't welcome a man into your bed unless you loved him. I figured you wouldn't have come to Coppermine that weekend if you didn't love me."

But what about his feelings for her? A man who had once patronized a brothel and kept a mistress could obviously make love to a woman without loving her in return. Honor shivered.

"Cold?" Nevada drew her against his own body to warm her and held her tightly. "I never thought I'd ever love another woman after Sybilla. But I sure do love you, Honor Davis, and that's the God's honest truth."

Relief and happiness lightened Honor's heart and she hugged him with a fierce possessiveness. "Even if I'll have white hair before I'm forty, and everyone will think I'm your mother?"

He grinned. "Even if you have white hair. But no one will ever mistake you for my mother." He trailed his fingers down her arm. "I've been meaning to ask you, why does your aunt call you Portia?"

"Portia was a lady lawyer in a famous Shakespearean play called *The Merchant of Venice*."

"Never read any Shakespeare."

She kissed him. "It doesn't matter. You have other

attributes." Suddenly she grew serious. "I felt awkward asking you here because I was afraid that you didn't love me in return. I didn't want you to think that I was trying to force you to love me."

"I don't have to be forced to love you."

"That sets my mind at ease."

"Sometimes it's hard for me to put my feelings into words." He flung back the covers, letting his gaze rove over Honor's naked body. "It's easier for me to show you what's on my mind."

Much to Honor's delight, he was most eloquent.

Later, when Nevada returned to his own room, he found sleep eluded him despite the lateness of the hour.

Theo's words kept echoing through his mind. "If you are not an honest man, Mr. LaRouche, you and my niece will never suit."

How could he declare his love for Honor and accept hers in return without being totally honest with her? She knew about August Talmadge's death, but like everyone else, she thought it had been an accident. Nevada had said nothing to disabuse her of that notion.

He rose and walked over to the window, flung back the curtains, and stared into the dark street below where not a soul stirred except a tomcat skulking in the shadows. Should he tell her the truth about that night? He could imagine the shock on her lovely face and the disgust that would fill her dark eyes. Whatever love she felt for him would surely die.

Nevada rubbed his jaw. No, there was plenty of time for the truth later, when her love grew and bound her tighter to him and he could make her understand. He returned to bed and slept a deep sleep unencumbered by dreams.

Although Honor and Nevada invited Aunt Theo to New York City for Christmas, she declined, so Honor spent Christmas Day with Nevada.

They exchanged gifts in the parlor.

When Nevada handed Honor a box so small that it could

only hold a ring, her heart sank. She opened it with trembling fingers to find a ring set with a square-cut emerald surrounded by sparkling diamonds. "Just like my earbobs," she said, her eyes brimming with tears. Robert hadn't been able to give her a betrothal or a wedding ring.

"I know you're not free," Nevada said in his soft drawl, "but I got you this ring to wear until that day comes."

He slipped it on the third finger of her right hand, and she kissed him. "Until the day I'm free."

Her gift to him was large and heavy, requiring the strength of a footman to convey it to the parlor.

"Now what could this be?" Nevada mused, tearing away the wrapping paper to reveal a two-foot-high bronze statue of a cowboy astride a galloping horse whose speed raised the brim of the cowboy's hat and plastered his shirt to his wiry body.

"A cowboy for a cowboy," Honor said softly. "It's by Frederic Remington. Aunt Theo found it for me."

Nevada ran his fingertips down the smooth black finish as he gazed at the statue in awe. "You can almost hear the hoofbeats and feel the wind whipping the tears from the rider's eyes."

"You like it, then?"

He took her hands in his. "Clovis LaRouche has never received such a fine gift, and he thanks you from the bottom of his heart."

Later, after a sumptuous Christmas dinner, they sat quietly in the parlor before a roaring fire.

Honor looked at him. "You're unusually quiet." And sad, she thought.

"I was just thinking about the Delancys."

She entwined her fingers in his. "It must be a terrible time for them, alone with their grief in a strange country. I remember the first Christmas after my father was hanged. We didn't decorate the house or have a tree or exchange gifts, though he was the kind of man who would have wanted us to go on. Every time I heard passersby wish each other a merry Christmas, I wanted to run outside and beat them for being so insensitive to my loss."

He squeezed her hand. "My mother wasn't one for keeping Christmas. She used to ask why she should celebrate the birth of a God who had forgotten her. But she always saw to it that I had some little present to open come Christmas morning. After she died, I never felt quite the same about Christmas. I guess loss takes off the shine."

Honor stared into the dancing flames. She thought of her first Christmas with Robert, when their love still had that shine. She thought of the owl he had carved, and how it symbolized the selflessness of his love. She looked down at the costly ring Nevada had given her, realizing that it meant more to her not because of its cost, but because the sentiment behind it was genuine.

Nevada stroked the nape of her neck. "What are you thinking about?"

"Robert. I was just wondering how he spent Christmas and if he regrets what he's done." When Nevada's hand fell away and he looked hurt, Honor added, "And if I knew where he was, I'd go there and serve him with divorce papers myself."

"For a minute there, I thought you were pining for him."

Honor brought his hand to her cheek. "Don't be silly. You're the only man I love."

"Hard to believe I'm so lucky."

"I'm the lucky one." She stared into the flames. "I felt so sorry for Aunt Theo when we saw her at Thanksgiving. She misses Wes so much and tries to numb the pain by acquiring paintings."

"She's trying to fill the hole in her heart, but she hasn't learned that you can't fill it with things. Only people."

She looked at him. "How did you become so wise?"

"Keeping company with smart lady lawyers."

He rose and poured two glasses of champagne. When he returned to the divan, he handed one to Honor and raised his glass in a toast. "To Catherine and Damon Delancy, and all our friends and loved ones who can't be here with us tonight."

Honor raised her glass and took a sip. "Do you think they'll ever come back?"

"And risk going to jail?" He stroked his mustache. "Damon left the country to save the doc. I can't see him returning and risk losing her."

They rose and went to the window to watch snow begin to fall, neither realizing that the coming of spring would prove Nevada wrong.

One Tuesday morning in late March of 1897, Honor stopped at Nevada's office on her way to court. She found him seated at his desk, staring so intently at something in his hand that he failed to notice her hesitating in the doorway.

"Am I disturbing you?" she said. "Miss Fields wasn't at her desk."

He looked up and rose. "I'm always glad to see you." But his eyes lacked their usual welcome, and he sounded preoccupied.

Almost wistful, Honor thought.

She closed the door behind her and took a few tentative steps into the room. "Are you sure?"

He gave her an exasperated look and rounded his desk purposefully. "Don't be silly. Of course I am." After kissing her swiftly, he held the item he had been studying out to her. "I was just looking at this old photograph of Sybilla and Bonette."

He had never showed her a picture of Sybilla.

Honor felt an unmistakable twinge of jealousy as she studied the lovely blond woman with the mischievous sparkle in her eyes. "She's very beautiful."

"Yes, she was."

Was. Honor reminded herself that Sybilla was dead and part of his past.

"And Bonette is"—she smiled—"too thin."

He grinned, took back the photograph, and put it away in his desk drawer. Then he pulled her into his arms and kissed her again, slowly, thoroughly, possessively, as if to reassure her and burn away any lingering jealousy she might feel.

A knock on the door interrupted their stolen interlude. Honor stepped away, her face flushed with guilt, and smoothed her shirtwaist as if Nevada's embrace were imprinted there for the world to see.

When Nevada bade the intruder enter, the efficient Miss Fields sailed through the door and stared at Honor reproachfully for not waiting outside. "A cablegram from Mr. Delancy." She handed it to her boss and sailed right back out again.

"Excuse me," Nevada said, opening the envelope and reading the cablegram. His eyes widened, he rocked back on his heels, and swore.

"It's not more bad news, is it?" Honor said. "Don't tell me that something has happened to Catherine or Damon now."

He handed her the cablegram. "Read it for yourself."

Honor read: "Both coming home April 12. Delancy."

She looked over at Nevada. "Why? I thought their reason for leaving was to keep Catherine out of prison. Surely they know they'll be arrested the moment they set foot in New York City."

"I don't rightly know why. Maybe they've decided to risk a trial. What are their chances of getting off the hook?"

Honor handed back the cablegram. "It's hard to say. First of all, they'll need a good lawyer. Second, you have to consider the climate of the times. People don't fear Anthony Comstock the way they used to. If anything, he's become a figure of ridicule. He's been losing more cases than he wins. That could work in Catherine's favor." She shook her head. "Still, a misdemeanor can carry a prison sentence and now they'll both be facing additional charges for fleeing the country."

"Such as?"

"Catherine will be charged with jumping bail, and Damon with helping her, unless their lawyer can persuade the district attorney to drop those charges. Even if he did drop them, I'm sure Catherine would still have to stand trial for her initial crime of violating the Comstock Act."

Nevada grew somber. "I don't think living in England suited them. I know Delancy misses Wall Street and with their little boy gone now, I guess they've decided to risk coming home."

Honor placed a hand on his arm. "Do you think Catherine would let me defend her? I'd give anything to argue such a controversial case."

He stroked his mustache. "She might agree to it, but I think Delancy will want someone with more experience."

Honor felt her excitement rising. "I could do it, Nevada, I know I could. Misdemeanors are tried in the Court of Special Sessions before three justices. There is no jury. The district attorney and the defense counsel don't even make opening or closing statements. They call character witnesses and cross-examine. Even the Graham divorce case was more difficult."

"But if you lost, the doc could still go to prison."

Honor nodded reluctantly. "There is that chance."

Nevada placed his hands lightly on her shoulders. "You can offer to represent Catherine, but don't get your hopes up. Delancy will do anything in his power to free his wife. Don't be disappointed if he wants someone with more experience."

"I'll keep that in mind."

He smiled, his eyes warm with anticipation. "I can't wait for you to meet Delancy and the doc. I know you're all going to get along just fine."

Honor had to find some way to convince Damon Delancy to let her represent his wife.

Chapter 18

"There they are," Nevada said, his usually calm drawl edged with excitement. "They made it."

He and Honor had arrived at the South Street Seaport just fifteen minutes ago and spent the time searching the long line of docked ships for any sign of Damon Delancy's seaworthy steam yacht, the *Copper Queen*. Now that they had found the vessel almost hidden between two ocean liners, Honor watched a man and a woman dressed in the unrelieved black of mourning walk down the gangplank, arms locked and heads held high, presenting a united front against a hostile world.

Honor took a deep breath to quell her fluttering insides. For Nevada's sake as well as her own, she prayed that she would like the Delancys and that they would like her.

Damon Delancy captured Honor's attention at once. A tall, broad-shouldered man who moved with the confidence and grace of a conqueror who owned the world, he scanned the crowded dock with contempt and defiance, as if daring policemen to come forward and arrest him.

Honor's heart sank when she realized that he reminded her of the arrogant man who had ruined her father.

When the Delancys reached the foot of the gangplank, Honor turned her attention to Catherine. She saw a woman of average height and ordinary looks, her chestnut hair cut in a fashionable curly fringe across her forehead. Though

Catherine's oval face appeared tired and sad, her pale blue eyes sparkled with inquisitiveness.

By Honor's side, Nevada called, "Delancy!" and waved. Then he broke into a face-splitting grin and strode forward, drawing Honor along with him.

"LaRouche!" Delancy called back in a deep, rough voice, a smile lighting up his handsome but saturnine features.

Nevada released Honor's arm so he could embrace his friend with a quick thump on the back. "Christ, it's good to see you again."

When they parted, Delancy's gray eyes roved over his friend in swift appraisal. "Still got the boots, I see, but where are the spurs and the Stetson?"

Nevada stroked his mustache. "I put them away in the attic. Thought it was high time I stopped being a cowboy and became a respectable businessman."

Delancy raised his brows and shook his dark head in disbelief.

Spurs and a Stetson? Honor thought. I didn't know Nevada ever wore spurs and a Stetson.

But the Delancys did.

Catherine smiled at Honor and extended her hand. "I'm Catherine Delancy. You must be Honor Davis."

Honor held her breath, waiting for a judgmental look that would tell her Catherine had compared her to Sybilla and found her lacking. She saw only warm approval.

Studying Catherine, Honor recognized in her the same resoluteness she herself possessed, an air of invincibility one acquired from always fighting against the winds of convention.

Honor liked her immediately. She shook hands and returned the smile. "The pleasure is all mine, Dr. Delancy. Nevada has told me so much about you."

"All of it true," Nevada said, hugging Catherine. "It's good to see you again, Doc."

When Catherine pulled away, tears brightened her eyes, and her lower lip trembled with the effort of maintaining her composure. "It's wonderful to see you, too, Nevada, but I wish we had returned under more pleasant circumstances."

His smile died and he grasped her hands. "Nearly broke my heart to hear about little Wild Bill."

Catherine closed her eyes and nodded wordlessly, a furrow of grief forming across her brow. Then she pulled herself together and turned to Honor. "This is my husband, Damon."

Damon stepped forward, his sharp eyes raking Honor over from hair to hem, assessing her. "Mrs. Davis, it's a pleasure. I've never met a lady lawyer before. Are you any good?"

Honor bristled at his challenging tone, but before she could utter a word, Nevada slipped his arm around her waist and faced his friend. "'Course she is."

Delancy shrugged. "I meant no offense."

Catherine gave him a reproachful look. "You must forgive my husband, Honor. He tends to be outspoken."

Something unspoken passed between the Delancys and Nevada, leaving Honor feeling excluded from their shared history.

Damon scanned the dock. "Where are the police? I expected them to be waiting for us the minute we stepped on shore."

"I'm sure the Harbor Police spotted you the moment your yacht arrived, and you'll be arrested as you go through customs," Honor said, tugging at her locket.

"Then what will happen to us?" Delancy demanded. He was obviously a man who took control of every situation and wanted to know his options.

"Since it's after four o'clock and no magistrates are holding court to set your bail, you'll have to spend the night in jail. Tomorrow morning you'll appear before a magistrate for a bail hearing. I can try to get you out on bail, if you like."

Delancy scowled at her. "Try? What do you mean, try? I don't want to rot in the Tombs. I want us free on bail, is that clear?"

Honor fought down her rising temper and reminded

herself that these were Nevada's friends. "What you want is immaterial. The magistrate will decide whether you remain in jail or are freed on bail. Since you have already fled the country once, he may fear that you'll run again and deny you bail."

Delancy glared at her out of gray eyes quick to go cold. He did not like being thwarted. "That's absurd. We wouldn't have come back if we planned to leave again."

"I will point that out at your hearing, but I can't guarantee the magistrate will accept that argument."

"If that's the case, I'd just as soon return to my ship and get out of here while the getting's good."

Catherine placed a hand on his arm. "Please, Damon. Before we left London, you agreed that we would accept the consequences of returning no matter what they were."

He touched her cheek, his eyes warming with love for her. "I'm having second thoughts. We left New York to keep you out of prison, and I didn't return just to put you there. You're not a criminal."

Catherine turned to Honor. "What will they do to Damon?"

"He's an accessory. He'll be tried separately."

Damon said, "If I'm convicted, how long will I spend in jail?"

"That will depend on the judge."

He took his wife's hand, his harsh expression softening with tenderness. "I don't care what they do to me. I just want Catherine to be free." He looked at Honor with an intensity that made her shiver. "All right. You can represent us at our bail hearing."

Catherine squeezed her husband's hand. "Let's get this over with, shall we?"

As Honor had predicted, when the Delancys went through customs, they were detained until the police came to arrest them.

Hours later, after watching the Delancys being led away to their jail cells in the Tombs, Honor and Nevada returned to the Fifth Avenue mansion.

The moment Nevada entered the library, he poured himself two fingers of bourbon and downed it in one swallow. Too preoccupied to offer Honor anything, he strode over to the fireplace and leaned heavily against the mantel.

She stared at his back, debating whether to go to him. She decided not to. Ever since the Delancys' arrival, she had sensed a profound change in Nevada. His old friends now filled his life, leaving Honor to feel like an interloper.

Don't be absurd, she chided herself. He is your lover. There will always be room in his life for you.

"Did the police really have to lead them off in handcuffs?" he muttered bitterly. "I thought Delancy was going to go hog-wild when they put them on the doc."

"I know it's humiliating, but they have to do that," she said gently.

He turned to her, his blue eyes tired and troubled. "What if their bail is denied tomorrow?"

"I don't think that will happen. After all, Catherine isn't a murderess. Despite what Anthony Comstock thinks, she poses no real threat to society, and no judge wants to lock up a woman for any length of time, especially one who has just lost her child." Honor walked over to him and placed a reassuring hand on his arm. "They did return to New York of their own volition. That should count in their favor when I see the district attorney about dropping the other charges."

"I hope so."

"Don't worry. I'll plan my strategy very carefully."

He covered her hand with his own and managed a wan smile. "I know you'll do your best."

"I may not have tried a criminal case, but I excelled in criminal law in school and assisted other lawyers when I was a clerk in Boston."

"I wasn't doubting you."

Honor took a deep breath. "I appreciate your confidence in my abilities, but I don't think your friend Delancy shares your view."

Nevada's expression changed to one of bewilderment. "What do you mean?"

"I don't think he likes me."

Instead of disputing Honor's assertion, Nevada said, "He'll come around once he gets to know you better. You have to understand that he's always been protective of the doc. When she's threatened, he gets as ornery as a sidewinder that's just been stepped on."

"Quite frankly, I found him arrogant and overbearing." The moment the words popped out of her mouth, Honor realized she should have kept her opinion of Damon Delancy to herself.

Nevada's brows rose in surprise, and he stared at Honor for what seemed like an eternity. "Are you saying you don't like him?"

Honor tugged at her locket. "He reminds me of the man who swindled my father."

He grew very still. "Delancy's not like that. He has his faults, but he's a good man."

"I'm sorry, but I can't help the way I feel."

"Damon and Catherine are more than friends. They're my family. I hoped you would like them."

And if I don't?

She shrugged helplessly. "I like Catherine, but I sense that Damon disapproves of me."

Placing his hand beneath her elbow, Nevada said, "Let's talk," and guided her over to the sofa.

Once they were seated, he turned his body so that he was facing her. "Damon is used to being the boss. I suppose I'm used to his ways, so I don't notice it." He shrugged. "That's just the way he is, and I accept it."

She stared at a row of books lining one of the shelves on the opposite wall. "I've fought against male prejudice for most of my professional life, and I resent his implication that I must somehow be incompetent because I am a female."

"He didn't mean that the way it sounded," he said gently. "His own wife's a doctor. He respects professional women."

"Perhaps he respects her profession because she is his wife and he loves her."

"You're wrong about him."

Honor smiled. "We'll see."

Nevada didn't return her smile, just stared at her as if she had turned into a stranger.

Feeling suddenly awkward, Honor rose. "I really should be going. I have to prepare for their bail hearing tomorrow." When Nevada rose, she said, "Unless you want me to stay."

"I have some things to see to before Delancy is released," he said. "Now that he's back, he'll be taking the reins of Delancy and LaRouche again."

Honor nodded. "Of course."

He walked her to the front door and dropped a kiss on her forehead. "I'll have the carriage take you home."

She managed a smile. "I'll see you in court tomorrow."

He smiled back, but his eyes remained remote. "Until then."

After handing her into the carriage, he returned to the house.

The moment Honor walked into her dark, empty apartment, she felt frustrated tears sting her eyes. She never should have told Nevada what she really thought of Damon Delancy.

She turned on the light in the sitting room and removed her coat and hat. Though Nevada hadn't said anything, she could tell that he was disturbed and disappointed by her reaction to his friend.

When Nevada had told her that the Delancys were returning, Honor had expected to fit right in and turn their close trio into a quartet. She hadn't expected to find that Damon Delancy reminded her of the man who had swindled her father. She hadn't expected that he would dislike her. It certainly made matters awkward if not downright impossible.

And what of Nevada? Though he didn't show it, he had been upset by the apparent friction between his lover and his best friend.

Honor recalled the meeting on the dock, when Nevada

had defended her to Damon. Yet tonight, when Honor offered to stay with him, he had rebuffed her with the excuse that he had to prepare for Damon's return. If Nevada chose his friends over her, there was nothing she could do about it.

Honor went to her desk and retrieved her tablet, then sat down and started planning her strategy for freeing the Delancys.

The following morning Honor faced a grim-faced magistrate at the Delancys' bail hearing.

Honor handed the magistrate a letter. "Because the Delancys returned willingly to stand trial, and because of their high standing in the community," she began, "District Attorney Rampling has agreed to drop the charges of jumping bail against Dr. Delancy, and the obstruction of justice charge against Damon Delancy. However, the previous charge against Dr. Delancy for violating the Comstock Act still stands."

The magistrate frowned as he read the letter. He sighed. "Very well. The charge against Damon Delancy is dismissed."

Honor sighed in relief.

The magistrate said, "Do you know of any reason why I should grant Dr. Delancy bail, Mrs. Davis? She left the country once before. What makes you think she won't do it again?"

"Sir," she began, "Mr. and Dr. Delancy returned to New York City of their own volition, knowing full well that they would be arrested as soon as they docked. If they intended to jump bail again, why wouldn't they just remain in England? Why return to this country at all?"

She paused and strolled around the table where the Delancys sat, watching her. She tried not to think of Nevada sitting right behind her, and how they hadn't said two words to each other before the bail hearing began.

"My clients pose no threat of flight. Dr. Delancy returned

to stand trial for the charges against her, and stand trial she will."

Honor studied the magistrate's stone face for any sign of how he might rule. Nothing. "Let us also consider the severity of the charges. Dr. Delancy is not a murderess or a thief. She has been accused of violating the Comstock Act by receiving anti-conception information through the mail, a misdemeanor, not a felony." She turned and shook her head in exaggerated bewilderment at the absurdity and insignificance of such charges. "Need I remind you that many have been released on bail despite far more serious charges."

"No, Mrs. Davis," the magistrate said with some asperity, "you don't need to remind us of anything."

"Before you deny my client bail," Honor continued, "I would also ask you to consider the great loss to society if Dr. Delancy were to be jailed until her trial."

"And what great loss to society would that be, counselor?" the magistrate said.

Honor raised her brows. "Catherine Delancy is a physician dedicated to providing free medical care for the poor. She has volunteered her services at the Women's Dispensary on the Lower East Side. She will be visiting squalid, overcrowded tenements not fit for animals, caring for women who are going to have babies, and treating their ill children—all at great risk to her own personal health and safety, I might add. Her humanitarian efforts would be lost if she were jailed for even a day."

Honor took a few steps toward the bench and spread her hands beseechingly. "And finally I appeal to your sense of compassion. Several months ago the Delancys' only child, a four-year-old son, died." She paused for effect. "Grant Dr. Delancy bail. Let her and her husband enjoy what little time they may have together."

She thanked him, sat down, and prayed.

After a minute of deliberation the magistrate said, "You have made a most convincing argument, Mrs. Davis. Bail is set at five thousand dollars." He slammed his gavel down with a crack.

Honor let out the breath she had been holding, rose, and turned to the Delancys with a gloating smile. "You're free—for now."

"I don't know how to thank you," Catherine said.

Damon extended his hand, his gray eyes cool. "You did well, but this was only a bail hearing."

"I kept you out of jail, didn't I?" Honor snapped. "Now if you'll come with me to sign some papers, we'll have you out of here as quickly as possible."

Turning to leave the courtroom, Honor saw Nevada waiting for them. His remote blue eyes rested on her in puzzlement for an instant. Then he was grinning and stepping forward to congratulate his friends while Honor stood by in silence. When they were ready to leave, she turned and headed for the door to avoid saying anything to Nevada.

She hadn't taken four steps when she felt a restraining hand on her arm. She turned to find him staring down at her.

"Good arguments," he said, his soft drawl gentle. "Thank you for keeping my friend out of jail."

His friend. "Only doing my job." She turned and resumed walking.

As they left the courtroom, a tall, heavyset man with white muttonchop whiskers and a fanatical gleam in his eyes accosted them. Honor had seen him around the courthouse often enough to recognize Anthony Comstock.

He shook his fist at Catherine, sandwiched protectively between her husband and Nevada. "So you've come back, have you, you spawn of Satan!" he bellowed, causing everyone in the hall to stop and stare. "You escaped me once, Catherine Delancy, but you won't get away with it a second time. You're going to jail where you belong."

Damon turned red and swore under his breath, but before he could take a swing at Comstock, Honor stepped between the two men.

"I'll thank you to stop harassing my clients, Mr. Comstock," she said coldly, "otherwise you'll find yourself in jail."

Though Honor herself was tall, Comstock towered over her. "I'm not afraid of your threats, Mrs. Davis."

"I don't make threats," she retorted. "No one is above the law, even you." Honor took a step forward, deliberately crowding him toe to toe. "Now, if you'll be so kind as to get out of our way . . ."

He stepped back reluctantly while glaring at her, only to be replaced by a swarm of newspaper reporters firing questions at the Delancys, who knew most of them by name.

"Dr. Delancy, why did you decide to return to New York and risk prosecution?"

"Mr. Delancy, what will you do if your wife is convicted?"

"Do you intend to have the lady lawyer represent Dr. Delancy?"

Ever since the day a pack of reporters had waylaid her outside of her office about *Graham v. Graham*, Honor had resented being crowded and questioned by members of the press.

"Gentlemen, my client has nothing to say at this time," she said.

"Oh, but I do," Damon said behind her, taking control in his customary manner.

Honor stopped, annoyed by his presumption, but she said nothing. The reporters fell silent, their pencils poised above their notepads, their expressions eager for a scoop.

Delancy's deep, rough voice commanded attention as it rang through the hall. "My wife and I decided to return to New York City because we were despondent over the death of our son." His cold gray eyes sought out Anthony Comstock standing on the edge of the throng and glaring back. "We also decided it was high time to fight these ridiculous charges brought against my wife by a malicious fanatic."

A reporter piped up, "But what will you do if she's convicted?"

Delancy smiled. "She won't be, Ransom, because we're living on the verge of the twentieth century, and it's time Comstock's reign of terror came to an end."

Another reporter, whom Honor recognized as Liam Flynn, said, "Do you intend to have Honor Davis defend your wife?"

She held her breath and pretended his decision didn't matter.

"I haven't decided. Now, if you gentlemen will excuse us, my wife and I are eager to get out of here."

Satisfied, the reporters dispersed.

After the papers were signed and the Delancys were free to go, a white-faced, tight-lipped Catherine said, "God, I had forgotten how much I hate that man! He has single-handedly done more than anyone else I know of to keep women ignorant and impoverished." She shook her head. "Miserable, small-minded, fanatical—"

"Hush," her husband said, patting her arm as they walked down the courthouse steps. "We're going to beat the bastard this time."

When they reached the foot of the steps, Catherine turned to Honor. "Will you come back to the house with us?"

"I can't today," she replied. "I have a pile of work waiting for me at my office."

"Can't it wait an hour or two?" Nevada said.

Before Honor could answer, Catherine said, "Please come. You're Nevada's friend, and we think of you as our friend as well. We'd like you to share in our homecoming."

You would, Honor thought, but your husband wouldn't.

She considered her lapel watch and made a face. "I'm afraid a client is coming to my office at eleven o'clock, and I can't reschedule him."

A faint line of displeasure appeared between Nevada's brows.

Catherine looked crestfallen but managed a warm smile. "I can certainly understand the demands of a profession. Perhaps you would join us for dinner tonight."

The persistent woman was not about to take no for an

answer, and Honor couldn't put off socializing with Nevada's dear friends any longer. "I'd be delighted to come."

Catherine smiled again. "We'll look forward to getting acquainted."

Nevada said, "I'll call at your apartment at seven."

Had anyone else noticed that only Damon Delancy did not express his pleasure to hear that she would be joining them?

"Good night, boss," Elroy called from the outer office.

Seated at her desk piled high with law books, Honor glanced at her clock. Was it five o'clock already? "Good night, Elroy," she called back. "See you early tomorrow morning. Don't forget that I have to depose Mrs. Elias about that rent dispute at eight o'clock sharp."

"Yes, boss, I won't forget." Honor heard his footsteps cross the outer office and the door open. Then she heard Elroy say, "Oh, hello, Mr. LaRouche. . . . Yes, the boss is in her office. . . . Sure, go right in. Good night."

The door closed.

Honor's heart beat faster, but she kept writing, listening to Nevada's slow, deliberate footsteps cross the outer office. She looked up to find his lanky frame filling her doorway, his eyes troubled.

"Did the Delancys get settled?" she asked.

He nodded. "The minute they walked through the door, the doc broke down."

"That's to be expected. She's been away from her home for . . . what? Over two years?"

He nodded again.

"I know I'd cry the minute I walked into my home after such an absence." Honor set down her pen. "You're early. I thought you were calling for me at seven, at my apartment."

He stepped into her office, stood before her desk, and came right to the point. "Why do you suddenly act like a horse with a burr under its saddle?"

Honor knew it would be useless to pretend ignorance, so

she rose and faced him. "Ever since the Delancys arrived yesterday, I've felt like an outsider."

Nevada's eyes widened in genuine shock. "I hope I haven't made you feel that way."

She tugged at her locket. "But you have. You three have shared so much together." She rounded the desk and went to the window, where she stared down into the street. "You've said that Damon is like a brother to you, and I can tell that Catherine regards you as one. When we met them at the dock, I saw that the three of you fit so perfectly together while I was like a puzzle piece that didn't quite fit."

Nevada crossed the room and took her hand, forcing her to look at him. "Of course we all fit. We've known each other for a long time. Once they get to know you a little better, you'll be like a sister to them."

She shook her head sadly. "I spoiled any chance of that when I told you that I found Damon arrogant and overbearing. He's your family. I should have kept my opinion to myself."

"I prefer the truth to a lie, no matter how much it hurts." He stroked his mustache. "Well, you're right. Delancy is arrogant and overbearing, but we've all got our faults. That doesn't mean that you can't get along, that you can't respect him as much as I do."

"He doesn't like me, Nevada. I can tell."

He placed his hands lightly on her shoulders and looked deep into her eyes. "That's not true. He told me just this afternoon that he thinks you're a beautiful woman and a damn fine lawyer."

"But not fine enough to represent Catherine."

He rubbed his jaw. "You have to understand how he is when it comes to the doc."

"I do."

"The doc likes you, too. She couldn't stop singing your praises."

"But Sybilla was her dear friend. Surely every time she looks at me, she must compare me to her."

With a heavy sigh, Nevada drew her into his arms and

held her tight. "Honor Davis, you make more mountains out of molehills than any woman I know."

She closed her eyes. "I never want to force you to choose between me and your friends."

He released her abruptly, but only to take her face in his hands. "You're not forcing me to choose. And even if it did come down to you or Delancy . . ." His hands fell away, and he shrugged helplessly, his composure finally rattled. "Hell, Honor, I love you."

There was her answer.

"And I love you." She bit her lower lip to keep it from trembling. "But last night, when I offered to stay—"

"I sent you home," he said, his soft drawl ragged with remorse as he realized the magnitude of his thoughtless act. "I chose the Delancys over you after all."

"That's how I saw it," she said, tears springing to her eyes.

"I didn't mean to." He reached for both her hands, laced her fingers through his own, and held them at his sides while he bowed his head. "Sometimes I can be an ass, Honor."

She rested her forehead against his own. "I wanted you so badly last night."

"And I turned you away." He took a deep breath. "What a fool."

She looked up at him. "You can make it up to me."

A smile played about his mouth. "How?"

She brushed her lips against his in a light, teasing kiss. "Tonight, following dinner at the Delancys', you can stay after you take me home."

"How late?"

"As late as you like."

"I don't know if I can wait," he whispered.

She raised her brows. "But the Delancys are expecting us for dinner."

Nevada groaned. "This is going to be the longest evening of my life."

The moment Honor stepped out of the carriage and entered the Delancys' mansion, she decided that no matter how insufferable Damon was, she was going to enjoy herself for Nevada's sake.

Catherine and Damon greeted them in the foyer.

"We're so glad you could come," Catherine said, smiling warmly and taking both of Honor's hands in her own. She had a way of listening intently, of giving her undivided attention to a person as if no one else existed. Honor could understand why Catherine's patients regarded her so highly.

Damon even kissed Honor on the cheek and echoed his wife's sentiments. Still wary, Honor noticed that he seemed more relaxed and congenial this evening, now that his wife was out of jail. In just the short time Honor had known Damon Delancy, she had seen that he loved his wife with an intensity that bordered on obsession and that her welfare ruled his actions. Yet Catherine could tame him with a look or a word or a touch.

As Nevada took Honor's wrap and handed it to the butler, Honor said, "I imagine it's good to be home."

Catherine looked around the foyer and shivered. "I never thought I'd see this house again."

Her husband placed an arm around her shoulders. "We're here to stay."

"I'll do my part to see that you do," Honor said.

Catherine sighed. "Let's go into the parlor and have some sherry before dinner, shall we?"

When they adjourned to the parlor and were all seated with drinks in hand, Honor said to Catherine, "Do you intend to resume your medical practice?"

She looked at her husband with a spark of defiance in her eyes that Honor could not understand. "Yes, when my future is more certain. For now I'll volunteer at the Women's Dispensary."

Damon gave her a long, level look, but said nothing, and Honor suspected Catherine's work in the tenements was a sore point with her husband.

Seated beside Honor with his glass of bourbon, Nevada said, "Two minutes after Delancy unpacked, he was down at the office, taking over the reins."

Damon raised his glass to his friend. "And you were only too happy to relinquish them."

Nevada smiled slowly. "I'll leave you with all the headaches."

While the men continued to discuss the turmoil resulting from Damon's sudden reappearance and resumption of control over his company, Honor sipped her sherry reflectively. How different Nevada was from the brash, bold Delancy. Yet remaining in his friend's shadow did nothing to diminish Nevada in the least. He was confident enough to step aside.

Catherine leaned forward and said, "I was so shocked to hear that Gordon and Genevra Graham had gotten a divorce."

"Yes," Honor replied, and proceeded to tell them about the case.

Damon looked at her with interest. "You represented Genevra and won?"

Honor nodded. "Up until that time, my legal work had consisted of negotiating contracts for circus performers and actors, writing wills, and doing some estate work. That divorce case marked my first appearance in a courtroom." She shook her head. "I had to persuade the judge to let me argue the case, and then he warned the jury not to be influenced by my beauty."

Sympathetic anger flashed in Catherine's eyes. "How infuriating! When I wanted to become a doctor, you can't imagine the stupid, illogical arguments that were used to try to discourage me."

Honor felt another surge of kinship with this woman. "They were probably the same ones used to try to discourage me from becoming a lawyer."

"My favorite was the theory that such taxing mental activity would wear a woman out physically."

"I was told by law professors and fellow students—all male, of course—that the rigors of arguing cases in the courtroom would cause me to die at an early age."

Catherine gave a derisive bark of laughter. "Women are physically able to work twelve hours a day in a sweatshop or as servants, but they're not strong enough to practice medicine or law."

"Then one day I showed my male colleagues an obituary for a male lawyer who died when he was only twenty-nine." Honor smiled. "I guess the rigors of the courtroom proved too much for him as well."

She looked at Nevada. "Thank God that not all men are so narrow-minded." He smiled and raised her hand to his lips.

Honor said to Catherine, "I've read in the newspapers about your dealings with Anthony Comstock, but I'd like you to tell me how you became one of his targets."

Catherine's gentle gaze hardened as she lowered her voice, creating an air of intimacy. "I was a doctor who treated tenement women. I saw firsthand how repeated childbearing kept them impoverished. I knew how they could prevent unwanted pregnancies, and I told them.

"One day Comstock sent one of his henchmen to my office posing as a concerned husband who wanted to limit the size of his family." She rolled her eyes. "He said he worked as a clerk and didn't make much money, so having a child every year was becoming too much of a burden. He wanted me to tell him how to keep his wife from having any more children.

"Comstock was waiting outside. If I had given his crony the desired information, they would have arrested me. But my intuition warned me there was just something not quite right about him, so I sent the man packing."

"Bastard," Damon muttered, his gray eyes turning as cold as pewter at the memory.

Catherine added, "Then Comstock went around to my patients in the tenements demanding to know if I had ever told them how to keep from having babies." Her expression softened. "They all denied that I had ever given them such information."

"They obviously appreciated how much you were trying to help them improve their lives," Honor said, touched by the loyalty Catherine inspired.

"Later, Comstock stood outside of my office for hours, harassing my patients." Her serene face twisted in anger.

"He did later have me arrested for supposedly performing an abortion on a young prostitute."

Damon's expression turned as black as a thundercloud.

Nevada said, "The police actually barged into the house here during a ball and arrested the doc."

Honor raised her brows in astonishment. "In the middle of a ball? In front of a houseful of guests?"

Damon nodded. "I could have killed Comstock with my bare hands for that." And he meant it.

Catherine knotted her fingers together in her lap, obviously distressed by the memories, but determined to continue. "Those charges were dropped when another doctor, a friend of mine named Kim Flanders, came forward and confessed to having performed the abortion, so I was freed. But Comstock later had me arrested a second time. He got a search warrant and found anti-conception literature that I had received through the mail."

Honor shook her head regretfully. "If that information hadn't been sent through the mail, they wouldn't have had a case against you."

Damon downed the rest of his bourbon in one swallow, and his expression darkened further. "That's why we fled the country. Comstock had too much evidence against Catherine, and my lawyer couldn't guarantee that he could win her case." He stared at Honor defiantly. "Breaking the law was preferable to my wife going to prison."

Honor put on her expressionless lawyer's face so she wouldn't reveal her annoyance. "You should have stayed and found a better lawyer, one more experienced in criminal cases. He could have found ways to keep Catherine from even going to trial for months, possibly years."

Enunciating every word slowly, Damon said, "I couldn't take the chance."

Honor said, "How did you manage to evade Comstock? Surely he had you watched while you were out on bail."

"We fooled the old buzzard," Damon replied. "I knew Comstock was watching the house, so on the night we were planning to leave, two friends of ours led him on a wild-goose chase. They took our carriage to Grand Central, so Comstock assumed we were leaving town by train and followed it. When he got there and accosted them, he discovered that 'the Delancys' were really a doctor friend of Catherine's and her maid cradling a ham in her arms as if it were our child. By the time Comstock realized he had been tricked, we were on the *Copper Queen* heading for England."

"An ingenious ruse," Honor said. She had to admire the man's guile.

"The end justified the means," Damon said. He looked at Honor. "I've thought about this long and carefully, and I'd like someone else to represent my wife."

Honor swallowed hard to hide her disappointment. "I understand."

"I hope you won't take offense," he said.

"I'm disappointed, but I know you're doing what you think is best for your wife."

"I disagree with my husband's decision," Catherine said. "Unfortunately, I can't make him change his mind."

"I don't want to be the cause of any friction between you," Honor said.

Damon just smiled. "Do you know of another lawyer who might take the case?"

"There's an attorney in Philadelphia named Philip Lyons who has a reputation for winning cases," she replied. "I can see if he's available, if you like."

"I'd appreciate it," Damon said.

Honor added hopefully, "I know I could learn a great deal from a lawyer of his stature, so I'd like to assist him with Catherine's case, if you have no objections."

"I have no objections," Damon said, "but Lyons may. I leave his choice of an assistant up to him."

So he didn't even trust her to assist in his wife's defense. Honor bit down her resentment and wished the evening would end.

By the time Nevada could bear to pry himself out of Honor's soft, warm arms and return home through hushed, deserted streets, it was three o'clock. Only Damon remained awake at this hour of the night, sprawled in one corner of the chesterfield sofa and so lost in thought that he started when Nevada entered the parlor.

Damon's bloodshot gaze took in Nevada's rumpled frock coat, tousled hair, and satisfied expression. He grinned. "Why didn't you stay with her until morning?"

Nevada took off his coat, flung it across a nearby chair, and grinned back at his friend. He yanked off his tie and rolled up his shirtsleeves. "Much as I hated to leave her, she needs her rest."

"She won't get any if you're around." Damon raised his glass. "Make yourself comfortable."

"Don't mind if I do." Nevada poured himself a bourbon, then seated himself across from his friend.

Damon dragged his hand through his hair. "Christ, am I glad to be out of that cold, wet, miserable country."

Nevada cradled his glass in one hand. "I take it you didn't cotton to England." Aside from frequent cablegrams concerning the firm, Damon had left the letter writing to his wife, and Catherine had purposely spared Nevada most of the hardships they endured as expatriates.

Damon snorted in derision. "You could say that, old friend. Everything was always cold and damp, even the food. And the people . . ." He looked at Nevada. "Do you know that a duchess once asked me how large my plantation was and how many Negro slaves I owned?"

Nevada stared at him, dumbfounded.

"Stupid woman. And her husband, the duke, wanted to know if red Indians had ever attacked my home!"

After Nevada finished laughing, he said, "Well, they did once, in Arizona."

Damon grinned. "That's what I told him. You should've seen his face." Then his smile died. He shook his head and added bitterly, "I didn't know the right people, so it was damned hard doing business there."

Nevada sobered. "It must have been hell for you."

"It was." Damon emptied his glass, and his expression

softened. "If it hadn't been for Catherine, I would have gone mad. I knew she was homesick and always blaming herself for forcing us into exile, but she refused to lose hope. Every day she said to me, 'It will get better,' but it never did."

Nevada thought of Honor. "A good woman sure lightens the load."

Damon rose, refilled his glass, and returned to the sofa. His voice turned ragged when he said, "Then Willie died."

There was such an unbearable darkness in Damon's eyes that Nevada had to look away. When Nevada had learned that Sybilla was carrying his child, the pain of promise unfulfilled had seared his soul, but his own pain must have been as fleeting as the touch of a feather compared to what Damon had suffered and was suffering still.

Damon's eyes glazed, and he stared at something only he could see. "One day he was laughing and playing tricks on his papa, and then he was gone. After he died, it rained for twelve days. I never wanted the sun to shine again."

Nevada glanced up to find Catherine standing in the doorway. How long she had been there and how much she had heard, he didn't know.

Her eyes hot and dry, her face tight with the strain of always remaining strong, she walked over to the sofa and placed a hand on her husband's shoulder. Damon looked at her, and something terrible and heartbreaking passed between them. He rose and slipped his arm around her waist, leaning against her like a sad old man. Without so much as a good night to Nevada, they went up to bed.

Nevada stared into the depths of his bourbon, suddenly wishing Honor were here. He needed her smile, her warmth, her life.

Philip Lyons had better be good, he thought, draining his glass and rising. Damn good.

CHAPTER 19

"YOU MUST FORGIVE MY husband," Catherine said to Honor two days later, when the women were having luncheon together, seated across from each other at one end of the long mahogany table in the Delancys' dining room. Her eyes sparkled with wry humor. "I'm afraid his tendency to protect me can make him insufferable."

Honor sensed that Catherine preferred honesty to the graceful social lie, so she said, "I have noticed."

Catherine laughed. "You speak your mind."

"And you really listen to what others have to say," Honor said. "I can see why your patients are so loyal." Indeed, the woman's warm and genuine interest in people made Honor feel as though she had known Catherine Delancy all her life.

Catherine beamed, obviously pleased.

Honor had accepted Catherine's invitation because she wanted to discover the real woman beyond the persecuted female doctor presented in the sensational newspaper accounts and the saint so glowingly described by everyone else. Without Damon around to dominate with his forceful personality, Honor found that the intelligent, humorous Catherine could hold her own.

Today she looked less tired than when she had first stepped off the *Copper Queen,* and she had relieved the stark black of her mourning clothes with a white shirtwaist sporting a flattering fine red stripe.

Honor picked at her salad. "How did you and Damon meet?"

"I first saw Damon ice-skating with a lady friend in Central Park," Catherine replied, "but we didn't actually meet until his horse threw him in the middle of a busy street near my office. He fractured his clavicle—his collarbone—and I set it for him." A mischievous smile played about her mouth. "I've never had a surlier patient. He was unbelievably rude and arrogant, accusing me of overcharging him, then refusing to pay my fee."

Honor sipped her cold Chablis. "Not an auspicious way to begin a relationship, was it?"

"Indeed." Catherine's smile faded. "My husband is a difficult man. Since we're both so headstrong and stubborn, our courtship and marriage have been tumultuous, to say the least. There have been times . . ." She shook her head, her gaze clouding at some remembered incident. "Yet we always resolve our differences because we love each other."

"Nevada has never struck me as particularly difficult," she said. "Remote, with a certain untamed quality, but not difficult." Except when he kept secrets.

Catherine fell silent for a moment as if contemplating some point she wanted to make. Then she said, "If Damon is a hurricane, all thunder and roaring wind, then Nevada is the eye of the storm."

Honor considered that metaphor and smiled. "The eye of a storm . . . calm in the midst of turmoil. Yes, that does describe him."

Catherine toyed with the stem of her wineglass. "Women as unconventional as we are can only be content with unconventional men who accept us for what we are. Yet because they are different as well, we can't expect them to act like ordinary men." She sighed. "Sometimes their differences can be aggravating, but that is the price we pay for loving them."

Honor ate the rest of her salad in silence as she thought about Catherine's assertion. She couldn't expect an extraordinary man like Nevada to behave like Wesley Saltonsall or

Amos Grant. Indeed, she didn't want him to. His upbringing in a brothel and life on his own in the lawless, violent West had shaped him as much as Honor's tragic loss of her father and privileged life with Aunt Theo had shaped her. But as Catherine had said, the women they loved paid a price.

Honor looked over at Catherine. "They pay a high price for loving us, too."

Catherine's expression clouded. "Indeed they do."

A footman entered the dining room to remove their salad plates and to serve sliced roast duck with orange sauce and rice.

When he left, Catherine said, "How did you meet Nevada? All he said in his short, infrequent letters was that he had met a wonderful woman who brought him great happiness."

Honor's cheeks grew pink with pleasure. "He said that about me?"

"Oh, yes. Our friend is a man of few words, but he chooses them carefully, from the heart."

"That is so true." Then she proceeded to tell Catherine about Lillie Troy and how her breach of promise suit had led to Honor's fateful meeting with Nevada.

By the time Honor finished, Catherine's shoulders were shaking with laughter. "Poor Nevada. I'll wager he didn't know what hit him."

"Then my husband, who is also a lawyer, went to work for Nevada, and we saw a great deal of each other."

"Your husband? Nevada never mentioned that you are a widow."

"I'm not," Honor replied, "but I might as well be." At Catherine's inquisitive look, she told her how Robert had left her after Nevada caught him stealing secrets for a competitor, and just disappeared without a trace.

Catherine's brow furrowed in sympathy. "So you and Nevada—"

"Can have no future until Robert is found. I can't even divorce him."

"How sad. Have you tried to find him?"

"Detectives are expensive, and I haven't been able to afford one because I've been slowly building up my legal practice."

"Perhaps Nevada could help you. He's a very wealthy man."

"I wouldn't dream of imposing."

Catherine smiled. "Somehow I don't think he'd see it as an imposition."

"I still couldn't ask him," Honor replied. "We Putnam women are a proud lot."

"I assume you're referring to your aunt Theo in Boston. Nevada told us about visiting her for Thanksgiving and how much he likes her." Catherine's gaze dropped to her plate for a moment. When she looked up, she leaned forward. "Have you accepted Nevada's violent past?"

Honor looked surprised. "Of course. Regardless of what he did years ago, he's the kindest, gentlest man I ever met."

A bittersweet smile touched Catherine's mouth, and her eyes turned bright. "That's exactly what Sybilla said when I asked her that same question."

Honor had been waiting for Sybilla's name to come up in conversation, and she had been dreading it. "He loved her very much, didn't he?"

"As much as he loves you now." Catherine placed her hand on Honor's, regarding her with that fierce intensity. "Sybilla was my best friend, but that doesn't mean I think Nevada is disloyal to her memory because he's found you. I don't."

Honor squeezed Catherine's hand and let out the breath she had been holding. "You don't know how relieved I am to hear you say that. I was worried that you would compare us and find me lacking."

Catherine shook her head. "On the contrary. I want Nevada to be happy. When Sybilla was murdered and we later learned she had been carrying Nevada's child, he—"

"Dear God!" Honor felt as though a bolt of lightning had struck her where she sat. "A child? He never told me." Never allowed her to comfort him for his double loss.

"Oh, dear, perhaps I shouldn't have said anything," Catherine said softly, "but I assumed he'd told you. On second thought, I'm not surprised. Nevada is a private man who tends to keep his pain buried deep."

Still stunned, Honor picked up her fork and tried to finish her duck, but found she had lost her appetite.

What other secrets is he keeping to himself? she wondered.

Then she remembered the night they had first made love, when Nevada had revealed his Christian name.

She gave Catherine a defiant look. "Did he ever tell Sybilla his real name?"

"Never. Even Damon doesn't know that." Then comprehension dawned in her eyes. "But Nevada told you."

Honor nodded, wondering why such a small matter should make her feel so triumphant. Yet to her it symbolized a profound trust that Nevada had never invested in another, even his beloved Sybilla.

"Don't expect me to reveal it to you," she said with a warning grin.

"I wouldn't dream of it," Catherine replied. Leaving the rest of her luncheon untouched, she set her napkin beside her plate. "I have an idea. I realize you're a busy woman, but could you possibly take the rest of the afternoon off?"

Honor considered her schedule, remembered that she had no appointments or court appearances, and said, "Yes, I could. Why?"

"I'd like to take you on a little tour."

Honor set down her own napkin and rose. "I'd like that."

As she followed Catherine out of the dining room, Honor could not stop thinking of the newest secret she had discovered about the man she loved. She wondered when Nevada intended to tell her that Sybilla had been carrying his child when she died.

A little boy, one huge dark eye swollen shut into a slit and the other filled with pain and fear, clung to his frail mother in the waiting area of the Women's Dispensary and stared at Catherine and Honor as if they were angels.

Unmindful of her long skirt, Catherine knelt down on the immaculate floor beside them and smiled as if no one else existed. She touched the boy's threadbare sleeve gently and said, "Why, hello, little boy. My name is Catherine Delancy. What's yours?"

The child hid his face against his mother's shoulder.

The woman's tired face softened as she tenderly stroked his clean dark hair with a chapped, work-sore hand. "His name's John, but we call him Johnny." She said his name proudly, as if he were a king.

"Johnny . . . what a distinguished name."

Standing behind Catherine, Honor glanced around the crowded waiting area, appalled by the human suffering. Among the dozen women and children seated on chairs lining the walls was a girl who couldn't have been more than fifteen years old, listlessly nursing an infant while another child clutched her skirts in one hand and a worn rag doll in the other. A toothless old white-haired woman wrapped in a moth-eaten black shawl rocked back and forth and conversed with herself, while a garishly dressed young woman with hair dyed too gold and lips painted too red stared back at Honor defiantly.

This was where Honor would find the real Catherine Delancy.

Still absorbed in the little boy, Catherine said, "Will you tell me how old you are, Johnny?" When he made no response, she frowned sadly and said, "I'll cry if you don't tell me."

His mother whispered, "You don't want to make the nice lady cry, now, do you?"

Without lifting his face from his mother's shoulder, Johnny blindly thrust out four fingers.

"Four years old?" Catherine exclaimed. "Why, you're the same age as my own little boy."

Honor held her breath. How could this woman even bear to look at another child, having lost her own so tragically?

Catherine rose and was about to go over to the garishly dressed young woman when a middle-aged woman with her arm in a sling came through the waiting room door, followed by one of the dispensary's doctors.

". . . and the next time your husband beats you," the doctor said, her tone so withering it could have blistered paint, "you'll be lucky if all he does is break your arm."

Honor stared. Despite her own sheltered, privileged upbringing, she wasn't unaware of violence, a lesson she had learned from Graham's two thugs. But she would never understand how a man could beat his own wife, someone he presumably loved.

The blonde gave a derisive snort and said to everyone present, "I'd be damned if I let a man do that to me."

The doctor glared at her and retorted, "But you let them give you a social disease, Bessie Hayward, so don't go turning up your nose at anyone else."

Head bowed, the woman with the broken arm quietly walked through the waiting area and disappeared out the door, no doubt returning to her abusive husband because she had nowhere else to go or was afraid of retaliation. Wealthy women like Genevra Graham obtained divorces; poor women like this one endured.

Catherine stepped forward. "Well, Hilda, I can see that you haven't changed."

Hilda, a Valkyrie of a woman with iron-gray eyes that matched her iron-gray hair, stared at Catherine as if she had seen a ghost. "What in the hell are you doing back here, you fool? This time they're going to lock you up and throw away the key."

Incensed, Honor was about to step forward and give the rude woman a piece of her mind, but Catherine just laughed and flung her arms around the Valkyrie for a crushing hug. "It's good to see you, too. You don't know how I've missed you, old fraud."

Then she turned and said to Honor, "You must excuse my friend here. Hilda doesn't mean half of what she says."

"I mean every word of it," the Valkyrie said, stepping forward and extending her hand to Honor. "Dr. Hilda Steuben, crotchety middle-aged doctor. And you are . . . ?"

"Honor Davis, attorney-at-law."

Dr. Steuben's iron-gray brows rose. "A woman lawyer . . . I didn't know there were such critters."

"There are, but very few of us. In fact, I'm the only one in this entire city."

Dr. Steuben said, "You're going to have to be mean and unscrupulous to get Catherine off."

"I won't be representing her," Honor said. "I'm here as her friend."

Catherine smiled. "Hilda was born with a black cloud hanging over her head. She always expects the worst to happen."

"And when it does," Hilda said, "I'm never surprised." She looked at Catherine. "Have you come to work or to talk? If you're not going to work, you can leave, because I'm short-staffed and I've got patients to see."

"I'll be in first thing tomorrow morning."

"See that you are. I'll put you to work." Dr. Steuben scowled. "I thought they would've arrested you the minute you set foot in New York City."

"They did, but Honor got me out on bail."

Hilda shook her head morosely. "Enjoy your freedom while you can."

Honor said, "Perhaps Catherine's attorney will call you as a character witness."

Dr. Steuben's gray eyes sparkled with relish. "I'd like nothing better than to butt heads with Anthony Comstock, that sanctimonious old hypocrite." Then she said, "Well, I've got patients to see."

Catherine hugged her again. "I'll see you tomorrow."

Dr. Steuben looked at the blonde. "Bessie, you're next."

Just as the doctor was about to stalk off to her office, Catherine said, "Hilda, Damon sends his love."

Dr. Steuben turned around and muttered something under her breath that sounded suspiciously like, "Tell him to go to hell," before disappearing through the door with Bessie.

But Catherine only laughed and said, "I will."

Puzzled, Honor whispered, "Doesn't she like your husband?"

Catherine rolled her eyes. "Hilda doesn't have much use for men, and there was a time when my overprotective husband tried to keep me from practicing medicine. For my own good, of course," she added. "Let's just say that his manipulations didn't endear him to Hilda."

Privately, Honor thought that Hilda was far too prickly to find anyone endearing, but that apparently didn't concern Catherine.

"Shall we go?" Catherine said. "I have much more to show you."

On the way out, she stopped to say good-bye to Johnny. To Honor's surprise, the little boy looked at Catherine and waved his fingers at her. A shadow of pain passed across Catherine's face, but she hid it behind a brave smile and tousled his hair before leaving with Honor.

"This," Catherine said, "is Mulberry Street." She frowned as she regarded a group of skinny, ragged children playing together next to a pile of ashes on the sidewalk. "I can see it hasn't changed."

Honor looked around, appalled by the tenement buildings huddled together, separated by dark, narrow alleys littered with refuse, which gave off such a choking stench that she wanted to press her handkerchief to her nose and gag. She caught glimpses of women staring listlessly out of windows so grimy that their faces were as blurred and unfocused as their lives, and she tried to ignore the hostile, resentful stares of men lounging in doorways. Catherine didn't. She looked at every one of them and nodded as if they had just been introduced at a ball.

As they walked, Catherine said, "You've never been to this part of the city before, have you?"

Honor shook her head.

"When I first went to work at the dispensary, Hilda brought me down here. One of the first things she did was buy a newspaper."

Honor frowned. "A newspaper? I thought you were going to heal the sick."

"She told me I'd need a newspaper because in the tenements, most people didn't have beds with clean sheets. The women usually gave birth on a pile of straw, so a newspaper was necessary to absorb the blood."

Honor turned white. "That's disgusting."

"I quite agree." She looked up at rags hung from drooping clotheslines strung between buildings. "It has always infuriated me to think of human beings living like animals."

Honor took a deep breath. "I'm glad I decided to become a lawyer because I could never be a doctor."

Catherine glanced at her. "Nevada told me about your father."

Honor reached up to anchor her hat as a sudden gust of April wind tore at them. "I suppose some people would consider me foolish for letting such a tragic incident rule my entire life, but"—she shrugged helplessly—"I loved my father, and I blamed myself for what happened to him."

Catherine placed a hand on her arm. "People said the same thing to me. Why should I choose such a difficult path in life just because of what happened to my mother? My becoming a doctor wouldn't bring her back."

Honor remembered that Nevada had told her that a careless male physician had caused the death of Catherine's mother in childbirth.

Catherine said, "But every time I save a life, I feel that I am doing something useful and honoring her memory."

"Every time I keep someone from being taken advantage of or I win a case, I feel as though I'm winning it for my father."

Catherine clasped her hand in mute understanding.

As they toured the squalid East Side, Honor felt her admiration for Catherine Delancy growing. Though the lady doctor had been away for a little more than two years, people remembered her. A boy no older than twelve came up to them and in halting English thanked Catherine for saving his mother's life. A young woman greeted "Dr. Dee" and proudly showed off her son, who could walk because Catherine had set his broken leg correctly, and another woman thanked Catherine for saving her baby from cholera infantum, the dreaded "summer sickness."

But the ones who haunted Honor were the women who thanked Catherine for helping them to have fewer children and told her how their lives had improved.

"My husband doesn't drink so much now that we don't have to worry about having another mouth to feed."

"Next month we'll have enough money to move out of this rat trap into a real nice place."

"Now there's enough money to send my Mabel to school instead of a sweatshop."

And Anthony Comstock wanted to throw Catherine in jail.

Later that night, awakened from a light, troubled sleep by the pattering of rain against the bedchamber window, Honor left Nevada sleeping and rose naked from their bed. As always, her body felt warm and soothed by his lovemaking, yet ready to be aroused at his lightest touch. She looked down at him in the darkness, his fair hair tousled against the pillow as he slept on his side, and she felt her heart constrict. Even in sleep he never let down his guard.

Honor padded quietly over to the window and peered through the curtain. A brisk April wind flung raindrops against the glass, blurring the deserted street below. The building across the way was dark save for one window where a light shone. Honor stared at it.

Why didn't he tell me about their child?

She heard him stir in the bed, sensed that he had reached for her, then quickly wakened when he realized she was no longer lying beside him. Only the bed's soft creaking betrayed him. Then she could smell the pleasant, pungent musk of their lovemaking, and she knew he had quietly crossed the room to stand behind her.

"Can't sleep?" he whispered, his lips against her hair, his hands lightly caressing her bare shoulders. "I know just how to cure what ails you."

She watched as the light in the window across the street went out, plunging the building into darkness. "Why didn't you tell me about your child?"

His hands stilled. Silence.

Finally he said, "The doc told you?"

Honor turned and looked into his wary eyes. "This afternoon."

He took a deep breath. "I didn't tell you because I've put it behind me."

She placed her hand against his hard cheek, feeling the muscles tense. "I love you. I don't want any secrets between us."

Something flickered in the depths of his eyes. "It was never real to me somehow. I know that sounds callous, but—"

She placed her fingertips against his lips. "I understand." And she did.

He sighed. "I would have liked a future with them both, but that wasn't in the cards. My future lies with you and our children."

Honor's eyes widened. Children. This was the first time Nevada had ever mentioned having children with her. She thought of a lanky boy with her black hair and black eyes, or a winsome little girl with her father's slow smile.

Honor said, "I'm still legally married. I wouldn't want any of my children to be illegitimate."

He took her face in his hands. "They won't be. That no-good husband of yours will turn up one of these days. And in the meantime . . ."

Nevada swept her into his arms and carried her over to bed, where his loving hands and lips erased all secrets.

Later, as they lay together among the rumpled sheets, she said, "I've never met a woman like Catherine Delancy. She's a saint."

Nevada propped himself up on one elbow and roared with laughter. When the bed finally stopped shaking, he wiped the tears from the corners of his eyes. "The doc a saint? That is a belly buster."

"Oh, is it? I'll have you know that in the Women's Dispensary and throughout the tenements, everyone thinks she can perform miracles. I was skeptical myself at first, but now . . ." She shrugged.

He sobered. "Just because lots of folks love and respect her doesn't make her a saint. She's got her faults, and she is just as stubborn and hardheaded as Delancy." Nevada wound a lock of Honor's dark hair around his finger. "After Sybilla was killed, Damon feared for the doc's life. The tenements are especially dangerous for a woman alone, even during the day, but just the thought of his wife going there alone at night was enough to drive him mad. He wanted her to stop practicing medicine."

Honor raised her brows. "Stop practicing medicine? That would be like someone telling me to stop practicing law."

"Well, the doc didn't take too kindly to being ordered around. One day, when she returned home, she found that Damon had taken down her shingle outside the house and converted her office back to a parlor."

"She must have been furious. What did she do?"

"She left him."

Honor sat up, pulling the sheet up over her breasts. "She *left* him?"

"She told him she wanted a divorce."

Honor stared at him, speechless.

"Hard to believe, isn't it? If ever there were two people more in love . . ." He grinned. "Except for us, of course. But neither one of them would bend an inch or meet the other halfway. So they went their separate ways for a while."

"Obviously they resolved their differences."

He nodded. "When Damon was blinded in a bomb explosion, Catherine went to Coppermine and tended him until he got his sight back. They obviously became lovers again because the doc soon discovered she was going to have his child. That's when she returned to him, but she resented it. Eventually they both decided to bend, and you know the rest."

Honor shook her head. "Catherine told me that she and her husband had a tumultuous marriage, but I never dreamed . . ."

"Oh, they fight like cats and dogs, but they don't stay mad for long."

"I can see why Catherine finds him so exasperating." She looked at Nevada thoughtfully. "You and Damon are so different, it's hard to imagine your being friends."

"I reckon that's why we've stayed friends for so long."

Honor rested her chin on her knees. "I couldn't live with a man who tried to tell me what to do, even if it was for my own good." Robert had tried.

"Delancy always thinks he knows what's best for everyone. I guess we're all used to his ways."

"When Gordon Graham had me beaten, you didn't try to persuade me to drop Genevra's case."

Nevada's blue eyes hardened possessively. "We weren't married. It wasn't my place."

"But even if I were your wife, you wouldn't forbid me to do my job, would you?"

He studied her. "You can't change the course of a river. All I would do is stand right by your side to make sure you didn't come to any harm."

Relieved, Honor touched his cheek. "Catherine said that Damon is like a hurricane, all thunder and roaring wind, but that you're like the eye of the storm." She let the sheet fall, reveling in the sound of his breath catching at the glorious sight of her. "I much prefer the eye of the storm to a hurricane."

The familiar heat flared in the depths of his eyes. "Is that how you see me, as the eye of the storm?"

She nodded. "Always calm."

He reached for her. "But what if I've a mind to be a hurricane?"

"As long as it's only in bed."

Laughing, he pulled her into his arms, and Honor felt herself swept up in a storm of quite another kind.

Chapter 20

MEMORIES OF SYBILLA WERE still there, warm, bittersweet, and poignant, but they occupied his thoughts less and less, fading a little more with each passing day like the faint scent of summer roses detected while quietly passing through a room. Even as Nevada sat in his office looking at a photograph of an ageless Sybilla frozen in time, he thought of Honor lying real and solid in his arms last night, a lifetime of experiences still waiting to be savored and shared.

He looked at the photograph for the last time.

As he put it away in the farthest corner of a bottom desk drawer, he thought he felt the barest brush of air against his ear and heard a whisper that sounded like "good-bye."

He shook his head. Impossible. He was much too practical a man to believe in ghosts.

"Mr. LaRouche?"

He looked up to find Miss Fields standing in the doorway. "Yes?"

"Mr. Stannard from the Pinkerton National Detective Agency is here to see you, sir."

They had found Robert Davis.

Nevada rose, anticipation heightening his senses, racing through his blood like a fever. "Show him in."

Aaron Stannard was an inconspicuous-looking man whose sharp gaze never rested, first darting around the room, then up and down Nevada as if committing height, build, hair color, eye color, and any distinguishing characteristics to memory. Once he completed this fast, penetrating survey, however, his eagle eyes held Nevada's and never wavered.

Nevada shook the man's hand, offered him a seat, and got right to the point. "I take it you're here because you have good news for me?"

Stannard shifted in his seat, but his gaze remained locked in place. "I'm afraid not, Mr. LaRouche. Our man tracked Davis to Georgia, then lost him."

Nevada stroked his mustache, his annoyance growing. "How can one man be so hard to find? He's a lawyer. Surely he'll try to set up shop somewhere."

"He hasn't yet. He's a man on the run, and he's clever about covering up his tracks. He works at different jobs under more names than a dog has fleas, and just as we're closing in, he bolts. It's almost as though he smells us coming."

Nevada swore under his breath.

Stannard's gaze didn't flinch. "We'll catch the slippery bastard sooner or later. We just need more time."

"You've been chasing him for six months."

"You want us to stop?"

Nevada placed his palms on the desk and leaned forward. "Not if it takes you six years."

The detective smiled slowly and nodded in understanding. "You must want him real bad."

"I do." He wanted Honor to be free, no matter how long it took, no matter what the expense.

An hour after Stannard left, Nevada received another visitor.

"May I interrupt you?" a familiar voice inquired from the doorway.

"Any time, Doc," he replied with a welcoming smile, rising as Catherine closed the door behind her and swept into his office.

She kissed him on the cheek. "I'm here to go to lunch with Damon, but he's in a meeting, so I thought I'd visit with you while I'm waiting."

Nevada indicated a seat. "You going to the dispensary today?"

Catherine sat down. "Work keeps my mind off the trial."

He leaned back in his chair. "When are you supposed to meet that Lyons fellow?"

"He'll arrive here the day after tomorrow and stay the week as our guest to familiarize himself with my case." A frown creased her brow. "I hope he agrees to let Honor assist him. She does so want to help."

"She's a good lawyer. He won't be sorry if he takes her on."

Catherine smiled. "I do like her. I wasn't sure if I would, out of loyalty to Sybilla, but now that I've gotten to know her better, I can see why you love her so much. You're a lucky man, Nevada LaRouche, to have found the perfect love twice in a lifetime." She paused. "Have your detectives had any luck finding her ne'er-do-well husband?"

"One of them was in here just an hour ago to tell me they tracked him to Georgia and lost him."

"He's obviously a man who doesn't want to be found."

"I don't know why he's on the run. I told him I wouldn't have him arrested for what her did. Guess he didn't believe me."

"Perhaps he's doing it just to spite Honor. If he can't have her, he's going to make sure no one else does."

"He's sure accomplishing that. As long as he stays missing, we can't marry."

Catherine studied him thoughtfully, as if choosing her next words with exquisite care. "Much as I hate to mention this . . . have you told her the truth about the night August Talmadge died?"

Nevada shook his head. "Haven't found the right time."

Her expression softened with sympathy. "No time is the right time, old friend. Honor is a lawyer, sworn to uphold the law, just as I am a doctor, sworn to heal the sick. You can't keep something like this from her too long, because when she does find out, she will be devastated. You may even lose her."

He rose and strode over to the window, where he hooked his thumbs in his belt and looked back at Catherine in despair.

"How can I tell her that the man she loves is a cold-blooded murderer?"

Honor paused before the gold-framed mirror in the Delancys' foyer to check her appearance one last time before meeting the famous Philip Lyons. Not a hair was out of place. Her mannish tailor-made shirtwaist with its starched front, modified wing collar, and jaunty blue tie made her look like a woman who expected to be taken seriously.

The tapping of boots on the marble floor heralded Nevada's approach. He looked her over as if she were something rare and precious, then glanced around the foyer to make sure they were alone. "I don't reckon you'd let me kiss you."

When Nevada took a determined step toward her, Honor raised her hands to ward him off. "As much as I'd love you to, I simply cannot meet Philip Lyons looking as though I've just tumbled out of my lover's bed." She smiled. "Which is exactly how I will look if I let you kiss me."

His blue eyes danced as he kissed her chastely on the forehead.

Honor reached for her locket, remembered she hadn't put it on, and let her hand fall away. "Where is he?" she muttered nervously. "What's he like?"

"He's in the parlor with Delancy and the doc." He drew her arm through his. "You can judge for yourself."

The moment Honor stepped into the parlor and Philip Lyons rose, she was awed by the sheer magnetism that radiated from him in palpable waves. He was taller than Nevada, with a straight, trim physique carried proudly. The youthful, energetic sparkle in Lyons's brown eyes made him look twenty years younger than his sixty years, despite a head of thick white hair and Vandyke beard. Honor noticed that his lower lip was full and sensual, like Robert's.

Lyons didn't wait for an introduction. He strode across the room, his gaze holding Honor's and assessing her man to woman. Then he took her hand and brought it to his lips with a flourish. He was a master of the dramatic gesture; like an actor, he used his body to illustrate the spoken word. "You must be Honor Davis," he said in a deep, authoritative voice that made judges and juries sit up and take notice. "I am Philip Lyons, at your service."

Up close, Honor could see the deep lines radiating from the corners of his eyes and scoring his cheeks, but they only made him look more distinguished, giving him the air of a wise elder statesman. The only flaw in his perfect features was the broken blood vessels that reddened the tip of his nose.

He drinks too much, she thought, dismayed.

She smiled. "The pleasure is mine, Mr. Lyons." Beside her, Nevada stirred restlessly.

Catherine stepped forward to take Honor's hands and kiss her cheek. "We were just telling Mr. Lyons all about you and how we hope he will accept your help with our case." She turned to her husband, who was standing near the sofa. "Isn't that right, Damon?"

"Yes, Catherine," he replied. "But as I told Mr. Lyons, the final decision is his."

"Why don't we sit down and discuss it?" Catherine said, ushering all of them to their seats.

Lyons fit himself in one corner of the sofa across from Honor, propped his elbow on the low arm, and rested his head casually against one hand, with two fingers touching his temple. He studied her. "In all my forty years at the bar, I've never before met a female lawyer, and I can't say that I approve of them in general."

Though Honor felt her temper rise, she decided that Philip Lyons was the kind of man who would be won over by reason and logic rather than confrontation. This was no time to be Steel Stays Elliott.

"I realize that even though I've argued several divorce cases," she said, "I still have much to learn. But all I'm asking is a chance to learn from the best, Mr. Lyons. There is so much that you can teach me, and I'd give my right arm to work with you."

Beside her on the sofa, she felt Nevada shift in his seat.

Honor added, "I can do research for you, gather character

witnesses, and take depositions. I can be your eyes and ears in New York while you're in Philadelphia."

Lyons tapped his temple, those sharp, youthful eyes staring at her intently. "I don't know New York at all, so that would be helpful."

Catherine glanced at her husband, seated next to her, and an unspoken signal passed between them.

Damon said, "Before you agreed to take my wife's case, you said that you had to be allowed to conduct it as you saw fit."

Lyons nodded. "I know what's best for my clients and how to give them the best defense. This isn't idle boasting. My record speaks for itself."

"You're certainly not known for losing," Honor said dryly.

Lyons smiled and shrugged. "I have lost one or two cases, but then, no one is perfect." He was not a modest man.

Damon said, "I would consider it a personal favor if you would agree to let Honor assist you."

Lyons stroked his beard. "Ordinarily I would refuse, because I prefer to work alone. However, after hearing about your victory in *Graham versus Graham*, I will make an exception in your case, Mrs. Davis. I would welcome your assistance."

Honor let out the breath she had been holding. "Thank you, Mr. Lyons. You won't regret this."

"See that I don't."

"When shall we start?"

Catherine said, "How about tomorrow morning? Damon and I would like to show Mr. Lyons around New York this afternoon. He'll be staying here as our guest, so you can see him anytime."

Honor said, "Tomorrow would be fine. Now, if you'll all excuse me, I have to get back to my office."

Nevada rose at once. "I have to go down to Wall Street, so why don't I drop you off?"

Damon rose to escort them to the door, and when they reached the foyer, Honor placed her hand on his arm. "Thank you for requesting that Mr. Lyons let me assist him."

His cold gray eyes warmed. "I know we got off on the wrong foot, but I'm not your enemy. I just want what's best for my wife."

She nodded in mute understanding and wished him a good day.

Once Honor and Nevada were seated side by side in the Delancys' carriage, she said, "You don't like Lyons very much, do you?"

"Not particularly," he replied, looking out the window.

"Why not? He does seem immodest, but his confidence is justified. He's the best counsel money can buy, and he knows it. Catherine will win against Comstock, mark my words."

He turned to her. "The law has nothing to do with my feelings toward him. The man is attracted to you, pure and simple." His cool gaze warmed as it lingered on her, a hunter staking his claim. "Not that I blame him."

"Nevada LaRouche, I'm surprised at you. He's old enough to be my father." Still, the thought that her confident lover could be jealous of another man delighted Honor on some primitive level she couldn't even begin to explain.

"A man like that wouldn't let a few years stop him if he really wanted you."

"Well, he can want all he pleases. My interest in him is purely professional." She reached for Nevada's hand and drew it to her lips, kissing each knuckle. "I'm a one-man woman, Clovis. You should know that by now."

He gave her an exasperated look at her use of his hated name and drew the backs of his fingers down her cheeks in a light caress, his eyes darkening with possessiveness. "I do know it, but a man shouldn't take his woman for granted."

"Or a woman her man." Honor closed her eyes and trembled at his tender, exciting touch. Her clothes suddenly felt too hot and unbearably heavy against her skin. "Do you have to go to your office right away?"

"No. Do you?"

"No."

"Shall we stop at your apartment?" His soft drawl had an impatient ragged edge to it.

Honor's heart raced at the delicious wickedness of a morning dalliance with him while the rest of the world went heedlessly about its humdrum affairs. "I have a feeling that neither of us will arrive at our respective offices today."

And they didn't.

Lyons spent the following day in Honor's office, where her desk was piled high with every newspaper Elroy could lay his hands on.

After spending the entire morning and half the afternoon reading and studying the accounts of Catherine Delancy's troubles with Anthony Comstock, Lyons finally rose, stretched unselfconsciously, and said to Honor, "Catherine will have a better chance of winning her case if she has a jury trial."

Honor knew full well that misdemeanors were tried in the Court of Special Sessions before three justices of equal rank, not before a jury. "So you're going to court to appeal for a jury trial?"

His youthful eyes gleamed like those of a fox getting ready to outwit the hounds. "Yes. The judge may not grant us one, but nothing ventured, nothing gained. This maneuver will also delay the trial, so we'll have more time to prepare."

She gave a knowing nod. "You think that a jury will be more sympathetic to her."

Honor knew as well as any lawyer that even though jurors were supposed to determine the issue without prejudice and base their verdict solely upon the sworn evidence, they were still fallible human beings.

"They will be more sympathetic to her," Lyons said. "Do you know why?"

Honor sat back in her chair and pondered his rationale. "Most likely they'll be family men, some young and others middle-aged. Perhaps several will have experienced the financial hardships of raising large families themselves. Perhaps others will even have practiced some method of limiting the size of their families."

Lyons held up his right index finger to emphasize his point. "During the voir dire, we'll look for those who have lost a wife or a sister to childbirth, or someone whose wife or daughter was saved by a woman doctor like Catherine Delancy. We'll seek those who once lived in the tenements and pulled themselves up by their bootstraps and got out."

He spread his hands before him. "But that's not all. Let's hope to get a writer or an editor because such men are intelligent and will doubtlessly find in Catherine's favor. The same would be true of artists. They're romantic and imaginative."

Honor knew from her own experience with *Graham v. Graham* and her other divorce cases that all lawyers, including herself, had their own prejudices when it came to selecting jurors.

She nodded. "Twelve jurors will give us much better odds than three justices."

Lyons leaned across her desk. "But that's only the start. Next we'll have to persuade the popular press to take our side."

Honor recalled Gordon Graham's skillful, but ultimately unsuccessful, manipulation of the press during his divorce case, and as much as she hated dealing with swarms of nosy reporters and hearing lurid headlines bawled by newsboys from every street corner, she had to admit that journalists could sway public opinion.

"Can't you see the headlines?" Lyons said, sweeping his hand across an invisible front page in yet another dramatic gesture. "'Angel of the Tenements Threatened with Prison,' or 'Lady Doctor Fights for Freedom.'" His eyes sparkled with youthful zeal, and his face turned red. "The outraged citizenry of this city will march through the streets in protest. They'll burn Anthony Comstock in effigy. They'll crowd the courtroom demanding justice for the fair Catherine."

Caught up in his infectious enthusiasm, Honor added, "The jurors will have tears in their eyes when they hear your moving, brilliant closing statement about this courageous woman doctor who is willing to risk a prison sentence to better the lives of her patients."

Lyons placed his closed fist over his heart. "Who could not be moved?"

Honor smiled. "That's a brilliant strategy, Mr. Lyons."

"Philip, my dear," he said, grabbing her hand and bringing it to his lips. "If we're to work so close together, we cannot stand on formality."

She felt her cheeks turn pink, and she was thankful that Nevada was not in the room and that Elroy was seated just beyond her closed door, pecking at his typewriter. "Philip and Honor it shall be."

Lyons released her hand and started pacing around the office like his restless namesake, staring down at the floor as if brilliant legal strategy were written there. Then he looked at Honor. "Your task is to make everyone in this city fall in love with Catherine Delancy."

Honor stared at him, dumbfounded. "And how am I supposed to accomplish that?"

"Listen carefully. . . ."

Catherine was skeptical when Honor cornered her in the dispensary late that afternoon and told her of Lyons's plans.

Her sleeves rolled up to her elbows and her shirtwaist spattered with dried brown bloodstains, Catherine dragged her forearm across her brow and sighed wearily. "But I'm not an angel of the tenements, Honor. I'm just a doctor trying to treat my patients, and as for turning me into a fashion plate"—she shook her head—"I wear my hair in a chignon to keep it out of my way, and I wear plain, serviceable clothes that clean easily and let me move freely." She rolled down her sleeves. "And as for talking to newspaper reporters, I'd rather be dragged through the streets by wild horses."

"Catherine," Honor said, trying not to watch Hilda Steuben sewing up a gash on a woman's head as if she were stitching two pieces of cloth together, "your husband is paying Philip Lyons a small fortune to keep you out of prison. The least you can do is take the man's advice. He knows what he's doing."

"I'm sure he does, but I'd still rather have you defend me."

"At least I'm helping him."

Catherine frowned in annoyance. "New clothes, newspaper interviews . . . this is such a bloody awful waste of time."

"It could keep you out of prison," Honor said.

Hilda, without missing a stitch, muttered, "Go ahead, Dr. Dee, be as stubborn and pigheaded as I am. Don't listen to your lawyers. And when you wind up behind bars on Blackwell's Island, don't expect me to come visit you."

Catherine smiled. "Hilda, the thought of not seeing your smiling face or hearing your sweet voice for five years is enough to make me reconsider." She said to Honor, "I surrender. When do we start?"

They started the following day to create the new Dr. Catherine Delancy.

Their labors bore fruit four weeks later when Elroy came rushing into Honor's office with a fistful of newspapers.

There in the *World*, beneath a headline that screamed, "Angel of the Tenements Faced with Prison," was a picture of Catherine, her severe chignon abandoned in favor of hair swept up beneath a charming hat, and her mannish shirtwaist replaced by a mourning outfit complete with black ruffles and ribbons.

The artist who had drawn Catherine had made her look appealing yet approachable, strong yet vulnerable, sad yet optimistic. She looked like a heroine out of Sir Walter Scott, a Rebecca looking for her Ivanhoe.

The illustration in the *Sun* was a romanticized depiction of her at a patient's bedside looking suitably noble and compassionate, holding a sick woman's hand and mopping her brow. The accompanying article rang with sympathy for Dr. Delancy and vilified her persecutor, Anthony Comstock.

But though the newspapers were on Catherine's side, the courts were not. Despite Philip Lyons's best efforts throughout the spring and early summer, his two appeals in the Court of General Sessions for a jury trial were denied.

On August 6, 1897, Dr. Catherine Delancy was scheduled to go to trial.

* * *

Honor had never seen so many people packing the corridor outside Special Sessions as she found gathered there on the Friday morning of Catherine's trial. With Nevada to her right, she and Lyons preceded Catherine and Damon, who walked arm in arm. In the milling crowd, she noticed an iron-jawed Hilda Steuben towering over almost everyone, several of Catherine's patients from the tenements looking bewildered and out of place, and the newspaper reporter Liam Flynn leaning against a wall as he tried to jot something down on his notepad. She assumed that the rest of the spectators were curious onlookers and Socialists, who had declared their support early on.

Honor scanned the crowd, observing facial expressions and listening carefully like a hunting dog scenting the wind, and she exchanged a satisfied smile with Philip Lyons when she detected a decidedly pro-Catherine mood in the comments she overheard.

"They can't send her to prison."

"She's only trying to help us have a better life."

"Comstock ought to be shot for persecuting the poor woman."

When Comstock himself appeared at the other end of the hallway, the crowd suddenly turned ugly, and Honor witnessed the mindless, collective savagery of a lynching party. The crowd surged toward Comstock like a human wave, sweeping past Honor and everyone else in its path. She felt Nevada grab her arm and shield her with his own body, lest someone shove her to the floor, but even he was helpless against the movement of the angry human tide.

Before outstretched hands could claw and tear at Comstock, several policemen appeared between him and the crowd.

"Order!" one of them barked. "Quiet down, or I'll throw the lot of you in jail!"

"Just try it," someone shouted back, causing the policeman to turn red and search the sea of faces for the transgressor.

But the crowd settled down, much to Honor's relief, and they were admitted to the courtroom.

* * *

Entering the large, well-lighted courtroom, Honor felt her blood race as though she were striding onto a battlefield where Catherine Delancy's freedom would be won or lost. Her heart sank when she saw the identity of the presiding justice.

She caught Lyons's sleeve and whispered, "The presiding justice is Cresswell Pike. You should know that he's not exactly sympathetic to passers of anti-conception information."

Lyons's youthful eyes sparkled. "But there are two other justices sitting there. Hambly and George could overrule Pike."

Honor hoped so as she, Nevada, and Damon found their seats behind the defense table. She took out her handkerchief and dabbed at her brow, for it was hot in the courtroom and she felt strangely light-headed. She dismissed the sensation as the result of too much excitement.

A clerk looked around the crowded courtroom, where spectators now filled the benches, and shouted, "Hearken to the call of the calendar!"

Pike consulted a long sheet of paper. "People against Delancy?"

District Attorney Rampling rose and replied, "The people are ready."

Lyons rose. "The defense is ready."

The clerk bellowed, "Catherine Delancy to the bar!"

Still dressed in deepest mourning for her lost child, Catherine approached the bench along with Lyons and District Attorney Rampling.

Pike gave her a stern look. "Catherine Delancy, you stand accused of receiving obscene literature through the mails and circulating said obscene literature. How do you plead?"

"Not guilty, Your Honor," she said in a clear voice that carried in the hot, hushed courtroom.

Honor knew that Lyons's defense strategy was aimed at

proving that the pamphlet in question was not obscene; therefore she was not guilty of the charges against her.

Anthony Comstock, who had secured himself a seat near the witness enclosure, glared at her, shook his head, and muttered, "How can she perjure herself by not admitting her guilt?"

"Mr. Rampling," Pike said, "call your first witness."

As Catherine and Lyons returned to their seats, the district attorney called Anthony Comstock to the stand.

Comstock heaved his bulk up and approached the bench, his eyes flashing self-righteous fire as he glanced back at the spectators, seeking Damon Delancy. "Your Honors, I have been told that if I pursued this case, I would be shot." He eased his bulk into the witness chair, his huge paunch shaking. "I have disregarded that threat, and have only brought it to your attention so you'll have all the facts in this case."

The district attorney thanked him for performing his civic duty and waited for him to be sworn in before questioning him.

Sitting between Nevada and Damon, Honor listened to Comstock relate to the court how Dr. Delancy had first come to his attention when one of his agents heard that a woman doctor was distributing obscene anti-conception pamphlets to poor women in the tenements. He later sent one of his agents, Homer Baggins, to the doctor's office to obtain one of the pamphlets, but a suspicious Dr. Delancy refused to give him a copy.

Later another agent saw her leaving a brothel called Ivory's one night. A young prostitute, when questioned, accused the doctor of having performed an abortion.

"Was Dr. Delancy prosecuted for that crime?" the district attorney said.

"She was arrested," Comstock replied, "but another doctor later confessed to it." He sounded disappointed. "Since Dr. Flanders was her friend, I suspect that he did so just to save Dr. Delancy, and—"

"Objection," Lyons said.

"Sustained." Justice Pike turned to the witness. "Mr. Comstock, you will only answer the questions and refrain from adding personal comments."

Comstock then told the court that he suspected Dr. Delancy of providing her patients with anti-conception devices and obscene literature detailing how to employ such godless methods to limit the size of their families. He said that he had interviewed her patients, but they had all played dumb and none would report the doctor.

Then he told how he finally found evidence that incriminated Dr. Delancy: "I obtained a search warrant, and with several of my agents, on October 15 in the year 1894, we went to Catherine Delancy's office. There we found a supply of anti-conception devices and a disgusting, obscene pamphlet entitled *A Married Woman's Secret*. As it says in my original complaint, Your Honor, the devices were still in their packaging with the postage affixed." Comstock glared at Catherine. "Before the state could prosecute, the doctor and her husband fled the country."

Honor risked a glance at Damon, sitting to her left, his body rigid with tension. He stared at Comstock out of narrowed eyes so cold they could have frozen fire, and a muscle in his cheek twitched with the superhuman effort to suppress his rage and loathing. She wondered if Damon had hired someone to threaten to shoot Comstock. As a lawyer she objected on ethical and moral grounds, but as a woman she wouldn't have blamed him.

Then it was Lyons's turn to question Anthony Comstock.

He rose and approached the witness enclosure with the confidence of a stalking lion assessing his prey. Honor leaned forward in her seat and clenched her fists. She held her breath.

Lyons said, "When you sent Mr. Baggins to Dr. Delancy's office, isn't it true that he did not inform her that he was a member of the New York Society for the Suppression of Vice?"

Comstock regarded him with utter contempt. "If he had done that, she wouldn't have given him the pamphlet, now, would she?"

Lyons grasped the enclosure's railing. "You tried to obtain

that pamphlet under false pretenses, did you not?" His voice rang out: "You tried to frame her! That's fraud, Mr. Comstock!"

The district attorney objected.

Comstock ignored his objection. "If she had been innocent, she would have had nothing to fear. She would have welcomed my scrutiny as a God-fearing woman, and I couldn't have trapped her." He stared out at the spectators. "When you're doing the Lord's work, the end justifies the means."

A low rumble of outrage rippled through the courtroom, causing Justice Pike to call for order.

When the noise died down, Lyons said, "When you couldn't prosecute Dr. Delancy for performing an abortion, didn't you stand outside her office and harass her patients, intimidating them and threatening them with arrest?"

"I was exercising my right of free speech by trying to make those sinful women see the error of their ways."

Beside Honor, Nevada stirred.

Lyons smiled coldly. "I see. You were exercising your right of free speech by harassing those poor women, but at the same time you prevented them from exercising their right to see their physician."

"Objection, Your Honor. That's irrelevant," Rampling said. "Mr. Comstock is not on trial here."

What a damn shame, Honor thought. She had never loathed another human being more than she loathed Anthony Comstock.

Lyons said, "On October 15, 1894, when you obtained a warrant and searched Dr. Delancy's office, was she present?"

"Of course not. I waited until she went out. If I hadn't, she would've destroyed the evidence before I had a chance to seize it."

"And according to your previous testimony, you found copies of a pamphlet entitled *A Married Woman's Secret* in Dr. Delancy's desk. Is that true?"

"Yes, an obscene anti-conception pamphlet."

Lyons walked back over to the defense table, retrieved a

copy of the pamphlet, and showed it to Comstock. "This is the pamphlet?"

"The very one."

Lyons stroked his chin and frowned as if in deep thought. Then he looked up. "How do you know this pamphlet is obscene, Mr. Comstock?"

The question silenced Comstock, but only for a second. He regained his composure almost immediately. "For over twenty-five years I have dedicated my life to destroying filth such as this, sir. In that time I have destroyed over one hundred and fifty tons of pornography. Do you think I don't know an obscene pamphlet when I see one?"

"I wish you to be more specific," Lyons said, his voice dangerously silky. "I want you to tell the court precisely what qualifications you possess that make you the arbiter of this country's morals, Mr. Comstock."

Comstock turned red and bristled with indignation, obviously not accustomed to having his authority and judgment challenged. "I possess the same qualifications as any God-fearing, law-abiding citizen who is outraged by the filth and degradation that is corrupting the morals of our youth. And I know the law. The act that bears my name empowers me to seek out 'every article or thing designed, adapted, or intended for preventing conception or producing abortion.' That certainly describes the pamphlet found in Dr. Delancy's possession."

Honor leaned forward, transfixed by Lyons's method of laying the groundwork for their challenge to the pamphlet's obscenity.

Lyons gave an exaggerated sigh. "You haven't answered my question, sir. I asked how you know this pamphlet is obscene."

Comstock bristled again, shaking his chair. "Any decent, moral human being would know it's obscene. It contains a lewd drawing and obscene references to private parts of the human body, using words that are never spoken in polite society."

Lyons opened the pamphlet and studied it, his brow furrowed. "The drawing you speak of appears to be a medical illustration of the female reproductive system."

"It is lewd."

"And I'm assuming you're referring to words such as 'genitals,' 'vagina,' and—"

"How dare you!" Comstock roared, jumping to his feet and shaking with righteous indignation. He turned on the three justices. "I object, Your Honors. There are ladies and gentlemen present in this courtroom. They should not be exposed to the reading of such filth."

Honor looked around at the spectators whose tender sensibilities Comstock was trying to protect. No one had gasped in outrage or fainted.

"Mr. Lyons," Justice Pike said, "what is the point you're trying to make?"

Lyons was the picture of innocence. "I am merely trying to determine Mr. Comstock's qualifications for judging this pamphlet obscene, Your Honor."

"It would appear that he is eminently qualified," Pike said dryly.

Honor's heart sank. It was obvious that Pike was on Comstock's side, a point that did not bode well for Catherine. Honor wished they had been able to obtain a trial by jury, for Lyons was renowned for his ability to move the common man.

By the time Lyons concluded his cross-examination of Anthony Comstock, it was almost one o'clock, time for the summer session to be adjourned until Monday.

Rising, Honor studied Justice Hambly and Justice George. She could not tell from their composed expressions if they shared their colleague's high opinion of Comstock.

CHAPTER 21

"SOMBER AND TENSE" MOST accurately described the prevailing mood in the Delancy carriage after the trial. Damon sat there seething with frustration, memories of Anthony Comstock burned fresh in his mind. Philip Lyons frowned and massaged his neck.

Catherine studied him out of sharp, inquisitive eyes. "Mr. Lyons, are you feeling well?"

"It's nothing," he replied with a dismissive wave of his hand. "I often get a headache or a stiff neck after a trial. I expect it's all the excitement."

"I'll give you a headache powder when we arrive," Catherine said.

Honor leaned forward. "How do you think it went today?"

Lyons spread his hands. "It's too early to tell. We'll know more on Monday when the district attorney puts that O'Neill fellow on the stand."

Catherine groaned. "I remember him all too well. When he found out that I had given his wife a copy of *A Married Woman's Secret*, he threatened to kill me for interfering with his authority over his wife and family."

"He's in the minority," Lyons said. "For every man the prosecutor can find to testify against you, we can find five who will testify on your behalf."

Damon looked at his wife. "I wanted to murder Comstock with my bare hands."

"That would accomplish nothing," Honor said. "You'd only go to prison, and possibly to the electric chair, for your pains."

Nevada gave her a strange look, but said nothing.

They rode in silence until they reached Honor's office, then all wished her a good day as she disembarked. Nevada kissed her on the cheek and said he would return that evening to pick her up for dinner at the Delancys'.

At six o'clock that afternoon, after Elroy had gone home for the day and while Honor was just finishing up some paperwork, Nevada returned for her.

One look at his pinched white face told Honor that something dreadful had happened.

She shot to her feet, her heart racing. "What's wrong?"

He went to her and grasped her hands tightly, as if to brace her for the worst. "Lyons has had a stroke."

Honor stared at him, dumbfounded. "A stroke? When? He isn't . . . ?"

"Dead? No." He eased her back into her chair and sat down on the edge of the desk. "After we ate luncheon, he kept rubbing his neck and complaining of a headache. The doc wanted to examine him, but he wouldn't let her. He said he simply needed to lie down for a while and he'd be fine.

"When he didn't come downstairs after a couple of hours, the doc got worried and went up to look in on him." Nevada's blue gaze clouded. "She found him on the floor, unconscious."

Honor sat back in her chair. "Oh, dear God."

"The doc had Damon send for an ambulance, and they took Lyons to St. Bridgit's Hospital." Nevada took a deep breath. "Honor, he can't talk, and he can't move his right arm or leg."

She felt the blood drain from her face. "He's paralyzed? Dear God . . . will he recover?"

"The doc says if he does, it's going to take a long time."

"And if he doesn't?"

"The doc says he'll never be able to practice law again."

Hot tears stung Honor's eyes. "The poor man." She took a deep breath to control herself. "This means Catherine's trial will have to be postponed."

"Or she'll have to get another lawyer." Nevada stepped

away from the desk and extended his hand to her. "We had best get to the Delancys'."

Sitting in the carriage beside Nevada, Honor felt overwhelmed by sadness for Philip Lyons. Years ago a friend of Aunt Theo's had suffered a stroke. Honor remembered the woman vividly, confined to a wheelchair because one leg wouldn't support her and one arm was useless. She had all her mental faculties, but because her speech was slurred and garbled, she couldn't make herself understood to those around her. Honor remembered thinking at the time that it must have felt like being buried alive in one's own dead body.

To take her mind off Lyons, Honor wondered what Damon would decide to do. Would he seek to have the trial postponed, or would he hire another lawyer?

In any case, Honor knew he wouldn't ask her to take over.

When they arrived, they found Catherine pacing around the parlor and Damon leaning against the mantel, their faces strained and worried as they wondered what to do about this latest turn of events.

Honor went to Catherine at once and took her hands. "How is he?"

Catherine held tightly. "I wish I could say that he'll be back in the courtroom before you know it, but I can't. He has regained consciousness, but his prognosis is still not good."

"Can I visit him?"

"In several days, if his doctors allow it."

Damon stepped away from the mantel, his expression grave. "As much as I feel sorry for Mr. Lyons, and as heartless as this may seem, we have to concern ourselves first and foremost with Catherine's trial."

Catherine rubbed her forehead and slanted an exasperated glance at her husband.

Damon said to Honor, "What do we do next?"

"Have the trial postponed for as long as possible and find another lawyer," she replied.

Catherine exploded, her blue eyes flashing. "I don't want a postponement," she said, smacking her right fist into her left palm for emphasis. "I want this trial over and done with." Her voice rose, stunning everyone with its vehemence. "I don't want to spend another week or another month or another year wondering whether I'll go to prison or remain free." She faced her husband squarely. "Do you understand?"

"Of course I do," he said softly, placing a soothing hand on her arm.

"I don't want another lawyer," Catherine said. "I want Honor to represent me."

A muscle twitched in her husband's jaw, and his sympathetic gaze turned stern and unyielding. "Catherine, we've been over this a thousand times."

She flung his hand away. "I don't care if we've been over this a million times. I want Honor to represent me!"

"Catherine—"

"Honor has been working closely with Lyons," Catherine pointed out. "She knows exactly how he intended to argue my case." She looked at Honor. "Don't you?"

"Yes," Honor replied. "We discussed it point by point and decided that Catherine's best defense would be to prove that the pamphlet itself is not obscene. If we can do that through expert testimony, Comstock won't have a case."

Triumph shone in Catherine's eyes. "Do you think you can prove it?"

Ignoring Damon's fierce warning glare, Honor raised her stubborn chin. "Before, I would have said no, but after working so closely with Lyons, I'm confident that I can handle it."

"Well, I'm not," Damon said. "You don't have the experience. I want to hire another lawyer as soon as possible."

"How do you know the new man will be as good as Lyons?" Catherine said.

Damon's mouth quirked in a wry smile. "Lyons is not the only outstanding lawyer in the world. I'm sure I can find one or two others."

"A new attorney will have to start from scratch. He'll need time to prepare," Catherine said. "And what about the newspapers? Will they keep writing glowing accounts about me while the trial is postponed?"

Damon said, "The longer your trial is postponed, the longer you'll remain free."

"I can't spend another waking hour wondering when I'm going to be carted off to prison," Catherine said.

Honor said, "She's right. Part of Lyons's plan to gain public sympathy was to have frequent articles about Catherine in the newspapers. If the trial is postponed and she's no longer newsworthy, those articles are going to stop appearing. When her trial is eventually resumed, interest will have died. That could ultimately hurt her case."

Nevada, who had been standing quietly with his thumbs hooked in his belt, spoke up. "Honor has a point, Delancy."

Damon looked from Nevada to Honor. "Those three justices didn't look as though they'd be swayed by public opinion. I want Catherine's case postponed, and I want her to have a new lawyer."

"Stop it!" Catherine cried, her face crumpling. Her slender shoulders shook, and loud, keening wails emanated from her open mouth. She lowered herself onto the sofa, buried her face in her hands, and sobbed as though her heart would break.

Damon exchanged a panic-stricken look with Nevada, then knelt at his wife's side. He touched her arm tentatively. "Catherine . . . ?"

She lowered her hands away from her tearstained, ravaged face and hugged herself, rocking back and forth and crying in great hiccuping sobs that filled the parlor.

Sobbing so hard she could barely speak, she managed to say to Damon, "I can't go on. I can't fight Comstock anymore. It's my fault that Willie's dead. *My* fault. He'd still be alive if we hadn't gone to England. He'd be alive if we had stayed here."

Damon sat down beside her and pulled her into his arms, hugging her fiercely. "It wasn't your fault. Damn it, Catherine! You mustn't blame yourself."

"I don't want to fight with you, Damon. I just want it to be over so I can have some peace."

He stroked her wet cheek tenderly. "You're tired and overwrought. You'll feel better once you've had some sleep."

"No, no, don't you see?" she moaned, pulling his hand away

and clutching at it. "It's not sleep I need. It's peace. I want Honor to defend me. I want this over once and for all. If I have to wait another month or another year, I'll go mad, I swear I will."

And because even a strong-willed man like Damon Delancy had no defense against the power of his wife's tears, he surrendered. "If you want Honor to defend you, you shall have her." He closed his eyes. "Just don't cry."

Catherine dabbed at her eyes with a handkerchief. "I just want this nightmare to be over, my love. I just want it to be over."

Later, after Catherine had gone to her room to rest, a visibly shaken Damon met Honor and Nevada in his study. With unsteady hands he poured himself a generous measure of brandy and downed it in two swallows that made his eyes water.

He sat at his desk and shook his head. "I never dreamed she would fall to pieces like that. She's always been so strong."

Nevada stroked his mustache. "Everyone has a breaking point."

Damon gave Honor a hard stare. "Catherine wants you, so against my better judgment, I'm asking you to take over from Lyons. Will you do it?"

Honor nodded. "I feel more confident of winning than I did several months ago."

Damon rose and extended his hand. "Then you're hired."

She shook it. "You realize that I can't guarantee an acquittal."

"Let me just say that if my wife loses her freedom, I shall hold you personally responsible." The coldness in his eyes caused a chill to slither up Honor's spine. "I don't care if you are Nevada's friend. If my wife goes to prison, you will pay and pay dearly."

Nevada stepped closer to Honor, his body tense. "You'll have to get past me first, Delancy," he growled.

Damon regarded his friend with regret. "Just so we understand each other."

If Honor lost this case, not only would Catherine lose her

freedom but Nevada would also lose an old and valued friend.

Later that night, curled up against Nevada in her bed, Honor couldn't sleep. She wouldn't be saving Catherine from the gallows, but hers was still an important case with far-reaching consequences for women, and the thought that she was going to argue it made her blood sing with excitement.

If she lost, the consequences would be just as far-reaching for the man she loved. After they had left the Delancys' and she had thanked Nevada for siding with her, he had looked offended and said, "I always defend what's mine." Though Nevada acted as if a rift with Damon wouldn't matter, Honor knew that the breakup of their long-standing friendship would exact a heavy price, not only financially but emotionally.

Then you just can't lose, she thought, gathering all the courage she could muster. Too much is at stake.

That Sunday, Philip Lyons's doctors at St. Bridgit's allowed him to have visitors, so Catherine arranged for Honor to see him.

Seeing her mentor as he lay there in an overcrowded hospital ward that smelled of sickness and carbolic, his right arm slack, Honor had to fight back tears when she thought of the vital man he used to be. Now she saw fear and hopelessness in the eyes that had once held such a youthful sparkle. Though he squeezed her hand with his good left one, he was too proud to try to speak.

Sitting by his beside, Honor told him that she would be taking over Catherine's case. Lyons smiled in approval and nodded, even as an indescribable sadness filled his eyes.

Leaving the hospital, she knew she was on her own.

The following day, a hot, steamy Monday, Honor went to court and informed the three justices that Lyons had suffered a stroke and that she would be taking over as Catherine Delancy's counsel, causing an uproar in the courtroom.

They reluctantly granted her a continuance until Thursday,

so Honor had three days to prepare for the most important case of her life.

The following morning Honor awoke with a sour stomach that she attributed to nerves. She was especially annoyed to find none other than Liam Flynn of the *Sun* waiting downstairs in the lobby of her apartment building as she left for her office.

"Ah, Mrs. Davis," he began with his most beguiling Irish smile. "Just the person I've been waiting to see."

Honor raised her brows. "This is a new low for you, isn't it, Mr. Flynn, accosting me in my home?"

He didn't have the grace to look embarrassed. "You know what they say, dear lady: the early bird gets the worm. I'm merely getting a leg up on the competition." He looked around the lobby. "Is there somewhere we can talk in private?"

"But I haven't agreed to talk with you."

"It will be to your advantage if you do."

Honor remembered what Philip Lyons had said about using the press, so she capitulated. "We can use the public parlor."

Once they were seated in a quiet, deserted corner, Flynn whipped out his dog-eared notebook and leaned forward. "I want to do a story on you, Mrs. Davis. It's not every day that a beautiful lady lawyer—"

"Just stop right there, Mr. Flynn," Honor said coolly. "If this is to be anything like the story you did about me when I argued Mrs. Gordon Graham's divorce case, I'll have none of it."

He looked perplexed. "What was wrong with that story, pray tell?"

"You dwelt more on my . . . physical attributes than on my legal expertise. I was quite offended."

He grinned. "New Yorkers want to read about beautiful, unconventional women, Mrs. Davis."

"Be that as it may, you must agree to concentrate on the legal aspects of the case, not the color of my hair and eyes. Agreed?"

"May I at least mention how lovely you are? It may garner your case some extra sympathy."

Honor sighed. "You may describe me as you see fit, but kindly don't dwell on it."

"Agreed."

Liam Flynn then spent a good half hour talking with Honor about the case. He was so skillful an interviewer that she almost didn't notice when his questions suddenly took a personal turn.

"You're obviously married, Mrs. Davis."

"Obviously."

"Why do we never see Mr. Davis in court?"

Honor paused and considered her response carefully. "He deserted me about a year ago."

Her reply jolted Flynn's composure, and he turned bright red beneath his rust-colored beard. He cleared his throat. "I'm sorry. I didn't know."

Honor heaved a theatrical sigh that would have done Aunt Theo proud. "He callously left me alone in the world to fend for myself."

Flynn's eyes narrowed. "For a woman who misses her husband, you seem to spend quite a lot of time in Nevada LaRouche's company. Whenever you appear in court, he's never far behind."

Honor felt as though she were dancing on ice, and she scrambled furiously to regain her footing. "Mr. LaRouche and I have been friends ever since my husband worked for his company."

Flynn scratched his beard and stared off into space. "He's always stayed in Delancy's shadow, except during that business with August Talmadge."

Honor frowned. "Talmadge was the banker who murdered Mr. LaRouche's fiancée and was later killed when he tried to murder Dr. Delancy."

"The very same." The reporter watched her as carefully as a cat studying a mouse. "As a matter of fact, it was LaRouche who killed him."

"It was an accident," Honor pointed out. "When he tried to stop Talmadge from escaping, the man fell and broke his neck."

"That's what everyone said."

Suddenly feeling uneasy, she tugged at her locket. "Am I to assume that you feel differently, Mr. Flynn?"

He closed his notebook. "That whole situation seemed a little too neat and tidy to me."

Her curiosity got the better of her. "Neat? In what way?"

Flynn slipped the notebook into his breast pocket. "Oh, that Talmadge just happened to break his neck while escaping, and that the Delancys just happened to witness the accident and provide LaRouche with a perfect unbreakable alibi."

Honor stared at him for what seemed like an eternity. When she spoke, she chose her words very carefully. "Are you saying that Mr. LaRouche deliberately killed Mr. Talmadge and that the Delancys conspired to help him conceal it? I hope you can prove it, Mr. Flynn, because if you can't . . ." Her voice trailed off in warning, her implied threat of dire legal consequences hanging in the air between them.

The reporter rose and raised his hands. "Hold on there, Mrs. Davis. Don't jump to conclusions. I'm not accusing anyone of anything. I was merely speculating, as we reporters are wont to do. But I know what I would have done if I had been in LaRouche's shoes."

Then he wished Honor a good morning and left.

And I know what I would have done, Honor thought.

"Did you deliberately kill August Talmadge?"

Honor faced Nevada as he stood behind his desk at Delancy and LaRouche, her fingers clasped tightly around her locket as if it were a truth talisman. Ever since Flynn had blithely strode away, leaving his horrible innuendo behind to fester and grow, Honor hadn't known a moment's peace despite her best efforts to put the Talmadge incident out of her mind and concentrate on Catherine's case.

Finally her burning need to know the truth had sent her flying out of her office to confront her lover.

Nevada's eyes were as solemn and as sad as Honor's father's had been the night before he was hanged, and with a sinking heart, she knew.

She felt light-headed. Black spots danced before her eyes.

Her corset squeezed the last ounce of breath out of her. Then Nevada was at her side, one strong arm around her waist, easing her into a chair. She breathed slowly until the light-headedness passed and she could think clearly.

"You all right?" he said, his soft drawl edged with a concern that brought tears to her eyes.

"I felt a little faint from the heat." She looked up at him, her bright, accusatory stare demanding an answer.

He sighed, a dismal sound in the quiet room. "To answer your question, yes."

"No!" Honor shook her head in emphatic denial. "You couldn't have. I know you. You're too proud a man. You—" She stopped, unable to go on.

"It's high time I told someone the truth about what happened that night."

Oh, dear God, it's true, Honor thought wildly.

She knew he had killed men, but only in self-defense. He could not have committed cold-blooded murder.

Bile rose in her throat and she swallowed hard. "I want to know how it happened."

Nevada sat on the edge of his desk and gripped it so hard his knuckles turned white. "I take it you learned about that night when you investigated me?"

Honor nodded, fighting to make the nausea subside.

"Then you know Talmadge murdered Sybilla and was trying to kill the doc when Delancy and I arrived just in time." When she nodded again, he said, "I told Delancy and the doc to leave me alone with Talmadge, and they did. We fought in the doc's office. Fear gave him strength, and he gave as good as he got."

Nevada frowned and rubbed his forehead as if coaxing out some long-forgotten memory. "Actually, I don't remember how it happened. It's like there's a piece missing to a puzzle. The next thing I knew, I was looking down at Talmadge lying on the floor. His neck was broken, but as God is my judge, Honor, I don't remember doing it. Yet no one else could have. When I told the Delancys what I had done, they both said I should claim it was an accident and they would swear to it."

She swallowed hard. "Did you intend to kill him?"

"No! I only wanted to beat him senseless. I must have killed him in the heat of the moment, and believe me, I've regretted it ever since."

"If you didn't intend to kill him, you would have been charged with manslaughter, not murder."

"What's the difference? Honor, I killed him."

"It's a legal position of intent. If you had killed him with malice aforethought, you'd be charged with murder. Like my father." She looked at him. "Why didn't you tell the police just what you told me?"

"I offered to turn myself in, but the Delancys talked me out of it." His eyes darkened and he looked troubled. "It seemed justified at the time. That bastard strangled Sybilla. She died scared and alone in an alley. And then he tried to kill the doc. Why should I go to prison for killing him?"

"As horrible as Talmadge was," Honor said, "his punishment should have been decided in a court of law, not by you, Nevada LaRouche. This isn't the wild West. You shouldn't have taken the law into your own hands. Damon and Catherine shouldn't have helped you."

He looked at her. "I'm not a saint, Honor. I warned you at Coppermine that I had broken laws. I've even killed men, but always to keep them from killing me first. I've never deliberately set out to take another man's life."

She rose, her eyes burning with the effort to keep from crying. A lump formed in her throat, making speech difficult. "Were you ever planning to tell me the truth about Talmadge?"

"Yes, when I was sure that you loved me so much it wouldn't matter." He stared at the toes of his boots. "But I guess it does matter."

She almost flung herself into his arms, but she knew that if she did so, she would be turning her back on her long-cherished principles. Honesty. Decency. A respect for the law. Nevada and the Delancys obviously thought they could twist and subvert the law to their own advantage. As always, the three of them were as thick as thieves.

Honor stepped away from him and crossed her arms. "I

know myself well enough know that it does matter, but I can't think about anything except Catherine's case right now. Perhaps it would be best if we didn't see each other until I can decide what to do."

Before she could blink, he was off the desk, his long fingers grasping her arms above the elbow. His eyes blazed with raw desperation. "I won't let you leave like this. We have to talk."

But she knew the time for talking was long past. Honor just stood there, wordless, not fighting, but not helping, either. Finally, Nevada released her and let his hands fall to his sides.

Honor turned and left his office.

"Honor, it's Catherine. Please open the door. I have to talk to you."

Honor tried to dry her red, swollen eyes with her damp handkerchief, blew her nose, and went to the door of her apartment. "Are you alone?" When Catherine answered in the affirmative, Honor unlocked the door and opened it.

Catherine regarded Honor with a mixture of reproach and sympathy.

"If you've come to try to talk me into forgiving him," Honor said, closing the door, "you can turn right around and go home." She dabbed at her nose. "Come to think of it, you and Damon have a few things to answer for yourselves." She headed for the parlor, the thin batiste of her dressing gown billowing out about her.

Catherine followed. "I know I'm the last person in the world you want to see right now, but—"

"No, Nevada LaRouche has that honor." Honor's eyes filled with fresh, senseless tears as she swept into the parlor and whirled on Catherine. "I don't mean to be rude, but please say what you have to say, then leave me alone. Unless you're here to discuss the case."

Catherine did not even ask if she could sit down. She stood before Honor nervously twisting her wedding ring. "When Nevada returned home today, he went to the stables to curry his horse himself. That may seem insignificant to you, but it's what he does whenever he's deeply troubled."

Honor folded her arms before her as if that simple act could keep Catherine's words from affecting her.

"He told me what happened today," Catherine said softly. "I've never seen him so—so devastated, and as you know, he's not a man who reveals his emotions readily."

"He killed a man and tried to hide it," Honor snapped. "What am I supposed to say? I'm an officer of the court. It's my job to bring people like him to justice, not condone what he did just because he is—was—my lover."

"Before you judge Nevada so harshly," Catherine said, "I'd like to tell you about August Talmadge."

"He was a murderer."

"He was much more than that." Catherine sat down. "Will you give me a half hour of your time?" When Honor sat down reluctantly, Catherine began her story.

"I first had dealings with Talmadge when his wife, Dahlia, became my patient. She had been complaining of severe abdominal pains, and when I examined her, I discovered more than an ovarian tumor." Catherine leaned forward. "I discovered that she had been whipped."

Honor stared at her. "Whipped? But who . . ."

"Her husband. He regularly tied her to the bedpost and whipped her to gratify his perverted sexual desires."

Honor's lip curled. "That's disgusting."

"I was appalled and outraged, and since my husband did business with Talmadge's bank, I asked"—she smiled—"no, I demanded that he pressure Talmadge to stop brutalizing his wife." Her expression clouded. "Little did I realize that I was signing Sybilla's death warrant.

"During the depression of '93, Talmadge's bank failed and he blamed Damon and took his revenge. He hired someone to plant a bomb in our stables, and Damon was blinded when it exploded." Catherine knotted her fingers together. "Luckily, the blindness was only temporary, but it could have been permanent. And of course you know that Talmadge tried to kill me." She leaned forward. "The man was a monster, Honor."

"That may be true, but Nevada still had no right to be his judge, jury, and executioner. And you had no right to protect him."

"Can you blame him? He loved Sybilla. And we protected him because we love him."

"Even monsters deserve their day in court. Talmadge would have gone to the electric chair for his crimes."

"Not necessarily. Justice is often blind. There's no guarantee that Talmadge would have been executed for what he did."

Honor thought of her father, an innocent man executed for a crime he didn't commit. Justice indeed could be blind.

Catherine studied her intently. "How would you feel if someone killed Nevada?"

A picture of Nevada lying dead in an alley flashed through Honor's mind, and she felt a terrible aching loneliness, like a knife wound to the heart. She shuddered, rose, and turned away. "That's not fair."

"Why not? If you were in the same situation, wouldn't you feel like killing your lover's murderer?"

Honor walked over to the window to escape Catherine's relentless hounding, closed her eyes, and rested her forehead against the cool windowpane. "I don't know."

Catherine joined her there. "What do you intend to do now that you know our dreadful secret? Will you turn the three of us over to the authorities?"

"Even if I did, it would be my word against yours. I wasn't there. I have no proof." She smiled wanly. "But I'm afraid it's going to be difficult for us to remain friends."

Without a warning, a wave of dizziness made her sway on her feet.

"Honor, what is it?" Catherine asked sharply, grabbing her elbow to steady her.

"I—I feel faint."

Catherine led her back to the sofa and made her sit down. "Has this happened before?"

"It comes and goes."

A knowing look flashed across Catherine's face, then disappeared. "My medical bag is in the carriage, so I can examine you, if you like. Since I still want you to defend me at my trial, I want to make sure you're up to the task."

Honor regarded her in disbelief. "After what happened

between Nevada and me, I assumed you wouldn't want me to defend you."

"You assume too quickly." Catherine looked at her. "I meant what I said to Damon. I want this over as soon as possible. I trust you, and I feel confident of your abilities."

"This won't change how I feel about your conspiracy."

"I don't expect it to."

She turned and headed for the door.

After retrieving her medical bag, Catherine made Honor lie down on her bed and proceeded to examine her. When she finished, she took Honor's hand and said, "There's a simple explanation for those dizzy spells. You're a little over two months pregnant. You're going to have a baby."

Honor stared at her, dumbfounded. Surely Catherine was talking about someone else. This was her revenge for Honor's breaking off with Nevada. It had to be. There was no other explanation.

"I am not having a baby," Honor said.

"But you are."

"You're sure."

"Positive."

Honor burst into tears.

"You have to tell him," Catherine said, sponging Honor's forehead with a cool cloth. "He is the father."

Still reeling from the shock, Honor muttered, "I can't be pregnant. I've always used Aunt Theo's pessaries."

Catherine raised her brows. "They're illegal. It would seem that our upstanding lady lawyer has been breaking the law herself."

Honor's cheeks turned crimson. "It's not as serious a crime as murder, Catherine, and you know it."

"Yes, I do. I was merely trying to make a point."

Honor sat up and grabbed Catherine's arm. "You mustn't tell him. Not yet. Promise?"

"As with lawyers, anything you tell a doctor is held in strictest confidence." Catherine closed her medical case.

"What are you going to do about this child now that you've broken off with Nevada?"

"I don't know. I haven't had time to think about it."

Catherine rose. "May I offer you some advice? First walk in Nevada's boots; then temper justice with mercy and let your heart guide you."

Then she wished Honor a good night and let herself out.

A baby. Nevada's child.

Sitting in her dark parlor, curled up in one corner of the sofa, Honor let the warm night breeze blowing slowly in through the open widow waft over her while she watched the square patch of moonlight crawl its way across the floor.

She still couldn't believe it. The queasy stomach in the morning, the dizziness, the two missed cycles that she had been too busy to notice—all the warning signs were there, but she had not heeded them.

What was she going to do now? She was a married woman whose husband was God only knew where, and she was pregnant with her lover's child. Not only wouldn't they allow her into a courtroom once her condition became apparent, but she would also be branded an adulteress. She would have to return to Boston.

But she didn't want Aunt Theo. She wanted Nevada.

Honor hugged her pillow. She wished he were here with her now, his eyes shining with pleasure at her news. He would take her in his arms and hold her with his customary strength and tenderness, her head cradled against his shoulder. Later he would take her into the bedchamber, and they would celebrate the conception of their child.

But he had concealed a crime, with the help of his friends. How could she possibly love and live with a man who flouted the very laws she was sworn to uphold?

Honor's heart felt encased in ice, and a deep hollowness filled her soul. As much as she loved Nevada, they now stood on opposite sides of a deep chasm, and no matter how hard they tried, they would never bridge the gap.

Honor decided to leave for Boston after Catherine's trial and never see Nevada LaRouche again.

Chapter 22

She saw him on Thursday morning when she entered the crowded corridor outside the courtroom for the continuation of Catherine's trial. No matter how well she girded herself mentally, the sight of him still made her traitorous pulse race.

His complexion was inordinately pale, and the dark smudges underscoring his eyes gave testimony to sleepless nights. Though deep in conversation with Damon, he looked dazed, as if someone had struck him hard on the side of the head. When he glanced up and inadvertently saw Honor through the crowd, a warm, expectant light flared in his eyes, then died.

Honor thought of the fatherless boy raised in a brothel, always seeing and hearing too much, and she felt her resolve weaken. She wanted to take him in her arms and tell him that all would be right.

Don't do this to yourself, she thought. He's not that little boy anymore. He's a grown man who wouldn't pay for his crime.

She finally wove her way through the crush to where the three of them stood. One look at Damon's thunderous, accusatory expression told her that he knew of her estrangement from Nevada. She squared her shoulders, refusing to allow him to intimidate her.

"Damon . . . Nevada," she said coolly to the men before quickly turning to Catherine. "Are you ready?"

Catherine smiled warmly as though nothing had happened and knotted her fingers together. "I can't stop shaking. I just want to be done with this."

Honor tried to ignore Nevada's solid, quiet presence and his ability to unsettle her. She said to Catherine, "It'll be over soon."

Just then the clerk summoned everyone into the courtroom. Honor was about to go in when she felt a firm, unyielding hand on her elbow. She looked up to find Damon's dark, glowering face inches from her own.

"I want to talk to you after the trial," he said between savagely clenched teeth.

"If it's not about the case, we have nothing to say to each other," she replied. "Ever again. That goes double for Nevada."

He muttered a curse under his breath, but she ignored it. She knew how to handle angry, bellicose men snorting steam through their nostrils.

She looked straight ahead and focused on the coming trial.

Patrick O'Neil took the stand.

Seated next to Catherine at the defense table in the hot, overcrowded courtroom, Honor forced all thoughts of her condition out of her mind, along with the man responsible, who was seated right behind her. She had to concentrate. She knew that the district attorney was so confident of a conviction that he did not intend to call any witnesses for the prosecution aside from Comstock and O'Neill. Honor would begin Catherine's defense later today.

". . . and when did you discover that your wife had received anti-conception information?" Rampling said, holding up a copy of *A Married Woman's Secret*.

O'Neill, a small man as skinny as a rat's tail, turned red with outrage. "I found that paper hidden under me mattress where she thought I wouldn't find it, Yer Honor."

"Did you ask your wife who gave her this pamphlet?"

"Aye, that I did, Yer Honor." He pointed a damning finger at Catherine. "She said she got it from Dr. Delancy."

The district attorney glanced at Honor. "Your witness."

Honor rose and approached the witness enclosure. "Mr. O'Neill, you gave your age as twenty-five."

"That I am."

"And you have *eight* children?"

"That I do."

"Is it true that you, your wife, and your *eight* children"—she let her voice rise incredulously—"all live together in a two-room flat in a tenement on Baxter Street?"

Before O'Neill could open his mouth, Rampling rose and said, "Your Honor, I fail to see what Mr. O'Neill's living arrangements have to do with this case."

Pike said, "So do I. Mrs. Davis, please stick to the pertinent facts."

"Yes, Your Honor. Mr. O'Neill, did your wife ask Dr. Delancy for the pamphlet?"

Rampling rose. "Objection. Whether Mrs. O'Neill asked for the information is immaterial."

Lyons had been right when he said Rampling wouldn't let him get away with this line of cross-examination, but Honor saw that at least Justices Hambly and George looked astonished to hear that a family of ten lived packed together like cattle in two rooms. Perhaps they could see the benefit to family limitation after all.

"I have no further questions of this witness," Honor said, and returned to her seat.

"Prosecution rests, Your Honor."

Now it was Honor's turn.

During the next hour Honor called three character witnesses to the stand, just as Philip Lyons had planned, all tenement women who were Catherine Delancy's patients, but she asked them questions of her own devising rather than relying on Lyons's strategy.

By use of skillful questioning gleaned from watching

Cleavon Frame in Boston, Honor drew the court a portrait of a selfless, dedicated doctor who spent long hours and risked her own life to help her patients. Everyone in the courtroom except Anthony Comstock listened transfixed, and when Honor glanced at the spectators crammed together on the benches, she saw only sympathy.

Rampling found little to object to in the testimony, but when he cross-examined the women, he asked only one damning question: "Did Dr. Delancy ever give you information or devices that would keep you from having children?"

Each one indignantly replied, "Yes, but I asked her for it, and I'm glad I did!"

Honor studied the justices' faces, hoping that the glowing character references would outweigh these admissions of guilt.

Then Honor called Dr. Hilda Steuben to the stand and got ready for fireworks.

When Hilda was sworn in, she glared at the bailiff as if he were a fractious two-year-old and said, "Young man, I am not a liar. Of course I'll tell the truth."

The spectators tittered, causing Justice Pike to bang his gavel and call for order.

Honor approached her witness. "Dr. Steuben, how long have you been practicing medicine?"

Seated in the witness enclosure, Hilda needed only a horned Viking helmet to complete the picture of an aggravated Norse goddess. Her demeanor telegraphed her scorn for these proceedings more clearly than mere words, especially when her gaze lit on Comstock, seated nearby.

"Twenty-five years," she replied.

"In that time you've read a great deal of medical literature."

Hilda rolled her eyes. "More than I care to remember."

Honor walked back to her table, picked up a copy of *A Married Woman's Secret*, and handed it to Hilda. "I'm not asking you if you've ever given this pamphlet to your patients, but have you ever read it? Just by chance, of course."

"As a matter of fact, just by chance, I have."

From his place near the witness stand, Comstock muttered, "Another peddler of filth lying to save her own skin."

Hilda's eyes narrowed into dire slits, and she glared at him. "There's no law against reading, you sanctimonious old goat. You might try it sometime and let the sunlight of truth into the dark recesses of your closed little mind."

"Dr. Steuben," Pike said, "please refrain from such outbursts."

"That wasn't an outburst, Your Honor. I was merely exercising my constitutional right of free speech."

The justice scowled. "Nevertheless, please refrain from making disruptive comments in the future." He gestured at Honor to continue.

"Doctor, what's your expert medical opinion of the pamphlet?"

Hilda bristled. "It's no more lewd or obscene than most medical books I've studied."

The district attorney jumped to his feet like a jack-in-the-box with a broken lid. "Objection! Dr. Steuben is a physician, not a lawyer. She is not qualified to make such a judgment."

Hilda reared back in her seat. "I beg to differ with you, sir. During all the years that I've been practicing medicine, I have seen the Comstock Act hang over the head of everyone in the medical profession like the sword of Damocles."

"Dr. Steuben—"

"No, Mr. Rampling, let me finish. This absurd obscenity statute has hindered me and other experienced, well-trained doctors in our efforts to aid those who most need this information."

Pike turned beet red. "My good lady, I'm warning you for the last time that I shall hold you in contempt of court. And I quite agree with the district attorney that you are not qualified to judge the obscenity of such a pamphlet."

Hilda turned a darker shade of red. "I may not be a lawyer, Your Honor, but you are not a doctor, so how can you presume to tell me what is best for my patients?"

Honor stepped in before Hilda went too far and wound up spending the night in the Tombs. "Dr. Steuben, how long have you known Dr. Delancy?"

"A little over six years."

While the courtroom listened, Hilda spent the next hour telling how her softhearted colleague had once arrived too late to save a young mother who had committed suicide by swallowing carbolic acid. She told how Catherine Delancy was almost murdered by a drunkard when she tried to deliver his wife's baby. She told of a young mother too poor to afford a crib for her newborn baby because she had so many mouths to feed, and how it had cost the softhearted Dr. Delancy many a sleepless night.

Finally Honor said, "Thank you, Doctor. I have no further questions."

Rampling obviously decided that Hilda was too much of an unknown quantity to cross-examine, so he said, "I have no questions of this witness." He looked relieved when Hilda stepped down and sailed back to her seat.

Pike noticed it was one o'clock, time to adjourn for the day.

Tomorrow Honor would call her final witness.

Tomorrow Catherine's fate and her own would be sealed.

Late that afternoon in Honor's hot, stuffy office, after she had evaded the irate Damon and managed to say a few words to Catherine about tomorrow's court session, she looked up out of tired eyes to find Nevada standing in the doorway.

Strange, she thought, how a man who looks so out of place everywhere else always looks so much at home here.

Though he appeared calm, anger skittered just below the surface of his composure. "Did you mean what you said to Delancy about not having anything to say to me?"

Where in God's name had Elroy gone? Why hadn't he warned her?

"I never say what I don't mean," she replied, wishing she were strong enough to resist this man's magnetic pull, wishing she didn't find him so damned attractive or love him so much.

He stepped into her office and closed the door. "We have to talk."

Honor rose and shuffled the papers on her desk while she eyed him warily. She sensed a volatile shift in his mood, an air of barely restrained male displeasure that left her edgy in his presence.

He moved as quietly as a cougar, and before Honor could blink, she found her wrists restrained by his strong yet gentle hands. "I love you," he growled, his remote gaze revealing complex emotions too deep and unsettling. "You've lain with me, so don't deny that you love me. We're mated."

He released her wrists just long enough to grasp her hands, lift them to his cheeks, and rub his face against her palms slowly and deliberately, leaving his scent on her skin. He closed his eyes and deeply inhaled the faint rose perfume she had dabbed on her wrists just that morning. Honor couldn't move, transfixed by the sheer eroticism of feeling his smooth warm skin stretched taut over fine, hard facial bones. She felt as though she were petting some powerful mythical beast.

"Mine," he whispered, lowering her quiet hands so he could reach her mouth with his own.

"No." She stiffened at the first electric touch of his lips and turned her head away before she succumbed. "I can't love a man who would kill another and not pay for it. I took an oath to uphold the law, damn you!"

He released her and stepped away, dragging one frustrated hand through his hair, mussing it. "God as my judge, Honor, if I had it to do over again, I would have turned myself in and served my time. But I didn't. Can't change history now."

"Don't you see?" Honor cried. "You're just like Robert, asking me to flout the law for your convenience."

He grew so still, nothing moved. "Why don't you just cut out my heart and be done with it?"

"I'm sorry," she said softly, "but that's how I see it."

"Guess there's no point in flogging a dead horse. I'm right sorry, too."

He turned and left her office without a backward glance.

When Honor heard the door to the outer office close and his footsteps die away, she sat down at her desk and cradled her head in her hands, feeling a bone-deep sickness that had nothing to do with her pregnancy. Nothing had prepared her for the soul-searing pain of losing him, not her father's tragic and undeserved death, not the shattering discovery that Robert didn't really love her.

Nothing.

But at least she would always have Nevada's child.

The following morning in the Court of Special Sessions, Honor called her last witness to the stand.

"Dr. Delancy," she began, "you have pleaded not guilty to the charges of receiving obscene literature through the mails and circulating said literature, yet the evidence against you would appear to be overwhelming. Why did you do it?"

"For the welfare of my patients," Catherine replied in a clear, strong voice. Today she was the heroine of the *Sun* and the *World* come to life, still in mourning for her son, her head held high. As she spoke, several artists sketched her for their newspapers.

Comstock piped up, "So you admit your guilt, you godless woman," making Honor wonder why Justice Pike never threatened to hold the pompous buffoon in contempt.

"I admit nothing!" Catherine retorted. "I have broken no laws because *A Married Woman's Secret* is not obscene."

Comstock shouted, "Liar!"

"Your Honor," Honor addressed Pike with some asperity, "may I please be allowed to question my witness without interruption?"

Pike looked annoyed that she should even dare ask, but he ordered Comstock to keep quiet.

Honor turned back to Catherine. "Why do you claim it's not obscene?"

"That pamphlet is no more obscene than the medical textbooks I studied in medical school."

Her answer was Honor's cue to return to the defense table and pick up the book that would be crucial to the defense. A hushed, curious silence fell on the courtroom as Honor returned to the witness stand and handed Catherine the book.

"Do you recognize this book, Dr. Delancy?" she said.

Catherine glanced at the spine, opened the book to the frontispiece, and smiled. "Yes. It is my copy of *Essentials of Obstetrics.*"

"Would you tell the court what this book is about?"

"It's a medical textbook detailing pregnancy, labor, and childbirth."

"Would you describe the beginning of the book?"

The district attorney rose and objected. "Your Honor, I fail to see the relevance of this line of testimony."

"I will show the relevancy shortly, Your Honor."

Pike made a face. "Be quick about it, Mrs. Davis."

Honor smiled at Catherine. "Please continue."

Catherine opened the book and perused the beginning. "There are several illustrations of the female genitals, and the first chapter describes the anatomy of female genital organs."

"Dr. Delancy, precisely what words are used to describe these organs?"

Comstock jumped up from his seat near the witness enclosure. "Your Honor, I really must protest."

"The sooner you keep quiet," Pike said, "the sooner we'll finish."

Honor could almost see the steam coming out of Comstock's ears as he reluctantly sat down.

Catherine turned her attention back to the book. "Words

such as 'external genitals,' 'mons veneris,' 'vulva,' 'hymen,' and 'vagina' are used."

Honor turned, her eyes scanning the courtroom. "In fact, the words used in your medical textbook are the same as those used in *A Married Woman's Secret.*"

"The exact same words."

Honor turned back to Catherine. "Dr. Delancy, was this book, *Essentials of Obstetrics*, in your office when Mr. Comstock searched it in 1894?"

"Yes. I always keep it right on my desk."

"So he would have seen it."

"He would have had to be blind not to see it."

Honor rubbed her forehead and gave the three justices a bewildered look. "Your Honors, would you care to tell me why this pamphlet, which uses the same so-called lewd words as the medical textbook, is considered obscene, while the textbook is not?"

The three justices exchanged uncomfortable glances. Pike, clearly at a loss for words and resenting Honor for putting him in such a position, turned as red as Comstock.

"And if it is not obscene," Honor added, her voice rising to fill the courtroom, "why was Dr. Delancy arrested?"

Her point made, Honor said, "No further questions of this witness," and sat down.

Pike, who had regained his composure, said, "Dr. Delancy, just because you don't think you're guilty doesn't mean you aren't in the eyes of the law." He looked at the district attorney. "Do you wish to cross-examine?"

"No, Your Honor," Rampling replied, obviously thinking that Catherine had just convicted herself.

After Catherine stepped down, Justice Pike said, "Since there is some disagreement on this point, the court will now determine if the pamphlet is obscene."

Once the three justices had copies of the pamphlet, they left the courtroom to decide Catherine's fate.

Honor sat back in her seat and let out the breath she had been holding and said to Catherine, "I hope your testimony and Hilda's convinced them."

Damon, seated behind their table with Nevada, leaned over the railing to say to Honor, "Do you think they will find in Catherine's favor?"

"It's anyone's guess," she replied, ever conscious of Nevada's gaze boring into her back.

All around them people were talking about the trial or rising to stretch their legs before the justices returned with their verdict. Many came over to the defense table to offer Catherine encouragement and support.

Fifteen minutes later Catherine whispered to Honor, "Have you told him yet?"

Her hand flew to her locket, then fell away when she realized she wasn't wearing it. "No. Perhaps when this is over."

Alarm flashed in Catherine's eyes. "By then it may be too late."

Before Honor could ask her why, the justices filed into the courtroom and the bailiff asked everyone to rise. When the justices had taken their places on the bench, Presiding Justice Pike asked Catherine to rise.

Honor rose also, her heart pounding so hard she thought she would faint. She didn't need eyes in the back of her head to know that Damon was sitting on the edge of his seat, his hands gripping the railing separating him from his wife, while Nevada stood ready to aid him, ever the faithful friend.

A hush descended on the courtroom. No one spoke, no one moved, no one dared even to breathe.

Then Pike's voice rang out. "Dr. Catherine Delancy, of the charge that you circulated a pamphlet that is immoral and indecent, we hereby find you guilty."

"No!" Damon shouted, jumping to his feet.

Pike pounded his gavel, the sharp crack echoing throughout the room. "Sit down before I have you thrown out, Mr. Delancy. I'm not through yet."

Out of the corner of her eye, Honor saw Nevada place his hand on Damon's shoulder and urge him back into his seat.

Pike wagged his finger at Catherine in patronizing, paternalistic disapproval. "People like you who circulate such pamphlets are a menace to society, Dr. Delancy. Too many people now believe it is a crime to have children. It is not. Children are a blessing from God, and each one is to be cherished, whether it be born to the rich or to the poor."

"Amen," Comstock muttered, his eyes glittering with zeal.

Pike next addressed the spectators. "If people like Dr. Delancy encouraged women to have more children, they would be doing society a greater service.

"Although I am in favor of sentencing you to five years in prison, Doctor, my fellow justices have overruled me. Therefore, we are going to suspend your sentence and fine you one hundred and fifty dollars."

Honor stood there, stunned. She had lost the case, but she had won Catherine's freedom. Catherine would not have to spend one day in prison. With tears streaming down their faces, Honor and Catherine hugged each other.

Later, looking back on what followed with the advantage of hindsight, Honor decided that Dr. Hilda Steuben was responsible for the ensuing riot. Seconds after Pike gave Catherine a suspended sentence, the redoubtable Hilda rose, let out a whoop that could have been heard all the way to the Tombs, climbed up on her bench, threw her hat almost up to the ceiling, then roared when it landed on Comstock's head.

Suddenly it was as if a gathering thunderstorm had finally broken. A volley of clapping grew louder and louder, followed by a medley of cheers and jubilant shouts of victory. Men and women alike climbed up on the benches and waved their bowlers and handkerchiefs.

The three justices, their faces red with fury, stood at the bench. Pike went on pounding his gavel louder and louder, keeping time to the clapping and cheering.

Well-wishers swarmed around Honor and Catherine, hugging them and shaking hands. At one point, Honor found herself swept up in Damon's crushing embrace.

"You've done it," he said. "Whatever you want, name it, and if money can buy it, it's yours."

"Money can't buy what I want," she said.

He held her at arm's length. "You don't need money to get what you want. All you have to do is go to him."

As harried court attendants and determined police reinforcements began herding the unruly spectators toward the outside corridor to clear the courtroom, Honor noticed that Nevada was gone.

"Where is Nevada?" she asked Catherine.

Catherine's fingers dug into Honor's arm. "He's gone to turn himself in for killing Talmadge."

If Honor hadn't been a civilized woman and pregnant besides, she would have clawed and kicked her way out of that courtroom. Instead she reined in her desperation and let the crowd move her like a paper sailboat carried along by a swiftly moving stream.

She had to find him. She had to tell him that she loved him and that she would stand beside him no matter what happened. If they sentenced him to prison, she would wait for him.

Panic rushed up to grab her by the throat when she got to the corridor and couldn't find his pale head bobbing among the crowd.

Then she saw him at the far end of the corridor.

Suddenly an earnest young woman stepped in front of her. "I've circulated many copies of *A Married Woman's Secret* among my friends and classmates, Mrs. Davis. Even if one of us is arrested, another will take her place."

Honor squeezed her hand. "If that happens, I'll be more than happy to defend the lot of you, but right now, you must excuse me."

After disengaging herself from the young woman, Honor looked around. Nevada had disappeared again. Swearing under her breath, she fought her way through the crowd like a salmon swimming upstream. Finally she broke free.

Honor looked around desperately. Just when she thought

she had lost him, she spied him striding down one of the mezzanines that led to the rotunda below. With her steel corset stays robbing her of breath, she rushed after him.

Honor caught up with him just as he started across the rotunda.

"Nevada, wait!"

He stopped and turned.

Suddenly the realization that she wouldn't be seeing him for years hit Honor like a bolt of lightning. She wouldn't hear his soft drawl, see his eyes burn with desire for her, feel him lying so warm and solid beside her when she woke up in the morning. He wouldn't be there when his child was born. Their child wouldn't have a father for God knew how long.

What had Catherine said the night Honor learned she was pregnant? "Temper justice with mercy and let your heart guide you."

Principles be damned, she thought. I can't let him throw his life away.

Out of breath, she went up to him. "Where are you going?"

"To the police station," he replied, his gaze caressing her, "to turn myself in."

"You can't."

He started walking away from her. "Why not?"

"Because I love and want to be with you for the rest of my life."

He kept walking. "You sure that's enough?"

"There's another reason," she replied. "I also don't want my child's father to be a convict."

He stopped in his tracks, then slowly turned to face her. "What did you say?"

"You heard me, Clovis."

"You're . . . ?"

"Two months along, according to Catherine."

He walked back toward her, his expression one of stunned surprise. He stroked his drooping mustache. "A child? Mine?"

A horrible thought skittered through her brain: what if he didn't want the baby? Honor trembled with that new uncertainty.

His hand shot out, grasping her by the elbow to steady her. "You all right?"

"You're pleased"—she reached for the locket that wasn't there and wound up twisting her fingers instead—"aren't you?"

He gave her an exasperated look and drew her out of the rotunda's traffic before she was jostled by a passing stranger. "Couldn't be happier."

Honor gave a small sigh of relief. "Then you won't turn yourself in?"

"Not unless you want me to."

"I don't."

He lifted her chin with his fingers and looked deep into her eyes, his own frightfully serious. "We have a lot to talk about."

"So you keep telling me."

"Well, it's high time you listened."

"Once more?"

Nevada lay back against the pillow with a satisfied moan. "Are you sure this . . . activity won't hurt the baby?"

Honor chuckled and nuzzled his ear. "Catherine says we can be as active as we like."

"You'll be the death of me, woman." He stared at the ceiling, his mood sobering. "Why did you change your mind?"

She propped herself up on one elbow and studied the sharp planes of his face. "It was something Catherine said to me about tempering justice with mercy and following my heart. When I saw you walking through the rotunda, heading for the police station to turn yourself in, I suddenly realized how much I loved you and how empty my life, and the life of our child, would be without you."

Honor placed her hand on his chest. "Talmadge was a horrible, horrible man. I'm not saying he deserved to die, but you didn't intend to kill him. What purpose would it serve for you to come forward now? Our lives would be ruined. Catherine and Damon would have lost a good friend."

"You know I would have done it for you," he said.

"I know." She kissed his shoulder. "But I also realized that I'm not honorable like Aunt Theo, who gave up Wesley Saltonsall for his own good. I want you, Nevada LaRouche, and if that's compromising my principles, then I'm guilty."

They both started when a clap of thunder split the summer night sky, followed by the welcome hiss of falling rain on the dry city street below. A gust of wind bursting through the open window sent the curtains billowing out.

"The rain's coming in," Honor said, rising from the bed.

Padding softly across the bedchamber to close the window, Honor recalled what another, more famous Portia had said: "The quality of mercy is not strain'd, It droppeth as the gentle rain from heaven."

Smiling, she closed the window and returned to bed.

EPILOGUE

December 1897

CHRISTMAS AT COPPERMINE WOULD be a mixed blessing this year for Nevada. He had Honor and he had his freedom, everything a man could wish for. Almost everything, he reminded himself, watching Honor napping soundly on the fainting couch in their upstairs sitting room, her softly rounded body ripe and heavy with their child.

The child that would be illegitimate. A bastard.

Watching Honor sleep, one hand curled around her locket, Nevada knew that she didn't want their child to bear the stigma of illegitimacy, no matter how often she reassured him that it didn't matter to her. It broke his heart when she tried to pretend for his sake.

He was so lost in contemplating how he had come to deserve such a woman that he failed to notice the carriage rushing down the drive toward the house, failed to attach any special significance to the rattle of wheels and the pounding of hoofbeats, beyond thinking fleetingly that Damon and Catherine must have returned from showing Theo, who had arrived just yesterday, around the snow-covered estate.

So when he heard a soft knock on the sitting room door and answered it, he was surprised to find Catherine standing there.

"There's a man named Stannard downstairs," she whispered.

Before she could say another word, Nevada flew past her.

He returned ten minutes later to kneel at Honor's side. He took her hand and stroked her silken cheek. "Honor, wake up."

She stirred. Slowly she opened her eyes, sleepy midnight pools that filled with the most wondrous light whenever she looked at him. She took one look at him now and knew that something momentous had happened.

She pushed herself into a sitting position, suddenly alert and afraid. "What is it?"

He squeezed her hand. "You're finally going to be free."

"Free? I don't understand."

He took a deep breath. "Your husband has been found."

Honor turned so pale that he feared she would faint, and her eyes widened. "Found? Where?"

He told her that he had hired the Pinkerton National Detective Agency to find Robert so that she could divorce him, but they hadn't had any success.

"Until now. They tracked him to Seattle, where he's been practicing law under an assumed name." He tightened his grip on Honor's hand. "You can divorce him, and we can get married."

"You realize that our child will be born long before I'm able to divorce Robert."

He kissed her hand. "Once we're married, he or she won't be illegitimate anymore."

Honor's eyes brightened. "You never told me you'd hired the Pinkertons to find Robert."

"I didn't want to get your hopes up if they failed. They've been tracking him around the country since last November."

"All this time?"

He nodded.

Tears of happiness glistened in her eyes. "My love, you've given me the best gift of all, my freedom."

"I guess we both gave each other that."

"My sweet Portia, she's a perfect little Putnam," Theo cooed, holding Honor's four-hour-old daughter, Chantal Putnam LaRouche. "She has the Putnam hair and eyes."

"And her father's smile, as well as ten perfect little fingers and ten perfect little toes," Honor said from the depths of her bed, where she was recuperating from a long, hard labor that had almost driven her to vow never to have another child and her poor, frantic Nevada never to allow her to go through such agony again.

While Theo rocked the baby, Honor smiled at Nevada, sitting on the edge of the bed by her side and looking as exhausted as she felt. She took his hand and brought it to her lips, her eyes dancing with mischief. "Are you sorry she wasn't a boy so we could name him after his father? I think Clovis Putnam LaRouche has a certain . . ." She stopped when she saw his warning look.

He glanced at his daughter being fussed over by her white-haired great-aunt. "I won't be sorry if she turns out like her mama."

Little Chantal let out an earsplitting wail that startled everyone.

"She's definitely going to be a lawyer," Honor declared when Theo handed the fussy baby back to her besotted mother. "She's arguing a case already."

When Theo left, Nevada gave Honor a worried look. "Are you sorry you won't be practicing law for a while?"

She glanced down at her baby's round dark head, and her eyes softened with maternal pride. "I'll go back to it someday, but right now, I can't bear to leave this little princess."

Nevada shook his head, still unable to believe his good fortune. "Our daughter . . . During all my years of wandering, I never thought I'd have a family."

"Well, you do. And someday Chantal will have a brother or two, or another sister to keep her company."

"Even if you think you want to go through this again, I don't know if I can." Memories of Honor's harrowing labor were still too fresh and raw.

She understood his fears. "When the time comes, we both will."

"If you say so." He stroked Chantal's cheek with his

finger. "Do you think she'll marry an outlaw like her papa?"

Honor looked at him, her heart fit to burst with happiness. "If she does, she'll find herself mated for life."

He gave her a long, lingering kiss just to prove that she was right.